Where Love Lies

Also by Julie Cohen

Dear Thing

Where Love Lies

Julie Cohen

St. Martin's Griffin
New York

WHERE LOVE LIES. Copyright © 2014 by Julie Cohen. All rights reserved. Printed in the United States of America. For information, address St. Martin's Press, 175 Fifth Avenue, New York, N.Y. 10010.

www.stmartins.com

Library of Congress Cataloging-in-Publication Data

Names: Cohen, Julie.
Title: Where love lies / Julie Cohen.
Description: First U.S. edition. | New York : St. Martin's Griffin, 2016.
Identifiers: LCCN 2016002087| ISBN 9781250081742 (trade paperback) |
    ISBN 9781250081759 (e-book)
Subjects: LCSH: Married women—Fiction. | Choice (Psychology)—Fiction. |
    Self-realization in women—Fiction. | BISAC: FICTION /
    Contemporary Women. | FICTION / Romance / Contemporary. |
    GSAFD: Love stories.
Classification: LCC PR6103.O417 W48 2016 | DDC 823/.92—dc23
LC record available at http://lccn.loc.gov/2016002087

Our books may be purchased in bulk for promotional, educational, or business use. Please contact your local bookseller or the Macmillan Corporate and Premium Sales Department at 1-800-221-7945, extension 5442, or by e-mail at MacmillanSpecialMarkets@macmillan.com.

First published in Great Britain by Bantam Press, an imprint of Transworld Publishers, a Penguin Random House company

First U.S. Edition: August 2016

10 9 8 7 6 5 4 3 2 1

To Ken

Part One

What can you do if you are thirty and, turning the corner of your own street, you are overcome, suddenly by a feeling of bliss – absolute bliss! – as though you'd suddenly swallowed a bright piece of that late afternoon sun and it burned in your bosom, sending out a little shower of sparks into every particle, into every finger and toe?

'Bliss', *Katherine Mansfield*

Chapter One

I know exactly where I'm going.

I've only been to the restaurant once before, but as soon as I step off the train at Richmond everything looks completely familiar. I touch my Oyster card and turn left immediately outside the station. A young busker with wild dreadlocks plays 'Walking on Sunshine'. He throws his whole body into it, strumming and twitching and singing to the darkening London evening, as if he can make it midsummer noon with the force of his will. I dig into my jacket pocket and drop a pound coin into his guitar case amongst the litter of money.

I check my watch; I'm meeting Quinn in five minutes. I'm cutting it fine, but from what I remember, I have plenty of time to get there. I pass familiar shopfronts and turn right at the junction. The restaurant, Cerise, is round the next corner: it's a brick building, painted yellow, with a sign made of curly wrought iron. It's a treat for both of us after our separate days of meetings in London – Quinn's idea because I've told him they serve the best crème brûlée I've had outside of Paris.

I turn the corner and I don't see the restaurant.

I stand for a moment, peering up and down the street. Maybe they have repainted it. I look from building to building, but there's no wrought-iron sign, no wide window with a view of the tables inside. Anxiety rises from my stomach into my throat.

A little bit late isn't a problem, said my editor Madelyne this afternoon, just a couple of hours ago, on the other side of London. *But this is more than a little.*

I shake my head. Of course. The restaurant isn't on this street, it's further on. How silly of me. I stride to the end of the road and over the junction.

Quinn is never late. Quinn is frequently early. He'd prefer to wait outside wherever he's going, looking around him or reading a newspaper, than to be rushed or rude. You'd think he'd know me well enough by now to build in some leeway when he's meeting me, but he never does. I tried suggesting this once, breezily, and he listened, as he always does when I try to explain something. 'I'd still rather read the paper for a little while,' he said, and that was it. I've learned that Quinn is Quinn, and he does not change.

And even though he never acts impatient or annoyed, I try not to be late so often. I even bought a watch. I hate to think of him waiting, over and over.

It's warm and I'm still feeling anxious, so I take off my jacket and drape it over my arm. The restaurant should be right here, on the left. Except it's not; it's a Starbucks.

I frown. I must have got turned around the wrong way, somehow. This Starbucks looks exactly the same as every other Starbucks in the world, and definitely not like a French restaurant. I probably went too far down this road. I turn around and start back the way I've come.

10

My phone rings. It's Quinn. 'Hello hello,' I say, as cheerfully as I think I should.

'Hello, love. Where are you? Are you still on the train?'

'No no, I'm in Richmond, I'm on my way. I took a wrong turn, I think, but I'll be there in a tick.'

'Right,' he says. 'See you in a minute, love.'

He hangs up and I put my phone back in my handbag. He always says *love*, always, leaving in the morning or greeting me when I come in the room or ending a conversation on the phone. It punctuates beginnings and endings. It's something his father does with his mother, and he's slipped into the habit as if he were born to it.

At the corner I catch a whiff of scent, something familiar, someone's perfume.

I stop walking. 'Mum?' I say.

My mother isn't here. Of course she isn't here. But the scent is so strong, it's as if she's just walked past me.

I glance around. Two teenage girls sharing earphones, a man walking a terrier, a young couple, her with a hijab and him with a pushchair. There's a woman near the end of the street, walking away from me. She's wearing a sleeveless top and rolled-up jeans, her shoulders tanned. Her hair is a long silver plait down her back. The scent of flowers trails behind her on the warm air.

'Mum?' I hurry after her. She turns the corner, and by the time I reach it, she's gone.

But I can still smell her perfume. It's so familiar I can't think of the name of it, and my mother never wore perfume anyway. This smell, though, is my mother: it tugs something deep inside me, makes my heart leap with hope and a kind of sweet agony. I run further along the street and think I see the woman ahead of me, crossing the bridge over the Thames.

It can't be my mother. It's impossible. But I'm still thinking of everything I need to tell her: *I'm married, I've bought a
house, I'm sorry. So sorry for what I made you do.*

I collide with the plastic shopping bag held by a man
coming the other way over the bridge, and it falls onto the
pavement with a clang of tins. 'Oi, watch it,' he says.

'I'm sorry, so sorry,' I say, maybe to him, maybe to the
woman ahead of me. I reach for his bag but he's snatched it
up again. He's eyeing me up and down.

'Don't worry, beautiful, it's my pleasure,' he says.

'Sorry,' I say again, and carry on over the bridge,
quickly.

'Smile,' he yells after me. 'It might never happen!'

People are between us and she's walking rapidly; my
moment with the man with the shopping bag has put me
even farther behind her. But the scent is as strong as ever, and
as I get closer, dodging around pedestrians, my heart beats
harder and harder. It's impossible that when I catch up to this
woman she will be my mother, Esther Bloom, and she will
turn around and say, *Darling*. It's impossible that she could
take me into her arms and I could be forgiven. I know it's
impossible, and yet I can't look away from her. It's as if my
body doesn't know what my mind does. I can't stop my feet
from following her, faster now, running, my ballet flats
pounding over the pavement, sweat dampening the cotton
collar of my shirt. My jacket slips off my arm; I stuff it into
my handbag, mindless of wrinkles, and hurry forward.

The woman opens the door of a pizza takeaway. Panting, I
clasp her by the shoulder.

It isn't my mother's shoulder. It feels all wrong, and this

woman is darker than my mother, with more grey in her hair, which is finer than my mother's was – but my body has that irrational hope that when she turns around, her face will be Esther's.

'Mum?' I gasp.

It isn't. It's a stranger. She looks nothing like my mother at all.

'My mistake,' I say, backtracking. 'So sorry, I thought you were someone else.'

She shrugs and goes into the takeaway. The scent of flowers is gone, replaced by a whiff of baking dough and melting cheese.

My mother didn't even like pizza very much. I rub my forehead and look around. It's starting to get dark; the street-lights have come on, and this street is entirely unfamiliar, even more unfamiliar because not ten minutes ago I thought I knew exactly where I was, exactly who I was following. It's as if the street has changed around me. As if the world has changed around me.

In my bag, my phone rings. I know without looking that it's Quinn, wondering where I am. I don't answer it; I'll be with him in a minute. I hurry back across the bridge and along the road, which seems quite busy now; the cars have their lights turned on. I see a sign pointing to the station and I turn that way. This street looks strange too, but if it takes me back to the station that's good because I can definitely find my way from there.

Though I didn't just now.

How did I get so lost?

I reach for my phone to answer Quinn's call. Sometimes it's better to admit defeat and get somewhere that little bit

13

quicker, and Quinn loves giving directions anyway. And also it would be sort of nice to hear his voice, his habitual calm. *Hello, love.*

Two things happen at once: my phone stops ringing, and I see the restaurant. It's thirty metres away, on the other side of the road from where I'd expected it to be, and Quinn is outside it, his phone in his hand. He's wearing the same grey suit he was wearing when he left this morning to get the train to London, though the tie's been removed and he's unbuttoned his collar. His dark hair, as usual, is sticking up in the front because he's been running his fingers through it. The restaurant is painted yellow, with a wrought-iron sign outside. Light spills through the window. Everything is exactly as it's supposed to be.

He spots me and runs across the street, dodging a cab. I kiss him on his cheek, where there's a couple of days' growth of beard.

'You had me worried, love,' he says, kissing me back. 'What happened?'

I look at my husband: slender, pale, serious, with his grey eyes and his dedication to facts. The newspaper he's been reading while he's been waiting for me is tucked underneath his arm. He's never been late in his life, and he's certainly never followed a woman who doesn't exist any more, except in his memory.

'Oh,' I say, 'I just took a wrong turn.'

Chapter Two

On the train out of London, I lean against Quinn's shoulder and half-doze, trying to recall the scent I followed in Richmond. It's fading already in my memory. Something floral, definitely. Something exotic. Something I've smelled many times before, though I'm not sure where or why.

It didn't necessarily belong to the woman I followed; maybe someone else was wearing the perfume, which is why it seemed to vanish when I caught up with her. Maybe it was a flower growing in a window box, or in a garden. Maybe it was a perfume exuded out onto the street from a posh boutique, and happened to be similar to another perfume that I know.

As we drive home to Tillingford from the station, I open the window so the fresh air will wake me up a bit. 'So Madelyne is anxious for your new book?' Quinn says, though we've discussed this already at dinner. Or at least we've discussed it as much as I want to.

'She says she's looking forward to it.'

'So am I. Did you come up with any ideas together?'

I sit up straighter. 'Pull over,' I say.

'Are you okay?'

'Yes, yes! Pull over!'

He pulls into a lay-by and I jump out of the car. 'Come on!' I say, and run to a stile between the hawthorn hedges.

'What are you doing, Felicity?' Quinn has turned off the engine, but left the car lights on. He stands with the door open, looking after me. The road is quiet, the night scented with growing things.

'Turn off the lights and come and join me! We need to see.'

'Are you— oh, all right.' The car door shuts. I swing a leg over the stile and jump over. A nettle stings my bare ankle, but I keep on going, threading through a stand of trees. There's just enough silver light up ahead for me to see. Behind me, I hear the rustle of Quinn's footsteps. I wait for him to catch up, and when I feel him standing beside me I walk forward, through the last of the trees into a field.

Without the trees in the way we can see the full moon. It's silver and enormous, perfectly round, hanging in the sky.

'Is this why you had me stop the car?' Quinn asks.

'Isn't it worth it?' I gaze up at the moon. He stands beside me and gazes up at it too. 'I wish I knew what all of those shapes on it are called.'

'Mare Tranquillitatis,' he says. 'Mare Serenitatis, Mare Imbrium.' He points to different parts on the huge disc. 'Sea of Tranquillity, Sea of Serenity, Sea of Showers.'

'They're beautiful names. How do you know them?'

'Many, many misspent hours with a telescope and a book. There's an Ocean of Storms, and a Lake of Clouds. All on a surface with no water at all.'

'It was worth stopping the car, wasn't it?'

He takes my hand. His fingers are warm in the night, which has become cool. 'Yes.'

I look up at the moon some more.

'I know whose field this is,' Quinn says. 'He'd be quite surprised to see me standing in it at this hour.'

'Let's sit in it, then.' I sit down on the rough grass at the edge of the field. As I do so, there's a crinkle from my handbag and I pull out a box of macaroons. I offer one to Quinn. 'Macaroon? It's only slightly crushed.'

He begins to laugh. 'You're as daft as a brush,' he says. 'I do love you.'

'I love you too.' I lean my head against his shoulder and let my thoughts float away into the tranquil seas of the moon.

'A little bit late isn't a problem,' my editor Madelyne had said, yesterday afternoon, 'but this is more than a little. It's been eighteen months, and we have schedules to think of. Don't you have anything to show me yet?'

We were in her office, in the corner, overlooking the park. Her assistant had made us tea in a proper teapot, on a proper tray. There was a little box of macaroons, which Madelyne insisted I take because she was on a diet. The whole office was so quiet, as if everyone was reading at the same time. Books lined every wall that wasn't a window. Above the door I'd come in there was a framed original of the cover of my first picture book. I could feel Igor's wide owl eyes staring at the back of my neck as I sat in the wooden chair.

'I've been working on it,' I said to her, lying. 'But nothing seems to come out quite right.'

We'd always met in restaurants before. Long, boozy lunches where we got the business bit out of the way at

17

the beginning and spent the rest of the time trading gossip, tossing around ideas. Behind her desk, Madelyne seemed different. Her posture was straighter, her pulled-back hair more severe.

'I'm sure it will all be fine,' I added.

'Even some sketches would be useful,' she said. 'A title, something we could bring to the Frankfurt Book Fair. We've already put back publication twice. I'm worried that we'll lose the momentum on this series, with such a long gap.'

'I understand. I completely agree.'

'We all love Igor so much! And we miss him.' She smiled then, for the first time, and put down her cup. 'I know you've had a very eventful couple of years. So many ups and downs, with getting married, and your mother—'

'Yes, but it's fine. It's fine. I'll send you some sketches.'

'I can help you with ideas, you know. That's what I'm here for. You can pass me anything and we can bounce it around together.'

But not if there aren't any ideas at all. Not if the only thing I've ever been any good at has gone for ever. 'Of course.'

'And you know that if you ever want to talk—'

'Yes. Of course. I'm sorry the book is so late, Maddie. I'm always late for everything. I was even late to my own wedding.'

And we both laughed, even though it was true.

The next morning, I wake up after Quinn has gone off to work and I go straight into my studio, pulling on a dressing gown and pushing my hair into an elastic. I turn on the computer and the scanner, even though I don't have anything to use them for yet, and I clear off a stack of books from my chair beside the window, pick up a sketch pad and a pencil and look out at the morning.

My studio is actually the back bedroom of Hope Cottage, the house Quinn and I bought when we married. It has better natural light than the front bedroom where we sleep, and looks out over the garden — a jumble of flowers and weeds, a lawn that needs mowing, gnarled fruit trees. Petals from the cherry and the apple have drifted over the grass like pink and white snow. On warm days, sometimes I take a cushion out to the metal bench, painted with flakes of peeling blue, and read in the shade. I fell in love with the garden as soon as we saw this cottage: overgrown, wild — the sort of garden that harbours fairies in foxgloves. I love the cottage too, with its crooked floors and bulging walls, the suspicion of damp in the dining room, and a thatched roof that really should be replaced soon, this summer or next. But the garden is my favourite place.

A blackbird hops across the grass. I make a mark on the page, a black curve of head and wing, then fill in sharp beak, gleaming eye. I sketch in the dandelions behind him. This is all very well, but it's not Igor the Owl.

I've drawn and written six *Igor the Owl* books in the past four years, all of them before meeting Quinn. They're not complicated things: Igor is a tiny, fluffy owl, much smaller than all of his owl family and owl mates. To make up for being so tiny and fluffy, not much bigger than a chick, he solves puzzles.

For example, in the first book, *Igor the Owl Takes to the Air*, Igor has a problem because his wings are too little. He can fly in a fluttery way, but he can't soar on silent wings like the rest of his family, and he's feeling quite down about it. He's worried he'll never be a proper owl. Meanwhile, he makes friends with a family of squirrels who are living in a hole in a dead tree by the river. When the river floods, Igor tries to help his friends but he's too small to carry them to safety, so he quickly invents a sort of hang-glider thing with wings made out of discarded feathers and a framework made out of twigs, and the squirrels use it to fly to safety. And then Igor uses it to soar with his family, on silent wings. He's the only hang-gliding owl in children's literature, apparently, and the book sold much more than I expected it to, so I created more of the stories for publication, though I would have continued doing so anyway.

Igor has also solved crimes, in *Igor the Owl and the Monkey Puzzle* (nobody else noticed the ants stealing the nuts), and saved lives, in *Igor the Owl and the Good Eggs* (he was so small he could crawl right into a broken eggshell). In his last book, the one I wrote and illustrated nearly two years ago now, before I knew my mother was ill, Igor the Owl had started his own Owl School; here he taught other woodland creatures to solve puzzles, but he was sabotaged by a jealous magpie. In the end, Igor worked out who the culprit was, and they became friends.

I press my lips together and draw Igor next to the black-bird I've sketched. Big eyes, smiling beak, stubby wings. I never have a problem drawing Igor; I've been drawing Igor for years, ever since I was a teenager and invented him to amuse my mother and me during long train journeys, or on candlelit nights when the power would go out because Esther had forgotten to pay the bill. My mother, a proper artist, worked best on big canvases; I liked scraps of paper and ballpoint pens. I would breathe on a window and draw in the mist. I could tell a story anywhere with a few lines and shapes, as long as it was a little story.

I've been on plenty of trains since my mother got cancer, and I've even been in a power cut. But I haven't found any new stories that I want to tell, any puzzles that a tiny owl could possibly solve.

Sighing, I rest my elbows on the sketch pad and stare out at the garden. The old glass is uneven, and when I move slightly to either side, the grass appears to swell and subside. Madelyne was pleasant and kind, charming as always, but she wasn't pleased with me. Perhaps I should do something else for a job. But this is the first thing I've done which I've really liked. Before I stumbled into it, I was waiting tables, working in bars or shops, earning enough money to travel and then spending it all. People said they were interested in my art, but that was just because of who my mother was. Drawing Igor, writing out his story, being paid for it, holding the book in my hands – all these made me feel as if I were finally taking root somewhere. Finding the sort of life I was meant to have.

What will happen if I can't think of any more stories? I'll be dropped by my publisher. I'll have to pay back my advance, probably, which wouldn't be a huge problem, but it would be humiliating. I'll have to find something else to do, something that the other wives in the village do to use up their time if they haven't got a job. Coffee mornings. Charity events. Book clubs.

I think back to the rising sense of panic I had yesterday on my way to the restaurant. Was it fear, because somewhere down deep I knew that Igor was finished for me, that I'd used up all the stories I made up to amuse my mother because I loved her, and I would have to decide to do something else with my life? Because I can't fall back on what I used to do now. I can't get a job in a bar somewhere and flit off to India when I've saved enough money. I'm married, I've chosen to live here in Tillingford with Quinn, and all the possibilities of my past life have faded into air.

What was the perfume that woman was wearing who passed me on the street? It smelled so familiar. It made me think of the past, some unspecified moment, something I've forgotten.

The phone rings and I sit up. Outside, it's started to rain and the blackbird has flown away; inside, my computer screen has gone to its screensaver of random moving lights, each one leaving a coloured meteor trail behind it. My sketch pad is empty aside from two birds, one real, one imaginary. I make my way through the dark cottage to the kitchen, where the phone is.

'Hello, love,' says Quinn. 'How are you getting on?'

'Slowly.'

'Can I help?'

'Oh, thank you, no, I don't think so. I'm just having an off day.'

'Envelopes keep on disappearing from the stationery cupboard here. You could have Igor solve that.'

I pick at an unravelling hem on the flowered tablecloth. People who aren't creative, people who spend their lives structuring real-life stories and checking facts, rarely have any idea of the energy that's generated by a really good idea. They think you can choose any old thing and make it work. My mother never used to make suggestions for the Igor stories; she would wait for them to happen, and then she would listen.

'I was joking,' Quinn says.

'I thought you were in meetings all this morning.'

'It's lunchtime,' he says, and when I look at the clock over the sink, it is. 'Anyway, I just thought I'd ring to see how you were getting on. You seemed . . .'

'I'm fine. Everything's fine.'

'. . . preoccupied.'

On the draining board are Quinn's mug and his bowl from breakfast which he has washed up and left to dry. He has, I see, left a mug out for me by the kettle, my favourite one with the leaves painted on it. I know without looking that he'll have put a tea bag inside it, so I wouldn't lose vital seconds when I could be drawing. It's sat here while I've been in my dressing gown, staring out at the garden, accomplishing nothing. I should thank him, I should say something warm and loving to make his lunchtime special after a morning of meetings, but I'm irritated by this as well because it reminds me of a future time when I may have nothing better to do but Quinn's washing up, nothing better to do but make tea.

I close my eyes. This is another thing about marriage: second thoughts. Doing what's best, saying what's best, instead of what you feel.

'Sea of Tranquillity,' I say. 'Wasn't the moon amazing last night?'

Quinn

The christening had gone well. Baby Jacob Edward Isaac Harrington, swaddled in antique white, slept through the water dousing, and the rain had confined itself to a tiny shower while they were all in Tillingford's twelfth-century stone church. Now most of the village was crammed into the Harringtons' back garden. The new family stood in the centre; the baby, now awake, bounced from one person to the next, emitting tiny gurgles. Quinn stood with his back to the yew hedge, holding a glass of prosecco and trading opinions about sheds with Patrick, his sub-editor, who lived in one of the new builds just outside of town.

'I'm telling you, it's the only five minutes' peace I get at home these days, when I go out to sort through the spanners,' said Patrick. 'You've got your nappies and your baby food for a start. Then you've got the Weetabix. Have you ever tried to get dried Weetabix off a wall?'

'Like cement, is it?'

'I'm thinking about using it to replaster the house. And the questions from the older one. "Why are snails, Daddy?" she asked me yesterday. Not why are snails slimy, or why do they have shells, no. *Why are snails?* Had me stumped. And then there are the toys everywhere. I stepped on a piece of Lego this morning in my bare feet. You probably heard the swearing all the way over in your house.'

'I wondered what that noise was,' said Quinn. He didn't take Patrick's complaints seriously; the man had three photos of his two daughters on his desk, and more in his wallet. Quinn was a great believer in the power of words – he used them for his living, after all – but sometimes, actions spoke more loudly.

'It'll be your turn next,' said Patrick. He drank his fizz with great satisfaction. 'Where is your missus, anyway?'

'She's underneath the apple tree.' Quinn gazed across the garden to where Felicity was chatting with Emma and Gurinder, all of them with glasses in hand. It was a sixth sense, almost, this awareness of Felicity, something he'd never experienced with any other woman or girl he'd known. Though it could also be because she looked different from anyone else in the garden. All of the other women were wearing pastel dresses, flowers and pashminas and pale shoes, with their hair carefully curled, straightened or combed. Felicity wore a bright green dress covered with a concentric-circle pattern, a lace underskirt, bare legs and red ballerina flats. Her hair was shoved up into a messy bun, tendrils escaping. Her eyes were lined with kohl, her lipstick the same colour as her shoes.

Before he met Felicity, Quinn had never known a woman who could make untidiness seem deliberate.

Before he met Felicity, Quinn had never known a lot of things. For example, how you could feel as if you understood your wife better when you were watching her across the garden, than when you were talking with her in the home you shared.

'She's got a style, hasn't she?' said Patrick.

'She's an artist. She has an artistic background.' Quinn finished his drink. 'She's wonderful.'

He had plenty of friends who were married; plenty of friends who claimed they loved each other. Yet they complained about each other when they were apart. They seemed to have petty difficulties rubbing like grit between them. He'd sworn he'd never do that, never let that happen.

'Newlyweds,' said Patrick. 'Do you want another drink?'

'Yes, please.'

Patrick went off and Quinn put his hands in his pockets and allowed himself to watch his wife. Even after being married for nearly a year, it was the purest pleasure he knew. The two other girls were still talking, but Felicity's attention had wandered. She stood with them, but her eyes gazed into the distance at nothing, and the smile had melted from her face, replaced with a more intent expression, as if she were listening hard to something just out of hearing range.

What did she think when she looked like that? What was she hearing and feeling?

At first, before they'd been married, he'd asked her. He'd wanted to know everything about her. But she'd been so startled, her answers so vague, that he had stopped asking. Even in a marriage, it seemed, even when everything else was shared, his wife needed privacy. If only within the space of her mind, during the short blank spaces where her body was with him but her attention was not.

Quinn, himself, would open his whole mind to Felicity. He couldn't imagine a single thought, a single feeling, that he would not be willing to share with her, if she cared to hear it. His past was an open book; they lived in the village where

26

he'd grown up, among people whom he'd known all his life, so even if he'd had any dark secrets to hide, there wouldn't be much of a chance of it.

He thought of last weekend, in the empty field with the full moon overhead, holding her hand and reciting the names of the seas. All those hours as a teenager with the telescope his father had bought him for Christmas: unknowing, he had learned about the moon for the sole purpose of holding Felicity's hand and saying those names to her in the silver-lit darkness.

Quinn began to walk across the crowded garden towards his wife, intending to take her hand again under the apple tree, to call her back to the reality of the two of them.

'Here, now, Quinn Wickham. I'm glad I caught you.' Irene Miller stepped into Quinn's path.

Mrs Miller was the town gossip, and fancied herself as a sort of investigative journalist, using mostly tea and eaves-dropping as tools. He resigned himself to several minutes of being told third-hand information he had no intention of printing. Lately, Mrs Miller had been angling to be given her own column, a gossip column or possibly an agony aunt feature. Patrick thought this was a hilarious idea and that it would increase their circulation considerably. Quinn was more of the opinion that it would cause all-out warfare on the common.

'Hello, Mrs Miller,' he said. 'I hope you're well.'

'I've got a word to the wise for you.' She sidled closer. 'I think you should go and have a word with that Bel Andrews.'

'Is that so?'

'She's over there near the cucumber sandwiches. You can catch her if you hurry. Word at the Tillingford Tea Pot is that there have been some unofficial council meetings lately.' Mrs Miller tapped her nose. 'Secret dealings. About the budget.'

Councillor Bel Andrews was, indeed, by the sandwich table, looking as stolid and unconspiratorial as ever. Out of the corner of his eye, Quinn saw Felicity turn and slip through a nearby hedge.

'Thanks for the tip, Mrs Miller. I will certainly talk to Bel as soon as I can. If you'll excuse me . . .' He began to edge away.

Mrs Miller followed Quinn's gaze. Felicity's glass and her handbag sat on the grass, abandoned. 'Why are you and your wife so mad keen to get into that hedge?'

'Damsons,' he said quickly. 'We're looking for a cutting for our garden. Thanks again, Mrs Miller.'

'Your father never crept through hedges!' she called after him. He waved acknowledgement, and felt her watching him.

Emma and Gurinder were chatting to each other when he approached. 'Hi, Quinn,' Gurinder greeted him. 'We were just talking to— oh, she was here a minute ago. She's really interesting, your wife. Different.'

'What were you talking about?' he asked, unable to resist the temptation.

'How Emma had a crush on you in primary school,' said Gurinder.

Emma blushed. 'I had a crush on *everyone* in primary school. Anyway, you fancied David Enright, and look what happened to him.'

'*I* didn't steal David Enright's pencil and keep it under my pillow, like you stole Quinn's.'

'Gosh,' said Quinn. 'I hope I didn't chew on the end. Listen, did Felicity say where she was going?'

Emma looked around. 'For another drink maybe?'

'It was all just a laugh,' said Gurinder. 'Ancient history. Felicity didn't seem to mind.'

Quinn didn't think that Felicity would mind about a primary-school crush. But why had she disappeared through a bush? He thanked Gurinder and Emma and went to examine the hedge. There was a small gap in it and he pushed himself through. A twig caught his jacket and he had to detach it, hearing the women laughing behind him.

The hedge separated the Harringtons' garden from the Thompsons' next door. The Thompsons were at the christening; the climbing frame and swing stood abandoned on the grass. Felicity was kneeling on the lawn by the patio, cradling something in her hands.

'Felicity?' he said, going to her. 'What's happening?'

He ignored the relief that washed over him. If he felt relieved, it would mean that he'd been worried that his wife actually would slip away. That in one of her blank, private moments, in one of those moments where he couldn't reach her or know her, she'd forget about him.

It was a side effect of loving her so much. Of not quite believing he was lucky enough to have her.

Some more of her hair had come loose from her bun and there was a long red scrape at the top of one of her bare arms. 'It's a bird,' she told him.

He knelt beside her. Moisture from the ground soaked into his trousers. The bird was a house sparrow, dun and black. It lay in the hollow of her hands, wings folded, eyes closed into near-invisible slits. Its feet were tiny commas.

'I heard a thump,' Felicity said. 'I think it flew into the glass

29

doors. At first I thought its neck was broken, but I can feel it breathing.'

'Should you have picked it up?'

'Well, I thought that if its neck were broken it could hardly make things worse. What should we do if it's hurt its wings?'

'Anil's at the christening,' he said. 'I don't know if he treats wild animals, but we can ask him to have a quick look.'

'I can feel its heartbeat,' she whispered. She touched the dun feathers on its breast with the tip of her thumb. 'It's like a vibration. The pauses are too small. Do they live faster than we do, do you think? Not just shorter, but faster? More intensely?'

He opened his mouth to answer, he didn't know what – possibly something about hummingbirds and how fast they lived – when the sparrow opened its eyes. It looked at him and Quinn just had time to wonder how it saw him, a monster or a giant, before the bird hopped to its feet and with a papery flutter, launched itself from Felicity's hands into the air. She laughed, surprised, holding her hands open and empty.

A sudden urge gripped him to fling his arms around her. To hold her tight, to lie down with her on the grass with the chatter of the party next door muted. To feel her heartbeat and compare it to his. But it was the Thompsons' garden; they couldn't roll around on the lawn next to the Thompsons' swing set.

'Well,' said Felicity, standing up, 'that was lucky.' She brushed twigs and grass from her dress. 'I suppose we should go back to the party.'

Quinn stood. 'Is your arm okay? You've scraped it.'

'Have I?' Felicity peered at it. 'Oh, I have. I'm fine.'

'Maybe we should walk round to the front rather than going through the hole again.'

'I'm sorry,' said Felicity, as they skirted bicycles on their way to the front garden. 'I know you were enjoying the party.'

'You saved me from Mrs Miller's conspiracy theories.'

'Did you know that one of the women in there stole your pencil when you were a child?'

'It'll be all over the Tillingford Tea Pot tomorrow, how Quinn and Felicity Wickham disappeared through a hedge.'

'Oh dear.' She frowned, and he put his arm around her waist. 'I don't think I'd have stolen your pencil,' she said.

'I'd have given it to you.' They reached the gate, and he opened it. 'I'd have given you anything,' he said.

Chapter Three

I keep on thinking about how it felt to have that sparrow fly away from my hands. One moment it was there, light as fluff. And then the next moment I felt its claws on my palms, a flicker of air on my face. Flit. Gone.

Quinn changes out of his suit but I stay in my dress. I slip off my shoes and lie back on the sofa, propping my bare feet on the arm. The prosecco has made me drowsy and relaxed. When Quinn comes back he lifts my legs, sits on the sofa, and rests my feet on his lap.

'Did you enjoy that?' he asks me.

'I thought it was dead. It was as if it came back to life, right in my hands.'

He smiles. 'Yes, but the christening?'

'Oh. It was all right. I still don't know the hymns.'

'Ed and Alice seem very happy. Apparently they've been trying for a while.'

'Yes, very happy,' I say. 'And taking full advantage of a new reason to go shopping. Did you see their new pram in the hallway? It looks like something off a spaceship.'

He murmurs assent, and begins to rub my foot. Quinn gives lovely foot massages. Apparently one of his ex-girlfriends, Maya, taught him because she always had sore feet. She never knew that I'd be the one benefiting from her penchant for ill-fitting shoes. It's odd that every relationship we have, aside from the first one, is patched together from things we've learned already, habits we've formed with other people. I close my eyes and wonder what I've brought to my relationship with Quinn. The thing is, he's quite different from anyone else I've ever been involved with.

'I've been thinking,' says Quinn.

'Oh dear.'

'Always dangerous, I know.' He runs his thumb up the arch of my foot, something that should tickle, but feels good. Sexy. 'And Patrick said something today, which made me think about . . . and how lovely the christening was, and how happy Ed and Alice are, and their parents. I mean, I was wondering, do you think . . .' He takes a breath. 'Don't you think it's time we started trying for a baby?'

'A baby?' I sit up, pulling my feet under me so I'm cross-legged, facing Quinn. He's looking at me.

'You know, little creatures,' he says. 'Drink milk. You've heard of them.'

'I've heard of them, yes. I didn't know you wanted one.'

'You don't think it's a good idea to have a family?'

'I . . . haven't thought about it, to be honest. I mean, we've only just got married.'

'A year next month.'

'Really?' A year, a whole year, stretches behind me. Behind us. 'That happened quickly.'

'I thought that was one of the reasons we bought this house,' he says. 'Three bedrooms: one for us, one for your

33

studio, one for a nursery. With room in the garden for an extension if we have more children.'

I thought we bought the cottage because we liked it. Because of the roses over the door and the cracks in the plaster and the golden colour the thatch turns at sunset. I thought the third bedroom was a spare one.

'I mentioned it at the time,' Quinn says.

'Did you?'

'Yes.' His voice is patient. 'I told you how Mr and Mrs Ogden lived here all their lives and brought up three children here and then they grew old together here. I told you how their son Michael was my maths teacher at school. I said it was the right sort of place for us to do the same thing.'

'I must have forgotten.'

He lets out a short sigh of exasperation or disappointment.

'I just haven't thought about it,' I say. 'I didn't know you had.'

'I thought it was the normal next step.'

'I don't know. Is it? Are we a normal couple?'

'Of course we are.'

But are we? I felt quite different from the other couples at the christening today, with their four-wheel-drive cars, the couples with babies in carrycots or toddlers in clothes that require ironing. The couples who refer to 'their other half' and who talk about the desirability of local schools.

'It's all quite sudden, Quinn. I mean, a year and a half ago, I didn't even know you yet.'

'Surely you've noticed my mother talking about it?'

'Well yes, but that's Molly, isn't it? I didn't think you were listening.'

He isn't exasperated; he's hurt. And now I've insulted his mother as well. I touch his arm.

'It's all new to me, Quinn. Probably, yes, I should have been thinking about it. You clearly have, but I haven't. But I'll think about it now. I promise. Okay?'

He leans over and kisses me on the forehead, then gets up. 'Thank you. Fancy a cheese sandwich? I'm making one.' I shake my head, and he leaves me alone in the sitting room, thinking.

The next morning, Quinn cycles off to get the paper before I'm out of bed. While I'm standing by the bedroom window pulling on my socks, I see him returning. He wheels his bicycle through our front gate and leaves it just inside, unlocked. No one ever locks up anything in Tillingford. At first I thought it was because no one ever stole anything, but that's not the case; it's because everyone knows everyone else and any thefts that do happen are easily remedied. Quinn's had his bike stolen twice, both times by Cameron Bishop, and both times Quinn has walked round to the Bishops' house and taken it back from beside their shed. I've run into Cameron's mother Lisa Bishop in the post office several times and she's never said a thing about it.

I didn't sleep much last night, though I went to bed before Quinn did and pretended to be asleep when he came up. Quinn is right, of course; Quinn is almost always right. People get married and then they have babies. It's the normal order of things.

Quinn would make a wonderful father. As a couple, we're in a good, sensible place to have a baby. We're financially secure. We have insurance and pay the mortgage on time. My career is something I can easily do from home. The baby would be brought up in the countryside, with loving family close by, one set of grandparents and an aunt. It's the ideal situation, really. It is quite different from how I grew up, travelling from house to house, country to country, with money either short or plentiful and somehow never anything in between. A baby created by Quinn and me would be confident and comfortable. It would know its place in the world. It would be a Wickham in temperament as well as in name.

It would be quite different from me. That would probably be a very good thing.

I come downstairs to the kitchen. The door jamb is marked with the heights of all three of the Ogden children, in half-inch and inch increments, each including the date. They begin about two feet from the floor and stretch over my head. Michael is the tallest; Sophia is the shortest. The most recent date is 1978. I've thought that was just another of the cottage's nice quirks, a little bit of history. Now it seems more like a map of the future.

Quinn's got the kettle on. From the washed-out tin in the sink, I can see that he's already put out food for the neighbours' cat. The paper and a carton of orange juice sit on the table. 'Morning, love,' he says, stretching up to reach the tea bags.

'Morning.' I get the milk and put it out on the table. Every Saturday and Sunday morning, tea and the paper in the kitchen. When there's a big story, Quinn sometimes buys two papers. He makes the tea and I add the milk to both mugs. He pours us each a glass of juice and he settles down to read.

I watch Quinn. His concentration is complete. If I asked

him a question later on about the story he's reading, he'd be able to recite it for me almost verbatim.

I've asked him several times why he's never moved to London, got a job on one of the broadsheets, instead of being an editor here of a local paper. 'I like living here,' he's said.

'But you could commute,' I've suggested. 'It'd only take an hour each way.'

'Long hours, long commute. Competition. I'm not ambitious, Felicity. All I want is to be happy.'

He'd be good working for a national newspaper, I think. He's curious. He remembers everything. But I can see that he likes living here, where he grew up, where he knows everyone. He likes being known as Derek and Molly's son, Suz's brother, a man who's made his own place in his own community, who's made something of himself. The paper was nearly defunct when he took it on, and increasingly irrelevant. He built up ad revenue, developed an online presence, widened the news to include more than Scout meetings and farming reports. He writes most of the copy himself; he chooses the causes to support, ways to improve this small part of the world. It's been commended in a Regional Newspaper of the Year competition and most of the people who work for him think that next year they'll win it. I only know most of this because Patrick has told me; Quinn wouldn't mention it himself.

He turns the page. I drink my tea and I look at the top of his head, at his hands holding his mug, at his eyes following the words. He hasn't forgotten what he mentioned last night. I wonder when he'll bring it up again.

I wonder what I'll say.

I get up to put on some toast. 'What are you up to today?'

'I was thinking of going for a walk after breakfast,' he says, eyes still on the newspaper. 'Before going round to Mum and Dad's. Do you want to come?'

'Oh.' I gaze at the sunshine outside. 'I . . . should try to draw.'

'It might give you some inspiration.'

I put butter and marmalade on the toast, give him both the pieces, and put in some more for me. His questions hang in the air: both the one about the walk that he's asking now, and the one he's really asking, the one he asked last night.

'Better not,' I say.

For the next week, Quinn doesn't mention a single word about babies or the possibility of having one. In fact, he does the opposite. He gets up to make a cup of tea when a nappy ad is on the television, his face a careful blank. Another time, we're in the Seven Stars having a drink and Rowan, the landlady, tells a story about leaning down into a pram belonging to a couple who came in for lunch and how the baby grabbed her hair with both hands and would not let go. Quinn actually interrupts before the story is over to tell us a news item about an eighty-year-old local man who is planning to climb Kilimanjaro for charity.

It would be funny if it weren't so truthful. Although the question goes unasked and ignored, it hangs between us in the house. I picture it, a plump pink baby hovering near the ceiling, crowded in with the other unanswered questions of this marriage. I draw the baby floating there, and then throw the piece of paper away. I draw some flowers with silly faces instead. I notice a new crack in the wall by the front door, and pin the flowers over it.

When the adverts come on television on Thursday night, Quinn gets up from the sofa. 'Brew?' he asks.

'Yes, please.'

I watch him go into the kitchen. I think about what it would be like on a Thursday night if we had a baby. There would be toys on the floor over there, under the window. The baby might be here with us, asleep in my arms. Or it might be upstairs and there would be a baby monitor on the low table where sometimes Quinn props up his sock-clad feet.

It wouldn't be much different. It wouldn't be cataclysmic. Things would carry on much as normal. Everything would be normal for ever, except for this other person depending on me to get it right.

Chapter Four

Dear Ms Bloom,

You may recall that several months ago I wrote to you to tell you of the major retrospective of your mother's work which the Gallery is holding in July and August. We're tremendously excited as it will be the first exhibition of her work outside of London since your mother passed away, and the first that will include several of Esther Bloom's pieces that have been held for many years in private collections across the world.

Some few weeks ago, I sent you an invitation in the post to attend the exhibition opening as our guest of honour. Many curators, art critics, historians and collectors will be present, along with international press, and we would be privileged to have you amongst us. We will, of course, cover your expenses for your journey and your stay here.

You may have already replied to this invitation, in which case please excuse me for writing again, or it may have been misdirected or misplaced, which is why I am contacting you once more . . .

I fold the heavy cream paper in half and in half again, and in half again. I twist it into a tight tube and drop it into the recycling bin.

Lying on her white pillow, her skin yellow like wax, her cheeks sunken, she took my hand in hers and she whispered, 'This was always going to happen. Let go, my darling. Travel lightly, my girl.'

And then the other things she said, later.

I don't need a retrospective to remember my mother. I wish I could *stop* remembering.

'Any post, love?' Quinn calls from upstairs, where he's knotting his tie, getting ready for work.

'Nothing,' I call back up. He appears at the top of the stairs.

'I thought I heard something.'

'Junk mail.'

I feel a bit sick, so I open the door and step out onto the flagstone path, into the watery morning sunlight. One day I'll remember only the good things. One day I'll stop seeing her on the street. One day I'll think about her with joy, and not with pain and regret.

I wish I could ask her what I should do. Whether she always knew that she wanted a child; how she knew that she wanted me. I know what she would say, but I want to hear her say it. I want her to send me a sign.

Sunday lunch is a Wickham family tradition. Quinn's mother Molly cooks something enormous, and the grown-up Wickham siblings and I gather at their parents' house, which is across the common from our cottage. Sometimes we have it at ours, and sometimes we have it at Suz's house, and sometimes we travel to various aunts' and uncles', but most of the time we have it at Molly and Derek's. Their house, the Old Vicarage, is 220 years old, made out of local grey stone, and furnished in chintz and watercolours of horses and flowers. Derek grew up in it.

This week, Molly has made roast lamb and a mountain of mash. I sit at the table beside Quinn, as I always do, across from his sister Suz. 'I made enough for an army,' says Molly, joining us at the table with a bowl of broccoli, her dark hair streaked with silver and pushed behind her ears. She smiles at her family. Molly Wickham – plump and welcoming, homely and conventional – is exactly the sort of woman my mother tried not to be. She is, however, a very good cook, and she always does make enough for an army.

Quinn helps his mother load everyone's plates with food, while his father and Suz pour the wine and water. I've noticed how they unthinkingly split down the middle when there are tasks to be done. Quinn and his mother, Suz and her father, neat mixed-gender teams. I mentioned it to Quinn once and he was bemused, as if it's something ingrained in his family that no one had ever questioned or even noticed before. Maybe all families with two parents and two children do this. I have no idea.

'How is the drawing going, dear?' Molly asks, passing me a full plate of roast dinner. In-laws are served first at Molly's table.

'All right, thanks, Molly. I'll take some photos later to use as backgrounds.'

'I was talking with Ella Richardson the other day about you. We were saying how marvellous it must be, to be so creative.'

'Yes.'

'You must love being a creative person? It must be so interesting?'

Molly asks a lot of questions that you have no choice but to agree to. On the day Quinn and I got married, in the car on the way to the church (the church where Derek and Molly were married, and the church where both sets of their parents were married too) she put her hand on my knee and she whispered to me, 'I hope you will always look upon me as your mother, Felicity?'

She had that soft smile on her face and tears beginning in her soft grey eyes, and there were many things I could have said to her, if I'd wanted to talk about my mother. My only mother, my real mother, my quirky and talented and loving mother Esther Bloom, who could never be replaced.

But really there was nothing to say but, 'Yes.'

'Yes,' I say now. 'Yes, it's very interesting.'

'I wish I could! I can't do anything but cross-stitch, and that's all to a pattern that's been printed on the canvas already, you know.'

'Cooking is creative,' says Derek, accepting his plate. 'You're a splendid cook, Molly.'

'Oh, well, that's just feeding my family. It's a pleasure.' She passes a plate to Suz. 'Ella was also saying that her nephew was visiting next week – you remember George, don't you, Susan?'

'Yes, of course. How is he?'

'Very well. Divorced.' Molly says the word in a lowered voice, as if it's bad luck. She says 'cancer' and 'heart attack' the same way. 'Maybe you could meet him for a quick drink in the Seven Stars? Ella thought he'd like to do that. Maybe you'll hit it off this time.'

'Maybe,' says Suz. 'Quinn, what do you fancy of Howarth's chances in the by-election?'

'Not bad, though I'd be sorry to see him win.'

'Slightly to the right of Attila the Hun, is Howarth,' says Suz, sipping her wine. 'Nice wine, Dad.'

'I think he's got some sound policies,' says Derek. 'Take what he said on housing—'

'There they go again, talking politics,' Molly says to me, rolling her eyes in mock exasperation. 'They'll be coming to blows in a minute.'

I smile at her joke, and spear a bit of broccoli. The conversation continues, not much louder than the scrape of forks and knives on plates, floating comfortably around politics and news about neighbours and friends. The dining room is large and airy, the biggest room in the house, adjoining the kitchen and with a view through sash windows to the neat garden. Most of the childhood photos Quinn has shown me were taken in this house or just outside it. The dining table is an expanse of glossy wood, covered with an ironed white cloth. It was bought by a previous generation to accommodate a growing family. It has plenty of room for grandchildren.

'. . . Felicity?'

Molly has asked me a question. I bring myself back to the present.

'Pardon?'

'I was asking if you had any plans for your anniversary?'

'Oh. We haven't discussed it.' I look at Quinn.

'I've got one or two ideas,' he says.

'What's the first year?' Molly muses. 'Paper?'

'I took your mother out for an expensive meal,' says Derek.

'You did not,' says Molly.

'I always take you out for an expensive meal. I know my duty. I remember it well. You had the lobster.'

'I didn't. On our first anniversary I was pregnant with Susan and we had a quiet evening at home.'

'Of course we did. You were sick as a dog.'

'That was with Quinn I was sick. With Susan, I felt wonderful. You were such an easy baby, Susan.'

I gaze at my mother-in-law. This is one possible future for me. Sitting at this table at Quinn's right hand in thirty years' time, serving roasts and reminiscing about my pregnancies with my grown-up children. It should be difficult to imagine, but in this room it seems almost inevitable.

'What would you like to do for our anniversary?' Quinn asks me.

I'd like to get out a map and close my eyes and stick a pin in it, and go wherever it lands. I'd like to spend the day with Quinn getting drunk in a cinema, watching as many films as possible and necking in the back row between sips of red wine from a hidden bottle. I'd like to learn a new dance, or go to a gig by a band I've never heard of, or spend all day in bed.

'Let's see what we feel like on the day,' I say.

Derek puts down his own knife and fork. He regards his family with affection. 'That was smashing, love,' he says. Just as he always does.

'You were quiet,' says Suz to me as we stand at the sink together. I wash, and she dries, because she knows where everything goes, and also (though no one says it) because she's less likely to drop something on the flagstone floor and break it.

Suz resembles Quinn. Or rather, they both take after their mother, and have thick dark hair and grey eyes. Suz's is straight, cut in a bob. Their hands are similar, with long fingers and short nails. Their mother's sister and brother also have these hands and eyes, this hair. Their belonging is signalled in their faces, but also in something about how they move and talk. Suz is a solicitor in the same firm as Derek, though she specializes in conveyancing while he's semi-retired and deals in probate. She helped us with the legal stuff for our house.

'Quinn wants to have a baby,' I tell her.

She takes the gravy boat from the draining board and dries it, paying careful attention to the scrolling round the handle.

'You don't seem surprised,' I say.

'I'm not surprised that Quinn would like to start a family, if that's what you're asking. He'd make a marvellous parent.'

'It would make your mother very happy.'

'Well, that too.' She puts the gravy boat in its place on the dresser. 'And my father – and me too, of course.'

'You've left me off that list.'

'I'm surmising, from the fact that you've brought up the topic, that you're not certain.'

'It's not that I don't want to. I've just never thought about it.'

'You should take your time, then. There's no rush.'

'It's just such a . . . commitment.'

'As is marriage. Or so they say.'

Her words are measured, neutral. I knew they would be, which was why I've brought this up with her, but now I'm not certain it was a good idea. Quinn is her little brother. He's always been her little brother. She has never had to worry about disappointing him, or about not being the person he wants her to be. She's never for a moment felt his love as something precious and mysterious in its matter-of-factness.

'If you've got doubts, you should talk them over with Quinn.' She sees my hesitation, and adds, 'He'll be all right with it, you know. He'd do anything for you.'

'That's part of the problem,' I say to the suds in the sink.

'You don't have to have children. Lots of couples choose not to. There's no point making yourself unhappy because you're trying to please other people.'

'I love Quinn.'

'That's never in doubt,' says Suz. 'Anyone would love Quinn.'

But what I don't ask aloud, what I don't say anywhere but inside my own head, is *But do I love Quinn enough?* Because if I did, I wouldn't be having these doubts, would I?

If I loved him enough, I wouldn't have any doubts at all.

As Quinn predicted, the weather has turned drizzly, but after the clearing up is done we all still get ready to go outside, pulling on wellies and anoraks that have been drying in the kitchen. The Sunday walk is nearly as important as Sunday lunch. I've always preferred umbrellas to anoraks – umbrellas are things of beauty, and anoraks are not. I have a lovely cherry-red one to use on Sunday walks.

We troop out of the door, en masse, a hearty cheerful clump of Wickhams with me at the tail. Although sometimes I really enjoy this, striding through the village and into the countryside, waving to neighbours and friends, part of a pack, today I'm quite glad I brought my camera along. It gives me an excuse to lag behind the others. I balance my umbrella in the crook of my arm and begin snapping pictures as I walk. Raindrops dripping off hedges, reflections in puddles.

The idea is to take pictures of things I'd like to draw, but I'm not really paying much attention. I'm thinking, instead, about Quinn suddenly wanting to have a baby at the same time his parents had a baby. As if there's a pattern for the correct time for major life events in their DNA, as well as for dark hair and grey eyes.

And what is wrong with this, anyway? There is nothing wrong with being predictable. There is nothing wrong with being happy. Is it because my own childhood was so chaotic, with us moving from place to place, school to school, that I can't quite reconcile myself to a life where I can anticipate every step in advance?

It's what I chose when I chose Quinn.

Plus, my life wasn't chaotic beforehand, anyway. It had a centre, a constant: my mother. Everything else around us – friends, houses, countries – might change, but she never did. She always loved me, her Felicity, her only child, her only family.

'Your father,' she would whisper to me when she kissed me good night, in whichever place we'd alighted on for a day or a month or a year, 'was the only man I ever truly loved. And though we weren't able to be together, he gave me the most precious person in my life.'

'Who's that?' I would whisper back, snuggling into my blankets, sure of the answer.

'It's you, my darling,' she would say. 'It is you.'

There is a ladybird perched on a leaf, vivid red against green. I frame it in my camera and take a shot. I glance up and see that the Wickhams are all far ahead of me now, walking with their purposeful gait. All except for Quinn, who is jogging back to me. His hands are in his pockets and he

48

is smiling. The sight gives me butterflies in my stomach, fluttering along with the undigested lamb and potatoes.

'Thought you could use an umbrella-holder,' he says. He takes my cherry umbrella from my hand. 'So you can concentrate on taking photos.'

I didn't really intend to have company, but it is kind of him, so I say, 'Thanks,' and squat down to take photos of some wild geranium. The rain has called up the smells of things and I inhale earth, green stems, and something else. Something heavy, exotic, flowering. I've smelled it before, not long ago, on a London street. And here it is again. White velvet petals, a sweetness that is not quite cloying.

I stand up; Quinn is holding my umbrella, humming slightly under his breath. We're in a lane about half a mile from the village, with no houses in sight. There's no one to wear the perfume, no exotic flowers to create it. It reminds me of my mother, but my mother is gone.

'Do you smell that?' I ask him.

He sniffs the air. 'Someone's having a bonfire?'

'No, the flowers.'

'Can't say that I do.'

Warmth rolls through me, a happy feeling of exhilaration. What a lovely husband I have, and how wonderful it is to be out in the countryside with him.

I fling my arms around him and kiss him on the lips.

'What have I done right?' he says when I've finished, but he looks pleased.

'I love you,' I tell him. My heart is beating fast and my fingers are tingling. My cheeks feel flushed. 'Isn't springtime fantastic?'

'Well, rather wet at the moment, but in general, yes.'

I inhale deeply. 'I love the air, everything growing. It smells wonderful.'

And I *feel* wonderful. Five minutes ago, I was worrying, wanting to be alone, missing Mum. Now a barely suppressed joy runs through my veins. The cherry-red umbrella, the grey of the sky, the frayed and well-worn collar of Quinn's blue anorak, the ladybird poised on the leaf. I've seen it all before, it's familiar and exquisite and it's all meant to be here, it's all here for a reason. It's all exactly right and correct, the way the world is supposed to be – and I'm in love with it.

It's the most amazing relief. I'm in love with my husband. Totally, wholeheartedly in love.

'What's so funny?' asks Quinn.

'It's not funny,' I say. 'It's . . . fantastic.'

I hug him and kiss him again, and then I can't contain it any more so I do a little pirouette in the damp lane in my wellington boots.

I feel as if I want to dance forever. I want to smile at the whole world.

Later, in bed, my husband falling asleep beside me, my body still warm from his hands, my lips tender from his kisses, I think about that moment in the lane. The perfume, so maddeningly familiar, out of nowhere.

I've wanted a sign, and maybe this is it. Confirmation that I've made the right decision in getting married, in choosing this life. That Quinn is my one, the person I'm meant to travel with, the one I'm meant to be with for ever. That even though I might have had a doubt or two, that can be over now.

I reach across the pillow and stroke his face with my hand. He shaved before he came to bed and his face was smooth against mine while we made love. For thirty, Quinn is quite young-looking, and he usually tries to keep a bit of stubble on his chin and upper lip so that people don't think he's younger than he is. Apparently the editor of a local newspaper needs to have a certain amount of gravitas. He shaves at night before he goes to bed, and only every few days. I found this careful ritual fascinating when we first got together. It was as if he were the opposite of every other man I'd ever met, all of whom shaved in the morning.

This Quinn, this clean-shaven man, only exists here with me at night. By the morning his chin will have become rough; his skin is pale and his hair is dark and the stubble shows through within hours and feels like fine sandpaper. Smooth-faced Quinn is mine alone.

It's one of the surprises of our marriage. My slender, courteous husband, the local-newspaper editor, softly-spoken and knowledgeable, is nearly another person in my arms in the dark. He is more solid. He feels taller and wider than he looks.

Drifting into sleep, I think about the myth of Cupid and Psyche. How Psyche only met her husband Cupid at night in bed, in the dark, and was never allowed to see him during the day. And then how Psyche grew more and more curious to know what her husband looked like. One night she was rash enough to light a candle. For a moment she saw him – the most beautiful man imaginable, the God of Love – and then a drop of wax fell from the candle onto his skin and awoke him, and he flew away and she lost him for ever.

But that's only a myth, with a moral: beware of curiosity. I don't need to be curious about Quinn. I know all there is to know. And finally, I feel the way I should.

Chapter Five

D r Johnson wraps the blood-pressure cuff around my arm and pumps it up. 'All good,' he says, letting the air hiss out. 'Everything all right in yourself?'

'Yes,' I say. 'Yes, fine.'

I nearly cancelled my appointment, but I scheduled it six months ago. I forget about appointments on a regular basis, so it seemed rather wasteful not to turn up to one that I actually remembered.

What will Quinn think, I wonder. He will have noticed the pack of pills on my side of the medicine cabinet emptying, and he will have seen the appointment written on the calendar. Will he ask whether I kept the appointment? And what if I say that I did?

After all, just because I've been given a repeat prescription for birth control pills, it doesn't mean I have to take them for the full six months. Or indeed that I have to take any of them. They're just handy things to have around.

Dr Johnson sits back behind the desk. He is the picture of a village GP: sparse white hair, tweed jacket. He has been treating Wickhams for ever. 'Migraines haven't come back?'

'No,' I say, as I always do. 'Not since I was a teenager.'

'Lucky you.' He clicks a button and the prescription prints itself out. But he's planted a seed in my head.

'I have been smelling things.'

'Smelling things?'

'Like cologne, or a flower. I've smelled it a couple of times now. Quinn couldn't smell it. It was really strong for about two or three minutes, and then it completely disappeared.'

He narrows his eyes through his glasses. 'That is odd. No headache associated?'

'No.'

'How often did you say it's happening?'

'Just twice, I think. Both times I was outside and it was really strong. I thought it was flowers, but then I thought it must be perfume. I even followed a woman because I thought she was wearing it. And then it disappeared.'

'Did you have auras with your previous migraines?'

'I don't think so. I didn't smell anything when I used to have headaches.'

'But visuals? Colours, shapes, anything like that?'

'No.'

'Well,' he says, frowning, 'it's probably nothing, but we should check a few things out. My guess is that this phantom odour could be linked to your previous migraines, but just to be on the safe side, I'm going to refer you to a neurologist for a specialist opinion.'

'Really?'

'It's nothing for you to worry about. Just being safe.' He takes a form from his desk and begins to write on it. 'What should happen is you'll receive a letter in two weeks or so with a date for an appointment.'

'Okay.'

'Meanwhile, I'm afraid I can't give you a repeat prescription for the contraceptive pill.'

'Because of a smell?'

'The pill could be causing it, and there's an association between migraines, the pill and stroke. Again, nothing to worry about, especially if we've caught it early, but it's not a risk we should take. You shouldn't take the ones remaining in your current packet, either.' He crumples the unsigned prescription form and tosses it in the wastepaper basket. 'I could give you a progesterone-only pill, or we could talk about other methods.'

I sit up straight. If the smell was a sign, this is an even stronger one. 'No. No, that's all right. Quinn and I were – we were talking about stopping it anyway.'

Dr Johnson beams. 'Now I think that is a fine idea.'

That night, Quinn's closest to the phone when it rings. He lifts the receiver and holds it in place with his shoulder as he's wiping dry the dishes.

'Hi, Mum.' As always, he sounds pleased to hear her voice, even though we only saw her two days ago and we'll see her again on Sunday. 'Thanks. What news?'

He listens and then looks over at me. 'My mother says that she saw Dr Johnson today in Waitrose and he told her some news. I think she expects me to know what she's talking about.'

My hands are wet, but I snatch the phone. 'Molly? What did Dr Johnson tell you?'

'He says you and Quinn have decided to start a family! Oh, Felicity, I'm over the moon! I've noticed you've been a little preoccupied lately and no wonder. I haven't said anything, but I don't mind telling you now that I was hoping you wouldn't put it off too long. There are so many women nowadays who start trying for a baby later and they find that they have problems. Not like when I was younger, when everyone started a family in their early twenties and before. Everything has changed, hasn't it? Of course, that's not to say that you'll have any trouble. Dr Johnson says there's no reason to worry at all, that you're very healthy.'

Quinn is watching me closely. He puts the tea towel down. 'I don't—' I begin.

'Derek is here too, he wants to say something.'

Before I can interrupt, Molly has passed the phone over to Derek. 'I'm so proud of you,' he says to me. 'You've made me very happy, love.'

My eyes sting with sudden tears. Quinn steps forward and puts one hand on my shoulder and holds the other out for the phone. I shake my head.

'Derek, that's – that's really nice of you, thank you. But I didn't think that the doctor would— I haven't talked about it with Quinn yet.'

'Talked about what yet?' asks Quinn.

'I understand,' says Derek. 'I just want you to know that I couldn't imagine a better person to carry on the Wickham name than you. You're a part of our family, and we'll do any-thing we can to help.'

'Baby-sitting!' calls Molly from close by.

'Okay. Thanks. Er . . . talk soon.'

Quinn takes the phone from me and replaces it in its cradle. 'What haven't we talked about yet? What are my parents on about? It isn't bad news, is it? Did the doctor find something wrong?'

'No. No, nothing wrong.'

'Why are you crying?' With his thumb, he wipes away the tear on my cheek.

'It's not bad news. I was just . . . your father was being really kind.'

'About what?'

'About our trying for a baby.'

Quinn's face transforms into something beautiful. 'Are you— you aren't pregnant, are you?'

'No, but I'm going to stop taking the pill. Dr Johnson was worried about it maybe causing headaches. But – but I wanted to stop anyway. You're right. It's a good idea.'

'Oh, Felicity,' he says, and he pulls me into his arms. He kisses the top of my head. 'I am so, so happy, love.'

I can feel his happiness pouring through his body into mine. He's nearly trembling with it.

'So am I,' I say. Now that the decision has been made for me, I feel lighter. I hug him back. 'I'm happy too.'

Chapter Six

I'm standing in the bedroom ironing Quinn's shirts. The unironed ones lie jumbled in a basket beside me, and the ironed ones hang cool and crisp in his wardrobe. Quinn doesn't mind ironing his own shirts, but I like doing it. It's relaxing: passing the hot iron over the cotton, smoothing out the wrinkles, pressing collars and cuffs flat and sleeves into perfect columns, tucking the point of the iron into gathers and around buttons. The room smells of warm fabric and Quinn underneath. Radio 4 plays in the kitchen, sending its murmur up the stairs to me, a counterpoint to the rain outside.

I place the iron on the board and reach for a hanger. Molly insists on wooden hangers instead of metal or plastic ones; she gave us about a hundred of them when we moved in. I never knew there was a difference between hangers, but apparently there is. As there is a difference between types of detergents and oven cleaners, brands of flour and salt, shower scrubbers and thicknesses of towel. Domestic harmony involves a world of knowledge, and Molly carries it constantly in her head, along with the dates of birthdays, anniversaries and holidays major and minor. Sometimes I think about how tidy her brain must be, everything filed away and labelled, like the shelves of her pantry.

Slipping the hanger into the sleeves of the shirt, I smell perfume.

I turn around to check if anyone's come into the bedroom, but there's no one there. It's the same perfume as before: strong, flowery, exotic, familiar. According to Dr Johnson, it hasn't come from anyone; it's come from my own head, a strange type of migraine.

It doesn't feel at all like the migraines I used to have when I was a teenager. I used to spend the whole day in a darkened room with a wet cloth on my forehead. I used to shrink from light and be unable to eat. My migraines have mutated from painful to fragrant. Lucky Felicity.

I inhale. I can smell what's really around me: cotton and hot metal, detergent and dust, faint remains of burnt toast. But the flowery scent floats over it all, stronger and more insistent. I hold my nose and I can still smell it, somehow. Sweet and velvety, warm and tropical, a hint of spice and honeysuckle. A round, ripe scent, full and soft and strong.

And I know it. It makes me smile. Where do I know it from?

Without anyone else to distract me, and without having to search for where it's coming from, I can concentrate on it more. I close my eyes and I see flowers: white with a yellow heart, five perfect petals like a child's drawing. There are clouds of them, with waxy green leaves, heaped up around a chair. The flower heads nod slightly in the breeze from an open window.

Frangipani. The flowers are called frangipani.

That summer, in London, there were armfuls of the

blossoms coming into the house every day for weeks, endless perfume and beauty. Cut, they wilted in the heat and their limpid petals released still more scent every evening, crushed underfoot on the unfinished wooden floors, and in the morning came the fresh blooms. It was the summer of frangipani and . . .

And then the feeling sweeps over me. The feeling that something wonderful is happening, that everything around me is beautiful and significant, that I am teetering on an even greater happiness. My pulse quickens and I am holding my breath. My fingers curl up into my palms. My skin tingles. I have found the centre of everything and everything is perfect. I hear my heartbeat racing in my ears and I want to sing, to laugh, to kiss.

I'm in love.

Chapter Seven

Then it's gone. I stagger forwards and the side of my hand brushes the hot iron. 'Ow!' I yell, and jerk my hand away.

The air doesn't smell of flowers. My heart is still pounding, but the huge happiness that possessed me a moment ago has mostly drained away, leaving a lingering warmth. A memory of love rather than the love itself.

'What happened?' I ask aloud, cradling my hand.

No one answers. I'm all alone, although while my eyes were closed I felt as if someone were close enough to touch me. What else could explain that anticipation, that desire?

I look around. Nothing has changed. A jumble of shirts in a basket, the hot iron, wooden hangers. The shirt I was hanging up lies on the floor where I've dropped it. Outside, it's raining. I sniff and sniff the air, but the magic has gone.

My hand hurts. The room, so substantial before, feels unreal to me. Where did the flowers come from? And that feeling? And the memories?

I stumble to the bathroom and hold my hand under cold running water. According to my watch, no more than a few minutes can have passed. But a few minutes of . . . what? Migraine? Recollection?

I turn around and walk straight out of the cottage into the rain. In the middle of the garden, I turn my face up to the clouds so the water can wash my face, clear my head.

What on earth just happened? And why was it different from the other times I've smelled phantom flowers?

The rain flattens my hair, drips down inside the collar of my shirt.

The difference is, of course, that this time I was alone. The first time I was on a street, and I thought it was about my mother. The last time I was with Quinn. I thought the smell was real. I thought the feelings that flooded through me were about him, because he's my husband and he was standing next to me.

I thought I was feeling a wave of love for my husband. Who I do love. Of course I love him.

But now I've had the – whatever it is, the migraine, the memory – alone, without Quinn near me, I know that this feeling, this specific, particular feeling, isn't about him. Why would I have an overwhelming attack of love while I'm standing in the bedroom, ironing shirts?

It's about someone else, a man in my memory who smelled of frangipani, who tucked a blossom behind my ear that summer. I know it like I know my own past, like I know the series of choices and actions that have brought me to live here, in this cottage, and to stand outside in the rain.

It was Ewan. This smell, this feeling, this memory: it's Ewan. Not Quinn. Ewan, whom I knew ten years ago, one July and August. I haven't spoken to him since; I've thought of him, but not often. But there's only one man who smelled of frangipani, who stood for hours surrounded by it and then took me to bed. My feelings for him have been dulled. You can't sustain intense love like that for ten years, not for someone you haven't seen. Not for someone you can't have.

But I did feel like that about him, once. I recognize it, as I would recognize him if I saw him on the street. It's not just any love I felt: it was love for *him*.

The real question is why this memory has chosen to surface again now, and so powerfully.

'Mum?' I say aloud to the rain. Nothing answers. I open the gate and walk across the lane, out onto the common. The houses and cottages of Tillingford surround it like rocks holding down a handkerchief in the wind. The pub on one corner, the Wickham offices on the other. Derek and Molly's house directly across. Stolid, certain, unmoving.

Ewan McKillan. His blue eyes, the way his brown hair gleamed red in the sun, the faint freckles on his arms, his faded jeans with the hole in the knee. I can't stop thinking of him now. He wore boots with scuffed toes and worn-down heels. His fingertips were callused, the nails of his right hand longer than on his left. Ewan smiling, Ewan tipping back a pint and swallowing, the line of his neck, the texture of his skin, how he frowned whenever he sang.

I don't know where he is now. I deleted his number and screwed up the piece of paper he gave me with his address written on it. For months after we split up, I thought I saw him on the street. I expected him to ring. But he never did – because I asked him not to, or maybe because he didn't want to – and gradually he slipped out of my mind, out of my thoughts. *Travel lightly, my girl.*

Past lovers are supposed to slip away, especially when you're married. Maybe there's an echo every now and then; sometimes when I hear a song on the radio I think of Ewan and how he would play it. But it's supposed to be an echo. Ten years distant, overlaid by more recent feelings and events. If you meet a past lover on the street, you're supposed to smile and spend a few minutes catching up, maybe go for a coffee, and then part again. That's what I thought I would do if I ever met Ewan again. Maybe there would be a pang, a slight trace of the desire I used to feel, but it would be reduced. Nearly gone, only a pleasant memory.

I wasn't supposed to be alive with love for him – for *him*, Ewan – in my own bedroom that I share with my husband. It wasn't supposed to be so near and close that I felt as if I'd gone back ten years in time.

'Felicity?'

The voice is right behind me. I whirl around. Suz puts her hand on my shoulder. She's in a suit, holding a golf umbrella up over us.

'Are you all right? I was looking out of the window and I saw you out here without a jacket or anything, just standing on the common.'

'Oh, I – I was thinking.'

She studies my face. 'You look strange.'

'Strange how?' I ask, suddenly worried that my sister-in-law can see into my mind, see what I've been thinking about. But she grins.

'You look like you've just smoked an enormous spliff, to tell you the truth. Totally blissed out.'

I touch my lips with my fingertips and yes, I'm smiling. I try to relax my mouth muscles but it doesn't seem to work. The feeling I had ten minutes ago is still inside me, still warming me. 'I haven't been smoking anything.'

'I wouldn't tell, if you were. I wouldn't mind trying some

of it myself, if it makes you feel as good as you look like you feel.'

'It's just . . . I like the rain.'

'Oh! I'm so glad you got to her with that umbrella, Susan.' Molly bustles up to us across the grass, scarf tied over her hair, wellies on her feet. 'Here, Felicity, I've got an extra mac for you. You shouldn't be out like this in this weather, you'll catch your death.'

She wraps the mac around my shoulders. Suz holds the umbrella above all of our heads. With the rain not falling on me, I can feel how wet I am. My hair streams down my back. My fringe is plastered to my forehead. 'I'm fine,' I tell Molly, beginning to shiver.

'What happened to your hand? It's bright red.'

'Oh. I burned it on the iron. It doesn't hurt.'

Molly tuts and puts her arms around me. 'Come along with me, we'll get you into a hot bath and then some dry clothes. A nice cup of tea.' She begins to draw me towards the Old Vicarage, but I stop.

'I think I might have left the iron plugged in.'

'Then we'll go to the cottage.' She pulls me the other way. Over Molly's shoulder, I see Suz wink at me.

'I'll get back to work and leave you in Mum's capable hands.'

'I honestly only came out for a breath of fresh air,' I say.

'A nice cup of tea, and some salve for that burn. You'll be good as new, you'll see.'

At Hope Cottage, she fusses. She makes me sit, wrapped in a blanket, on my sofa while she draws a bath for me and finds me dry clothes. While I'm in the bath she brings me a cup of tea, carefully averting her eyes from my body among the lavender-scented bubbles which she gave me for Christmas. She perches the cup on the edge of the bath. 'You could get a lovely white bathroom suite for this,' she says, backing out, 'it would just brighten up the room. Now relax, warm up.'

We haven't redecorated the upstairs bathroom; the tub, sink and toilet are a violent salmon pink, to match the flowery wallpaper which is peeling in one corner. The tiles have contrasting flowers. We don't use the pink bidet so I've put a spider plant in it. It seems to be doing quite well.

I lie back in the hot water, my burned hand propped on the side of the bath so it doesn't sting. I'd like to think more about this feeling about Ewan, and why it hijacked me. But I can hear Molly in the cottage, talking to herself busily. It sounds like she's finishing ironing Quinn's shirts, and then I can hear pots and pans going in the kitchen.

I rest my head on the back of the tub, gazing up at the ceiling. Maybe it's the presence of my mother-in-law, but the euphoria I felt on the common has drained out of me, leaving me feeling heavy and tired. Lavender has always reminded me of a jumper I found in a charity shop once. It was pale blue wool, lovely and light, but washing didn't remove the smell, and whenever I wore it I smelled like an old lady. Now, because of the bubble bath, it reminds me of Molly. The gold-coloured wrapping paper she used at Christmas, sprigged with holly. Molly holly. All the gifts kept till after Christmas lunch, just as the Wickhams had always done it.

A light knock on the door makes me start and open my eyes. The water is tepid and the bubbles have nearly all gone. The door opens and Quinn pokes his head in. 'Hello, love. Did I wake you?'

His hair is wet and when he comes into the bathroom, he smells of rain. He touches my shoulder with a cool hand. 'Mum's downstairs. She says you were traipsing around the common in the rain like a water nymph.'

'She never used those words, did she?'

He shakes his head. 'She's made us a stew.' He puts down the toilet seat and sits on it, gazing at me. 'Sorry about that. I know you're a grown-up who should be able to walk in the rain if she wants to, but you know what Mum's like.'

'She's only being kind. Besides, Suz was out like a shot with an umbrella.'

'It's a bit like a goldfish bowl, the common. Are you all right? You burned your hand?' He picks it up gently, examines the bandage his mother put around it.

'It's fine. I'll live.' I yawn. 'I'm worn out though.'

'I'll tell Mum you want an early night. I'm sure she'll take the hint.' He stands and picks up his toothbrush.

'Quinn? Do you ever think about your ex-girlfriends?'

He catches my eye in the mirror and gives me half a smile. 'You mean, besides the ones I run into in the pub and on the street on a daily basis?'

'You make it sound as if you dated most of the village.'

'Only one or two. And no, I don't think about any of them, or not in any way except as friends.' He looks down, squeezes toothpaste. 'Do you think about your exes?'

'Oh, something today reminded me of someone I used to know a long time ago.' He begins to brush his teeth, his back to me. He's waiting for me to say more, and for a moment, looking at the back of his neck, how the hair curls there when it's damp, I think I might tell him. *Isn't it weird*, I'd say, *that I felt ten years of distance vanish.*

Isn't it strange that I could still feel anything about him.

But this isn't what you say to your husband, in your bathroom, as he brushes his teeth. You don't admit these feelings about another man, not if you still have them, not even if, until today, you thought they had faded.

'A long, long time ago, in a land far away,' I tell him. 'It's not important. How was your day?'

Quinn

Sometimes when he came home from work, Felicity was trying to draw. Sometimes she was waiting for him, full of questions, wanting to share in his day. Sometimes she was in the middle of a spontaneous DIY project. He came home one evening last September to find she'd ripped up every single downstairs carpet and thrown it into the front garden. Which was fair enough – they were hideous patterned things from the 1960s, which was apparently the last time the Ogdens had bothered to decorate – but he'd been planning to get some professionals in.

'Look!' she'd told him, standing in the middle of the dining room, their furniture pushed to one side so she could get up the underlay. 'These floorboards! Aren't they gorgeous? I knew they would be. Look at this.' She dropped to her knees and pointed.

'I think that's woodworm,' he said.

'Yes. But it's beautiful, all the curved holes.' She frowned. 'We have to get rid of it though, I suppose, before we fall through.'

He kissed her, the only person in the world who would find woodworm beautiful. Then he rang Patrick to ask for recommendations for a woodworm treatment firm and a place to hire a sander.

Occasionally, not often, he came home and she wasn't there. A light might be on, or maybe none. The house would be full of traces of her: lipstick mark on a glass, discarded shoes, the radio left on. But he'd know as soon as he walked in that she was gone. The cottage's heart was missing. At times, she left a note, or he'd get a text later. Other times, she didn't. She'd return with a bunch of wildflowers, her boots muddy from walking. Once she left her phone on the kitchen table, and as the hours went by he'd imagined her lost, injured, running away. He didn't want to be the sort of husband who checked up on his wife, but he'd been just about to ring her best friend Lauren when Felicity walked in with a box containing two perfect éclairs, one for each of them, which she'd taken the train into London to get.

Today when he propped his bicycle against the shed wall and entered the house through the kitchen door, he could hear her upstairs in the back bedroom she used as her studio. Loosening his tie, he climbed the stairs. They'd agreed on signals months ago. If her door was closed, she was working and didn't want to be disturbed. If it was open, he could go in, chat with her, look at her drawings. More often than not, her door was closed, and the drawings he saw were un-connected with her book.

He knew she was stuck. He pictured her sitting in her studio, battering her head against an invisible window. Trying to think up a story that wouldn't come. He was as helpless as she was. When he asked her about it, she waved it off as if it wasn't important. When he offered to help, it seemed to make her cross. He could see when she was thinking about it, when she was trying to break through that barrier inside her. It made her quiet and distant, the way she'd been when they'd first met on that train, huddled inside herself, frowning at the page in front of her.

The door was ajar. He hesitated outside it, catching an odour of white spirit and flowers. 'Hello, love, I'm home,' he called. When she opened the door, the scent assailed him. 'Whoa,' he said, lifting his hand to his face. 'Did you drop a bottle of something?'

'It's an experiment.' Felicity was standing by her desk. She'd moved the Mac and her scanner to the floor, and covered the surface of the desk with bottles and boxes and objects. He saw the plastic bottle of white spirit, and a bottle of perfume. A joss stick and an orange studded with cloves and a pale blue cardigan.

'An experiment on what?'

'Smell.' She picked up the orange and held it out to him. 'This, for instance. Smell it and tell me what you feel.'

He sniffed. 'Christmas.'

'Christmas in general, or a very specific Christmas?'

He closed his eyes and smelled. His grandmother's kitchen, scrubbed flagstones and herbs drying from the beams. 'Gran used to make mulled cider. Suz and I would always nick some. It was the first time I ever got drunk.'

'Try this one.' A pine-scented air freshener.

'A million taxis.'

'What about this?' She passed him a small bottle filled with yellow liquid.

'I don't know what this is. Some sort of oil?'

'It's linseed. It's used in oil painting.' She closed her eyes and inhaled it. 'It's what my mother smelled like.'

Felicity never spoke about her mother; not at length, anyway. He knew Felicity had been an only child, and that her mother had been a well-known artist. He knew they travelled around a lot, that there wasn't a father in the picture, that they didn't care much about money or timekeeping or material objects. He knew that her mother had passed away about six months before he'd met Felicity; he knew, though he wasn't sure if he was supposed to, that Esther Bloom's ashes were in a metal urn inside a plastic bag underneath the armchair in Felicity's office.

Quinn watched Felicity breathing in the scent of her mother. His own mother smelled of talcum and lily-of-the-valley and melted butter. He wondered if, when Molly was gone, he would try to recreate that scent.

'She could be in the next room,' Felicity said. 'It's extraordinary.'

'Smell does that,' he said. 'It's supposed to be the sense that's most connected to our memory. It's closer in our brains or something. Once, I remember, I picked up a book at my parents' house and opened it, and something about the smell of it reminded me of a cat we used to have. I hadn't thought about the cat for years. And the odd thing was, the memory was of the cat dying. I remembered hugging him after he was dead, and his fur felt the same, but his body was limp. I must have been four or five years old. I remember my dad putting him in a box to be buried in the garden, and I put his catnip mouse in the box with him because that was his favourite toy.'

Felicity was looking at him intently. 'All that, from a smell?'

'I must've opened that book at the same time, or maybe the catnip mouse got into it. I don't know. But yes, all that

71

from a smell. I can still feel it now when I think about it.'

He waited for her to reciprocate. To tell him something about her mother, or one of her memories. But she was gazing at him and he couldn't read what she was thinking.

'Do you miss her?' he asked, finally.

It seemed to bring her out of a sort of trance. She nodded and put the cap back on the bottle of linseed oil. 'I'm not sure I like it,' she said, and picked up another bottle, this one rectangular and decorated with flowers in relief. She took off the cut-glass stopper and handed it to him. 'What do you think about this?'

It was perfume, cloying and tropical, too sweet, like a room full of lilies. He wrinkled his nose. 'Where'd you get this?'

'I bought it. Have you smelled it before?'

'No. I don't think so.' He turned the bottle over in his hands. *Frangipane.* 'Not the sort of scent *you* would be likely to wear, is it?'

'Not me, no.' She took it back from him and sprayed it in the air. 'It's different in a perfume. No, it's not quite right.'

'Not quite right for what?'

'Just – not quite right. It's got vanilla or something in it. Something mixed in.' She put down the bottle, firmly, as if she'd made some sort of a decision. 'Anyway, it's not important. It doesn't matter.' She went to the window and opened it wide, to let the fresh air in.

Chapter Eight

The letter comes from the hospital a few days later, when Quinn's at work. I open it up and skim it; it gives me a map of the neurology unit, and an appointment eight weeks away, in August.

I've never been to a neurology unit, but I've spent plenty of time inside a hospital. I picture sterile white walls and crêpe-soled shoes on polished floors, a big machine for looking into brains like the ones I've seen on television. I picture a doctor trying to work out why my brain is giving me these memories, treating them like a symptom or a sort of headache, which is ridiculous because I'm not ill at all.

I may be haunted; I may have a brain that is trying to tell me something, to remind me of something I've forgotten. But I'm *not* ill.

When it comes down to it, these memories are happy ones. A scent of flowers, and a sensation of overwhelming love. Who goes to the doctor to diagnose the cause of happiness?

Away down at the bottom of my thoughts, the place where the worries live, I think, *But what if there's something really wrong with me?*

I fold up the letter and put it in the bottom of my in-tray where I file bills. I feel fine. In fact, I feel better than fine. If the memories get weird, or if I start having any headaches, I'll call Dr Johnson and ask if he can move the appointment forward. If they go away, I'll cancel it.

Until then, I'd prefer to understand what this smell and this feeling mean, and a big machine or a doctor won't be able to tell me that. Any more than they were able to save my mother.

The loft in our cottage is low-beamed and full of cobwebs and the scent of damp thatch. The first time I go up there, on the rickety aluminium ladder, I forget the torch, so I have to go back down and search for it. The beam picks out the outline of boxes, suitcases, the decorations we bought for our first Christmas together. My plastic box of photographs is shoved right under the eaves near the back. I pull it over to the open loft hatch, where there's more light, and sit with my feet dangling over the edge.

There's a certain amount of hazard in looking at old photographs. On the one hand, they're just pieces of paper, frozen memories. They can't act; they can't hurt you in new ways. Everything in that box is finished. On the other hand, once you've opened the box, it's difficult not to look at everything in it. It's hard not to remember things you'd like to forget, not to regret choices you wish you hadn't made. Even the happy photographs are dangerous, if the happiness captured in them is gone.

I know I have photographs of Ewan inside this box somewhere. There's at least one strip we took in a photo booth in Boots, pulling funny faces, kissing each other. I seem to remember another one taken by one of the members of his band, Matt maybe or was it Dougie, in a nightclub so dark that you can only see Ewan's face in a blur. But mostly they are photographs I took myself. I took photographs of Ewan laughing, running, sleeping. I took photographs sitting in the bath with him, in the park with his shirt off in the sunshine. There were several rolls' worth of film, which I had developed and kept in a shiny plastic envelope. I captured so many moments because they felt precious to me, because he was so beautiful I could hardly believe it. I took photographs and printed them out to keep, even before Ewan went away.

Is that because I knew they were all I was going to have left of him?

I don't have as many photographs of Quinn – not physical ones, anyway. There's one, framed, in our living room: a black and white one of us on our wedding day, with Quinn holding an umbrella up over our heads. I'm wearing my ivory wedding dress and he's in his morning suit. He's kissing my cheek and I'm looking up at the sky. It's a beautiful photograph, very well composed, and I remember that moment too, the warmth of his arm around my waist, the raindrops pattering on the umbrella and us safe beneath it, the way he laughed afterwards and told me I had muddy feet.

Over the past ten years, technology has changed. We take photographs on our mobile phones and text them to each other for immediate consumption. My Nikon is digital. I download my photos onto my Mac, but I don't print them out. It's too much bother. My photographs of Quinn are electronic information, instantly accessible. I don't have to look at them because Quinn is here living with me.

I regard the box. If I could put my hand inside it and immediately find the envelope of pictures of Ewan, I would probably do it. But there are lots of other pictures in there. Pictures of my mother when she was well. Pictures of myself, as a child, holding her hand.

I push the box back under the rafters, and climb back down the aluminium ladder.

I meet Lauren at her office in the City. Lauren is my oldest friend. My childhood was too itinerant to form any lasting friendships, though I still remember Jodie, with whom I used to eat lunch in Year Four, and Aisha, who taught me how to put on make-up at age twelve, and lots of other girls who were my best friends for a while. Sometimes I wonder if I've passed these people on the street since, not recognizing how they've grown into adults.

Lauren and I met in a youth hostel in Mumbai when we were both eighteen, both backpacking around the world, both drunk on the different languages, all the different people, strange sights and smells and tastes. She had dread-locks then, and small round glasses, and practically bathed in patchouli oil. These days she has had her vision corrected by laser surgery and wears smart suits and handmade shoes, works as a financial consultant and spends half her time in London or Brussels and the rest of the time flitting around Asia helping the super-rich save money.

As always, when she walks through the glass doors into Reception it takes me a moment before I recognize this sleek, well-groomed woman. In my mind, despite all the evidence that time has moved on, she's still teenage Lauren, a little bit overweight, bouncy on her feet, with all those woven bracelets made out of string.

Then she smiles and it's my friend. 'Fliss,' she says, kissing both cheeks. Her skin is cool, her hair straightened. Everything about her is expensive except for the warm way she squeezes my hand. 'Do you mind if we have our lunch on the go? I need to do my steps for today.'

'Steps?' I say, walking with her out of her building. She's wearing trainers with her suit.

'Fitness programme. I'm dating a personal trainer in Brussels – Hans. Did I tell you? He is really cute. But sort of a body fascist. Come on, five hundred more steps and then I'm allowed to have a high-protein wrap. I brought one for you, too. You'll hate it.' She starts some sort of app on her phone, and we set out at a pace down the street, swerving around fellow pedestrians.

'I thought you were seeing that trader, Frank Whatsisname.'

'He was married.' She pulls a face. 'That's the third American I've dated who's turned out to be married. Remind me never to touch another American again. I'd rather run a marathon, which by the way Hans wants me to do next spring. How's Lovely Quinn?'

'Good.'

'How's Annoying Mother-In-Law?'

'Also good.'

'Stepford Village?'

'It's not that bad. It is a bit Stepfordy. But it's very sweet.'

'And the book?'

'Slow. It'll get there.'

'Any news?'

Lauren likes certainties. She's not the type to be visited by memories of her past or buffeted by unexpected emotions. When I met her in that youth hostel in Mumbai, she already had her mental checklist of What Lauren Will Do With Her Life. She'd deferred her entry to the Sorbonne to study economics for a year, so she could travel the world and experience everything. I, on the other hand, was travelling because I had no idea what else I should have been doing.

If I told her about the sudden feelings I was having about Ewan, the phantom smells and the mad being in love, she'd want to investigate them. She'd want to find a rational explanation, and I'm not quite ready for that yet. Besides, Lauren absolutely adores Quinn. 'Love him,' she told me in private, after the first time I'd introduced them. 'Keep this one. He's good for you. I'll marry him if you don't.' But I knew she wouldn't; she'd told me that at the age of thirteen she'd determined that she would only marry a man who had as much personal wealth as she did.

'Not much news,' I say.

She passes me something wrapped in cling film, and I unwrap it and take a bite. I immediately spit it back into the wrapper. 'That is really, really gross.'

'I know.' She chews hers. It requires a lot of chewing. 'Hans loves them. Zero carbs.'

'Is he your financial equal?'

'He's independently wealthy. Old money. Here, have a protein bar.'

The protein bar is slightly more palatable. My ballet flats aren't quite up to the pace that Lauren is setting, and I'm obviously not as fit as she is, either. It's safe to say that Quinn is not a body fascist. Besides, I've spent most of the past few weeks sitting in my room, staring at a blank sketch pad. Or wandering in the rain after having feelings I can't explain. We power-walk up Bishopsgate into the gardens.

'Do you remember Ewan?' I ask her.

'Ewan who?'

'Ewan McKillan.'

She stops. 'The one who broke your heart?'

'Well, I don't know if he broke my heart as such . . .'

'He broke your heart. I recognized the symptoms. You washed up in Paris a complete wreck. Spent an entire month wandering around the Père Lachaise cemetery. The bastard.'

'Ewan didn't break my heart on purpose,' I say. Lauren never even met him, after all. None of my friends met him; Ewan and I were a unit unto ourselves, until we weren't. 'Our timing was wrong. We couldn't be together.'

'As I recall, he got some other woman pregnant.'

'That was before he'd met me. He didn't know she was pregnant when we were together.'

She snorts. 'According to him. It's hardly star-crossed-lover stuff, Fliss. He was a creep. You were better off without him.'

'Did I really seem heartbroken? Properly heartbroken?' It seems so distant now. The heartbreak, that is. I try to remember how I felt that autumn, wandering around the tombs, watching the cats frolic on the tombstones. I can think it in words, but I can't feel it any more.

'You were a skeleton. You hardly ate anything.'

'To be fair, I spent a lot of time living on love before that. I can't remember ever eating with Ewan in the same room.'

'Too busy shagging. And shagging isn't real life. A man who you can't eat with is a man you can't stay with.' I point at her high-protein wrap, and she grimaces. 'Point taken. Anyway, we do eat, Hans and I. It's just never anything nice.'

'Ewan was my first real love,' I say. 'He was beautiful and exciting. I'd never met a man like him before. When I was with him, I felt . . . that we were meant to be together. That I was exactly where I was supposed to be, and everything was right with the world.'

'Which obviously wasn't true at all, since you're not still with him. Good riddance, I say. Anyone who can make you so unhappy doesn't deserve a single moment of your time.' We've reached a bench with a bin beside it. Lauren chucks the wrap in the bin and sits on the bench, and I join her. 'Fuck it. You're right. I'll ring Hans and tell him it's over.'

'That's not what I meant,' I say, alarmed. But Lauren is already reaching for her phone.

'Oh. He'll be busy now anyway, doing his Pilates class. Okay, as soon as I get back this evening, I'll ring him. He's got a half-hour slot between half eight and nine.' She turns to me. 'Anyway, look at you now, Felicity. Everything's really right with your world these days.'

'Do you think so?'

She looks me up and down. It is always a little disconcerting when Lauren does this, because it's hard not to feel that she has evaluated every single part of you. Fortunately, from years of long-distance and close-distance friendship, I know how kind she is inside.

'I'll tell you something,' she says. 'Seeing you and Quinn together has almost made me change my checklist.'

'Change your *checklist*?'

'I said *almost*. Listen, when you invited me to your wedding, to be a bridesmaid no less, I won't say I wasn't surprised. A church wedding never seemed like your thing. Nor did settling down in a country cottage. But on your wedding day, it was so obvious. Everything was perfect.'

'It rained.'

'The two of you are meant for each other. Anyone can see it. You've put on weight, you look contented.'

I tug down my top. 'His mother is a good cook.'

'You're calmer than you used to be. More grounded. Quinn adores you. He looks at you as if he's won the lottery. I always thought that it should be one hundred per cent equal between a man and a woman – income, background, ambition, everything – but you and Quinn make me think I might be wrong.'

'No,' I say. 'We're not equal. Quinn is much better than I am.'

She laughs. 'See what I mean?'

'Don't you feel . . .' I begin. I've never said this aloud before. 'Don't you feel that love like that is a responsibility, though?'

'How do you mean?'

'Like how you said I've changed, for example. What if I'm calmer and I'm slowing down because that's how Quinn expects me to be? If I'm changing to please him, but I'm not *meant* to be that way at all?'

Lauren shakes her head. 'You'd rather be miserable and moping around with a broken heart?'

'No, but—'

'Listen,' she says. 'Forget about the dickhead ex-boyfriends who broke your heart. You're past that now.'

'Yes, but the thing is, Lauren—'

'Hi, Lauren,' says a guy, walking past pushing a cart of sandwiches. He's got curly hair and is wearing a T-shirt saying TWO SLICES CATERING, LET US MAKE YOUR NEXT PARTY EPIC!

'Hey, Bill,' she says. I watch her as she watches him walk down the path.

81

'You really have changed your checklist,' I say.

'What? No, I said I *almost* changed it. He's just a bloke I say hi to.'

'I didn't spend all that autumn wandering around the cemetery,' I tell her. 'I spent some of it looking for my dad.'

'Did you find him?'

'No. I don't know what he looks like.'

She touches my hand. 'This proves what I've been saying, Fliss. If you're happy, you don't go looking for a dad you've never met. You stay with the man who loves you and you settle down. And you're happy with Quinn, in a way you never could have been happy with Ewan, whoever he was. Right?'

My mother met Lauren a few times. After the second time, she tapped her chin with her finger and said, 'There's a woman who knows where she's going. I wonder if she'll know when she gets there.'

'In a different way than I was with Ewan,' I say. 'I'm happy, yes.'

But after I say goodbye to Lauren at the door to her building, I don't go straight back to Paddington to get the train home. Instead, I take the Central Line to Stratford.

It has changed completely since I was last there. The station is new, and Westfield shopping centre hunkers like an alien spaceship. I take a slow circle around and try to guess the direction I used to take, ten years ago. In the end, I decide to cross the road and follow my instincts.

I was a student, and I walked from the underground nearly every day. It was a hot summer, hotter than it is now, though it's June. The streets seemed crowded with cigarette smoke and steam. As I walk, I begin to see landmarks that I recognize, placed between the new buildings or old buildings used for new purposes. This is the small grocer where they stocked hair henna and chai tea, where the owner was friendly and greeted me in broken English. The vegetables outside look tired and wilted, covered with a fine layer of grime. The pub has been bought by a chain and renovated into something with chalkboards and pictures of burgers in the windows, but the building is the same. I pause on the pavement outside, remembering flashing lights on fruit machines and the taste of sweet cider. It used to be a horrible pub of soiled carpeting, yellowed walls and cracked vinyl, but there was a small wobbly table in the corner which was not visible from the road. I wonder if it's still inside.

The house is further down the street. It's a three-storey brick terrace with big windows on the ground and first floors. The door is painted red. I stand outside it, holding my hair piled on top of my head with one hand.

My mother, Esther Bloom, lived in this whole house for three years. I lived in it for one while I was starting art school, which I never finished. The studio was on the first floor, to catch the best of the light. My mother's bedroom adjoined her studio; it had a mattress on the floor, because we didn't own any proper furniture. I slept on the top floor in the back bedroom that overlooked the weedy patch of garden, in a proper bed with a single pine bedframe which had been left in the house when we moved in.

My mother had become successful, but we still didn't have curtains. We nailed swathes of fabric to the tops of the window frames and tied them back with twine. Some of the fabric was beautiful, woven by our friend Maria; some of it had been used as dust sheets and was spattered with paint, still smelling of linseed oil. In my own bedroom, I used a blue and red woollen blanket I had bought in Greece with Lauren.

We had a new kitchen: worktops, appliances, cupboards, flooring. There hadn't been anything when we moved in and Esther had cash by that point, so she went to John Lewis and spent it. She bought the entire kitchen, including the crockery, glassware, cutlery, and a set of expensive copper-bottomed pans which lived untouched in a cupboard. Esther rarely cooked, and I was pretty hopeless at it myself. Once I bought a tin of okra from the grocer's and boiled it. It looked like pond weed and tasted like urine. Often, visitors brought us meals, or came to stay and cooked. There was always wine. I remember a giant man called John who made bread, his dark hands kneading the pale dough. He might have been one of the people who wrote to me, after my mother had died.

I walk up the tiled path and up the steps to the front door. There's a row of doorbells, and after some deliberation, I ring them all, one followed by another. After a little while, the door is opened by a short woman in her early twenties, with black hair extensions and a neon-pink sweatshirt. 'Yeah?' she says.

'Hi,' I say. 'My name's Felicity. This might sound sort of funny, but I used to live in this house, and I wondered if I could have a look inside? Just for a minute?'

She looks at me and then shrugs. 'Whatever,' she says, and turns around to go down the corridor. I follow her. For the first time it occurs to me that no one knows I'm here and I'm lucky that a woman answered the door, and not a six-foot-five crazed axe murderer. This woman could be a crazed axe murderer, I suppose, but she's not really dressed for it. Her trousers are too tight.

The corridor has hardly changed, though where we had a table for keys and post and shoes, there's a large fly-specked mirror and a half-dead pot plant. The walls are a dull magnolia. What used to be an archway to the front room has been filled in, and there's a flimsy-looking door set in what was the middle of it. There's a similar door leading to what used to be the kitchen.

'Have you lived here long?' I ask her.

'Three weeks. Did you leave something in the flat?'

'No, I—'

'I don't pick up any post that isn't for me, so I don't have any of yours.'

'I really just wanted to have a glance around,' I say. 'Which . . . er, which flat is yours?'

She gives me a look like I'm crazy. 'The one you rang the bell for?'

'Oh. Yes, of course.'

She begins to climb the stairs and I follow her to the first landing, where she pushes open another flimsy door. 'Go ahead and look,' she says. 'But I have to go out in like five minutes, so . . .'

I step through. It's a bedsit, with a folded-out sofabed strewn with clothes. A small television blares in the corner. The tall window lets in a grimy light. It looks entirely unlike any place that I've been in before.

'This was my mother's studio,' I say slowly, trying to super-impose a vision of the past onto the present. There used to be two windows; a partition has cut the room in half. The bare floorboards, spattered with paint, have been covered over with cheap carpet.

My mother's easel would have been near the other window, in what's now presumably a different bedsit. Canvases were stacked against this wall where there's now a small kitchenette. There was a leather chaise longue where I would sit talking with my mother as she sketched. When the light failed she would put down her pencil and we would prop our feet up on boxes and look out of the windows as the orange streetlights came on. On some nights we could hear an owl, even here in the city. I incorporated her into my stories about Igor: Adrienne, the city owl.

I move over to one side of the sofabed. This is where they set up the vases of frangipani. This is where he stood. I watched him from beyond where the flimsy door now stands.

I breathe in and smell stale perfume and carpet cleaner. On the TV, there's an advert for yogurt that will get rid of bloating. I know this is the same house, I know this is more or less the spot where Ewan stood for days and days while he was being painted. But I can't feel it.

'Everything's changed,' I tell the woman. She looks at her watch. 'Thanks,' I say, and she nods.

On an impulse, instead of going down the stairs at the landing, I go up a flight. The carpet is new, but the stairs are the same. My hand trails on the banister, polished by many hands, including mine. I ran up these stairs, with Ewan behind me, both of us in a fever of anticipation. He carried me up them once, when we had drunk too much, and he nearly dropped me at the top.

The wood is smooth and holds no trace.

The door to my old bedroom is unchanged and for a split

second, gazing at the white-painted pine and the bronze doorknob, I slip back through time. My bed is through there, the single bed which we fitted into as if we'd been made for it. My books and my alarm clock that ticked too loudly and the Greek blanket that let the sun through in the mornings so it would slant against my cheek and wake me up, and then him.

Then I see the metal number 6 on the door, and the Yale lock that's been added over the doorknob.

It's all gone. I remember it, but it's with the knowledge that it was a long time ago and it is over now. The immediacy I felt the other day, the love as fresh as new, isn't there. It's finished. It's like when I smelled the bottle of *Frangipane* perfume: there are hints of what I once experienced, but it's been overlaid with change.

I don't have to do anything about this feeling for Ewan. I can leave it in the past where it belongs. It's a relief and a sadness, all rolled up into one.

Chapter Nine

'Can I look yet?'
        'Not yet.'

'It's been *hours*, Quinn. My eyelids are going to grow together.'

'It's been one hour and seven minutes exactly. You have your eyes closed for much longer when you sleep at night.'

'How do you know? You're always asleep too.'

Quinn doesn't answer. He hums lightly along to the radio as he drives. We're on a motorway, but I'm not entirely sure which one, and haven't a clue what direction we're driving in. All I know is that tomorrow is our anniversary, and this morning when I woke up, Quinn put my suitcase on the bottom of the bed and told me to pack for a weekend away. He'd already packed his own bag, and he wouldn't tell me what kind of clothing I'd need, so I filled my bag with dresses, rain gear, high heels and hiking boots. After breakfast he tied this scarf around my eyes and led me, by the hand, out to the car.

'Give me a little hint, at least. The time will go faster if I'm guessing.'

'No.'

'Anticipation is half the pleasure, you know. You're robbing me of it.'

'Tough.'

I sigh happily and lean back in my seat. This is exactly what I wanted to happen for our anniversary. *Exactly*.

I've been thinking about what Lauren said, about how Quinn has changed me for the better. And I've decided that what's really important is the here and now. My relationship with my husband who loves me, and whom I love in return. Memories, even intense ones, belong in the past.

And the proof is what's happening right this minute. Quinn's obviously put a lot of effort into arranging something especially for me, something that will make me happy. He knows I like surprises, even when I'm complaining and saying I don't. He knows that the pleasure of wherever he's taking me will be enhanced a hundredfold by the fact that I haven't had to plan it or think it through beforehand . . . just as I know that a great deal of his pleasure will have been in the planning.

The car slows and I enjoy trying to follow its progress. We've pulled off onto a slip road now. Stopped, waiting for traffic, and here's a roundabout. I can hear us going through a tunnel and then I feel several more roundabouts, and then the car slows further, almost to a crawl. Over speed bumps. Quinn pulls it into a parking space – I can hear that, because the engine noise changes as the car is closely hemmed in by others – and he switches it off.

'Now can I look?'

'Not yet. Open the glove box first.' I fumble for the catch and open it. 'Now take out what's inside.'

It feels like paper. 'Got it. Can I look now?'

'Yes.'

I snatch the scarf off my head. In my hand is a sealed envelope. I rip it open and inside are two plane tickets to New York.

I scream. 'We're going to New York!' I try to launch myself at Quinn, who is smiling like crazy, but the seatbelt stops me. I snap it open and then actually do launch myself at him. The gear stick bangs my leg and my elbow hits the horn. I don't care.

'This is brilliant,' I say, kissing him on the cheek.

'It's only for two nights, I'm afraid. I have to be back on Monday, so we're flying back on Sunday morning.'

'I don't care! It's New York!' I kiss him over and over and over again.

'I'm glad you like it,' he says, laughing, 'but we have to get to the terminal. You took ages packing, and check-in opens in five minutes.'

'You don't actually have to be there two whole hours before your flight,' I tell him. 'There's plenty of time. I've been late for lots of flights. They usually let you on.'

'I prefer to be on time.' He kisses me on the cheek and gets out of the car. I tuck the tickets and the scarf safely in my handbag and get out, too.

Quinn carries both our bags to the car-park bus stop, where we catch the bus to take us to the terminal. I laugh and point to the pods going by on rails. 'How long have you been planning this?' I ask him.

'A little while. I had some help.'

'Lauren helped you, didn't she?' He nods. 'She was singing your praises not long ago. I didn't know you'd been plotting together in secret.'

'I thought you were going to find out once or twice. You kept walking in when I was on the phone with her.'

'Did I? I never noticed.' I think back, and can't remember anything. 'I suppose I thought you were talking about work.'

He shakes his head. 'It's incredible. You notice all these little things when you're drawing or when you're interested, but when you're not, everything passes you by as if it's not happening.'

'Not everything. I notice . . . well, I noticed Cameron Bishop nicking your bike again yesterday. I actually caught him at it.'

'It's not a criticism. I'm a lucky chap, knowing that I could carry on a clandestine affair at any time and you'd be none the wiser.'

I elbow him.

'Or three or four affairs, maybe,' he says. 'Why not?'

'Well, I hope you can get one of your fancy friends to wash your socks.'

'Seriously, I'm glad I could surprise you.'

The bus drops us in front of the terminal. Quinn doesn't bother with a trolley, though my bag, at least, is pretty heavy. Inside, he peers at the information screens and leads us across the glossy floor towards the check-in desk. I've never been to this terminal before. I haven't travelled, properly travelled, for years. Everything is new and shiny, full of possibility and *now*ness.

I dance across the tiles after him.

Because of the time difference, we arrive in New York two hours after we left London. In the taxi, I wind down the window even though the driver gives me an irritated look

91

for wasting his air conditioning in the July heat. I want to smell the city, breathe in the hot concrete and oil, petrol fumes and rubbish. 'I love New York,' I tell Quinn, holding my hair back from my face and closing my eyes. 'I'm going to show you everything.'

All through the seven-hour flight, I've been listing things that Quinn has to try and do. He's never been to New York before. I've been several times; my mother taught here for a while, and I visited with Lauren, too. But the city is so large that I don't have to be worried about being hijacked by memories. 'It's lunchtime, isn't it?' I say, picking up Quinn's arm and twisting it to read his watch, because I haven't adjusted mine yet to local time. 'We should go straight to a deli and have enormous sandwiches. Reubens. You'd love a Reuben, it's got corned beef and sauerkraut and some sort of mayonnaisy dressing and cheese, and—'

'Let's go to the hotel and drop off our bags first,' he says, laughing. 'I can wait an extra half an hour for a sandwich named after a man. Aren't you tired at all?'

'No!'

'Well, I'd like a shower and a change of clothes. And then I'm all yours.'

'I can't believe you booked us a weekend in New York and you didn't plan a single thing for us to do. That's not like you, Quinn.'

'Well, I do have some plans for tomorrow, City Girl.' He touches the tip of my nose with his finger. 'Sometimes I can't quite believe that I convinced you to live in a village with me.'

'Just don't start chewing straw and spitting in Times Square, that's a good country boy.' I widen my eyes in mock surprise. 'Oh no, I just thought of something. Who's going to feed the neighbours' cat its second breakfast?'

'I have a bit of a surprise for you myself,' I say to Quinn, that night in the Lebanese restaurant I've chosen. The restaurant is crowded, with tables crushed together and the noise of many diners. My dessert is decorated with rose petals and a dusting of crushed green pistachios.

'What's that?'

I wasn't going to say anything. It's too early, and I know what Quinn is like. But today has been so great and he's done it all for me. It seems mean to keep anything to myself when it could give him pleasure.

'My period's late.'

Quinn slowly puts down his spoon. 'It is?'

'Yes. I only realized this morning when I was packing and I wondered if I should pack any tampons. So I counted, and it is.'

'Felicity. Do you think you are?'

'I don't know. We've been doing enough of what we need to.'

'That is fantastic.'

He looks as though he wants to jump up from his chair and plant a big kiss on my lips across the table. But he's far too English and Wickham to do such a thing. He just sits there, smiling, looking at me, his eyes shining.

'So in retrospect,' I say, 'it probably wasn't a great idea for me to order this glass of wine.'

'What? Oh, I see. You're right.' He pushes my glass of wine away from me, and then does the same with his. 'Do you really think . . . ? Do you feel any different?'

'Maybe. It's hard to tell, seeing as we're in New York all of a sudden.'

'I hope it's true,' he says, and touches my hand on the table. 'That would be – that would be everything, love.'

'I can do a test tomorrow maybe. I'm assuming they have pregnancy tests in New York.'

'They do,' says the woman at the table next to us. 'Go to CVS. I'm sorry for eavesdropping, but these tables are so close together and I couldn't help but hear the happy news. Mazel tov!'

'Mazel tov!' says her friend, also grinning.

'Thank you,' says Quinn. 'And it's our first anniversary.'

'Oh!' cries the woman's friend. 'What wonderful news. I won't put a jinx on it by saying anything else, but I hope it all works out for you.'

'Thanks,' I say. 'Me too.'

Quinn stands up, leans over the table, and kisses me. Beside us, the other diners begin to applaud.

Here and now is perfect.

Chapter Ten

'Wake up, sunshine.'

I open one eye. Quinn is standing beside the bed. He's had a shower and got dressed.

'Mmph,' I say, and pull the Egyptian-cotton hotel sheet up over my head.

'It's half past seven.' Quinn gently pulls the sheet back down.

'Half past seven? I only just got to sleep.'

'I've ordered breakfast. It'll be here any minute.'

'I've got jet lag,' I say. 'I need to sleep.'

'Jet lag doesn't work like that. It's half past twelve in the afternoon in England, so if it's jet lag, you should be wide awake.'

He's been wide awake for hours. I can tell by just looking at him.

'It's a holiday, Quinn. Come back to bed.'

'We came all the way to New York, and this is the only full day we've got. We're not staying in bed.'

'Isn't that sort of what having an anniversary is all about? Especially now while we're still young enough to *do* fun stuff in bed?'

'If we only wanted to do fun stuff in bed, we could have stayed at home.'

'Yes, but fun stuff is so much more fun in a New York bed.'

He chuckles and kisses my forehead. 'Definitely. Later. We've got breakfast and then I've bought us tickets for the Empire State Building.'

'I've never been up the Empire State.'

'Yes, exactly.'

I sit up and rub my eyes. My head feels woolly inside, despite my only having drunk half a glass of wine last night. 'It is jet lag, you know. I always have to sleep a couple of days when significantly changing time zones.'

'Coffee will sort you out.' Whistling, he strolls to the television and turns it onto the news channel.

'Do you have to go up the Empire State at a certain time?'

'No, but it's less busy before nine o'clock. We've got plenty of time, if you get up now.'

'Couldn't we go later?'

'Not without changing everything else.'

'What is everything else?'

'It's a surprise. All stuff that you'll like.'

I fall back onto the pillows. I knew this being-spontaneous thing wasn't going to last. It was the same on our honeymoon: Quinn likes to plan. We went to Sicily and he packed every minute full of interesting things to do. Yesterday was evidently my free-choice day, and today he's filled up our entire schedule.

'I just like New York beds,' I say, pouting a bit.

There's a knock at the door and Quinn opens it so a waiter can push in a little table, draped with a linen cloth and with silver-covered dishes. There's a crystal vase with a rose in it, two pots of coffee, and a jug of orange juice. At the smell of coffee and breakfast, my mouth starts to water. Travelling makes me hungry, even when there are important staying-in-bed-related principles at stake.

Quinn tips the waiter and closes the door after him. He pushes the table closer to the bedside and uncovers the dishes.

'Waffles and bacon,' I say.

'With maple syrup.'

'You remembered that was my favourite American breakfast. In bed.'

'And though I think it is a quite frankly insane combination, and I'm not mad about sticky syrup and crumbs on the sheets, I'm willing to put myself through it.' He grins at me, and looks so pleased with himself that I have to smile back.

'Thank you,' I say. 'Sorry for being grumpy.'

'Forgotten,' he says, and hands me a plate. 'We've got time to pick up a pregnancy test, if you like. Though I think . . .'

'Maybe it's best not to know today, in case it's not the right answer. Maybe it's best to wait until we're home.'

'Exactly. Let's concentrate on us.' He picks up a piece of crispy bacon from his plate, dips it in maple syrup, and crunches it with a grimace on his face that makes me laugh.

Seven hours later I am grumpy again, though I'm trying my best to hide it. We have 'done' mid-Manhattan with clockwork precision: Empire State, Times Square, Lincoln Center, Central Park. He's let slip that he's got theatre tickets for tonight, though he won't tell me which show. Quinn has planned this break to the millisecond, and all of it especially for me.

He's listened to me. He's thought of me. He's been absolutely entirely considerate and loving to me, and he's tickled pink that he's able to do this really incredibly sweet and wonderful thing for me on a day when it's not only our first wedding anniversary but when I may well be expecting our first child, too.

My feet are aching and I have indigestion from the hot dog that we shared from a street cart, but I'm not going to say anything. Quinn has worked hard to make me happy and he deserves for me to be happy. If I'm not bowled over with joy, it's not his fault. It's mine.

'This is the big thing,' Quinn's telling me. 'This is why I decided we'd go to New York, actually. I'd been thinking about it for ages, but when I discovered this was happening, it made up my mind.'

'What is it?' I ask. We're walking down a street, and I don't see anything in particular. Nothing that would tempt Quinn to fly me three thousand miles. Though that bookshop across the road looks interesting. I slow my pace to look at it, hoping he'll take the hint.

'It should be around this next corner.' He tugs my hand in excitement and I have to hurry up if I don't want to be positively pulled along.

We round the corner, and this street looks much like the last street, except without the bookshop. And then I see the sign.

ESTHER BLOOM: AN INTERNATIONAL RETROSPECTIVE

I stop on the pavement. It's one of those long banners, attached to the side of the gallery, with the lettering running vertically up it. At the top, there's a reproduction of one of my mother's pen and ink portraits. I dimly remember it being of one of our landlords.

'You've taken me to my mother's retrospective.'

'Yes! Isn't it a lucky coincidence? I never would have known it was even on this summer if I hadn't seen it in the *New York Times* online. Did you even know this was happening?'

'Yes.'

'You did?'

'I had an invitation. They wanted to fly me out here to be the guest of honour.'

'And . . . you said no?' Quinn's face has fallen. I've completely ruined his big surprise for me.

'No, I think I lost the invitation,' I say quickly. 'Plus, I thought it was too far to come for basically one party.'

The second excuse is completely unbelievable, but the first is probable enough. Quinn still looks devastated.

'You've never gone to any of the exhibitions of her work, have you?' he asks. 'Not since I've known you. I should have thought of that.'

I squeeze his hand. 'I met you just after she died, and it was too difficult then. It's all right now.'

I am lying.

'Really? Do – did you ever go to them?'

'Yes, we used to go together, but even then it was a little weird. It was like sharing my mother with all these strangers. I ducked out of them when I could. But it's fine now, Quinn. Really.' I smile. It's forced, but hopefully he won't notice.

'You don't mind sharing it with me?'

'Of course not. I want to.'

Quinn hesitates. 'I went . . . I went to an exhibition not long after I met you. I wanted to try to understand.'

'Her, or me?'

99

'Both. I'm sorry. I probably shouldn't have; we'd only known each other a few weeks. It felt like snooping. That's why I didn't tell you.'

It feels like snooping to me, too, but there's no rational reason for it. My mother was an artist. Though she belonged to me, her paintings and drawings were made to be shown. She wanted them to be shown. And Quinn wanted to know more about me. 'Did you find out anything?' I ask.

'They were beautiful. A little terrifying, sometimes, but still beautiful. I felt that I might have liked her.'

'You would have,' I say truthfully, my throat tight.

'We don't have to go in.'

I gaze up at the building. It's large. Who knows how many memories it can hold. I want to close my eyes and run away. I want to take Quinn's hand and go somewhere new with him, somewhere with no traces of anything I know.

'Of course we have to go in,' I say.

Even with my brave face on, I have to hold my breath when we walk into the gallery. All these pieces of my mother, all these visions she saw in her mind and created with her hands. Along with the photographs in our loft and the ashes in my studio, these are all that's left of her.

As an artist, my mother favoured large canvases; she painted her subjects several times bigger than life-size, the better to examine every flaw and beauty. The canvases line the tall white walls like frozen explosions of colour and feeling.

I wish they were all gone, that they'd all been burned with my mother's body. It's unfair that they still exist when she doesn't. It's wrong that these people who are wandering through the rooms, who probably came in on a whim from the street, can see what she painted and think that this is all that she was. And the fans, the art connoisseurs, the collectors, the students, the curators are worse: they think they know her, they think they own her. For a moment I hate them all and I want to scream at them to get out, *get out*, and leave us alone.

'Are you all right, love?' asks Quinn quietly. 'We can go if you want.'

Quinn has brought me here, Quinn has planned this hoping to please me, and for Quinn's sake, I can't leave.

I let out my breath, and draw another one in. I dread the smell of linseed, but it isn't there. It has evaporated away, out of these paintings. Maybe if I put my face right up close to one, I would smell the odour I associate with Mum. But the gallery itself smells of floor polish, and that makes it easier for me to look.

I've never seen the painting closest to the door before. It's the portrait of an elderly man, standing on an empty beach. He holds the skull of a bird in his hand. The small sign next to the painting says it was done in 1982, before I was born. It should be easier to see a painting I don't know, but it reminds me of all the time my mother existed and I never knew her. All the parts of her that I couldn't hold on to if I wanted to. Mum usually got rid of her paintings as soon as she could. If necessary, she gave them away.

There could be a painting of my father here. I wouldn't even recognize it.

'That's you, isn't it?' asks Quinn, quite close to my shoulder. I follow his gaze across the room and there I am. I'm four years old and I'm sitting on the back of a baby elephant.

This is easier to see. I walk across the room, Quinn by my

side, to look at it. In the painting, I'm draped in a green sari embroidered with silver thread. My fringe is too long and I look straight at the viewer, as I looked straight at my mother when she was taking the photograph that she painted from.

'Do you remember that?' Quinn asks me, and I nod. 'Were you in India?'

'No, it was a circus. I think it was in Norwich.'

Quinn laughs. His laughter is never loud, but it's the loudest thing in this hushed room. I gaze up at myself as a child. I remember sitting on that elephant very well, because it stank. The hair on its back chafed against my bare legs and its skin was more wrinkled than anything I'd ever seen in my life before. It was entirely alien. Its trunk stretched back and touched my knee as if to check on this strange thing on its back. The sari had tiny bells stitched onto its bottom hem and every time the elephant moved, the bells chimed.

Up until I was about fourteen years old, I believed that thirty seconds after that photograph was taken, the elephant started walking and I tumbled off it, straight into my mother's arms. She stopped me from falling onto the straw-strewn concrete floor and then she put me down safely on my feet. But then at fourteen I fell off my bicycle and broke my arm, and when the doctor showed us the X-rays he commented on the old, healed break in my radius. 'Oh yes,' said my mother, with that glimmer in her eye that meant she thought the doctor was fanciable, 'that was when she fell off the elephant.'

The doctor laughed, as he was meant to, and I said, 'But you caught me when I fell off the elephant that time.'

'No, darling, you fell off and broke your arm, don't you

102

remember? You had to wear a cast for weeks. You wanted flamingos drawn all over it.'

Gazing at the picture now, I don't remember breaking my arm. I must have broken it; I could see the thin line of healing on the X-ray, and I didn't remember any other time I could have broken it. But my memory is of being caught in my mother's arms. Surrounded by her hug, put safely back on my feet again.

'It's funny,' I say to Quinn now, 'how you remember some things and not others. Isn't it?'

He makes a sound of assent and I feel him waiting to hear more. But it's so quiet here. I'll be overheard.

'It's quite difficult,' I tell him. 'It makes me miss her.'

'I understand. We can leave if you want.'

I shake my head. 'No, you planned this. And now that I'm here, I feel that I should look. I just . . . I don't think I can talk about it. So much of it is so hard to explain.'

'You don't have to say anything.' He takes my hand. 'I completely understand.'

But he doesn't. How can he? He hasn't lost his mother. He's always known his father. He's always been secure of his place in the world, knowing he belonged there, and there's nothing that could shake it away from him. Quinn doesn't carry layers of loss and grief and guilt. He's straightforward and sincere. He's never been hijacked by the past when he was least expecting it.

'Let's just look at the pictures,' I say.

So much for the here and now.

I last about forty-five minutes before my head starts to throb with everything I'm containing in it. I rub my temples, which is enough of a hint for Quinn, who's been watching me much more attentively than he's been looking at the paintings.

'Do you want to take a break?' he says immediately. 'There's a café on the second floor.'

'Yeah, that's a good idea. I'll meet you there. I need to find a loo.'

'Maybe they have proper tea.'

'I wouldn't count on it. This is America. Tea bag with a string in a cup of lukewarm water.'

'I'll do my best.' He squeezes my hand, kisses my cheek. 'See you in a minute, love.'

As soon as he's gone, I can feel that I'm exhausted. My legs are shaking and though I don't actually need the loo, when I reach the cloakroom, I put down the seat in one of the cubicles and sit on it, my head sinking into my hands. I'm sure that Quinn planned to spend at least another hour here, but I've had enough. I need to stop remembering and clear my head.

The coolness inside the ladies' room makes me feel a bit better. I sit until my legs are steadier, then I emerge from the cubicle, splash my face with water, put some more lipstick on. It makes me look more like myself in the present. We've seen three portraits of me, aside from the one of me on the elephant, and in none of them am I wearing lipstick. Or a wedding ring.

As I head back through the gallery, looking for the stairs, I wonder what my mother would think of all this. The paintings are on loan from various collectors, mostly wealthy ones, although some have been lent to the gallery by Esther's friends. Those are ones she would have given away. She never

104

treated her work as if it were of any value. She wrote notes to my teachers on the back of old sketches; she sometimes used drawings as kindling in the fire.

Of course it's that cavalier attitude to her own work that means that her paintings now, after her death, are worth so much money and are so in demand. I've lost count of how many phone calls and emails I've ignored, how many letters I've binned, asking if I have any more work of hers for sale.

It was the same way with all of her belongings. If someone complimented her on a hat, say, she would pluck it off her head and press it on the person who'd spoken. People came and went in her life in a similar fashion. Some lovers she stayed friends with, some − like my father − she let go. She never went backwards and she never held on to anything or anyone, except for me.

'Walk lightly,' she always told me. 'Take nothing you can't leave behind.'

I have tried to walk lightly but I can't. Not as thoroughly as Esther could. I hold on to things and re-use them. I have favourite books which I have carried with me from country to country, house to house. I've kept my favourite jacket for nearly fifteen years. I have a plastic box of photographs. I collect pretty items, postcards and dried flowers and rhinestone hair clips and shoes.

I have a husband. I have a cottage and a mortgage. I've accumulated a whole life, much of it since my mother died.

I stop. I dig in my handbag and take out a handful of leaflets and maps about New York. There's a comb and an extra lipstick and an unused tissue and a mirror and some acorns that I found in Central Park yesterday. I squat down and put it all on the polished floor in an untidy pile, an

105

offering to my mother. For a moment I'm tempted to pick up the spare lipstick, because I quite like the colour, but I stand and walk away, a little lighter.

Against the odds, I'm smiling, and when I turn the corner I'm completely unprepared for what I see.

Chapter Eleven

Frangipani.

It surrounds him in clouds of white and yellow, brighter because he stands half in shadow. He's naked from the waist up, and the flowers give a glow to his skin, or perhaps his skin lends it to the flowers. It's golden, his skin, golden and perfect. His hair is dishevelled, too long, glinting with warmth; one hand holds a flower, about to drop it.

I stand, mouth agape, eyes wide, staring at him. He's nine feet tall and rendered in strokes of oil paint.

'Hello, Ewan,' I whisper.

His eyes are bright blue. They gaze out of the painting as if they're alive, as if the frame and the blank walls around it don't exist. As if years have been erased and he's standing here in front of me again.

The first time I saw him, he looked like this. Except he was naked.

I was late, of course. It was July and I had a sunburn from spending all morning reading on one of the carved benches in St Pancras Gardens. The strap of my shoulder bag rubbed against my skin and I had to keep on stopping to switch sides. It was completely my own fault that I was late; I'd left the garden late, reading an extra chapter, because I was procrastinating. I hated life drawing. I wasn't particularly good at it, even though I'd watched my mother effortlessly drawing people for all of my life. Maybe because I'd watched her, I knew how rubbish I was. My own drawings of human beings were awkward and half-imaginary; I could never quite translate what I saw in real life to what I put down on the page, so they ended up looking cartoonish. Freakish. And of course in a life-drawing class, there was always someone looking over your shoulder and you couldn't take your drawing away to fix before you showed it to anyone else.

But I wanted to go to art school, because drawing was the only thing I was halfway good at. Drawing owls, mostly. And if you wanted to go to art school, you needed a portfolio. And if you scraped by doing the minimum of work in your art A-levels and then spent the next eighteen months faffing around the world having fun, you needed to take summer classes at Central Saint Martins to bump up your portfolio.

When I got to the correct room I was dripping with sweat and it felt as if I had a blister on either side of my neck. I pushed open the door with both hands and burst in.

'Sorry,' I gasped. A dozen heads swivelled away from their drawings and towards me. From this vantage point, I couldn't see the model, but I could see the beginnings of drawings in charcoal and pencil. It was a man, a young man from the looks of it.

'There's a space over here,' the instructor said quietly to me and I gave all my attention to weaving between the other students and not knocking over their easels with my bag. I didn't like drawing young people, especially. Older people were more interesting. I preferred drawing wrinkles. If a life model had a perfect body, if they were beautiful, it only highlighted how faithless and ugly my drawing was. The first week, we'd had a stunning, slim young woman who was probably a catwalk model in her other life, and I'd made her look pretty much like a nude Cruella DeVil.

I set up my pad on the easel and I selected my charcoal and I wiped sweat away from my forehead with the back of my hand. Then, steeling myself for failure, I looked at the model.

He was looking directly at me.

It was like sticking my finger into a plug socket. My burned skin tingled. The hairs on my arms and on the back of my neck rose. I stepped backwards and exhaled an audible squeak.

His eyes were this incredible blue, ridiculously blue, as if they'd been coloured in with a swimming-pool-coloured crayon in a brighter hue than the rest of the room. Eyes should not be that blue. He should not be looking at me. He should be staring fixedly into the distance because he was a life model.

There was half a smile on his face. He'd heard me squeaking. He was looking at me because I'd just made a spectacle of myself crashing in late and then I'd been squeaking instead of calmly drawing, like a woman of the world who had seen countless naked men before.

I had in fact seen a lot of naked men. There were always naked men and women going in and out of my mother's studio; I frequently brought them cups of tea and sometimes had to lend them my dressing gown. Also, I was twenty years old and I had been around the world. I'd had boyfriends. I'd had sex. I was staring at this life model as if he were Adam and I were a gobsmacked Eve.

He was beautiful, all lean muscle, smooth chest, flawless skin. The ripple of his ribs was visible, and the scattering of hair on his chest and belly. He sat on a wooden stool and, probably fortunately for me, his genitals were hidden by his thigh. He was, of course, looking in my direction because that was the pose he had chosen. He just happened to have his head turned to this side of the room, where he could see the woman whose brains had temporarily deserted her.

'Are you all right?' whispered the instructor. She knew my mother and was inclined to be kind to me because of it. Though that made it worse for me, because my work could never live up to my genetic inheritance.

'I'm fine,' I said, with lips that had gone numb. 'Just . . . observing.' I raised my charcoal to my page. My palm was slick with sweat. My fingers were trembling. I made a mark – tentative, random.

'Interesting,' murmured the instructor and then, mercifully, she walked away.

I tried to draw. I tried to look at the page. I made other marks, supposedly the line of his arm, the tilt of his head. They were wrong, and besides, he kept on looking at me. His face had gone serious now. He looked as if he were thinking. Thinking about me.

I tore off the top sheet and tried again. But it was so hard to keep my eyes on the paper. And I should be observing his body, but his gaze kept catching mine. All this eye-contact. In a normal situation you would never stare at someone like this, right into their eyes, without speaking. It would never feel as if their gaze had taken hold of you, captured you with all that blueness, stolen all your thoughts, erased everyone else from the room.

'Shall we take a break?' The instructor's voice broke the silence and the people around me started to move, to stretch, to speak to each other. The model turned his head to something said to him and I was able, at last, to see what I'd done on my paper. It was a mess. It was random lines and smudges, the drawing of a four-year-old. My skin hot, I hurriedly ripped the page off and crumpled it into a ball.

'Hi,' said someone, and I knew without looking that it was him. Sometimes, quite often, the models moved around the room to see what people had drawn. I shoved the crumpled paper into my bag and tried a nonchalant smile.

He'd wrapped a cloth around his waist. But it was his eyes that I saw. 'Hi,' I said. I felt breathless. 'I'm sorry, my drawing was crap.'

'Fancy a coffee, after?'

That half a smile he'd had when I came in, had widened to a full one. Oh no. He'd seen me staring at him. He thought I was an easy conquest. He thought I was a silly little girl with clumsy feet and shaking hands. I should say no.

'Okay,' I heard myself say.

'I'll meet you at the front of the building,' he said. 'Once I'm dressed.'

'Are we ready for the next pose?' called the instructor.

I stand, now, in front of this painting of Ewan done by my mother. Two shadows of people who have left my life, in this one piece of art and memory. I check the white plaque by the painting, which says it is on loan from the owner, Mrs T. Kilgore from Florida. It's been in her house, sheltered

111

from the tropical sun, for ten years. Mrs T. Kilgore of Florida has gazed at Ewan every day without knowing the story of the painting: what happened before, what happened next, what has happened since. She has only known the title: *Portrait of a Young Man in Love*.

And Ewan stands there unchanged. He's so fresh. So tender. Of a piece with the petals before they fall.

My arms are gooseflesh. If I took a step forward I could step into the painting – a shadow myself – and touch him again for the first time, palm to palm, across a table.

Live it all again.

I stood on the pavement with sweat collecting in the small of my back, running the strap of my bag through my hands. It had got hotter while we were inside, as the asphalt and buildings collected the heat and radiated it back out again. All of the rest of the people in the life-drawing class had already filed past me, several of them giving me curious looks. He wasn't coming. I wouldn't be surprised if he'd nipped out of the back door as soon as he was dressed. He'd been looking the other way during the other poses, but I still hadn't been able to draw anything. Tracing the line of his back or the curve of his buttocks with my charcoal was too similar to touching him. And I wanted to touch him so much that I couldn't bear any substitute.

He was probably a wanker. He was probably full of himself. You had to be pretty full of yourself to stand in front of a whole load of people in a room and let them draw you naked, right?

Well, actually you didn't. I knew several artists' models and they were generally nice, normal individuals. But this one

112

probably targeted the women in the room, the ones who seemed flustered by his nakedness, attracted to him. He probably asked them all for dates and kept a score sheet, and then went to the pub with his mates and laughed about the silly art students. Even if he didn't, I didn't know anything about him. I'd just spent an hour and a half staring at him and failing to draw him. I might not even like him when I spoke to him.

I was going home. I turned on my heel and had started to walk towards the bus stop when I heard him behind me shouting, 'Hey!'

I whirled around, my heart leaping into my throat with irresistible joy. 'Hey,' I said, trying to sound calm and failing. He was wearing jeans and a leather jacket, in total disregard for the weather, but I didn't really notice that because he was looking in my eyes again.

I felt drunk. 'Do you . . . are you still up for that coffee?' I asked.

'There's a café on the Caledonian Road.'

He was almost unbearably close. He was smiling at me with more than a little bit of triumph. As we passed the side of King's Cross station, I decided I'd forgive him that smile because I fancied him so much.

It was an Italian café, and it was even hotter inside. He took off his jacket and hung it on the back of his chair and I could see damp patches on his T-shirt. He was as comfortable as he had been naked. 'What'll you have?' he asked me.

'An espresso, please.'

He ordered two, then held his hand out to me over the table. 'I'm Ewan.'

'Felicity.' I was too eager to touch him, so I took his hand casually, as if I couldn't care less. His palm was hot, and he held on to my hand for a beat too long. When he released it, I involuntarily put my fingers to my lips, then realized what I'd done and blushed.

'So, Flick. You're an art student.' He leaned back in his chair, resting his arm along the back of the one beside him. He had a soft Scottish accent, burrs in his r's.

'Not really. I'm trying to be one, but I've spent most of the past couple of years travelling so I need to build up my portfolio.'

The espresso and the travelling were to impress him. He raised his eyebrows slightly in acknowledgement, and then the coffees came and he began ripping open sugar packets and pouring their contents into his cup. I expected him to start talking about himself, but instead he asked, 'Where have you been?'

My mouth seemed clumsy, prone to stammering; I took a sip of the blistering coffee and told him anyway. As I spoke the words, named the countries, it became easier, because I could see that he was listening. Actually listening, not nodding and waiting for his turn to speak. He asked me which had been my favourites, what had been the most amazing thing I'd seen.

'I'd love to do that,' he said when I'd finished. 'I will, one day. I'll travel the world.'

'Why aren't you doing it now?'

He laughed, a sharp laugh that was almost a bark. 'Haven't got the dosh, have I? When I travel, I'm going to get paid to do it.'

'As an artists' model?'

He shook his head. His longish hair brushed his neck. 'I

sing and play guitar. I'm in a band up in Glasgow. "Magic Fingers Ewan", that's what they call me.' He held up his hands and twiddled his fingers.

'Really?'

'No, not really. But I am in a band. We're down here in London trying to get signed. On the verge of it, too. I sit for artists for a bit of extra cash.'

'Does it pay well?'

'Not much, considering half the time I've got a cold breeze blowing up my crack.'

The laughter that exploded from me had less to do with how funny his joke was, than my needing to do something to release tension. 'Do you like it?'

'I don't mind it.' He shrugged, and traced patterns in the sugar he'd spilled on the table. He had a tattoo on his arm, a complicated woven Celtic symbol; I hadn't even noticed it when he was naked. 'It's something to do with my days, anyway. This artist mate of mine set me up with it. I'm doing it for this sort of semi-famous artist next week. So I might be immortalized for ever.' He said it with just enough self-mocking irony for me not to mind. 'Do you want to be a famous artist?'

'No.'

'I want to be famous,' he told me. 'Properly famous. Not for the money; I want to have people all over the world listening to my music.'

'I just want to find something I'm good at,' I said. Inside I was marvelling. We'd known each other less than a couple of hours, had only been speaking for twenty minutes, and we were already sharing our deepest ambitions.

'You will,' he said. 'I bet you're good at lots of things.'

'Even if I don't find anything, I don't want to be normal.' My hands were shaking. I'd never said this to anyone before. 'I want to be extraordinary.'

'You're a beautiful girl. Really beautiful.'

He said it with emphasis. I knew I wasn't beautiful. *He* was beautiful. I was the mediocre artist who couldn't draw him. But that moment, I didn't just desire him; I loved him for seeing me as beautiful. As extraordinary.

Ewan reached over the table and he put his hand on my wrist. 'You should come to our gig at the Barfly in Camden tonight,' he said. 'It'll be a laugh.'

The room heaved and steamed, reeking of beer and sweat. I clutched half a pint of lager, was jostled on all sides. The floor was sticky underfoot.

There were four of them in the band, but I only registered them as variations of skinny and scruffy. My eyes were fixed on Ewan.

He was the lead guitarist and singer and he stood on stage like a young god. Cocky, sure of himself in tight jeans and a shirt unbuttoned to mid-chest, his guitar the same colour as his gleaming hair.

The music was loud and although I would learn all of it, eventually, by heart, that night I felt it rather than heard it, as a pulse through my body, a promise in his rough voice.

I shouldn't be so obvious, I thought, through the pounding and jostle and heat. *I should be cool, play the game. Go outside and scrounge a fag. Speak to someone else. Maybe flirt a little with the barman.*

I couldn't. I didn't. I watched him, enthralled. His hands

116

moved over his guitar, alternatively caressing and demanding. Every time his eyes met mine I burned.

When their set was over he picked up a bottle of beer from the floor near his mic stand and drank from it. I watched his lips purse, his throat move. He drank and drank while the other band members left the stage, until the applause stopped and conversation swelled again, and then he put the bottle down, handed his guitar to someone, and jumped lightly off the stage near me.

'Flick! Did you like it?' He was breathless and his hair was damp with sweat.

'I don't think I heard anything,' I said, basking in the fact that he'd given me a nickname.

'You were watching me the whole time,' he said. His voice was hoarse, nearly ruined. 'I didn't think you'd really come.'

'Ewan!' called one of the boys from the band. I thought it was the drummer. His accent was stronger than Ewan's. 'We need you over here, mate.'

'Just a minute.'

'This is important!'

'So's this.' He turned to me. 'Oh fuck. I don't know how to say this.'

'Say what?'

'Want another drink?'

Mine was still half-full. I nodded. He took my hand and led me to the bar at the back of the room. I felt the calluses on his fingers against my skin. He ordered a pint and a half of beer and leaned against the bar. His thumb stroked the back of my hand.

Neither of us said anything, but inside I was jumping

around. There was something different about him. Something elemental and sexy. Something urgent.

'Ewan!' The drummer appeared over his left shoulder. 'We need you over here. There's A&R from White Angel, man. He wants to talk with us downstairs.'

'I'll be there in a minute. Promise.' He never looked away from my face. Dimly, I heard the drummer make a noise of disgust and stalk away.

'I need to go,' he said, but he didn't go.

'That'll be four pound fifty,' said the barman who I'd neglected to flirt with. Ewan shook his head, as if waking up, and dug in his pocket for the money.

'Listen,' he said to me, pushing a litter of coins across the bar. 'I shouldn't be here.'

'You have to go to your band. I know. It's okay.'

'No, I mean – I'm not – there's . . .' He bit his lip. 'Okay, the truth. The truth is, I wasn't expecting to meet you. Not someone like you. I wanted you to come tonight, but I thought it would be better if you didn't. I shouldn't have invited you.'

'You shouldn't?' I stepped back and tried to pull away my hand, but he held tight.

'I've a girlfriend,' he said quickly. 'In Glasgow. I'm sorry, but I do.'

It was like a concrete block on my chest, pressing out all the air. 'Oh. I . . . I see.'

'Ewan, for fuck's sake!' Bellowed across the club.

'Like I said this afternoon, we came down here to get noticed by record companies. Like the one here tonight. Alana has a job so she stayed.'

'It's okay. It's fine. Thanks for telling me.' This time

118

I did pull my hand away, to flee through the crowded club.

Tears burned in my eyes. Stupid, stupid fool. I had only got two steps before I bumped into someone, and they said, 'Watch where you're going, mate.'

I heard Ewan swear behind me and then his hands were on my shoulders, gripping me. 'Stop.'

'It's okay, it's just bad timing. I've got work to do anyway.'

He turned me around. One of my tears had escaped and it rolled down my cheek.

'Flick, I want—' he began, but the drummer appeared again and grabbed Ewan's arm.

'What the fuck are you playing at?' he demanded. 'You've got to get over here – *now*.'

'I'm sorry,' said Ewan again, and this time I broke free and ran downstairs and out of the building, onto the hot Camden street.

Chapter Twelve

Ten years later, I pause in the doorway of the gallery café. Quinn is sitting at a table by the window. He has two pots of tea in front of him and he's reading the *New York Times*, which he's carried rolled up in his jacket pocket since this morning. His cheeks are rough with the stubble he cultivates to look older and there is a faint line between his eyebrows as he concentrates on his newspaper. He says he'll need glasses before long.

Quinn is grown up. We're both grown up. Grown up isn't meeting a man posing naked and immediately throwing all thoughts and plans to the four winds, forgetting everything in the hope of touching him again. Grown up isn't sitting with your hands shaking because you've told someone you want to be extraordinary, whatever that means.

Grown up is here and now, with my husband, both of us at thirty years of age, with me not able to tell him when I don't want something that he does.

I don't know quite how this happened. I can remember every decision and every step, but not how it led to adulthood, to responsibility. To home ownership and a steady income and insurance payments and lunch every Sunday and a schedule to follow and the baby that may be growing inside my womb.

To the loss of walking lightly. Or ever walking away.

My husband looks up from his paper and when he sees me, the frown grows between his eyebrows. He jumps up and takes my elbow. 'You're not well,' he says.

'I'm all right.' But I feel dizzy, as if I've landed in the wrong time.

'You're pale as a ghost.' He helps me into a seat and pours me tea. 'Oh dear, it's gone cold. Hold on a tick, I'll get some more.'

'No, don't bother, it's fine.'

'I'll put some sugar in it. That'll help.'

'Sugar isn't going to make any difference.'

He's tearing off the top of a packet of sugar, but he stops. 'What's wrong? Are you feeling sick? That could be a good sign, couldn't it?'

Only a man obsessed with having a family would be optimistic about his wife being unwell.

'No, I'm not sick,' I snap. 'I'm exhausted from being dragged around New York to a schedule and then tour-guiding you around an exhibition of my dead mother's work.'

He puts down the sugar. 'I'm sorry.'

I shouldn't lose my temper, but it's a relief after pretending to be pleased all day. 'I didn't want to come to this, Quinn. I tore up the invitation.'

'You said it was all right.'

'I *had* to say it was all right! You'd made such a bloody great effort.'

'I said, several times, that we didn't have to come in if you didn't want to.'

'And how kind would that have been, to make you turn away when you'd spent so long planning it as a surprise?'

'More kind,' he says quietly, 'than arguing with me about it in a café after it's too late to change.'

He's right, and I should stop, say something nice. But after so much silence, I can't stop the words. 'My mother's dead, Quinn. It hurts me to remember her, even if it's to satisfy your curiosity.'

'I'm not curious, not merely curious. I want to know you better.'

'Well, now you know me better. I'm the type of person who gets upset thinking about the past and what I don't have any more. Are you satisfied?'

I've hurt him; it's clear on his face. I bite my lip, too late.

'What's happened?' he says. 'You were fine a few minutes ago.'

'Let's just go,' I say, exhausted, sick of myself. 'Let's just go back to the hotel.'

I lie in the hotel bath, letting the hot water lap around me. The mirrors are fogged up and droplets of steam float in the air. The door is closed.

I left Quinn lying on the bed, reading the *New York Times* again. Dinner tonight wasn't anything near as joyful as our dinner last night. No surprises, no applause, no kisses. Barely any conversation, even though I said I was sorry, and afterwards we sat through the show side by side without touching.

This is my fault. My husband has done absolutely everything he can to make me happy.

We'll fly home tomorrow and I'll apologize again. I'll tell him I'm tired. And this could all be down to hormones, after all, although when Quinn dared to suggest that before dinner, I nearly bit his head off. There's nothing quite as infuriating as a man refusing to take your emotions seriously and putting them down to mysterious female chemicals, as if women were inherently irrational. As if the female mind were nothing more than a loosely connected bundle of electrical impulses, blown willy-nilly by the slightest physical influence.

Even so, I don't deserve him and how kind he's being to me.

This bubble bath supplied with the room is supposed to be calming and soothing, according to the words on the little bottle. I reach for another one and pour it into the bath, turning on the hot tap with my foot. Bergamot and jasmine rise up along with the cloud of bubbles, along with something else. Something that's stronger and that rapidly becomes more real.

The scent of frangipani.

I know it's in my mind and when I close my eyes it gets stronger. My hands curl around the sides of the tub and I relax into what's coming next.

It was eight days before I saw him again. I didn't go to the life-drawing class; in fact, I avoided that entire part of town. I stayed in my room with the Greek-blanket curtain, or sat in a park, drawing trees.

And then one Thursday afternoon I walked into my mother's studio and there was Ewan with his shirt off.

Standing surrounded by vases holding white and yellow flowers with a heady perfume.

'What?' I said, before I could help myself, before I remembered that he'd said he'd got a modelling gig with some semi-famous artist, and realized he must have meant my mother.

'Flick?' said Ewan, at the same time that my mother, out of sight behind her giant canvas, said, 'Now if you could manage *not* to move, that is entirely the point.'

'Nothing.' I tried to turn around and walk straight back out again, but Ewan came after me, touching my shoulder.

'Flick, what are you doing here?'

'I live here,' I said, shrugging him off.

'Darling, do you know my frangipani boy? Lissa sent him over and I'm trying him for this flower series.' Mum put down her brush and peered around her canvas, intrigued.

'He was the model in my life-drawing class,' I told her. 'Anyway, I'm just off out. See you later, Mum.'

'Esther is your mother?' Ewan asked.

Mum had come all the way out from behind her canvas now. She glanced from him to me and back again. 'Oh, it's like that, is it?'

'No,' I said, 'it's not at all.'

'We should talk,' said Ewan. I shook my head.

'Well, you'll have to wait until I've finished for the afternoon,' said Mum. 'Some of us have work to be getting on with.'

I ran down the stairs and out into the afternoon. I got on a bus and rode it, staring out of the window. When I got home, Ewan was gone. The house still smelled of frangipani.

Mum was in the kitchen she'd had installed, making a cup

of tea. 'I'm sorry, darling,' she said, the minute I walked in. 'I'll send him away.'

'No, don't do that. It's nothing, Mum.'

'It's not nothing.' She came to me and stroked my hair. 'It's not nothing at all. I won't finish the painting. It doesn't matter.'

'I don't want you to send him away. It's fine. He's got a girl-friend, and that's that. If you send him away, it'll make me look even more of a fool.'

She kissed the top of my head. 'What a funny, precious girl you are. Just say the word, and I'll send him packing.'

Fresh flowers arrived every day. I hid in the kitchen or in my bedroom. Ewan arrived after the flowers, so when his knock came on the front door, the house was full of their scent. I couldn't escape it any more than I could escape the sound of his footsteps as he went upstairs to my mother's studio, or the awareness of him in the same house, breathing the same air. Once, I heard him laugh, and I had to go out for a long walk so I wouldn't be tempted to run down the stairs and burst into my mother's studio. Even then, I found myself walking in circles, turning down streets that led me back to the house, back to the front door, back to the scent of frangipani.

Every day, I woke up thinking, *I'll go to Paris and see Lauren.* But then the flowers came, and so did he, and I couldn't leave, even though leaving would put all of this to an end.

'Darling, let it go,' said my mother on the evening of the sixth day. 'Let *him* go. You're obviously unhappy, and he's developing a sort of tortured expression. It's getting deeper by the hour.'

'Good,' I said, pouring us both another glass of wine.

'It's quite interesting for my painting, but it's not good for you. I'm ringing him and telling him not to come tomorrow.'

'No!' I said quickly. 'Don't.'

'You want him that badly that you'd rather this than nothing,' said my mother. She sighed. 'I recognize the feeling. It's horribly romantic, but is it worth the agony?'

'Don't send Ewan away, Mum.' Even saying his name was painful pleasure.

'It's silly, you know. If he wanted to be with her, he'd be with her, this girlfriend or whoever she is.'

'I like him better for being loyal.'

She clinked her glass with mine, then took a deep drink. 'He's quite an intense young man. He reminds me of your father.'

Usually when my mother mentioned my father, I was all attention, hoping for more information about him other than that he lived in France, other than that he was an artist, that he was married to another woman, that he didn't know I existed, that he was the love of my mother's life. But I had more pressing concerns right now.

'Do you think Ewan likes me?'

She snorted. '*Likes* you? His posture's terrible and he's got a face like a wet Wednesday, but you could bottle what's in his eyes and sell it to weary lovers.'

'Mum, I think I'm in love with him.' It felt like a momentous announcement.

'Of course you're in love with him. And he's in love with you.' She pulled me to her. 'I'm sorry it has to be so hard.'

I tucked my head under my mother's chin. He was in love with me. The wonder and the happiness of it swept through me. Even if I could never touch him again, even if we never spoke, he was in love with me.

On the seventh day, I went for a long walk in the sunshine. I swam through heat without noticing it. I saw the sunlight glimmering off the sides of buildings and I thought about one thing: *He loves me.*

It fizzed through my veins like champagne. It stirred my skin into wakefulness and bounced off the pavements.

He loves me. Even if I can't have him, he loves me.

I laughed to the sky.

I closed the house door behind me and kicked off my shoes. My feet whispered on the wooden floor as I walked upstairs, into the scent of frangipani.

'Oh,' said Ewan's voice above me. I stopped.

He was two steps down, as I was two steps up. He was bare-chested, wearing jeans, barefoot as I was.

'I didn't hear you come in,' he said.

He wanted me. He loved me. There was no explanation and no letting it go. I could see it in every line of him, his dishevelled hair, the clench of his hand. The look in his eyes that could be bottled for weary lovers. I took a step up.

'I was walking,' I said, my voice unsteady. 'It's a nice afternoon.' Our eyes met and held.

'I'm not a very good person,' he said.

'I don't care.'

One of us moved first, or maybe it was both of us at the same time. Me running up, him running down, taking the stairs by twos. He caught my face in his hands and I grabbed hold of his arms and for a moment, we just looked at each other, faces close. His heart pounded, his skin was hot.

127

We stumbled and he caught us with one hand braced against the wall.

We kissed, on the verge of falling, with no need to breathe.

I open my eyes. My bath has gone cold and the feeling of being in love is gone, though the traces of it echo in my heart. I get out of the bath, shivering, and wrap myself in a towel. My fingers and toes look like prunes and my hair is a wet straggle.

Cautiously, I open the door between the bathroom and the bedroom. Quinn is lying on the bed, fully dressed, his shoes off. The paper has fallen to one side and his eyes are closed. His dark lashes make semicircles on his cheeks.

Poor Quinn. I'm so sorry for making his last night here miserable. I pull the bedspread up over him and he makes a soft sighing noise before turning over onto his side in his sleep.

I gaze down at him. Quinn is handsome. He's good. He's clever and polite and intelligent, careful and loving and tidy. Punctual and considerate, kind and generous, pleasure-giving in bed, a cuddler in the darkness. He pulls the curtains open every morning, hums when washing up, leaves food out for the neighbours' cat.

He's my husband. He's the man I've chosen. He loves me entirely and without reservation. I love him.

Have I ever loved him like I loved Ewan?

I kneel beside him on the king-sized bed. When he doesn't wake I trace my fingers in the air over his features, knowing the shape of his nose, his cheeks, his closed eyelids, his lips. I remember his smile, the pain in his eyes this afternoon.

I love him. But do I love him with my whole heart and body, with a hunger and a need that don't leave room for anything else?

A drop of water falls from my hair onto my husband's cheek. Quinn stirs and opens his eyes.

'Oh, you're finished,' he says, and he sits up, blinking and rubbing his eyes. He yawns and stands, gets his pyjamas out of the drawer and goes into the steam-filled bathroom, shutting the door behind him.

In the morning, we're kind to each other. He brings me a cup of tea in bed. In the newsagent at JFK I buy him the *New York Times*, the *Wall Street Journal*, the *Weekly World News* (headline: BAT BOY FOUND IN WHITE HOUSE CHIMNEY), and a snow globe with the Statue of Liberty in it. He shakes it and the snow swirls around the lonely woman inside.

On the flight, he puts his arm around my shoulders and we watch a film together, pushing up the arm rest so we can both see the small seat-back screen. It's easier than talking. His special celebration has been marred and we both know it was my fault.

Of the two of us, only I know that I've discovered I don't love Quinn as I should. As he deserves.

The knowledge makes me more tender to him. I snuggle into his chest and I stroke the soft cotton of his shirt. I don't want him hurt. I hate myself for being the one who has the power to do it.

I watch the film – something about spies in suits and glasses, something I never would have chosen to watch if I weren't trying to please Quinn – and I decide: if I'm pregnant with Quinn's baby, I'll forget what I've learned. I'll embrace my marriage, my child, my husband, I'll do my best, I'll be happy with what I've got, and I won't look back.

It's only as we're fastening our seatbelts for landing that I realize I've made a decision very like this before.

Chapter Thirteen

'Surprise!'

When we walk into our cottage, Quinn's family is there. Derek and Suz are holding bottles of beer and our dining table has been spread with a flowered cloth and plates of food. Molly bustles up to us and hugs us both.

'Welcome home!' she cries. 'I hope you're not too tired. We couldn't resist throwing you a little party for your anniversary.'

'Good to have you back,' says Derek, clapping Quinn on the back and kissing my cheek as if we've been gone for weeks.

I glance at Quinn to see if he's planned this, too, but he looks as surprised as I am.

Suz hands Quinn and me each a bottle of cold lager. I start to take a sip, before I realize that I possibly shouldn't. 'How was New York?' she asks.

'It was lots of fun,' Quinn says. I think that only I can detect the hint of strain in his voice.

'I loved it,' I add. 'I wasn't expecting it at all.'

'And did you like the exhibition?' Molly asks. 'Of your mother's work? I was telling Quinn before you left what a wonderful idea that was.'

'It was very thoughtful of him,' I say.

'I think I would rather have a cup of tea,' says Quinn. 'Do you want one, Felicity?'

'There isn't anything you two have to tell us, is there?' asks Molly. 'If you're not drinking, Felicity?'

'Well . . .' begins Quinn.

'We haven't had a decent cup of tea in two days,' I interrupt. The last thing I want is for all of the Wickhams to know the pattern of the rest of my life before I'm certain of it. 'Americans just chuck a tea bag in a mug of semi-hot water and call it good.'

Quinn throws me a look and I raise my eyebrows.

'Well,' says Molly, 'you must be starving if you've only had that terrible airline food today. Come and have something to eat, and tell us all about your trip.'

Molly insists on doing the washing up before they leave, although Quinn's clearly exhausted from our weekend of travelling and sightseeing. He sits at the kitchen table, rubbing his eyes and running his fingers through his hair until it stands on end, answering his mother's questions about every single thing we did. *Tell your mother to go home*, I think at him, but he doesn't. He loves her too much to send her away, even when he'd prefer to go to bed.

I wipe the dishes and put them away into neat stacks. When my mother-in-law isn't around, I let them air-dry, but I need something to do. I'm full of energy. I feel that I want to go for a walk or a long bike ride – something physical to tire me out until I'm as tired as Quinn is so we can feel the same thing and I can stop thinking, over and over again, about what I decided on the plane home from New York. About how all of this might end.

'I'm glad the two of you had a good anniversary,' Molly says for at least the fifth time, drying her hands on a tea towel and hanging it neatly on its peg. 'You did well, choosing this one as a wife. The two of you really suit each other.'

'Yes,' says Quinn.

'And you,' she says, kissing me on the cheek, 'you take care of my boy for me, will you?'

'I will,' I say.

'Mum,' says Suz from the doorway, 'let's allow these poor people to get some rest.'

Molly collects Derek from the front room where he's been watching the sport and they say several more goodbyes before we watch them walk down the flagstone path.

Quinn is quiet. 'Well,' I say, 'that was nice of them.' I turn for the stairs, thinking about a shower.

'Why didn't you want to tell them you might be pregnant?'

I stop. 'It's so uncertain,' I say to the banister. 'I didn't want to get their hopes up.'

'You were happy enough to talk about it in the restaurant in New York, to strangers.'

'Strangers aren't going to be disappointed if it's not true.'

'I'll nip out and get a test now,' he says, and reaches for his shoes on the mat. 'It's Sunday, but George will give me one from his shop; he owes me a favour.'

'No.'

His head goes up, eyebrows raised.

'Don't buy it in the village.'

'Why not?'

'Everyone's already talking about our business, Quinn. I'll go to the chemist in town tomorrow morning and

133

get one. I'd rather we knew before the rest of Tillingford.'

'Fine.' He puts down his shoes. 'I'm knackered, love. I think I'm going to lie down on the sofa and read for a bit.'

'I'll tell you when the shower's free.'

I'm halfway up the stairs when Quinn says, 'Felicity?'

I stop.

'You do want to find out, don't you?'

'Of course.'

I don't sound as if I believe what I'm saying at all. But Quinn nods.

'I really love you, you know,' he says. He goes into the front room and picks up his book.

'I know,' I whisper.

I drive into Brickham the next morning while Quinn's at work and I buy a pregnancy test at the big anonymous Boots in the shopping centre. I also select hand lotion, cotton buds and some shampoo, so as not to be so obvious, but the lady at the till doesn't bat an eyelid. I suppose when you spend your life scanning incontinence aids and diarrhoea remedies, a single pregnancy test isn't that interesting.

Knowing that Quinn is waiting for me to ring him with the results of the test, I dawdle around town window-shopping and text him to say I'm going to have lunch here. But I'm not hungry, so I browse around a bit more and buy myself a pair of Green Flash trainers that remind me of school PE lessons. I hesitate outside the Apple store, shiny and full of people trying out seductive hardware.

I haven't caught a glimpse of Ewan for ten years, but people lead more public lives now. He must be on the internet. He'll have a Facebook page or a website, where there'll be pictures of him with whatever band he's in. He might even be famous. I'm not exactly *au courant* with pop culture these days. If I wanted to look him up, this would be the place to do it. The people in the shop might try to sell me a computer but nobody would be watching me and nobody would care, and my search wouldn't be traceable to me.

I shake my head. I'm not going to try to find Ewan, no matter how everything seems to be conspiring to make me think of him. It would be too much like contemplating cheating on Quinn.

If this pregnancy test is positive, I'll ignore all of these feelings. I'll forget all about Ewan and what we used to have, and if I smell frangipani and feel love again, I'll try to move up that appointment with the neurology department because this feeling isn't a sign, it's a headache. I will try to get myself cured of this love, so that I can concentrate on the good relationship I am in.

If it's negative . . .

I lean against the window of the Apple store, watching people walk by. All of them appear to be so purposeful. They're carrying their bags of shopping, pushing their pushchairs, or walking their dogs. Talking and feeling and going about their business. I watch a frowning girl in skinny jeans and sunglasses, a middle-aged man barking laughter into his phone. A toddler scaring pigeons into a flapping cloud.

Seen from outside, like this, they appear complete. They know who they are, they know what they're doing. Each one has a whole world within their heads.

Do I look the same way to them? I must. They can't know that my reusable canvas bag, better for the environment, is filled with things I only bought as distractions. They can't know that in the next few hours, my life is going to change one way or the other. Buffeted by memory and circumstance and feeling.

I used to have a friend, Ollie, who would never make any sort of decision at all without consulting the palm reader who had a stall in the marketplace near her house. Before she went on a date, before she moved house or changed jobs, before she bought an outfit sometimes, she'd have her palm read and sometimes her tarot, too, to see if the signs were auspicious. When the date turned out awful or the outfit unflattering, she would claim it was because she'd misinterpreted the signs. Eventually she married the palm reader's son, who was a property developer and quite charming, with the added attraction of a steady discount at her mother-in-law's stall.

I breathe in deep, trying to smell frangipani. Some sign that I'm on the right course.

If it's you, Mum, trying to give me a hint, I would really appreciate it if you'd turn up now.

There's nothing.

But maybe that's a sign in itself?

I had some hope that the pregnancy test would need to be done in the morning as soon as I got up, therefore putting off the moment of truth for another day, but when I get out the instructions at home, it says it can be done at any time after you've missed your period. I've wasted so much time in town that if I want to get it done before Quinn comes home, it has to be now. Even though I'm not ready.

I used to change my life so easily, moving from city to city, temporary job to temporary job. I should be ready for anything. I'm not.

There's a wait of several minutes between peeing on the tab and replacing the cap, and seeing a result. I leave it on the edge of the sink on a piece of tissue and I go outside and walk down the lane, stopping to stroke the Hoffmanns' cat. At the end, where it joins the main road, I stop and count to one hundred before I turn around and walk back. Mrs Taylor is in her garden weeding her beds and she waves a gloved hand at me in greeting. She gets up, grimacing at the pain in her back, and comes over to her gate. 'Lovely day!' she calls.

I'm glad of the distraction. 'How's your back, Mrs Taylor?'

We spend a good ten minutes chatting about her sciatica in the sunshine, and I'd gladly spend more, but she glances up at the sky and says, 'Well, these dandelions won't get rid of themselves.'

So I go back home. I take baby steps to the bathroom, linger in the doorway, thinking about ringing Lauren or maybe Naomi, deciding this isn't a good time and that it would be disloyal to talk about this with anyone before I talk with Quinn, wishing Lauren would ring me anyway. But the phone doesn't ring and I pick up the test.

It's negative.

I turn it over, looking for something I might have missed. But it's unequivocal: it says, in big bold letters, NOT PREGNANT.

I stand there holding it. I don't feel anything. It's as if my brain, my body, my heart, have all frozen in shock.

I was sure I was pregnant, I think, after an immeasurable time, and then to my surprise, I start to cry. Tears roll down my cheeks and I have to put down the test and sit on the toilet, my head in my hands, sobbing.

Even as I'm crying, there's a part of my mind that is calm and is wondering why I'm upset. I didn't think I wanted a baby. I thought I was doing it for Quinn. Am I crying in relief, then?

It would have been a good life with him, I think, and I cry harder.

My phone rings. Vision blurred by tears, I grope my way out of the bathroom and down the stairs to where I've left it in the kitchen. It's Lauren ringing, ten minutes too late. 'Hello,' I answer, on a sob.

'Felicity? What's the matter?'

'I'm not pregnant.' Saying it out loud makes me wail.

'You're trying to get *pregnant*? Why didn't you tell me?'

'Because – because I wasn't sure I wanted to have a baby.'

'So why are you crying because you're not?'

'I don't know.' I wipe my nose with my hand. 'Really, I don't know.'

'You're strange. You know that?'

I laugh shakily. 'Can I come and stay with you if I need to? For a little while?'

'Of course you can. Why?'

I find a paper towel and wipe my eyes. 'I'll tell you later. Can I come tonight?'

'I'm on my way to Brussels this evening. Should be there for the rest of the summer. I can leave a key with the neighbours if you want. You can have the place to yourself.'

'Yes, please. That would be good.'

'Are you okay, Fliss?'

'No,' I say. 'No, I'm not. But it's fate. It'll be all right.'

138

As if to confirm it, my body chooses this moment to shoot cramps up my lower belly and back, a physical confirmation of the test I've just taken.

By the time Quinn comes home, I've stopped crying. I've had an incredibly long shower and put on a comfortable pair of jeans and a patterned top. I've pulled my hair back into a scarf and put on a bit of lipstick and mascara to stop myself looking so pale and frightened. I've also taken two ibuprofen.

I don't know what I'm going to do. I hadn't thought any further than the pregnancy test, which I now know I believed, deep inside, was going to be positive. I don't know what words to say to change everything, or if I'll have the courage to try. Or even if I should. Is the crying a sign, too? If it is, is it more or less important than my feelings about Ewan?

Although I'm expecting him, I still jump up from my seat at the kitchen table when the back door opens and Quinn walks in. He's holding a large bag filled, from the smell of it, with takeaway Chinese food.

'Hi, love,' he says. He sounds cautious, and when I check the clock on the cooker, he's also half an hour later than usual. 'There was a little bit of a queue.' He puts the takeaway on the kitchen table. 'I didn't think we'd feel like cooking tonight. Whatever happened.' He doesn't pull out a chair to sit down, or go to turn on the kettle, or take off his shoes. He just stands in the kitchen, looking at me.

He knows, I think, but then that confuses me because he seemed even more certain than I was that I was pregnant. He was ready to tell his family and buy a pregnancy test himself, in a shop where it would be incredibly obvious why he was buying it.

'What *has* happened, Felicity?' he asks, at last.

'I took the test.'

'And?'

He knows, he *knows*, and he's making me say it. I don't know why he's making me say it — if he knows that my saying it will hurt him. Why can't we ignore it and carry on as usual?

Because we can't. I've already decided that we can't.

'I'm not pregnant,' I say.

'You must be relieved.'

I step backwards in surprise.

'What?' I gasp.

'You didn't ring me. If you were upset, you would have rung me. Therefore, you must be relieved.'

'I *was* upset.'

'I'm not stupid. I understand now. You don't want a child. You never wanted a child. Why did you say you did?'

I sit down again. 'You wanted it so much.'

'So you went along with it to please me? You can't do that.'

'It . . . seemed as good a reason as any.'

'It's not. It's *not*. This is something we should both want, Felicity.'

'I didn't feel that I could say no.'

'Why not? I didn't pressure you into it.'

'Of course you did,' I mumble.

'What? I didn't say anything. I asked you if you thought it was time that we tried, and then I let you—'

'You were thinking about it, all the time. I could tell.'

Quinn pushes his hand through his hair. 'I was thinking. How can I help that? That's not putting pressure on you.'

'It is. It is, Quinn. It's so obvious when you . . . when you want something. And then Suz—'

'I never discussed it with Suz.'

'—and your parents were so pleased, and Dr Johnson, and everyone. Everyone wants a baby, Quinn, and you most of all. It's in the atmosphere, all the time.'

'You should have told me so. What good does it do to lie to me? How am I supposed to know that you don't mean what you say?'

'I did mean it,' I say. 'I was going to try.'

He's pacing the kitchen now, his hair in disarray. Quinn is usually so calm and cheerful; I've only ever seen him angry at politicians and Rupert Murdoch. This is, I realize, our first real argument. My heart is pounding in my ears.

'I can't read your mind, Felicity. I try so hard to please you. I try all the time.'

'If you're trying so hard to please me, how am I supposed to disagree?'

'What? That's completely unfair. I only want what you want.'

'That's exactly the problem!' I push my chair back, because it seems wrong to be sitting when he's pacing. 'How can I even know what I want, when you're always trying so hard? When I never get a minute alone to think?'

'You're alone a lot. I'm out at work—'

'But everywhere I look, I can see you! Everywhere I go in the village, everyone knows you and they've already got our lives sorted out for us, bit by bit, stage by stage. You might not say anything, you might not even *be* here, but I can see what you want, I know what you want – and who am I to stop you having a baby because you only want one because you love me!'

141

'Felicity,' says Quinn, 'that doesn't even make sense. Just say what you want. Just say it.'

'I can't. It'll hurt you.'

'You're hurting me now, by pretending everything's okay. This whole weekend in New York – it was awful, and it wasn't supposed to be.'

I shake my head. Now that it's come to it, the time to enact my decision, I can't do it.

He drops to his knees on the flagstone floor in front of me. He takes my cold hands in his. He did this when he proposed to me, completely out of the blue, completely uncharacteristic, on a windy walk on the Ridgeway, with a ring in the pocket of his waterproof.

'Where do you go?' he asks me, his grey eyes boring into mine. 'Where do you go in your head, when you leave me, Felicity?'

He knows that, too?

'I think,' I say, short of breath, knowing that I have to say it now, before he starts asking more, before I tell him the whole truth and hurt him even more deeply, 'I need a little time.'

'Time for what?'

'Time to think. By myself. I have to sort my head out before I know what I really want.'

'You can have all the time in the world.'

'By myself,' I say again.

He looks at me. 'What you mean,' he says, 'is that you're leaving me.'

And wasting all that Chinese food, my errant brain thinks. 'I need time,' I repeat.

'Felicity,' he says, and now his face is full of pain. He was angry before, and exasperated, but now it's hit him. This isn't a little married spat. This is real.

I want to take it back, but I can't.

'I don't know how long for,' I go on, trying to make it less awful. 'Only a little while, maybe. I just need a clear head, Quinn.'

'Where will you go?'

It's the same question he asked a few minutes ago, but this version is answerable. 'Lauren says I can stay with her. In her flat, I mean. She has to go to Belgium.'

'You've planned this?'

I don't answer.

Quinn drops my hands. He gets up.

'I suppose you've packed already,' he says.

'No.'

'Then if that's what you want, I'll leave you to it.'

'It's probably a good idea anyway,' I blurt out. 'It will give me time to draw. To work on the book.'

He walks out of the kitchen, out of the cottage. He closes, doesn't slam, the door behind him.

And then the house is quiet, as quiet as I could want. And of course, now I have to go.

Quinn

Two pints in the Seven Stars, brooding at the end of the bar, were enough. He wouldn't have gone there if he didn't know it was Dad's night to be at the golf club, but everyone there knew him. Everyone asked, 'How's Felicity?' and he had to lie. And then Eric and Ed wanted to discuss the football, and Rowan was interested in talking about Boscombe House, the day centre for the elderly that the council wanted to shut, and Miranda the barmaid wanted to ask him confidentially his opinions on placing lonely heart ads, and all the time he knew that Felicity was packing, she was calling a cab, she was going to the station and getting on a train to London to stay in Lauren's flat.

How had it come to this? How, when he'd tried every-thing he could?

'It's unequal,' he said to Miranda, and quickly corrected himself. 'I mean, it's unpredictable. You could find love anywhere.'

Even in a crowded train.

And you could lose love anywhere, too.

He didn't even have a paper with him, and the Seven Stars had stopped carrying the dailies, threaded onto wooden wands, in the 1990s. Finally, he pretended to be absorbed in his phone so he wouldn't have to speak to anyone. They respected it – the local-newspaper editor engrossed in Important News.

Felicity didn't ring, or send a single text.

To himself, he couldn't pretend that he hadn't seen it coming. Otherwise, why had he run after her every time she was lost and late for dinner, or when she slipped through a hedge? And not only those times. In the past, he'd changed film tickets, rearranged lunch dates, read the same front page over and over again while he waited for her to turn up.

She'd never come after him. She'd never chased him or asked him to come with her. And although that didn't bother him most of the time, had never really bothered him other than the odd niggle, tonight he felt that he deserved, every now and then, to be run after. That he deserved not to be lied to, or to have things hidden from him. Because he loved Felicity so much – more than he'd ever believed was possible.

Tears pricked his eyes and he dashed them away under cover of a yawn. It wasn't going to work so he went into the men's cloakroom and stood in the single closed cubicle, his head bowed, gritting his teeth and letting the tears fall into a tissue. When he came out, face scrubbed with cold water and a paper towel, his half-full pint still stood at the end of the bar and Miranda was watching him, a frown on her face. He collected his pint with all the smile he could muster and took it to the snug, where he'd be less obvious. No one approached him. He wished he could be certain it was because he looked as if he were working.

Eventually, he finished his second pint and waved goodbye to Miranda and Rowan and Eric and Ed, the entire pub. It wasn't quite dark as he walked across the common. A bat swooped by his head.

In Hope Cottage, the lights were on but none of the curtains were drawn. Even from the other side of the gate, it looked empty. He unlocked the kitchen door and it swung open.

She was gone. He could feel her absence as keenly as he could her presence, even though the kitchen looked the same. By the door, her red umbrella was missing, and her favourite jacket, the patterned one that was threadbare at the elbows. He went upstairs. Her side of the wardrobe was thinner. The bed was desolate. There was a dent on the bedspread where she had laid her suitcase to pack it.

He knew, then, that not only was she gone, but she was not coming back.

Quinn sat on the bed. The dressing table had been denuded of make-up and hair clips. He gazed at himself in the mirror, saw himself alone.

The heart was a metaphor. It was muscle, not emotions.

His was breaking.

Part Two

Tell me where is fancy bred.
Or in the heart, or in the head?

The Merchant of Venice, *Shakespeare*

Ewan

In the murky light that pushed around the edges of the drawn blinds, Ewan McKillan sat at his dining table in Shoreditch and regarded the objects in front of him. Funny to think that everything he'd done, every decision he'd made, every road he'd travelled, had led him here to this room and these objects.

The table was wide and scarred. Originally it had been a laboratory bench, but it had been rescued and restored after the original lab had been refurbished. Ewan hadn't rescued it; it came with the flat, which he rented furnished. Even though he couldn't take credit for it, he liked telling people that he ate off a surface that had once been used for mixing chemicals.

Used to like telling people.

The dining table stood at one end of the open-plan living area, where the walls were plastered and painted a minimalist, modern half-grey; the rest of the room was taken up with squashy, worn leather chairs (they'd come worn, too, had probably been manufactured to look worn) and a low, wide glass coffee table. The far wall had been stripped of plaster and was raw red brick. He'd driven Y-shaped fittings into the brick, but they'd been empty for two days now, ever since he'd thrown the three guitars they used to hold out of his third-storey window.

He had checked first, to make sure there was no one on the pavement below his window to get hit by the guitars. The electric guitars were pretty heavy, but even a Martin acoustic could cause serious damage when it was travelling at several miles an hour, and he didn't want to be responsible for anyone else.

The acoustic, as he'd expected, shattered into pieces of golden wood and string. The Les Paul actually bounced – once, twice – before collapsing on the pavement with a deep crack running through it. The Strat's neck snapped clean off.

It was too similar to what had happened on that motorway in Texas. Ewan withdrew, shuddering, into the shadows of his flat and was about to draw the blinds when he heard a voice shouting, 'Oi!'

It was a teenage boy. He'd picked up the Strat, body in one hand, neck in the other.

'This a sixties Stratocaster?' the boy called up. 'What d'you throw it out of the window for?'

He was a different colour from Ewan, with a North London accent and shapes shaven into the hair at the side of his head, but Ewan saw himself in the boy's face, in his shoulders, in his hands.

'Nineteen sixty-four,' he said. 'You can keep it, if you like.' He closed the window.

That was the last person he'd spoken to. He didn't know if the boy had taken away the Strat in hopes of repairing it or using it for firewood. He didn't know what had happened to the other two ruined guitars. Yesterday, it had occurred to him that he should have kept the guitars so that someone could have sold them. Petra could have done with the money, maybe. Or he could have added it to Rebecca's bank account.

Pathetic to think that those carcases of guitars that he'd smashed in the street had been the most valuable things he owned after thirty-three years of being alive. The flat was rented; he didn't own a car. The other guitars and amps that he'd never bothered to retrieve from the lock-up were worth a little bit of money, and he thought, now, about writing someone a note, something so that it would be understood that whatever money he had should go to Rebecca and to Lee's wife Petra: half to the life he had created and half to the survivor of the life he had destroyed.

But that was a distraction. If he got up from this table to write a note, he would notice the unanswered messages on his phone, or he'd pick up a piece of unopened post on the floor, or he'd think about something else that he'd left undone that had better *be* done because otherwise it never would, and that would take up another five minutes. Another ten. Another whole day maybe, of action and inaction.

He'd made his decision. There was only one remedy for the things he'd done and the things he'd left undone. Only one more thing, now, to do. And so Ewan sat at his table, formerly a lab bench, and gazed at the objects in front of him.

The first was a one-and-a-half-litre bottle of blended whisky from Tesco, the kind that would make your mouth furry and your body exhale sour fumes. Good whisky would have been an affront; it wasn't pleasure he was after.

Beside it stood the packets of pills. These, unlike the

whisky, were the good stuff. His doctor had prescribed them to knock him out at night, on the nights when he couldn't get to sleep because of the dreams.

Nevertheless, Ewan hadn't taken any of the tablets so far. He preferred to lie awake, thinking about the dreams he didn't want to have, forcing himself to get up and walk around when he felt himself nodding off, wondering if that was what death was like – a final dream that you couldn't escape.

What the hell? He pushed his hair back from his face. Just because he was intending at any moment to take a fatal over-dose of whisky and sleeping tablets, didn't mean he had to go all Hamlet and think nonsensical shit about what it felt like to be dead. He'd find out soon enough anyway.

The last item was the worst. He picked it up, holding it between his fingers as if it were hot. HAPPY BIRTHDAY said the card, above a Quentin Blake drawing of a girl on a bicycle. He'd written the address on the envelope, but he hadn't written anything inside the card. It was too late to send it. Her birthday was today. But that was irrelevant, because he wasn't going to send it anyway. It would still be sitting here on his table tomorrow, and the next day. Until—

He sat up in his chair. Until when? Who was going to find him? His cleaner, Julia, came on Wednesdays. Would she be the one to find him? That hardly seemed fair. She wasn't a great cleaner – in fact, she was pretty rubbish – but she deserved better than to find a dead body, particularly one stinking of the cheapest whisky in Tesco.

Ewan swore and gnawed his lip. He couldn't phone any-one, or text anyone, or email anyone, because there was a chance they'd get to him before he'd finished dying. Once upon a time you could phone people's offices on a Saturday like this, and no one would pick up the messages till Monday. Now, he couldn't be certain.

Then he rolled his eyes. The answer was in his hand, of course. He put down the card and got up from the table. It took a few minutes' searching before he found a sheet of paper and an envelope. It was a used envelope, but he crossed out his own address and wrote the address of Ginge, his last tour manager. Ginge was the most practical and unflappable man Ewan had ever met, and Ewan knew this from hard experience.

Mate, he wrote, *sorry for this. As soon as you get this letter, the exact minute, call the police and ask them to go to my flat and break in. Don't go there yourself*, he added. *Really, don't. Thanks, mate. Ewan.*

As last letters went, it was markedly underwhelming. But if he stopped and tried to make it a heartfelt, profound letter, he'd be delayed again. And he'd delayed long enough already.

He folded it carefully, creasing down the edges.

If you keep finding excuses not to kill yourself, maybe you don't really want to do it.

'Bullshit,' he said aloud. 'I've always found excuses not to do what I'm supposed to do. This is no different.' He stuffed the letter in the envelope. There was some Sellotape to seal it in another kitchen drawer. But no stamps, though he pulled the drawer contents out onto the floor: takeaway menus, corkscrews, chopsticks, single-serving packets of sugar and coffee, old laminates and, for some reason, a sock.

Right. He'd nip out to the post office for a stamp and to post the letter to Ginge. Then straight back here to drink the whisky and take the tablets. He reckoned it would take a

153

good few hours to die, once he'd drunk and swallowed himself to oblivion. He'd get a second-class stamp, to be certain. If he was going to all the trouble of buying the cheap whisky and writing what was, more or less, a suicide note, he wasn't going to have his plans foiled by an unexpectedly efficient postal service.

He thrust the envelope into his back pocket. On the way from the kitchen to the door he passed the table and stopped again, caught by the birthday card.

He could send the card too. What harm would it do? It wouldn't get there in time, but that would hardly matter now, would it? He reached out his hand for it, to scrawl his name inside it and then something else. Maybe only *sorry* again.

Maybe *love*.

Ewan turned away, his hand empty. *Sorry* and *love*, what was the difference? It might not do any harm to send the card, but it would definitely do no good. And he'd delayed long enough. He strode across his flat, grabbed his jacket and pulled the front door open.

Someone stood there, her hand poised in the air to knock. Her mouth widened into an O, and though she was the last person on his mind, her eyes were the exact shade of green that he remembered.

'What the hell are you doing here?' he demanded of Felicity Bloom.

Ewan

'I—' she began, and even in that one word her voice sounded the same, as if they'd been interrupted mid-conversation ten years before and they were picking it up again.

'No,' he said, shaking his head. 'No, never mind. Don't tell me, I don't want to know. Just go away. Get out of here.' He backed into the flat. 'Now,' he added, and slammed the door so hard the floor shook.

Even with the door closed, he could feel her out there. She wasn't leaving. How long had she been standing outside, while he was talking to himself and trying to screw up the courage to do himself in?

'Fuck,' he said.

Felicity Bloom. Appearing like a ghost from the past, a reminder of another possible life that he had thrown away.

She knocked on the door. By itself, Ewan's hand reached for the knob, but he pulled it back sharply. He didn't need any more distractions. If he started thinking about why Felicity had appeared, he'd start thinking about other things. He'd get interested and he'd get sidetracked and he'd get caught up in the complicated dreary business of living again, of carrying on exactly as flawed as he was now.

But there was still the letter in his hand, without a stamp. He had to post it, and he couldn't leave the flat if Felicity was standing there.

He could give her the letter to post. No, that was a bad idea. She'd try to talk to him. She'd draw him in.

What was she doing here?

Ewan leaned against the wall and closed his eyes. He had not thought of her in years, but now he remembered the first time he'd seen her, in that drawing class when she'd come in late, dropping everything on the floor.

There had been no shortage of girls in London that summer. Tight clothes, short skirts, high heels, offering him fags after the gig, their eyes on his hands and his crotch. Plenty of the type he'd liked then, with big boobs and long legs, pierced tongues, eyeliner, the ones who looked like Alana did when he'd met her. It was only a matter of time before he broke his promise to Alana; they'd both known it when he left, they both knew him too well. But he promised to be faithful anyway and Alana pretended to believe him.

It was supposed to be with one of those girls, in the dressing room after a gig or back in his bedroom in the flat he shared with Gavin and Dougie. He'd held out for weeks but it was going to happen, awaiting only the combination of too much booze and a new girl with the best kind of smart mouth.

It wasn't supposed to be with someone like Felicity Bloom.

She was nervous and wore mismatched clothes that were too big for her and she had dreams in her face and he'd wanted to touch her. It wasn't even a sexual thing at first. He just wanted to draw his fingertips across her cheek or put his hand on her narrow shoulder. He'd been young and stupid and he wanted to connect himself to her because she seemed to be made of pure feeling.

Outside, Felicity stopped knocking on the door.

'Why do you want to see me?' he muttered. 'What would be the point?'

The silence was very loud and very long.

He'd been young and stupid but Felicity Bloom, if only for a few weeks, was possibly one of the only good decisions he'd ever made.

Ewan swore again and yanked the door open. She was gone.

He went down the stairs two at a time, the sound of his boot heels echoing in the stairwell. He emerged into the sunlight and had to blink several times before he could see properly. She was thirty metres or so away, walking down the pavement. She wore a blue spotted dress and a red cardigan and there was some sort of silk flower in her hair. He ran up to her and seized her by her shoulder.

She turned around.

'What?' he demanded, his voice gruff in his own ears. 'What do you want? Why did you find me? Make it quick, I've got something to do.'

Felicity smiled widely, delightedly, as if they'd met by fortunate chance at a party. This was a very, very bad idea. He should turn around before it got any worse.

'I just wanted to see you,' she said.

'Well, you've seen me now. Is that all?'

She looked him up and down: his unwashed clothes, his unshaven chin, his battered jacket, his dirty hair. He was certain that he looked exactly like what he was: a man who had spent the last couple of weeks hardly leaving his flat, not sleeping or eating, planning his own death and throwing guitars out of the window.

'Do I look older to you?' she asked.

Fucking hell. He'd forgotten how she spoke in non sequiturs. 'You came and found me because you wanted me to be your mirror?'

'I saw the picture that Mum painted of you,' she said. 'You look exactly the same.'

'Of course I don't. That was ten years ago, and I wasn't—' He swallowed, to contain his fury with her, with himself, with time.

'You've changed, but you look exactly the same.' She tapped her chest above her heart. 'In here.'

It was an incredibly cheesy thing to say, the sort of thing he would snort at and deride if he saw it on television or in a film. It pierced through him like a twisting knife.

'Hunky dory,' he said. 'Lovely to know. Eternal youth on canvas and also in your heart. How sweet, and also reassuring that the painting of me, wherever it is, isn't doing a Dorian Gray.'

'The painting's in New York.'

'Great. Thrilling. Now if you don't mind—'

'You came after me just now. You must have wanted to say something yourself.'

'I didn't come after you, I . . .' He sighed, sharply, to cover up the lie. 'I needed a stamp.'

'Then let's walk to the post office together.'

What was she trying to do? Annoy him? Stalk him? Rekindle their relationship somehow? Every possibility was so ridiculous he had no idea how to counter it.

158

'Fine,' he said. 'But only because I have to go there anyway. I don't need the distraction and I'm done with reminiscing. I've got something to do.'

He started walking down the street, quickly, swearing under his breath. Felicity trotted beside him.

'So,' she said. 'What's this important stuff that you have to do?'

He grunted and walked faster.

'What have you been up to for the past ten years?'

He didn't answer. The post office was close by. Stamp. Post box. Home alone. Whisky and tablets. Done.

'Ten years is a long time,' she continued. 'We haven't been in touch at all. Aren't you curious about what I've been doing?'

I assumed you were happier without me so I stopped thinking about you. 'No,' he said.

'I'm curious about what's happened to you.'

He swerved abruptly and pulled open the door of the post office, letting it swing shut behind him. Felicity stood outside. He could feel her through the glass door, watching him.

The post office was empty. He stormed over to the counter. 'Second-class stamp,' he growled at the woman behind it. 'Make it quick.'

'Do you want a book of them, or—'

'I said one stamp, for fuck's sake!'

She pushed over the stamp, took his money and gave him his change without a single additional word, which was exactly the way he wanted it.

When he got back outside, Felicity was standing with her fists clenched. 'Okay,' she said, 'I can understand why you might not want to see me. You're probably happily married and you have a bunch of kids and you don't need your ex-girlfriend coming back into your life even for a few minutes. That's fair enough. But you could say that, you know, instead of being so rude.'

He stared at her. Was this a joke?

It wasn't.

'Yeah,' he said. 'Rudeness is definitely the worst of my problems. Thanks for clearing that up for me.' He stuck the stamp on the envelope, which was pretty crumpled now. 'I need a post box.'

'You and I haven't seen each other for ten years, Ewan. Surely after all this time you can at least be civil to me.' She put her fists on her hips. 'Besides, you were the one who broke my heart.'

He'd stepped towards the red pillar box, but at this, he stopped. 'I broke *your* heart? Do you have memory issues or something? You're the one who sent me away.'

'Because you were going to have a child with your girlfriend.'

'And who in the world except you thinks that just because a woman's going to have a man's baby, that the two of them have to be together?'

'You didn't marry her?'

What was that emotion on her face? He used to be able to tell them all. Confusion, or panic, or disappointment?

'Oh, I married Alana all right.'

'And you had a baby together?'

'We have a daughter.' He continued his path to the pillar box and shoved the letter towards it. His hands were shaking. The letter hit the side of the slot and fell to the ground. 'Dammit.' When he bent to pick it up, he bumped into Felicity, who had followed close behind him.

'So I was right,' she said. Before he could recover himself, she swooped down and picked up the letter. 'I was right. You were meant to be with her, it was the right thing to do.'

'Give me that letter.'

'I'll give it back to you when you admit that we didn't make the wrong decision. Also, you have to go and apologize to that lady in the post office. She didn't deserve for you to be rude to her, either.'

He grabbed for the letter, but she skipped back out of reach. His reflexes were slowed from not eating or sleeping, from everything that had happened before. But he didn't really want to wrestle the letter from Felicity anyway in the middle of a London street. Though it made no difference, he'd just as soon not make himself even more of an arse.

'Fine,' he said, and stormed back into the post office. The woman at the counter flinched when he approached. Her hand went under the counter where he assumed they had a panic button or something in case of aggressive nutters like him.

'I'm sorry for being so rude to you,' he told her. 'Your customer service was exemplary and I was a cock.'

'Er—'

'Have a nice day.'

He rejoined Felicity on the pavement. 'Satisfied?'

'Now tell me that we didn't make the wrong decision when we split up.'

'Every single decision I have made in my life has been the wrong one, Flick.'

She blinked, and he nearly glanced over his shoulder to see what had startled her, when he realized what it was. Flick.

Her old nickname had come back to him without his even thinking.

'Okay,' she said.

She turned and posted his letter. His suicide note. One moment it was there, the next gone, into the bowels of the post box. The first step of its second-class way to Ginge, who would open it on Tuesday, or possibly Wednesday, and call the police to find Ewan dead.

It was done. The last thing. All that was left now was the whisky and the tablets. To fill up this emptiness for the last time with a cure. *'Tis a consummation devoutly to be wish'd.*

He fucking hated Hamlet. Indecisive moody bastard.

'Thanks,' he said dully to her and he began walking back to his flat.

She walked beside him, not saying anything. He didn't look at her, in case she started up a conversation again. In case he saw that he'd caused her pain. He didn't want to have to carry that too, even for the short time he had left.

He paused at the door to his building to take his keys out of his jacket. 'Well,' he said, looking somewhere in the vicinity of her left ear rather than at her face, 'goodbye.'

'Goodbye,' she said. 'I'm sorry this was all for nothing.'

She sounded defeated. He looked into her face. This was probably a mistake.

But from the minute he'd found her on his doorstep he had felt more emotion – more true, raw emotion – than he'd felt for what seemed like a very long time.

This was definitely a mistake.

'Do you want to go for a drink?' he asked.

Chapter Fourteen

'A drink?' I ask. 'Right now?'
'Yes,' says Ewan. 'Right now.'

'Don't you have this urgent thing to do?'

'Twenty minutes isn't going to make much difference. Come on.'

Once again he launches himself onto the pavement and I have to hurry to keep up with him. He's heading in the opposite direction than last time, though.

He looks so real, so much more three-dimensional than in my memories. It's as if the smell and the feeling I've been having have been embodied in this man who should be a stranger to me but isn't. Everything about Ewan, even the things that have changed, seem familiar to me.

Strange to think he's been living his own life for the past ten years as I've been living mine. He hasn't been frozen in time, frozen in memory. He's carried on, turned into more of himself.

His hair's thick and rumpled. He has lines around his eyes from smiling or squinting. His leather jacket might be the same one he wore ten years ago, more battered and soft and faded at the elbows and collar. He looks as if he's slept in his clothes. His accent has softened. His hands are exactly the same.

When he opened his door my heart made a great leap and I couldn't help but gulp the air, expecting it to taste of frangipani. In that moment, I didn't feel guilty. I didn't think about Quinn at all. The thoughts of Quinn came after, when Ewan had slammed the door, when I was walking back to the underground station and thinking that it was maybe for the best that Ewan didn't want to see me. Thinking that I'd had a strange feeling about my first love, that I had tried to find him again, and that nothing had happened. I'd appeased whatever my mind, or the universe, was trying to tell me, and I now could move on. I could work out what I wanted to do about my marriage without these thoughts of another man.

Then he came after me and I'd been simply, totally glad. Then I'd been furious. And then . . . lost. Without any feeling to guide me any more.

And now we're going for a drink together.

Though he doesn't seem entirely happy about it. His face is grim, his hands shoved into the pockets of his jacket, and his strides are angry.

'Where are we going?' I ask him.

'Pub.' He veers suddenly to the right down a side street and there's a pub there at the end. It looks pretty seedy from the outside, with several men leaning against the wall smoking, and when he pushes open the door and I follow him in, the inside isn't much better. It's dingy, airless and full of people who look as if they haven't left their seats since 1986.

Ewan goes straight to the bar. 'Whisky,' he says to the barman. 'House double. Cheaper the better. I might as well get started.' He turns to me. 'You?'

This is all so surreal that I'm not certain that drinking alcohol is a good idea. Also, I haven't eaten much today; I've been too nervous.

'Me too,' I say anyway. Ewan nods at the barman, who goes off to put our whisky in two cloudy half-pint glasses. Ewan carries them both to a table in the corner.

I sit on the cracked vinyl seat of one of the chairs. It's sticky. Ewan slumps across from me. He takes a drink of his whisky and drums his fingers on the table, looking off towards the fruit machine.

I sip my own whisky, and shudder at it. On the other hand, a cheap double whisky seems exactly the appropriate drink to have in a pub like this, and perhaps drinking it will give me some clue as to Ewan's state of mind. Every part of his body language tells me that he doesn't want to be here with me. And yet this was his idea. He could have slammed the door in my face, like he did at first.

'So,' I say, 'you never told me what you've been up to for the past ten years.'

'Playing guitar.'

'And what about your . . . daughter?' I wait for him to supply the name of the child he had with Alana. He drinks his whisky instead and doesn't reply. The minutes stretch out. His hand has stopped drumming and is clenched on the table. The blinking lights reflect in his eyes.

'I got married last year,' I tell him. 'We live in Tillingford – it's a village in Oxfordshire. We've got a tiny cottage, but it's big enough so that I have a studio in the back bedroom. That's what I do, now. I draw. Illustrations mostly, just little things. Children's books. I'm doing a series called *Igor the Owl*.'

I wait for him to react, to the news that I'm married, or maybe some sort of recognition of Igor.

'It's doing quite well,' I add.

'How's Esther?' he says as if he's had to drag the words out reluctantly.

'She's dead.'

Ewan's head snaps up. He appears to focus on me for the first time since we've entered the pub. 'I didn't know.'

'She died nearly two years ago.'

'I need another drink,' he says. He gets up and goes to the bar without asking if I'd like anything.

Across the room, one of the solitary drinkers is watching me. Leering. He raises his greasy eyebrows when he sees I've spotted him, and raises his pint in my direction. I bow my head and study the table, dreading Ewan saying the usual platitudes about how sorry he is, about how wonderful she was, about it being a shame.

When Ewan gets back, he doesn't say anything. He concentrates on drinking his whisky as if it's a job he must accomplish. This annoys me even more than if he'd mouthed the clichés.

'She had liver cancer,' I tell him.

He grunts; he doesn't seem to be listening any more.

I stare at him and my hand tightens on my smeared glass. This is not Ewan not knowing what to say. Ewan always had something to say. He swallows whisky as if I don't exist. As if my loss doesn't matter, as if he never spent any time with my mother. As if she'd never painted his innermost self, the way he looked when he was in love.

I stand up. 'You're not interested. I'm leaving.'

'You were the one who wanted to meet.'

'Not any more,' I say. I turn around and walk out of the pub.

The air smells much better out here. One of the smokers mutters something to his companion and they both snicker. I ignore them and hurry down the street, not sure where the underground station is from here. Not caring. My heart is hammering and my face is flushed with rage.

'Flick!'

Ewan shouts from behind me. I keep going. I hear him catch up with me, though he doesn't grab my shoulder this time. I whirl around to face him.

'You don't care about me at all,' I say furiously, 'or about how I feel. You act like an arrogant arse and take me to the most horrible pub in the universe and then when I tell you something important, something that really matters to me, all you can do is grunt. You don't care about me, that's fine, but my mother cared about you. She saw something in you and she tried to share it with the world, and you don't give a shit. I don't understand why you keep coming after me or why you invited me for a drink.'

His face screws up and he rubs his eyes with both palms. 'I don't know. I don't know why. It was stupid.'

'You're telling me!' I shout at him, and I step backwards. I should go back to Lauren's, go back to Tillingford, pick up my life again.

All this. For nothing.

I turn away so that Ewan won't see me crying.

'I'm sorry,' Ewan says behind me. 'I don't know what I thought would happen. You were just − unexpected. A distraction. It might have been another path.'

'I'm sorry too,' I say, and begin to walk away. He catches my arm.

'Do something for me,' he says urgently. 'I know I don't deserve it and I know I shouldn't ask. But do one last thing.'

'Why should I?'

'Because you're right, your mother saw something in me. Because you did.' I can smell the whisky on his breath. His hand is hot on my arm.

'Agree to meet me on Monday,' he says. 'No, Monday's too early, I could still do it. Tuesday. Agree to meet me Tuesday.'

'Why?'

'I can't tell you, not now. Say you'll meet me somewhere, anywhere, somewhere away from here. Meet me in Greenwich, near the Meridian Line. That'll do. At noon.'

His words are so urgent.

'Why?' I ask again. 'I've given you enough chances. Can't you tell me whatever you need to tell me now?'

'I can't. And I might not be able to tell you then, either. But if I can't tell you, I won't show up.'

'You want me to agree to meet you all the way over in Greenwich but you might not even be there.'

'If I'm not there, it won't be your fault. It'll be mine. Don't wait for long. And if I don't turn up, forget all about me. Forget I even asked you. It'll be for the best.'

'I don't understand.'

'You don't need to. I probably won't be there. Just say you will. Tuesday, at noon. It'll either be too late, or it won't.'

This close, I can see more changes in Ewan. There are threads of silver in his hair, at his temples. I don't recognize his scent.

This intensity, however, I know. The colour of his eyes, too, though they are tired.

'All right,' I say. 'I'll be there.'

Chapter Fifteen

The scent doesn't come until Ewan and I have parted and I'm walking towards the underground station. But then suddenly the air is filled with frangipani and I stop and look around, convinced that Ewan has followed me again, that he's behind me and is about to put his hand on my shoulder, and this time when I turn around he'll say all the things that he was supposed to have said. About how he's missed me and has thought of me all these years. About how he remembers this feeling, this love love love.

He isn't there. He didn't say any of those things. I lean against the metal railing that's meant to stop people crossing the road at the wrong place and I do the only thing I can do, which is to close my eyes, ignore my surroundings, and give myself up to bliss.

'Are you all right, miss?'

I pull myself back to reality, as much as I can, and see an elderly gentleman nearby. His skin is dark, his hair is grizzled, and he is wearing a tweed suit in full summer. This is so brilliant. I love people who utterly disregard the weather in their choice of clothing.

'I am fantastic,' I tell him. 'I'm the best I can be.'

'That is good to hear. You don't need help, then? Only you're holding on to that railing as if it's about to fly away.'

I laugh. 'I don't need help.' And yes, the feeling is fading. It's not so overwhelming; I can stand up straight (somehow I'd sunk down, so I was nearly kneeling, without noticing it).

'I'm in love,' I tell him.

'Well, that is also good. Love is good.'

'It's the best thing in the world. I know it is. It has to be. Otherwise, what have we got?'

'You be careful now. Look where you are going.'

I let go of the railing, flexing stiff fingers.

'Are you certain you're feeling well, miss? You seem unsteady.'

'I'm fine,' I say. 'I'm just on my way to . . .'

I don't know this street. I thought I was near the underground station, but I must have taken a wrong turning when I was paying attention to the frangipani.

'To where?' asks the gentleman, concerned again. But I don't care; I feel great and I'll find the station eventually. It can't be hard. I smile at him, the smile of a woman in love who knows that everything is going to be all right.

Lauren's flat in Canary Wharf is sparkling new and beautifully designed, climate controlled, with tall windows that look out towards the Thames. When I return to it, Lauren's spare laptop is still open on the table, asleep. If I pressed the space bar, it would come up immediately with Ewan's Facebook page, which includes his address and his telephone number and says that he is a professional guitarist. The profile photograph shows him on stage playing guitar, recognizable only by his hair and his stance. He has 1,453 friends and his relationship status says *It's complicated.* He has been here, online, ready to be found, at any time. But I only looked him up this morning.

It's taken five days. That's how long I've waited between leaving my husband and trying to find another man. Of course, that other man appears to have spent the last ten years turning into an utter tosser.

And yet I still felt as if I loved him.

I stumble across the polished hardwood floor and collapse on one of Lauren's twin sofas. It's composed of straight lines and not all that comfortable, but I'm exhausted. Bone-deep tired. There's a lot to sort out in my mind: should I meet Ewan again? Should I tell Quinn about him? Should I forget about all this and go back to Tillingford?

But my eyes close by themselves. I dream Ewan as a crow, leggy and wild-winged, with his eyes reflecting the lights of a fruit machine. He opens his beak and a ringing comes out.

I blink awake. My phone is ringing in my bag. I grope for it and see it's Quinn calling. Habit makes me answer.

'Hello, love,' he says.

'Sorry, I've only just woken up.' I sit up on the sofa, pushing my hair out of my face.

'Are you all right? Do you want to go back to sleep?'

'No, no. Just taking a nap.' I glance at the big digital clock glowing over the door to the kitchen; it's half past six, which is the time Quinn has rung me every day since I've been in London. Right after he's got home, made himself a cup of tea. My head feels full of cotton wool. 'How's your day been?'

'Summer fêtes. Charity walks. We've got a meeting with Tamsyn Ford next week to discuss the campaign for keeping Boscombe House open. She's our MP,' he reminds me,

172

without my having to ask. 'Cameron Bishop stole my bicycle again.'

'Have you got it back yet?'

'He only stole it five minutes ago. I saw him through the window.' He doesn't quite sigh.

I know where he is: in the armchair by the side of the telly, the one we rarely ever sit on. That's the one with the best view through the side window. One of the wooden arms is coming loose and I can hear it creaking when he talks.

I imagine him in the cottage, sitting in different chairs to make it seem less empty.

'Are you going to the pub later?' I ask him. I want him to be with other people, talking, laughing.

'Not tonight. What have you done today? Have you had any inspiration?'

I look around at the living room of the flat. Modern, bright, with windows looking out onto the grey and brown river. 'No, not really. Not yet.'

'It'll come.'

When I left, I mentioned spending the time to do some work as an appeasement. So that my leaving wouldn't hurt so much, so that I had a good, non-emotional reason to be in London. By tacit mutual consent we seem both to have latched on to it. We're both pretending that I'm only here to work. It's easier.

'I met up with an old friend,' I say. 'We might meet up next week, too. But I'm not sure.'

'That's nice.'

'Well, he's a bit of a tosser to be honest. But you know . . . old times' sake.'

He's silent. Our phone calls are like this now, with these

173

pauses. The weight of everything we're not saying. Mentioning Ewan to Quinn doesn't help me feel any better. But that's what I've done, after all. Met up with an old friend, who's turned out to be not as nice as I remember. I might meet him again.

I staggered down Shoreditch High Street, drunk with love for him this afternoon.

'So what are you going to do about Cameron and your bike?' I ask. 'That can't keep on happening.'

'I might have to get a lock. But I'm worried that then he'll bother himself to get a pair of bolt-cutters, and he could get hurt that way.'

'He could also ride your bike into the path of a car. You wouldn't be responsible for that, either.'

'I don't know why he likes my bicycle so much. It's not anything special. His mother says he has a BMX in the shed. Anyway, I can't get a lock. Every time he steals it, he says he'll never do it again. If I get a lock, it stops him being able to prove himself.'

It's a conversation we've had many times before, over tea, over supper, walking down the lane. I'm suddenly certain that if I'd been pregnant, we'd have done this: talked about our baby to cover up these silences.

Come back, he doesn't say. I can hear it in his breathing, in the creak of his chair.

'Anyway,' I say, 'I'm really tired. I might get an early night. It's supposed to get hotter tomorrow.'

'For the next few weeks. Proper summer weather for once. Mum's fretting about her flowers.'

What has he told his parents and Suz? Anything besides the fiction that I'm here working? I doubt it; Molly has already sent me two cards. One had a kitten on the front, and the other had a fake 1950s housewife on it. Both of them said, in her cheerful handwriting, *Good luck with the book!*

'Well,' I say, 'I suppose I should find something for supper. Lauren hasn't left much in the cupboards except for some protein bars. I think they're from her personal-trainer boyfriend.'

'Do you have any plans for tomorrow?' He asks it in a rush. 'Shall I come up to London? We could meet for lunch.'

The ring on my finger tells me to say yes. It was Quinn's grandmother's – rose gold and diamonds. I twist it round and say, 'I'm not sure. The whole thing about having space, Quinn, is that I have space.'

'I don't need to come to Canary Wharf. We could meet somewhere.'

'I don't know. It's . . . I need to think about things.'

'I'm your husband, Felicity. You can meet me for lunch.' For the first time since that night I left, there's an edge of impatience to his voice.

I twist the ring on my finger. Tuesday. Ewan asked me to meet him Tuesday. I can't be certain of anything until then.

It would be so easy to meet Quinn for lunch, fall into our relationship, our companionship, our routine. Our pretending. It would be easy to go home with him. Go back to Tillingford with nothing having changed. Like our conversation about his bicycle, running in well-worn tracks.

'Give me another week. We can meet up next weekend. Okay?'

'I suppose it will have to be.'

'Good night, Quinn.'

'Good night, love.'

Chapter Sixteen

Greenwich is hot. The sunlight bounces off the big white buildings of the Old Royal Naval College and steals the coolness from the Thames. I make my way through the park, up the path between swathes of grass towards the oniony dome at the top of the hill, the spike with the red ball impaled on it.

Ewan told me not to wait for long, which implies that he wouldn't stick around long himself, and I don't want to miss him. So, for once in my life, I'm early. Even on a hot Tuesday morning, the path is thronged with tourists calling to each other in their own languages, pushing buggies, taking photos, wheezing from the climb. Some people have spread blankets on the grass and are laying out picnics.

I reach the top of the hill. The Meridian Line is in a court-yard behind big black gates. People are queuing up behind it, waiting to stand on it and have their photograph taken with one foot in the east, one in the west. Did Ewan want to meet me actually on the line, or somewhere near it? I hesitate, but decide to stand outside the gates on the top of the hill. This way I can see him coming if he's not here yet, and I can see him inside the courtyard if he's beaten me here.

I station myself next to the clock set into the wall near the gates. I'm five minutes early — that's not very early, but it's quite a bit for me. It would be better if I had a newspaper or something to read, something to take my mind off waiting, like Quinn always has. I crane my neck, looking for Ewan, trying to peer around tourists. 'This is it,' says one of the tourists near my shoulder. 'This is where time begins.'

Is that what it is here? I must admit I have only the shakiest idea of what the Prime Meridian even means. Below the clock there are displayed Public Standards of Length, in iron bars. So that everywhere in the world, things are measured the same. This is a yard. This is a foot. This is certainty.

I spot a black leather jacket to my right, coming up the hill. My heart leaps, but it's a teenage boy with a pierced lip, not Ewan at all.

I think about what he said to me. *Don't wait for long. And if I don't turn up, forget all about me.*

It's all very well, his saying that. But I don't seem able to forget about him.

Last night, I Googled 'frangipani'. Wikipedia told me that it was another name for the plumeria flower, a tropical and sub-tropical species. It has a sweet scent but no nectar. In many places in Asia the flower is associated with funerals, cemeteries and death.

I kept looking, but there was nothing about a disease that causes you to smell frangipani.

I could ask for an earlier appointment with the neurologist and see if there's something physical causing me to have the scent and the memories. There might be some medication I could take. Or perhaps it's something more serious. I've seen what cancer does. Perhaps I'm carrying something around in my mind aside from memories, something growing and changing, something that may eventually eat all my memories away.

Perhaps this love is a sickness.

I leave the clock and the measurements and go to the other side of the path, leaning on the railing to gaze down at the view. The white symmetrical buildings below, the columns, the towers, the upright architecture, rational and perfect. Beyond it, across the river, are the jagged peaks of Canary Wharf, where I've been living since I've run away from my life.

And all love is sickness, isn't it? Something that comes from outside of you, like a virus, or from inside of you, like a cancer. It changes everything about you. It's temporary or it's permanent. You can't rip it out without causing more damage.

'Flick,' says Ewan behind me, and I jump. He's not wearing his leather jacket, just a T-shirt and jeans.

'You came,' I say, breathless.

'I wasn't sure you'd be here.'

'I am.'

We stare at each other for a moment. He's breathless too, as if he's run up the hill to get here.

'I'm sorry I'm a little late,' he says. 'I had to wait around for the postman, and then there was a bit of an argument.'

'You weren't rude to another member of Her Majesty's Postal Service, were you?'

'Apparently it's against the law to give a person a letter addressed to another person, even if the first person was the one who wrote it.'

'You were trying to get a letter back that you'd written? Why?'

'It's a long story. And a boring one. Let's get out of here, there are too many people.'

We slip through a gap at the top of the railing. I sniff, but there's no frangipani, just a faint scent of shower gel. He's shaved since I saw him last, and washed his hair. He doesn't say anything as we walk past the crowds of people snapping photos of the view.

Ten years can change a lot. Since we were lovers, Ewan has become a father. He's been places, lived in houses, met people, had what looks like a successful career. The visible signs of change on his face, in his clothes, are only the surface of what could be seismic changes inside. I used to know him in the past, but that doesn't mean I know him at all any more. And even then, ten years ago, we only spent a summer together. This man is a stranger.

It's safer to think that way, anyway.

We reach a tree and Ewan sits down on the dry grass underneath it in the shade. I do the same and lean my back against the trunk.

'It's a nice afternoon,' I say. Something you would say to a stranger. Something I might say to Quinn, these days.

Ewan looks out across the grass, down the hill to the historical buildings and all the people milling around them, like tiny insects. He glances up at the blue sky and he rubs the palm of his hand against the scrubby grass.

Then he barks a laugh. 'It's a beautiful day,' he says. He throws himself backwards onto the ground, and sweeps his arms and legs to and fro. If he were in the snow, he'd be making an angel. 'A strange and beautiful day to be

179

alive. Since when do *you* talk about days being "nice"?'

Ten years ago I would have flung myself down beside him. Rolled and rolled down the hill, laughing.

'Well,' I say, 'it is. Nice.'

He sits up and brushes grass out of his hair. 'I'm sorry about Esther,' he says. 'I thought she would go on for ever.'

'Oh,' I say. 'Yes. So did I.'

'You saw the painting she did of me? With those flowers?'

'Yes. In New York.' This isn't how I was expecting the conversation to go. I was expecting an argument. I didn't even think he'd listened to what I'd said the other day about my mother.

'Is that why you found me?' he asks. 'Because you saw the painting and you wanted to tell me about your mother?'

'It was partly because I saw your painting.'

He glances sideways at me, briefly. 'How did she die?'

'Does it make a difference?'

'No. I suppose not. Death is death.'

'Except it's not,' I say with more vehemence than he must have been expecting, because he looks fully at me now. 'Some are worse than others.'

'Was she very ill?'

'She had cancer. She was in a lot of pain. She wanted to die.' I rip handfuls of grass from the dry ground and drop it in clumps.

Ewan looks down. He offers no comfort, as Quinn would. He doesn't ask me for any more details.

'Sometimes it's the best thing,' he says to the grass, or to himself, or maybe to me. 'The world's going to carry on existing whether you're here to see it or not. I don't think it makes much difference.'

180

'It makes a huge amount of difference to me.'

'Because you loved her. But if there's no one to love you, there isn't much difference.' He stands up and dusts the dry grass and dirt from his trousers. 'Right. Well. Thanks for meeting me.'

'That's it? You're going?'

He shrugs. 'I'm not all that interested in the view. I wanted to say sorry for Esther. I've said it. So I'll go now.'

I jump to my feet. 'I don't understand you. You begged me to come here, and now you're just leaving. You haven't told me why you wanted to meet me. You haven't told me anything about yourself at all.'

'You don't want to know.'

'I do want to. That's why I came.'

'What do you want to know, then?'

I gesture with my hands. 'What do you do? What have you done? It's been ten years, Ewan.'

'I'm a guitar player. I play session guitar for bands. We go on tour. I play guitar for them on their songs. That's pretty much it.'

'What about your band? With Dougie and Gavin and that other guy?'

'That didn't really go anywhere. I went back to Glasgow. As you know.'

'And you married Alana.'

'And I married Alana.' His voice is singsong, as if he's mocking me.

'And you had a child.'

'Rebecca. Yes. Didn't we go through all of this the other day?'

'And . . .' Any question I could ask seems somehow

181

inadequate. I have butterflies in my stomach, anxiety in my throat. 'How are they?'

'I don't know.'

His hands are on his hips.

'I haven't seen them for two years,' he says. 'I send them a cheque every month. Alana got remarried. She has other children, a brother and sister for Rebecca. I assume that they're happy.'

'You don't see them? Not at all?'

He shrugs again. 'It didn't work out.'

'But you're her father.'

'They've got a new life. They're better off without me. Is that what you wanted to know?'

I stare at him. This was what I suffered all that heartbreak for, wandering around a cemetery in Paris, crying? So he could have a child with Alana and then leave her? What kind of father says his daughter is better off without him?

'Lauren was right,' I say. 'You are a bastard. I shouldn't have met you.' I turn to leave, and then it all changes.

The air, the hot summer air, dry and dusty, is suddenly filled with the scent of frangipani. It weighs down the trees with sweetness, presses on the grass, brightens the sky.

I throw my arms around Ewan's neck and kiss him on the mouth.

Oh, touching him is so wonderful. His lips are warm and full like I remember, slightly rough, chapped, his shoulders are broad, his body against mine is a perfect memory of happiness. I twine my fingers in his hair, shorter now than it was then but the same texture. Through my pleasure and my desire and the drugging scent of frangipani I can feel that his muscles have stiffened and he's standing completely still.

His hands aren't touching me to pull me closer or to push me away, and his mouth is slightly open, in surprise or to take an interrupted breath. Kissing him is like kissing a single moment of time, frozen, not moving forward.

I love him. It's a ball of heat in my chest where my heart is. I have never stopped loving him somewhere deep inside, and Ewan makes a sound in his throat and his hands grasp my hips. He holds me. His mouth moves, softens and opens, and then presses back against mine. He's kissing me too. Like he used to kiss me, when we were hungry for each other, when we couldn't get enough. Secret kisses, stolen kisses, kisses under the duvet in my bedroom as the stars rushed across the sky towards daylight.

Happiness makes tears spring up under my closed eyelids. I'm lost, I'm in love, it's the feeling everyone searches for through their entire life and I can feel it now. It doesn't matter what's happened since. And I'm kissing Ewan and he loves me too . . .

And then he releases me and steps backwards, not out of my arms but far enough so that our lips break apart. 'What are we doing?'

'Kissing,' I tell him, although one wouldn't think it was necessary to explain, and I kiss his top lip, where it bows down slightly in the middle, and his bottom lip, plump and hot, and the side of his mouth, and he makes that sort of groaning sound again and he kisses me right in the middle of my mouth. Our tongues touch.

He takes hold of my wrists and removes my arms from around his neck, and then steps back some more so that we're not touching at all except for his hands on my wrists. I can taste him on my tongue.

'Why are we kissing?' he asks me.

'Because –' *I love you, I'm in love with you and frangipani is in the air and nothing else matters* – 'because you're a very good kisser.'

'Felicity, this is crazy. We don't know each other.'

'We used to.' I try to step closer, but he holds me away.

'You think I'm a bastard.'

'It doesn't matter.'

'And didn't you say you're married?'

It's like a slap. I am married. I have somehow forgotten that in my rush to kiss him, in this overflow of emotion. I have forgotten Quinn.

'Oh my God,' I say. He lets me go and I cover my mouth with my hand. My lips are tender. I back away from him, staring. He's dishevelled and he's breathing hard, like I am. I'm still feeling a tug to him, all the love I felt a moment ago, so I find the tree we've been sitting underneath and lean against it, trying to glue my body to the bark so I won't be able to grab Ewan again.

'What's going on?' he says.

'I'm so sorry,' I say. 'I can't . . .' Oh, I want to touch him again so badly.

'It's not a good idea,' Ewan says. 'Not that I'm the most practical person in the world. Or the most moral, come to that. But even I can see that it would be foolish at this point.'

'We don't even like each other,' I remind myself.

'Then why are you looking at me like that?' Ewan wipes his mouth with the back of his hand. 'Maybe I should leave.'

'You should definitely leave.' I hold on to the tree.

'Are you all right, Flick? Is there something wrong?'

'I don't want to kiss you any more. Go away.' I close my

eyes and rest my cheek against the rough bark. I can feel every beat of my heart, every pulse of emotion pulling me to him. Without looking I can feel Ewan walking away from me, down the hill, walking on the grass without bothering to join the path. I can feel it as vibrations on the earth that we share between us. I keep my eyes closed until I know he must be out of sight, and still I feel him.

Chapter Seventeen

I was sitting on a train from Cornwall, holding a thick paperback in front of my face, my mother's ashes in an urn in a plastic bag at my feet.

I had spent the afternoon on Porthmeor Beach in St Ives, not far from where my mother had lived for her last four years. She had asked me to scatter her ashes there. The sea was clear, a lambent grey. I sat on the sand and I pictured myself going through the motions of opening the bag, taking the cap off the urn, reaching my hand in, throwing all that remained of my mother's body, the grit and the dust, into the air. She had been dead for six months.

She had told me about the funerals she'd gone to growing up, with the mourners intoning the Kaddish, the black clothes and the bowed heads, all the heaviness. She had trusted me to let her travel lightly instead, even after she was finished travelling.

Her ashes were too light for all that they meant to me, and I could not let them go. I could not reach inside the urn and let her ashes fly away. It was another betrayal, but she was gone and I was untied.

The plastic bag made snapping sounds in the wind. I

wrapped the urn more tightly inside it, and left the beach for the station.

'I love that book,' someone said. I looked up; a man was seated across the table from me, though I hadn't noticed him before. He was young-looking, fair-skinned and dark-haired, wearing a neat grey hoodie, a polite smile. He had a broadsheet newspaper and a takeaway cup.

'Are you enjoying it?' he asked.

'I don't know what it is,' I told him, and turned the book over so that I could see the cover. 'Oh. It's *Middlemarch*. Yes, I love this book. I haven't read it in ages though.'

His polite smile turned into a real one. 'You've won.'

'Won what?'

'You proved me wrong. I noticed you hadn't turned a page since you got on at St Erth, but I never suspected that you didn't know what book you were holding.'

'We were playing a game?'

He shrugged, looking a bit sheepish. 'I was. Sorry. I try to guess what my fellow passengers are thinking about. It helps pass the journey. Sometimes I can't resist finding out whether I'm right.'

'What are you, some kind of a detective?'

'Journalist.'

I sat up, wondering if he knew who my mother was, if he was looking for a story. I had received lots of phone calls and emails after she died. I didn't return any of them.

'Don't worry,' he said quickly. 'I'm not the kind who lurks with telephoto lenses. I work on a regional paper in Oxfordshire. This is more of a game that I used to play when I was a boy and wanted to be a spy. Silly, I know. I didn't mean to make you feel uncomfortable.' He looked genuinely embarrassed. He had slender hands and a voice that was slightly too deep for his body.

'It's okay,' I said. 'It's my fault.'

'No, no, not at all.'

'Because I am in fact hiding a deep dark secret. I stole this book from the bed and breakfast I stayed in last night. They had a bookcase in the lounge. I didn't even look at the title, I just wanted something nice and thick.'

'I understand. You didn't want to speak to anyone, and I've gone blundering in against all English codes of behaviour. Pretend I never said anything. Your secret is safe with me.' He passed his finger over his lips as if he was zipping them, folded over a page of his newspaper and returned his attention to it.

I went back to my stolen book. Although I hadn't read a word of it, it was open to page 220 and I saw that I'd been staring at a paragraph about Will Ladislaw's friend showing him Dorothea as if she were a piece of art in a gallery. I turned to the beginning of the chapter and tried to read on, but it'd been years since I read the book and I didn't remember most of the names any more. I deliberately chose it not because I wanted to read but because its thickness would work as a shield. Outside, the landscape rushed by. If I'd done what my mother wanted, her ashes would be behind me. They would have been embarking on their own journey into the water cycle, into the sea to evaporate in the sunshine and fall down as raindrops. Maybe that was the purpose of scattering ashes into the sea. So that you can feel that your lost beloved person could be in any drop of water.

I glanced at the man across from me, but true to his word, he didn't take his eyes from his newspaper. He wasn't as young as I had originally thought he was, but around my age. Suddenly, though there was no reason for him to know, I wanted to ask him when this raw, empty feeling would end. When I wouldn't see women resembling her in the street, when I wouldn't reach for my phone whenever it rang and expect it to be her.

'Tea, coffee, sandwiches, crisps?' said the woman pushing the refreshment trolley. I asked for tea and she reached for a cup.

'Make that two, please,' said the man. 'You'll let me buy you a cup of tea, won't you? To make up for being rude.'

'You weren't rude,' I told him. 'It's a day in the life of a superspy.'

'I do in truth like George Eliot. I wasn't just telling you that to ferret out your misdeeds. Though to be honest I haven't read that book in a very long time, either.'

The woman put two cups of tea on the table between us. I watched the man digging in his pocket for the money. 'Sugar?' he asked me, and I noticed that his eyes were clear grey, exactly the same shade as the sea had been in St Ives.

I awake completely, with no confusion. I know I've been dreaming about the first time I met Quinn. I know I'm in the flat in London with the light that's always in London even at night seeping around the blinds, and that yesterday afternoon I kissed another man in Greenwich park. I know that I'm dreaming about Quinn because I feel so horribly guilty and wrong, because I'm thinking how kind my husband is and always has been, and how I've repaid him by clinging on to him as if he could save me from sadness, when at the same time I've been shutting him out.

I close my eyes and I try to conjure up Quinn's scent. Non-biological washing powder, shaving lotion, tea, newspapers, his favourite jumper, the back of his neck, the sweat under his arms on a hot day, the scent of his skin naked after his shower.

I can't do it. It's like looking at words on a page without being able to read them. He's not there.

My phone is near my bed. I press his number, then notice the time. It's the middle of the night, and I'm about to hang up when Quinn answers it. He must have his phone by the bed as well. 'Hello, love,' he mumbles. His voice is rough from sleep. 'Are you all right?'

'I just wanted to hear you,' I say.

I want to tell him about all the confusion I'm feeling. About how guilty I am for kissing Ewan, and yet how much I want to know why Ewan has changed. How I'm curious about why he asked me to meet him in Greenwich, and about why I keep on having these emotions towards him. I want to ask Quinn what I should do, because Quinn has become my best friend. He has become the person who is always there.

He's the one person I can't ask.

I hear him shift in bed, the rustle of the sheets and pillow. 'I miss you,' he says.

'Let's pretend I'm there. Let's just go to sleep.'

So I lie there in bed, phone pressed to my ear, listening to him breathing, knowing he is listening to me. The sounds are familiar and comforting. I listen harder, trying to hear his heartbeat.

I remember how, after he bought me the cup of tea on the train, I asked him to remind me of what happens in

Middlemarch and he admitted he didn't remember, either. Instead he told me that he was on the train going home early because his weekend in Penzance with his mates had gone wrong when one of them had broken an ankle leaving the pub on the first night. The story had me laughing, and when the train pulled into Paddington he took down my case for me from the overhead rack and asked me, blushing, if I'd like to have a drink with him. When I asked if he didn't have to catch a connecting train, he admitted that he'd been supposed to get off at Reading and hadn't. 'Some spy I'd make,' he said ruefully, and when I laughed again, I realized that this was the first time I had forgotten about the emptiness. It hadn't gone away, but I had forgotten about it.

If I put my hand out, I would know that Quinn isn't here in bed with me. But with my hand tucked under my cheek, the other one holding my phone, I can pretend to feel the warmth of his body, the security of his presence. I listen to his breathing deepen in sleep, and when the scent of frangipani comes to me, I try to pretend that this feeling I'm having is about him, too.

Chapter Eighteen

All morning, I've tried not to leave the flat and find Ewan. I've tried to come up with an idea for a new story.

Igor the Owl and the Eagle Enigma
Igor the Owl and the Pellet Puzzle
Igor the Owl Kisses His Ex

Why is Ewan so sad? When I knew him, he was full of energy and life. He was optimistic and sure of himself. And now he's changed in every way except for the way he kisses.

At eleven o'clock, which is noon in Brussels, Lauren rings. 'Have you burned down the flat yet?'

'No, the flat's fine. Don't you meet your trainer boyfriend at lunchtime?'

'Hans is history. I've got another trainer called Gordon who does not fancy women. Going out with an MEP called Jan tonight. I don't have high hopes.'

'Lauren, is your life the way you thought it would be?'

She pauses to think. 'In some ways, yes. In some ways, no.'

'In which ways no?'

'I thought I would be married and have a yacht by now.'

I can't help but laugh at that. 'Which are you more disappointed about?'

'The yacht, of course. Why are you asking?'

'Oh. No reason. I was thinking about how you believe your life is going to go one way – you think it's a straight line, and then it turns out to be curved.'

'Have you spoken to Quinn? Have you made up and decided to have babies?'

I haven't been thinking of Quinn. I've been thinking about Ewan. He was supposed to carry on with his band. He was supposed to be famous; he was supposed to be a father. What went wrong?

'I speak to Quinn every day,' I tell her.

'Because I was lying. Marriage is more important than a yacht. Except in my case. I want the big boat, baby. Do you want me to come back? I can get the Eurostar tonight.'

'No, no, no, there's no need. I'm fine.'

'Have you left Quinn? Tell me the truth. I can sense that you're up to something.'

'I haven't left Quinn. We're having a break so I can work and so I can sort my head out.'

'Tell me the truth, Felicity.'

'I've . . .'

'Please tell me you haven't met someone else.'

I slump into Lauren's structured sofa with a sigh. 'I haven't *met* someone. It's someone I already knew. I . . . ran into him. And I can't stop thinking about him.'

'It's Ewan the Tosspot, isn't it?'

'How do you know these things, Lauren?'

'I work in finance. I can put two and two together. You're

not having an affair with the man who broke your heart, are you?'

'No! No, I'm not having an affair. Nothing's happened.' I cross my fingers. 'But he's changed. He seems . . . defeated. Angry. I want to know why. I'm curious.'

'Quinn is good for you, Fliss.'

'But Lauren, I'm not sure I'm very good for him.'

She's quiet, but says at last: 'Don't leave him for someone who's a phantom in your mind. Just . . . don't. Okay?'

'I have no intention of doing that,' I say.

I put down the phone and I immediately leave the flat, my heart pounding. It doesn't slow down for the entire tube journey. Ewan looks surprised to see me at his door, but not as surprised as he was last time.

'What is it, Flick?'

'I'm not going to talk about it on your doorstep.'

He hesitates, but eventually steps back so I can enter his flat. I walk into the open-plan living room and look around: one bare brick wall, leather furniture, a glossy stereo system including an actual turntable. 'Nice place.'

'I rent it.' He's standing with his arms crossed. 'Now can you tell me what you want?'

'Don't worry. I'm not going to attack you and kiss you again.' Although if the urge hit me, would I be able to resist it? I've been wondering this all the way here, but I've decided it doesn't matter. I won't stay long enough to find out. If I get the merest whiff of frangipani, I'll leave like a shot.

'I want to know why you're sad,' I say.

'Are you taking something?' he asks.

'Taking something? Like drugs, you mean? I didn't kiss you because of drugs.'

194

'I wasn't thinking that.'

'I forgot how healthy your ego is. Of course no one would need drugs to want to kiss *you*. Everyone wants to kiss you. Stone-cold-sober people fall at your feet.'

I'm not normally an argumentative person, but it's the way Ewan regards me, as if I'm strange or dangerous.

'Grabbing and kissing someone who's practically a stranger isn't out of character for you,' he says. 'It was the way you looked afterwards that was weird. You looked stoned.'

'I'm not on drugs.' I sit in one of the leather armchairs. It's cool against my bare legs. 'It's good manners to offer someone a cup of tea when they come to visit you.'

'You've come here to ask me why I'm sad, and then demand a cup of tea?'

'No. I'm also here to apologize. I'm sorry for forcing kisses on you yesterday. It was out of order and I shouldn't have done it.'

The corner of his mouth quirks. 'I never said I didn't like it.'

Desire rises up so quickly I have to catch my breath and I nearly bolt from my chair. But there's no scent. I can control myself.

'We can't do that again,' I say.

'Agreed.'

We look at each other. I'm remembering how, after he got over his surprise, he held me tightly and kissed me back. I'm thinking of how it was the same as ten years ago but different, because his body has filled out, because we're both older. I wonder what differences he found in me and whether they mattered.

'Because I'm married,' I say. 'And you're a father.'

195

'I'll make the goddamn cup of tea.' He turns and goes into what I presume is the kitchen.

I don't want a cup of tea. I don't think it's a good idea to stay here long enough to drink it. I have come to satisfy my curiosity, and that's it. I look around Ewan's living room trying to work out what his life is like now. The room is neat and bare. There are no books, no empty cups, no clutter. The long, high dining table is empty, with no decorations. There aren't any photographs on the walls; there are no personal items here at all. It could be a hotel suite. Lauren's flat is austere, but she has a couple of vases, some photographs, even a knick-knack or two. Ewan's flat has nothing. It could belong to anybody. He could be anybody.

Also, there are no guitars.

'Tea,' he says, coming back into the room and handing me a black mug. He doesn't have one for himself. He sits in the other armchair, watching me.

'You don't have much stuff,' I comment.

'My cleaning lady was here this morning and her life is hard enough. I cleared out the clutter for her.'

'Even the guitars?'

'I . . . got rid of my guitars.' He looks away.

'I thought you played guitar for a living.'

'I did. I'm finished.' He folds his arms. 'Is it impolite to ask you to drink your tea and then leave? I ask for information's sake. I've got things to do.'

'If you're this unwelcoming to everyone, you must not have many friends.'

'I don't. Not any more.'

'You didn't ask me to meet you at Greenwich because you

needed a friend. If it was because of that, you'd have been much nicer to me.'

'Maybe I would have let you carry on kissing me, as well. Would that have been more friendly?'

He purses his mouth in a way he always did when he was trying to be provocative. He's probably trying to get me to go away, but he could equally be trying to flirt with me.

If he starts actively flirting with me I will be doomed. He's so beautiful, even slumped in a chair, even wearing jeans with holes in the knees and no shoes, with an expression on his face like he wants to cause trouble. I should go. And yet I'm still curious. I want to know why I'm having these feelings for him, aside from the obvious attraction. I want to know why he keeps sending me away and then pulling me back. I want to know if I made the right decision ten years ago when I broke up with him for what I thought was for ever.

'Why are you sad?' I ask him again. 'Is it because you don't see your daughter?'

'That is none of your business.'

I take a sip of my tea and wrinkle up my nose. 'You forgot the sugar.' He makes an exasperated noise and starts to get up, but I beat him to it. 'I'll do it,' I say. 'I can find the kitchen. Don't exert yourself on my account.'

The kitchen is just as modern and spotless as the living room. There are no child's drawings on the stainless-steel refrigerator, no fruit bowl, no signs of cooking or eating at all. There's a stainless-steel canister saying SUGAR by the stainless-steel kettle, but I ignore it and check under the sink for the bin. That, at least, has several takeaway containers in it along with my used tea bag so I do know that Ewan eats occasionally. Quietly, I start opening cupboards. They probably won't give me any of the answers I'm looking for, but then again kitchen cabinets can tell you a lot. For example, in our cottage we have a cabinet half-full of cat food for a cat we don't own. A psychoanalyst would have a field day with that.

One cabinet is full of glasses and black mugs like the one he gave me. One is stacked with crockery. One is empty, one holds a single can of baked beans, and the one by the stainless-steel sink contains a one-and-a-half-litre bottle of whisky, three packets of prescription sedatives and an empty glass.

I stare at it. I notice that the bottle hasn't been opened. Quickly, I check each of the packets. They are all in Ewan's name, and aside from one missing pill, all the blister packs are full.

I close the cupboard just in time, before I hear Ewan's footsteps approaching the kitchen on the hardwood floor. When he enters the room I'm stirring my tea.

'Thought you got lost,' he says.

'I like to stir it a lot. So why don't you have your own band?'

'Are you going to drink that?'

I take my cup to the sink and put some cold water into it to make it a better temperature to drink. 'Why don't you have your own band?' I ask again, focusing on the tap.

'It didn't work out.'

'What happened to your guitars?'

'I threw them out of the window.'

This makes me look at him. He's serious. 'You what?'

'I threw them out of the window. You wanted to know, so I've told you. I didn't want them any more.'

'Why?'

He stands there in the doorway, silent. We were standing about this far apart when I kissed him. And I'm feeling agitated, nervous in my stomach. I've started to notice I often get this feeling before I smell frangipani. I'm becoming able to predict when I'm going to feel love. That must be pretty unusual – not for me, of course, but for humanity in general.

'Where's your husband?' he asks. 'Does he know you're spending so much time with me?'

I drink down the mug of tea, standing at the sink, all at once without pausing. 'Okay, bye then,' I say. I head for the door, but of course Ewan is standing in my way.

'Flick,' he says. 'You're not lying about the drugs, are you?'

'I'm not lying to you about anything,' I say, quickly though, because any moment now, I might not be responsible for my actions. 'Though I think you're hiding the truth about one or two things. Now, weren't you eager for me to leave?'

He stands aside and I go.

Quinn

'What's that part? It says, where do I work. What should I put for that? Should I put down Chair of the WI, do you think?'

'It's up to you, Mum. It's your profile.'

Molly leaned over him, one hand on his shoulder, squinting at the computer screen. Quinn turned aside slightly, to pick up his cup of tea. This afternoon was too hot for tea, but Molly always insisted.

'Or maybe the bit of bookkeeping I do for Turner and Wickham. Yes, put that down.' Quinn began to type it in. 'But will the WI ladies get upset, do you think, if they see that? Will they think that I think it's not really a job, being Chair? Because it is a lot of work, as you know.'

'I think you should be able to put whatever you like.'

'It isn't easy, though, is it? I don't want to offend anyone.'

Quinn rubbed his eyes. On reflection, today was not the best day for him to volunteer to help Mum with her social networking projects. That phone call from Felicity last night, saying how she wanted to pretend to be in bed with him. How it had taken every ounce of will not to shout out, *Come home! I'll get in the car and fetch you now!*

If she needed time, he had to give her time. If he crowded her it wouldn't work. They would be back to where they'd been before; she'd be full of secrets, disconnected.

He hadn't slept. He'd controlled his breathing, slowed it, deepened it, so that he could listen to her. It reminded him of being a child, when he'd heard his parents arguing downstairs, and he'd lain in bed trying to hear and not to hear at the same time. His mother would always check on him afterwards. She would come up, her breathing quick, her hands smoothing his bedding. He would pretend to be fast asleep. She would push back his fringe to feel his forehead, as if he were the one who had something wrong with him, and he would want to open his eyes and say, 'Mum? What's wrong with you and Daddy?'

But if he said it, it would be real. All the pretending they did that everything was all right, all day long, would be for nothing. The thin walls would collapse and it would be his fault.

He never said anything. He breathed steadily with his eyes closed and felt his mother watching him, as if to confirm he was the one who was keeping it all together with his silence. She would kiss him softly, and in the morning at breakfast everything would be normal again. A full set of thin walls up, growing thicker and stronger with each passing day.

It had been ages since he'd thought about that.

'Maybe we should see what Dad has on his page,' said his mother.

'Dad has a Facebook page?'

'Of course he does, doesn't everyone? How do I find it?'

Last night, over the phone, as he pretended to be asleep, Felicity had caught her breath and then breathed in, deeply and long. She was dreaming about something. He wanted to ask her what that was, too, and he knew he never would. He listened for a long time, not saying anything, not asleep. And then she must have rolled over onto her phone because it disconnected and he lay there in his bed alone until it was time to get up.

'There! Look at that! Doesn't he have a lot of friends?'

Derek Wickham had sixty-seven friends on Facebook. From the looks of it, they were all people Derek knew from the village, from the golf club, from the council. His mum pointed at the list and Quinn clicked it, so they could see all sixty-seven. Suz was there, and their cousins Catherine and Frederick, and one or two people Quinn recognized distantly.

'Why aren't you one of his friends? You have a thing, don't you?'

'I haven't checked my personal one in a while.' Why would Dad need a Facebook page? Was it, as Mum said, just because everyone did?

'Look, he likes Felicity! Oh, I want to like her too. Do you like her, on your page?'

'It's a fan page for her books, not really for her. Her publishers made her set it up. I don't think she uses it much.'

'It's a whole new world, isn't it, liking and friending and all that? I think Marian said the WI had one. Should we have a look?'

He pushed back the office chair and stood up. 'Maybe it would be better if you did this instead of me. It's good practice for you.'

'No, no, Quinn, you know me, I'm hopeless with computers. Sit back down, please, sweetheart. Can you help

202

me with my M&S order after this? Speaking of Felicity, how is she? How much longer is she staying in London for?'

He closed his eyes, only briefly. 'I'm not sure, Mum. The deadline's pretty tight and she has a lot of work to do.'

'That must be so hard, the two of you being apart when you're trying for a baby. I hope she can finish quickly. Have you decided what she'll do yet, about her work when the baby comes?'

'No.'

'Well, I was thinking I would pop round tomorrow and help you with a bit of housework. These old houses get full of dust so quickly. I hope she's back soon. There's no point in wasting time when you're trying for a baby, especially in your thirties. I was reading an article about it the other day, how so many couples leave it too long to try to conceive and run into all of these problems. But I'm sure that won't happen with you. And work, of course, is important too these days.'

There won't be a baby. She's not dreaming about me. It's over. We just haven't admitted it yet.

'Was there anything else you wanted to add to your profile, Mum?'

'I don't know, I think I should try to be friends with all the people he's friends with, don't you? Look at Suz's photo, isn't that a lovely one. I wonder how many friends she has. She was always so popular. Oh, wait, what does your father say he does for employment? Semi-retired? Do you think I should put that too?'

Chapter Nineteen

I've met a group of my illustrator friends in Clerkenwell for dinner and drinks. I haven't seen several of these people in a while; they all live in London and I haven't always been able to get here for their meet-ups. Quinn and I went to Andrew and Tom's wedding a few months ago, which is the last time I saw most of them. As always, we slide into a familiar conversation about editors and agents, deadlines and falling book sales, the projects we're working on and the projects we're working on next and the projects we wish we were working on but aren't because we've been told they won't sell.

It's quite a different type of discussion from the ones my mother used to have with her artist mates. Esther wasn't interested in commerce. Even when her paintings started selling for quite big sums she would immediately change the subject or leave the room whenever someone started talking about money, or working on a commission. To her, art was life, not a living.

I met Andrew and Tom, Naomi and Yvonne and Bindu and Yann at a lunch arranged by a children's illustrators' society. At first I was shocked by how frankly they talked about the fact that they got paid for their work. Then I realized that I found it rather refreshing. These people had passion, but they were practical, too – much more practical than I've ever been.

I've told them that I'm down in London on my own working on the latest Igor book. Bindu, who has three children all under the age of six, went into raptures of envy. 'You must be getting so much done without any interruptions.'

'I am.' The flat is covered with sheets of paper, abandoned sketches, things torn up. After leaving Ewan's flat earlier today, in the nick of time, I spent the afternoon drawing, and failing. 'I wish I could say any of it was good. I can't seem to concentrate.'

'Too quiet. You can borrow my kids if you like.'

'It'll come,' Naomi tells me over the rim of her virgin mojito. 'You have to work through the bad stuff before you get to the good stuff.'

'Like life, unfortunately,' sighs Yvonne, who also does theatre design and is the most self-consciously artistic of anyone around the table. She always wears black and has stopped straightening her hair, so it stands up in gorgeous curls all over her head.

'How's that scrumptious husband of yours, Fifi?' Tom calls to me across the table.

'Tom has a crush,' explains Andrew, though it isn't necessary because Tom has a crush on everyone.

'I'd drop you in a minute for him,' says Tom.

'Oh, I wish you would.'

'Quinn is fine.' I turn to Yvonne. 'What bad stuff are you going through?'

'Aside from that hair,' Tom calls.

'Plumbers,' says Yvonne, and launches into her unfortunate domestic story.

I'm on my third margarita before I get up the courage to ask my friends about what's been on my mind since earlier. 'Imagine you're at someone's house and you're looking through the kitchen cupboards. Mostly they're empty, except for one of them which has a bottle of whisky in it. A big bottle, a litre and a half. And several packets of sleeping tablets. And an empty glass. What would you think was going on?'

My friends are creative. They love problems like this.

'Self-medication,' says Andrew immediately. 'Person has trouble sleeping.'

'Except the bottle hasn't been opened, and practically none of the tablets have been taken, either.'

'They've just got new supplies in?'

'They're an alcoholic,' says Naomi, who doesn't drink, and doesn't tell us why not.

'They could be an alcoholic,' I conceded. 'I didn't find any empty bottles, though. Just this one that was untouched. And he hasn't seemed drunk when I've spoken with him.'

'Could be concealing it well, though. People do.'

'Any kids?' asks Bindu. 'They could be hiding the party stuff.'

'No one takes sleeping tablets to party,' says Tom. 'Are you sure they weren't Es?'

'They were prescription, all in his name.'

'I hide my prescription medicine in the kitchen cabinet,' says Bindu. 'Up out of reach. I keep the Pimm's there too.'

'Is that all you keep there?' I ask.

'No, there's a bunch of stuff there that I don't want my kids to get their hands on. Matches, glue, the good chocolate.'

'Was it good whisky?' asks Tom. I shake my head. 'He's a drunk, then. A drunk who's recently done the recycling.'

'Who does he live with?' asks Bindu.

'No one, I don't think. Although he said his cleaning lady had been in. So maybe he was hiding them from her.'

'Or she'd tidied them away.'

'He actually said he'd done the tidying before she came over. So he chose to put all of them away together in the same place. Maybe they weren't supposed to be together. But why was there a glass there too? The glasses were all in another cupboard.'

'Probably wants to have a glass handy in case he needs to take a sleeping tablet in the middle of the night.'

'Chased down with whisky?'

Tom shrugs. 'Makes them work quicker?'

'I used to hide my knife,' says Yvonne. She's been quiet up till now. 'Not all the knives. Just the special one I cut myself with. I liked to know it was there, all ready for me if I needed it.'

We all know about Yvonne's unhappy past, and she's promised us all that she's left it behind her now, but we fall silent in sympathy. Naomi puts a hand on her arm.

'That's what I'm worried about,' I say. 'I'm worried that it's an emergency suicide kit.'

'Ask him,' says Naomi. 'If he's feeling like that, he'll need the support of his friends.'

'If he really wants to do it, he'll do it anyway,' says Andrew.

'I didn't have the nerve to ask him,' I say. 'He was avoiding all of my other questions. But I do know that he's lost his job. And that he's given away some of his belongings. And he seems sad.'

'Maybe alert his family, or some of his other friends?'

'I don't know if he has any.'

Naomi is gazing at me. 'Are you worried about him right now?'

'Well, yes.' And more so, since I've said my thoughts out loud.

'Do you want to ring him?'

'I don't think he'd tell me anything over the phone.'

'I can drive you to his house, if you like. I have the car.'

I feel a wave of gratitude for my kind friends, along with guilt that I've hidden my own problems from them.

'He's not far,' I tell her. 'That would be great.'

In the car, though, I start to feel foolish. It's nearly eleven o'clock, and I'm about to barge in on Ewan without invitation for the second time today, all because he happens to keep alcohol and medication in the same kitchen cupboard. But then I remember how bad-tempered he's been, how erratic. How eager to get rid of me. How sad. And then what was that fatalistic thing he said in Greenwich? Something about how days went on whether you were there to see them or not, and how it didn't make much difference either way?

'Quinn and I have separated for a little while,' I tell Naomi as we're driving.

'Oh. I'm sorry. Can I help?'

That's Naomi – offering help without asking for details. 'It's ongoing. I'm not ready to talk about it yet.'

'It's easier to help other people,' she agrees, and I wonder if that's what I'm doing: focusing on Ewan because I don't want to think about Quinn, or about the strange things going on in my head.

I wonder if Naomi focuses on other people because she has things she doesn't want to think about.

Naomi's sat nav takes us to Ewan's street, and I direct her to his building. She parks opposite and we look up to his third-storey windows, which are dark.

'He's probably asleep,' I say.

'Hopefully.'

'What will I do if he doesn't answer the door?'

'Call 999. Do you want me to come with you?'

'No, stay in the car. I'll come back if I need to call the police.' I sigh. 'I'm going to feel a right berk if I ring the police and he's only been at the pub.'

'Sometimes friendship means feeling like a berk,' says Naomi. She turns up Radio 4 and settles more comfortably into her seat. I let myself into Ewan's building and knock on his door. He doesn't answer right away, so I knock again.

He answers wearing nothing but a pair of boxer shorts. I step back and reach for the wall to steady myself, though I didn't finish my third margarita and haven't felt drunk up till now.

'Flick,' he says. 'Been at the tequila? You reek.'

'I need to come in,' I say.

'You're the strangest girl I've ever met,' he says, but he steps aside so I can come in. His eyes are tired but not unfocused; he doesn't look like a man who's downed a bottle of whisky and a load of tablets. I inhale as I pass him and he doesn't smell of whisky, either; in fact, I happen to know that he's never smelled of whisky any of the times I've seen him, except for in that horrible pub when he actually was drinking whisky, because I keep on trying to smell frangipani on him and not smelling that either.

I go straight through his darkened sitting room to the kitchen and open the cupboard. The bottle and the packets are still there. He's followed me; I turn around and face him.

'Is this your suicide kit?' I ask him.

'Yes,' he says.

I have to steady myself again, with a hand on the kitchen worktop. He looks exactly the same as the man who opened the door to me, except now he's admitted he wants to die.

'Why – why haven't you used it?'

'Because of you.'

He gazes steadily into my face. My phone rings in my pocket. Without breaking eye-contact I take it out.

'Is he all right?' asks Naomi.

'We're going to talk,' I tell her. 'He's okay right now. Thank you so much for the lift. I'll get a cab home.'

'Let me know how it turns out.'

I slip the phone back into my pocket and it's only me and Ewan.

'Because of me?' I ask. He nods.

I've felt this before. It was the time we were in the café and I was trembling because I'd been honest with him and he'd been honest with me. Because it was so close to stripping off our skin, letting each other see the raw vulnerable insides.

'You turned up at my door when I was about to do it,' he says. 'I had to get a stamp for my suicide note, and there you were.'

'You posted your suicide note? Isn't that a little stupid? What if it got lost?' I am asking irrelevant questions because I am shaking.

'You posted it,' he says. 'And then I had to intercept it before it was delivered. I spent two mornings outside my tour manager's house and the postie nearly called the cops.'

'And you – and you asked me to meet you because . . .'

'Because it gave me an excuse not to go ahead and kill myself anyway. If I'd arranged to meet you.'

'You can't have really wanted to die if you put it off to meet me at the Meridian Line.'

'Oh, I did,' he says. 'But I wanted to see you more.'

I stare at him, a person who wanted to die but didn't because of me. Another person.

'If you wanted to see me so much, why weren't you nicer?'

'Well, to be fair, I did kiss you.'

'We agreed that was a bad idea and we weren't going to talk about it any more.' I'm still shaking.

The corner of his mouth quirks up and for the first time, he moves. He runs his hand through his hair, dishevelling it more. 'I don't know if I really wanted to die,' he says. 'I've been thinking about it a lot. Maybe I didn't want to kill myself. God knows, I was dithering enough that day. Maybe I was looking for an excuse to live and you gave it to me. Maybe I haven't lost the habit of living yet, even though I don't have anything to live for.'

'You have things to live for.' Though as soon as I say it, I realize I don't know if it's true. I don't know him well enough.

'If I really wanted to die I could have found a gun. Or stepped in front of a train. Or jumped off a building. Booze and pills aren't a sure thing.'

'It's sure enough for me,' I say. 'In fact . . .' I take the packets of tablets out of the cabinet and begin popping them

211

out of their blister packs and flushing them down the kitchen sink. 'How did you get so many sleeping tablets?'

'I don't sleep.'

He doesn't sleep. He's depressed. This is why he's been acting so strangely, being so aggressive and angry and erratic. He needs professional help, but right now, he's got me in his kitchen.

The tablets are white. Some of them drop down the plughole and some of them fall onto the stainless steel of the sink, making small taps. I finish one pack and start on the second.

'You could just put them in the bin,' Ewan says behind me.

'I'm not taking any chances.' Pop, pop, pop. He wanted to die but he didn't really want to die. He's still alive maybe because of me.

Did Mum have a kit, when she discovered what was happening to her? Somewhere that I never looked? Did she flush it down the drain because of me?

By the time I've finished emptying the blister packs the tablets have backed up a bit in the plughole, so I take down the bottle of whisky, crack it open, and wash the tablets down the drain with it. The smell is overwhelming: a cheap pub.

'I could get some more,' Ewan says.

'You could. But first you're going to tell me what happened so that you got them in the first place.' I put down the empty bottle by the side of the sink, and turn to face Ewan again. He's quite close, still wearing only a pair of boxers.

'We're going to need coffee,' he says. 'I'd offer you something stronger but you just poured it down the plughole.'

'I'll make it. I think you should get dressed.'

212

I can't help watching his naked back as he leaves the room. Then I run cold water in the sink to wash the smell of whisky away. I make two mugs of coffee, black because there's no milk, and stir sugar into both of them. When I come back into the living room he's sitting in a leather armchair, wearing tracksuit bottoms and a T-shirt. I take the sofa. The furniture here is big, designed for a man to use.

'What happened,' he says, 'is that my best friend died. Lee – that was his name. It was my birthday, and he died, and it was my fault.'

Chapter Twenty

'We were on a tour bus,' he says. 'I've spent a lot of my life on tour buses.'

He pauses, gazing at the blank brick wall, and seems disinclined to say anything else. But he's said enough so that now, I need to know.

The Ewan I loved was intense, exciting, and somehow innocent. My mother got it right in her portrait of him, standing among white and yellow flowers. This man is just as intense, and maybe as exciting. But the innocence is gone. There's a darkness, as well as a sadness. Things have happened to him since the short time I knew him. Two months. An eye-blink in the scheme of things. Such an insignificant time, if it had never been captured in an oil painting and the scent of frangipani.

'You used to want to travel the world,' I say. He laughs without humour.

'I've done it. All over the world, every continent. Some of it's exciting. But most of it's on tour buses. You get on the bus, and you drive to a hotel that's the same as any other hotel. Or you go to a gig that's the same as any other gig. You're travelling, but you're standing still. You're going to the same place again and again. You don't feel like you're moving at all.' His face crumples. For a moment I think he's going to cry, and I don't know what I'll do if he cries. I can't touch him to comfort him. But I don't think I could sit here and watch him crying, either.

But he takes a deep breath.

'I've done it myself,' he says. 'You wake up and the bus is noisy. You think you're on the road somewhere between New York and Ohio. Or Paris and Geneva. Or Sydney and Melbourne. The bus is always the same inside, so you could be anywhere. The windows are tinted and the engine is running. You get up, thinking you're moving, and there's no one else on it, and you find out that you're in a car park and everyone else has gone for a shower.'

I know what he's doing: he's talking about something else so that he doesn't have to talk about the painful thing. I do it too. He's rubbing the tips of his fingers on the arm of his chair, as if he's trying to get rid of an itch. And he's lapsed into silence again. But I think he needs to talk about the painful thing, to let it out. It's weighing him down.

'Tell me about Lee,' I say.

'He was a sound engineer. A bloody good one. We met years ago and kept on recommending each other for jobs so we could work together. He was sick of travelling, though. He wanted to stop and settle down, spend some more time with his wife. That was the last thing we talked about, in fact. He said he should go back to his wife, and I should go and visit my daughter.' He rubs his fingers harder on the chair, hard enough to leave a dent in the leather. 'I didn't want him to stop touring. I wanted him to keep on going. Even though I knew he was right, because touring was going to ruin his

215

marriage as much as it ruined my being a father. Because I knew that if he stopped, if he stayed with Petra, I'd be lonely without him. How pathetic is that?'

'And what happened?'

'We were in Texas. I really bloody hate Texas. It goes on forever.' He closes his eyes, and speaks like that. 'It was my birthday so Lee and I were drinking rum. It was something like four in the morning, so I suppose it wasn't my birthday any more, but we were pissed and everyone else on the bus was asleep. We were supposed to be stopping in Amarillo. We had hotel rooms there for the day. So Lee had given me a couple of Cuban cigars as a birthday present and we got off the bus to smoke them.'

His life is so different from mine, I think. Travelling and drinking, smoking cigars. Life on the road, with no connection to any of the places you pass through: is this what walking lightly is like?

'Except the bus hadn't stopped,' says Ewan. 'It was still going at seventy miles an hour when Lee stepped out.'

He holds out his right hand, the one that he's been rubbing on the arm of his chair.

'I tried to catch him. I had hold of him, or nearly. I could feel his shirt right here, in my fingers, and then I didn't. He was gone. I still feel it here. It won't go away. I still feel it.'

He spreads out his fingers in the air. Each one imprinted with memory.

Ewan

'But that's not your fault,' Felicity said. 'Shouldn't the bus door have been locked?'

'He was on the bus because of me. He was drinking because of me. I wanted to go outside for a smoke. It should have been me opening that door, not him.'

He hadn't told anyone about Lee, hadn't discussed it with anyone who didn't already know, and avoided discussing it with people who did, which was pretty much everyone in the business. He had never admitted his guilt out loud, though he knew he wore it on his face like a scar. He had told the doctor that he had bad dreams, but not what they were about.

Not about the wind, the sound. The way he woke up feeling the back of Lee's shirt on the tips of his fingers, how he felt that every time he tried to play guitar.

Why was he telling Felicity Bloom all this? A random woman from his past, someone he had never thought to meet again?

Because she had saved his life. She had caught the back of his shirt and stopped him from leaping.

'I can understand why you feel guilty,' said Felicity. 'But

that's not the same as actual guilt. Would Lee have blamed you?'

'He would, if he'd known what I was thinking. How I didn't want him to go off to be happy with Petra.'

'It's not what we think that matters. It's what we do.' She ducked her head when she said it, and began playing with the hem of her skirt. 'What does Petra say? Does she blame you?'

'I haven't spoken to her. I didn't go to the funeral. It was too much.'

'But you need to speak to her. How can you even start to forgive yourself if you haven't heard that she forgives you too?'

'I don't think I want to forgive myself.'

She looked up then, and met his gaze. She looked at him for what seemed like a very long time. It was so late that there was barely any noise from outside on the street. He found himself remembering what she felt like in his arms, not a few days ago, but ten years ago. When they were lovers, and it had seemed like anything was possible.

'Okay,' she said softly. 'Okay. I understand that, too. But maybe you can do something that will help someone else. Maybe that will make you feel better.'

'How can I help anyone?'

'Do what Lee told you to. His final request, if it was what you were talking about just before he died. Go and see your daughter.'

'That won't help anyone.'

'It might help you.'

He tipped his head back on the chair and looked up at the ceiling. 'I thought I'd forgotten all about that painting. But I've been thinking about it since you turned up and told me about Esther. It was full of flowers, wasn't it?'

'Frangipani.' Her voice was even quieter.

'It's odd to think about it still being out there in the world, unchanged. I'm still young, those flowers are still alive. You were still there in the room with me and we were lovers. When really, everything that produced that picture is dead.'

The room, nearly silent. Far away, the whisper of a car passing.

'It's not all dead,' Felicity said.

She was still looking at him and when he met her gaze again he could feel an attraction deep in his belly. A cord binding him to her, something he'd nearly forgotten but now, tonight, as fresh as the first time he'd seen her, a bright summer daytime.

Felicity didn't move from the sofa. He remembered how she'd flung her arms around him in the park in Greenwich, as if no time had passed.

'Does your husband know you're here?' he asked her.

'No.'

That hadn't been her husband on the phone, then. This husband of hers seemed to be often missing. But the fact of him stood in the room between them. 'Don't you think he should know?'

'There are a lot of things I can't tell him. Not yet, anyway.'

'It's late,' he said. 'I'll call you a cab.' But he didn't get up to fetch his phone.

'Will you sleep?' she asked.

'I doubt it.'

'I don't think you should be alone tonight. Not after talking about all of this.'

'What am I going to do? You've poured my suicide kit down the drain.'

'You've already listed several other ways you could kill yourself.'

'Flick, I'm guilty enough as it is. Go back to your husband.'

She dropped her gaze. 'I don't think I can,' she said to her lap.

They were both poised to fall. Or step back safely. Unlike on the bus, he could think, this time. He could choose.

Experience told him that the most appealing choice would probably be the worst.

He got up, but he didn't go to her. Didn't sit beside her, didn't take her head in his hands and kiss her.

'You can have a blanket and a pillow from my bed,' he said. 'The sofa is pretty comfortable, and I'll buy you a bacon butty in the morning. To thank you for saving my life.'

Chapter Twenty-one

'It was on this corner,' I say. 'I'm sure of it. Look, this is the pub, and then there was a newsagent, and then there was a launderette, and then there was the café. Here.' I point to a block of flats where the café used to be. A block of 1960s flats. Their architecture stubbornly insists that they have been standing here for a good forty years before I ever had a coffee with Ewan in this location. 'Wasn't it?'

'It was on the other side of the road,' says Ewan.

'I was certain it was on the right.'

'Look at the windows.' I examine them: plate glass, wide and tall, framed in black. Yes, that's where the gingham curtains used to be. But now it's a chemist, with displays of sun cream and allergy medication.

'So much for a bacon butty,' I say.

I'm not hungry, to tell the truth. I feel a bit hungover: fuzzy-brained, vague, headachy. I didn't get much sleep on Ewan's sofa last night, and what I did get was fitful. Every time I moved, the leather cushions squeaked, and I could hear Ewan in the next room. I lay awake, dreading the scent of frangipani, something that would propel me off the sofa and into the bedroom, where I would either make a fool of myself or even worse, he would welcome me.

The scent didn't come. I was awoken by a text from Quinn: *Good night out?*

Too much tequila, I texted back to him. *Talk to you later.*

It's the first outright lie I've told to him. When Ewan came into the living room, rubbing his hair dry on a towel, I told him I needed a walk to clear my head before I had the breakfast he'd promised me.

But the walk hasn't cleared my head. It's hot already, though it's before ten o'clock. I'm still wearing my going-out clothes, my hair bundled into an elastic. I've done the best I can with a wet flannel to erase the mascara trails under my eyes, but I feel as if I'm on what we used to call the Walk of Shame, where everyone can tell that you've been out all night. Perversely, this doesn't make me feel like a mess; it makes me feel sexy.

Dammit.

I should not be allowing myself to feel sexy. I'm with Ewan because he needs my help. Last night, lying awake, it occurred to me that perhaps the memories I've been having are a different kind of sign than I'd thought. Perhaps they've led me to Ewan because he needed me there, in his life, at that precise moment. Perhaps it has nothing to do with attraction, or feeling in love.

And yet I've lied to Quinn.

'There are plenty of other cafés,' says Ewan.

'I don't think I even fancy a bacon sandwich,' I say. 'I'm too hot.' And I should be getting back to Canary Wharf, to have a shower and wash myself back into my normal life. But I'm reluctant to leave Ewan. I don't think he's in imminent danger of committing suicide, not today; he seems more

222

cheerful this morning, as if it's helped him to admit what happened with Lee. It will probably get bad for him again, but today is a good day. And on a good day, he's so much more like the man I remember.

'I might have a better idea.' Ewan starts striding purposefully down the road. Around the corner there's a park, with a few toddlers playing in the sunshine while their mothers sit under trees with the buggies. An ice-cream van idles on the corner, the driver reading the *Sun*. Ewan goes straight up to it and in a few minutes he's back with two enormous cornets, each with a Flake.

'Ice cream for breakfast?' I ask him, taking mine.

'Why not?' He licks his. 'We're grown-ups. Bench?'

We sit together on a bench, eating our ice creams and watching East London go by around us. Whippy soft ice cream is, in fact, the perfect breakfast on a day like today. And this is exactly the sort of thing that Ewan and I would have done ten years ago, with no jobs, no responsibilities. Except ten years ago we wouldn't have been able to keep our hands off each other.

'Let's do whatever we want today,' I say, and then realize that could be misconstrued as being sexual. My cheeks heating, I amend, 'Let's wander around London and look at whatever we fancy. Eat whatever we want, drink whatever we want. Just spend a day being alive.'

'You're trying to convince me that life is good, aren't you? That it's worth living?'

'I don't think I can do that with a day wandering around London. This isn't a Christmas movie. I think you need to see a professional, Ewan. If you're having suicidal feelings, you can't mess around. You need to work out some stuff. Promise me you'll do that?' I turn and look directly at him; he's mid-lick, but he swallows and presses his lips together.

'Promise,' I insist. 'In words.'

'Okay. I'll see a doctor.'

I look hard at him. 'I'm not certain I believe you.'

'I'll spit in my palm and shake your hand if you want, but you might get a bit of Flake in it.'

'Call your GP right now and make an appointment. Then I'll be satisfied.'

I watch him call and make the appointment for later in the week. I am aware that in some ways I am being a hypocrite.

'Okay, and also put the Samaritans' number into your phone. In fact, give it to me and I'll do it for you.'

He hands it over, still warm, and I look up the number. When I open his contacts list I see that he still has Alana's number, right at the top. I make a new entry for the Samaritans. 'I'll call them Sammy. And here's my number too.'

As I'm keying it in, I think that this might be a dangerous thing to do. But I can't imagine Quinn ever checking mine or anyone else's phone. He's far too principled and trusting for that; he doesn't even have a lock for his bicycle, even though there's a nine-year-old poised to steal it at any moment.

Of course this makes it much easier for me to betray him. I swallow and close my eyes for a moment, dizzy at the enormity of what I'm doing.

I send Ewan's number to my phone. And because he's not watching me, but gazing across the park, I send Alana's number, too. In case anything happens to Ewan and I need to tell his next-of-kin.

'There,' I say, hearing my own phone dinging twice as it

receives the numbers. 'Done.' I give him his phone back and resume licking my ice cream.

'So, a day wandering around London,' he says. 'Don't you have anything better to do? Job to go to? Husband to see?'

'This is the most important thing I have to do today.' I throw my slightly ice-creamy serviette into the bin, and stand up. 'Ready to go?'

The day is hot, so we don't cover as much ground as we might have done otherwise. We pop into a vinyl-record shop where Ewan educates me about the bands I've been missing all of my life. We jump on a bus and ride for a bit on the top deck, until the heat drives us off it. For lunch we buy cold samosas and chunks of watermelon from an Asian grocery and find another park so we can spit the seeds at each other. The juice runs down my arm and wets the sleeve of my dress. By early afternoon my feet are beginning to hurt in my going-out shoes, so I buy a cheap pair of flip-flops. The pavement burns through them with every step.

We look in bookshops and delis, sweetshops and museums. A Hawksmoor church where we linger, cooled by the shadows and marble. By instinct, we avoid any parts of London where we might run into someone we know. Or at least I do, and we don't run into any of Ewan's mates, so he may be doing the same. School has finished for the summer and the pavements are full of teenagers, riding scooters and skateboards and laughing into their mobile phones. Ewan tells me about a boat trip he took in Thailand. I tell him about a waitressing job I had once, for two weeks, in Paris, before I was sacked. We talk about nothing of significance at all. When my phone buzzes, I ignore it.

One day. I can have one day with Ewan, before I think about my real life and my responsibilities. Before I think about who I could be hurting if I have any more than this.

I do not touch him.

We stop to sit outside a pub, at a table usually claimed by smokers. I drink a half of lager and lime, something I haven't had since I was a teenager.

'I met Petra a few times,' Ewan says suddenly. 'Lee's wife. She came to some of the gigs. Lee could never stop touching her when he was with her. He always had his hand on her knee, or her arm, or was stroking her hair. It was as if he knew he only had so long with her.' He looks at me with his bright blue eyes, the same colour as the summer sky. 'Do you think that's what love is like?'

It's exactly the sort of question that I have been trying desperately to avoid. I cast around for something to say, a change of subject, and spot a toy shop on the other side of the road. 'Wait here,' I tell him.

Inside, I'm a bit stunned by the amount of toys on offer. So much plastic, so many boxes with names in shouty fonts, so much buzzing and flashing and squeaking, segregated into gendered sections. Guns and cars for boys on the right, pink everything for girls on the left. I pause in the shop, bemused at how different this version of childhood is from my own childhood, or the one that I'd envisaged for Quinn's and my child.

It's difficult to find anything that isn't pre-gendered, but finally I find what I'm looking for, right near the back, in the section marked EDUCATIONAL. At the counter, I ask them to wrap it, but they only have plastic bags. I carry it out to Ewan, who has got us each another drink.

'A toy,' he says. He takes it out of the bag. 'A ukelele.'

'I thought it was a crying shame that you didn't have any guitars left. So this is the start of a new collection. A small start, but a start.'

'Well, I do have some guitars still in storage. I haven't thrown them out of any windows yet.' He strums it, fiddles with the knobs that tune it, and then strums it some more. 'I don't think I've ever played a ukelele before.'

He's smiling. The instrument is too small for his hands, but he coaxes a tune out of it. Something jaunty; probably you can only play jaunty tunes on its plastic strings. It's too small and ridiculous to play the blues on, which is one of the reasons I bought it. Passers-by hear him and smile. Like ice cream for breakfast, a silly tune on a ukelele seems like the perfect thing for a London summer day. The men sitting at the table next to us laugh, and give Ewan the thumbs-up.

'I'd forgotten how good you are,' I say.

'I've had a lot of practice.' He starts another tune.

'Do you think your daughter is musical?'

He stops playing. 'Oh, I knew this was too easy to last.'

'Tell me about her.'

'They moved to Manchester with her stepfather. She's got a half-brother and sister. She probably talks like a Manc by now.'

'What colour hair does she have?'

'Red. Same as Alana's. She doesn't look much like me. I don't know if she's musical.'

'Do you at least speak to her on the phone?'

He shakes his head. 'No point. Rebecca doesn't need me confusing her. She's got a dad. Alana has a husband. They're happy. I'm happy for them. That's all.'

'I never met my father,' I say, tracing my finger around the wet circle left by my glass on the table. 'He was married when he met my mother in Paris. They split up before I was born. She didn't keep any photographs or sketches. She's never told me anything about him, except that he was French, and she loved him. I had a happy childhood. I loved Esther and I never felt as if I needed anyone more than her. And still, every single time I went to Paris, I was looking for him. I expected to see him everywhere I went. I knew I wouldn't recognize him, but I looked for him anyway. Any man of my mother's age, or a little bit older, with dark hair or green eyes – I would look at him and hope I'd see something, anything, so I would know he was mine. Even when I was happy, even when I knew he couldn't give me anything I didn't already have, I wanted to meet him.'

'Well,' he says, picking up his pint, 'that's you.'

'If Rebecca feels even the tiniest little bit like I did – like I do – don't you think you owe it to her to keep in touch?'

He puts his glass down without taking a drink. 'Flick. Listen. I know you think this will help me. But it's complicated, okay? I can't just pick up the phone.'

'If you have her number, you really can. What's the worst that could happen? Alana hangs up on you? At least you've tried.'

'I thought you were trying to make me feel happier?'

'I'm just trying—'

'I know what you're trying to do. It isn't working. Do you want another drink, or should we go?'

He's already out of his seat. 'Let's go,' I say, and he walks off rapidly, in a seemingly random direction.

Well, that was an error. But I have learned enough of this

228

new Ewan to know that this is what he does when he's sad, so I walk silently along with him.

I remember how we broke up all those years ago. How, when he told me the news that Alana had rung to say she was three months pregnant, he seemed angry. Surly, close-faced. I'd been furious with him, even though I didn't know Alana, even though I'd helped him to cheat on her and then break up with her. How could he be angry at her? It wasn't her fault she was pregnant. It was both of them together. Something they'd both done before I met Ewan, planting the seeds that would take him from me.

'If she's going to keep the baby, you have to go back to her,' I told him, choking, imagining already how I'd feel if he didn't, how our relationship would become heavy and guilty. He'd turned to me, his blue eyes flashing. I'd never seen his temper before; I shrank back.

'If that's how much you care about me, then I will,' he said. And he left.

And that was that. Both of us making our choices for what we thought was for ever. As I recall, it took less than ten minutes.

The memory and the rapid walking makes my lager and lime slosh in my stomach. We were so young and so dramatic. Now, we walk up a hill and into yet another park. London is alive with green spaces today; we have bounced from one to the other and all of them have been full of people. Dogs bark, children shout. A man on roller skates narrowly misses us. All of the shady bits have been colonized by families with picnic blankets; Ewan flings himself onto a sunny patch of ground and I remember what he said in Greenwich: 'It's a strange and wonderful day to be alive.' Now I know he was being ironic.

I sit beside him and watch a football game. The children wearing shirts are drenched, and the ones without are sun-burned. In the heat, their movements are sluggish. My phone rings, and rings, and falls silent.

The scent of frangipani coalesces around us.

'I'm a prat,' says Ewan quietly. 'You were trying to help.'

'Can you smell that?' I ask him. Because maybe he does. Maybe it's something meant for both of us. Sweet and spicy, heavy and exotic.

'Smell what?'

'I need you to help me,' I say to him. I reach for his hand and it clasps around mine. His skin is even hotter than the air. 'I need you to sit here and not let me move. Just for a few minutes. Don't say anything, don't look at me. Don't touch me any more than this. Just sit here and hold my hand.'

'Why?'

'It's . . . something like meeting you in Greenwich,' I say. 'You just have to do it without knowing why. I'll be all right in ten minutes.'

'Okay,' he says, and I have barely enough time to draw my knees up and hide my head between them, hair dangling around my face, to keep him from seeing it or me from see-ing him. I sit there, on the hot dusty ground with the shouts and laughter around me, the sun beating down on my head. I will myself not to move, to stay rooted, to stay sane.

I hold Ewan's hand and I love him. My heart is beating so hard that I can feel my body moving with every beat. I tense my muscles and let his hand hold me in place. I clamp my lips together to stop laughing aloud.

I don't know if it's ten minutes, or fifteen, or half an hour. Eventually I feel it ebb. My heartbeat slows. The sounds of

230

the park begin to filter in. My back hurts. I stretch out one leg, then the other, and look up. True to his word, Ewan is staring straight ahead, not looking at me.

'Thanks,' I say. I feel there's a silly smile on my face, but I can't seem to get rid of it. Just like I can't seem to let go of his hand, not quite yet.

He turns to me. 'Are you all right?'

'Yes. Absolutely great.' I've got through it without doing anything stupid. This proves something, though I'm not sure what – that I'm more powerful than fate? That I have the ability to choose what I do?

Yes. That's it. I have the ability to choose. And despite all this elation buzzing through my body, I know what the right thing is to do. I drop Ewan's hand and stand up, brushing down the skirt of my dress.

'I've got to go home now,' I say. 'Thanks for a great day.'

He jumps to his feet too. 'Are you certain? You look a little . . . woozy.'

'I'm fine.'

'Was it the lager? On a hot day it can go to your head.'

'Yes, probably.' I laugh. 'I'm going to go now. Don't forget to see the doctor, all right?'

'But when will I see you again?'

I'm too light to answer that right now. I don't know what the right answer is. If I can resist Ewan, then that's the right thing to do. If I was only meant to see him to save his life, then maybe I've done that already.

'When it has to happen,' I say. And I head across the park, in a direction I'm not certain will lead me back home.

Chapter Twenty-two

Eventually, back at Lauren's, I go straight to bed, my limbs still tingling, and sleep until the intercom to the entrance door rings. Ewan, I think, and then I remember that Ewan doesn't know where I'm staying. Quinn?

I pull on Lauren's dressing gown and stumble to the door to pick up the phone. My head feels clearer for a bit of sleep, though I'm still tired. If it's someone selling something, I'm going to be cross.

'It's Suz,' she says over the phone. 'I tried to ring, but no luck, so I thought I'd come by on the off-chance.'

I buzz her into the building and have a moment of panic whilst waiting for her to take the lift to this floor. Will she be able to tell what I've been doing all day? Who I've been with? I dash to the bathroom and splash water on my face, try to finger-comb my hair into something respectable. I'm scrubbing traces of mascara from underneath my eyes with the corner of a towel when she knocks on the door to the flat.

Suz looks good. Not having seen her in nearly three weeks, I can see her for what she is, rather than just another piece of the Wickham family: a tall, attractive, professional woman. She's wearing smart, tight jeans, high-heeled sandals and a summery top. Her hair's been blow-dried into a pretty, tousled style and she's wearing a bit more make-up than she does around Tillingford. It emphasizes her grey eyes, which are the same shade as Quinn's.

She kisses me in a businesslike fashion on the cheek. 'It's lovely and cool in here. Did I wake you?'

'Just from a nap. Come through to the kitchen, I'll make tea.'

'Quinn said you'd had a late one last night.' She follows me, looking appreciatively at the modern, airy flat. 'Out with friends?'

'Yes, old friends. This is a nice surprise. What brings you to London?'

'Seeing a friend, too. I thought I'd pop in, see how you were getting on before I caught the train back.'

I fill the kettle, and then hesitate. 'Would you prefer something cold?'

'A glass of wine, if you've got it. I think the sun's past the yardarm.' Some loose papers are scattered on the table. She picks one of them up. 'I see you've been able to get some work done. That's great.'

'Oh, that's just . . . it's only some sketches I've been doing. I don't think they'll go into the book.' On the way to the fridge I see which sketch she's picked up. It's a robin, his head cocked with curiosity at the viewer.

'I love it,' she says. 'That's Quinn, isn't it? Quinn as a robin.'

I pause, my hand reaching for the bottle of white wine that Lauren keeps in here. 'How can you tell?'

'That's exactly the expression he gets when he's interested in something. The eyes, the mouth – the beak, I mean. It's marvellous. Do you have any more?'

I do. 'Er . . . not really.'

'Any of me? What about Mum? She'd be a magpie, don't you think?'

'Chattering.'

'And collecting shiny objects.' She sorts through the drawings, which are mostly half-finished, scrawls of lines, or studies of wings. 'Is Igor supposed to be you, then?'

'I don't know. Not really. Maybe. I suppose I liked drawing him as part of a big owl family. Because I never had a big family. Not before marrying Quinn, I mean.' I uncork the bottle and find two of Lauren's roomy, elegant glasses. 'And he's an oddball, so he's like me that way.'

'You're not that odd, Felicity. Oh, I love this sketch. What a handsome crow.'

The crow is Ewan. Swaggering, once glossy, now leggy and a bit rough around the edges. Because the drawing's in pencil, you can't tell that he has blue eyes.

'Here you are,' I say quickly, handing Suz her wine. 'It's probably nice. My friend Lauren's got expensive tastes.'

'Chin-chin.' Suz chimes her glass with mine and raises her eyebrows when she takes a sip. 'Very nice. How long do you think you'll be staying here in Town, Felicity?'

Here we are: the point of her visit. Suz is a solicitor, after all. Like Quinn, she likes facts. I take a slightly longer sip of wine than I would usually do, trying to decide which tone to take.

'I don't know,' I say finally. 'As you can see, I haven't really got much useful work done. It's all in the sketch stage. I haven't even really come up with a good book idea yet.'

'Because you probably can't tell it from his phone conversations, but Quinn is miserable.'

I put my wine down on the granite worktop. 'I know he is.'

'And unlike Mum, I'm not interested in interfering with your relationship. I don't need to know the ins and outs. I just want to know, as Quinn's sister, what we should be prepared for. If this is really a work retreat for you.'

She doesn't look angry, or accusing. She looks concerned, and like the robin in my drawing, she looks curious. Not because she wants shiny gossip, but because she wants the truth.

Suz picks up the wine bottle from where I've put it beside the sink. She fills my glass, right up to the rim. Then she fills up her own. The glasses are so big that now the bottle is pretty much empty.

'Get that down you,' she says. 'Then tell me.'

Because I trust Suz, I do what she says. I drink the wine straight down as if it were water. It probably has a wonderful bouquet and subtle hues of elderflower and lime, but I don't taste them. Suz also drinks hers, but more slowly. She watches me with her calm, grey eyes.

I gasp when I've finished half the glass. I can already feel the alcohol seeping through my system, causing a weakness in my legs that isn't unpleasant at all. It reminds me of how I felt this afternoon in the park with Ewan.

'My friend Lauren who owns this apartment,' I say. 'Do you remember her? She was at our wedding.'

'I remember her.'

'She's always had this theory that she could never go out with a man who wasn't her equal. She wants someone equally career-focused, with more or less the same salary as her. Equally intelligent, equally attractive, equally sociable.

She thinks that it's the inequalities in a relationship that make it go sour. Fortunately it's one of her talents to be able to estimate the probable wealth of a person just by looking at them. From then on she says it's a simple process of discovery and elimination.'

'You don't feel that Quinn is your equal?'

'No, no, I do – if anything, it's that I'm not *his* equal.' The wine is sort of helping. I take another sip to fortify myself. 'In our case it's emotional. He – I'm sure you know he fell in love with me right away when we met. He was the one who wanted to get married. He's the one who wants to have a baby.'

'I thought you were in love with him too.' Suz is neutral, non-judgemental.

'I am! But I never . . . I mean, I love him. There's no way anyone could not love Quinn. He's wonderful. And he loves me so much that it would be wrong if I didn't return it. He deserves for me to love him back.'

'But you don't feel that you do. Not at the moment.'

'When I met him, my mother had just died. I mean, she'd died a few months before that, but it felt as if it had just happened. And he . . . he made me laugh. He made me feel alive again. He helped me.'

'That isn't love?'

'It's . . . I don't know.' I sit in one of Lauren's kitchen chairs, miserable. 'I wish it were simple. I really, really do.'

'I don't think anything's ever simple when it comes to love.'

Suz joins me at the table. She takes the last little bit of wine from the bottle and pours it into my glass and we sit there together, drinking, for a while.

I like my sister-in-law; I've liked her from the moment Quinn introduced us. She's sensible, warm, reliable, good-humoured. She doesn't waste words. There's never been an inequality in our relationship that we had to hide. Even if I'd never met Quinn, I'd have liked to have Suz for a friend.

But if I lose Quinn, I'll also lose his sister.

I look at her hand on her glass. She's got clear varnish on her nails, which is unusual. As is this level of make-up, and this pretty new blouse. I remember what she said when she came in, about being in London to see a friend.

'If I were you, I'd meet up with my dates in London too,' I say. 'Tillingford's too small by half to have any romantic relationship without everyone gossiping.'

'And Mum's one of the worst for gossip.' There's something about the way she glances at me sideways as she says it, that makes me sit up suddenly.

'It's not a man you're seeing, is it? It's a woman.'

Suz nods.

'I just thought you weren't keen on any of Molly's blind dates,' I say, but then I realize that's not true. I'm not really surprised that Suz would date a woman. 'Does Quinn know?'

'I've always presumed he does.'

'He's never said anything.'

'There are a lot of things that our family know, but don't say.' She drinks her wine, quite unruffled. 'For example, I've known you weren't certain about your life in Tillingford for a while. It's only recently I've suspected it might be because you're not certain about my brother.'

'Are you – are you in love with your girlfriend?'

'Time will tell. What are you going to do about Quinn?'

'I don't know.' Suz's quasi-revelation has distracted me

237

from my misery for a few minutes, but now it's back. 'It's a tangle.'

'You can't just stay here and hope that he forgets you. He's not going to do that.'

For the first time, I detect an edge of anger in her voice. I've never seen Suz get angry. I have a feeling that it would be quite formidable.

'I know he won't forget me.' Especially not while he's living in that cottage, which we chose together, decorated together, full of the things we found together.

An emptiness sears through me. I miss our cottage. I miss living in it, sharing it, Quinn's washed-up mug on the draining board, his notes left by the phone, the wild garden, the uneven floors, us cuddling together on the sofa, all the warmth and comfort that isn't here in this flat.

'Maybe I shouldn't have married him,' I say. 'But I wanted to, Suz. I really wanted to.'

Suz gives me an odd look. Then she glances at her watch and stands. 'I'm going to catch my train. For what it's worth, I don't want you to leave Quinn. I want him to be happy, and I think you could make him happy, if you tried. I think you could both be happy. If you decided to be.'

'I have been trying. I did try. I don't know if you can decide things like that.'

'I suspect that it's possible. I suspect that a lot of people do. But while you're deciding, Felicity, please consider: if you're going to hurt him more than you already have, it would be better to hurt him quickly.'

Ewan

E wan had been in love dozens of times, and never. From the age of thirteen, there had been a new girlfriend every few months. He was known for it at school: Romeo, they called him. And later, there was never any shortage of girls. Women liked men in bands, though he tried to steer clear of overt groupies. He had no desire to sleep with someone just because they were available. He liked the first meeting, the chase, the game of does-she/doesn't-she. He liked talking with women. He liked the exchange of glances, the flare of attraction. He liked learning about them, getting to know how they ticked.

His mates had always taken the piss. They called him a charmer. They said he traded on his looks. 'Oh, another notch on the bedpost.' But it wasn't like that. He didn't keep score; when he thought of how many relationships he'd had, it was more depressing than boastful. He didn't start a relationship with a woman, all the time having an end-by date in mind. He started a relationship because he had started to fall in love. Because he was enchanted with someone.

'I'm a romantic, actually,' he told his friends, and when they laughed, he would explain: 'I love to fall in love. It's the best feeling in the world. The problem is, it doesn't last.'

Most of the time, it ended in an amicable way. But there were casualties, people he'd misjudged, angry break-ups, women whose feelings he had hurt. Because Ewan usually ended it himself. His job was quite convenient in that way. Other friends, the more perceptive ones, pointed out that Ewan never chose to fall in love with women who had children, or anyone who was in the music business. His romantic urges were purely directed at single, uncomplicated women from whom he could escape as soon as the tour started.

After years of travelling with one band or another, years of transient relationships, he had come to suspect, when he allowed himself to think about it, that falling in love so many times was very similar to never having your heart touched at all.

Or maybe it was the opposite, because every time, with every relationship, he started out so happy, so excited, so certain that this one was *the* one. And with every relationship he became disillusioned. It was heartbreak, of a sort.

Felicity Bloom was different, if only because she broke up with him before he was ready for it to be over. Even more, she broke up with him in order to send him back to another woman. He'd left her, angry and resentful and still in love with her, still touched by her inner happiness, the brush of her hand on the nape of his neck, the way she wrinkled her nose and how she whistled when she thought no one was listening. He'd gone back to Alana with Felicity still imprinted on his body and heart. It was no surprise that his marriage was doomed.

Maybe if it had run its full course with Felicity, he

wouldn't remember her so well now. He would have fallen out of love with her as naturally as he fell out of love with everyone else he had ever met: he would have noticed a previously unsuspected neediness, or an annoying habit of kicking at night, or abhorrent political opinions, or a tendency to nag or bully, or a complete ignorance of The Smiths. He would have started the slow or rapid process of disenchantment and disappointment.

Or maybe she would have been different. Maybe with Felicity, he would have stayed in love. Ewan wasn't such a fool that he didn't know that you had to work at love: you had to ignore the annoying habits, learn to shut your ears when it came to discussing politics. You had to descend from the rarefied heights of poetry and sex to deal with who was going to empty the bins and trying to remember to put the toilet seat down. He knew married couples who negotiated these hazards and still managed to love each other. Lee and Petra, for example.

Lee had never called Ewan a Romeo or talked about bed-posts, though he was one of the people who pointed out Ewan's almost uncanny ability to choose the correct women to fall in love with, ones who were strong enough not to require too much of him, who wouldn't haunt him when he inevitably ended it. 'Maybe it's because you choose women who you know are smart enough to see through you eventually,' Lee said. 'So when you break up with them, it's not really a surprise.'

'And can't Petra see through you?' Ewan had asked.

'She can see straight through and out the other side,' Lee said. 'Where I'm lucky is, she likes most of what she sees.'

Ewan had tried to make it work with Alana. He'd been in love with her once, after all, and she was carrying his baby. He did the right thing, the thing that he'd got so angry with Felicity for telling him to do. He went back to Alana and he married her in front of her parents and her friends. He got a job in a second-hand record shop and used every penny to pay the rent on the house they moved into together, a terrace with a second bedroom for the nursery. He emptied the bins and he tried to remember to put the toilet seat down. He played his guitar at night and on the weekends, in the pubs and clubs he used to play in before he'd left for London, and tried to channel his thoughts away from what Dougie and Gavin and Brian were doing, away from Felicity Bloom, and back to all the things he had once found to love in Alana.

Pregnancy made her softer, made her almost glow. It was easier to try to be in love with her when she was expecting his baby. And then afterwards, there was Rebecca to keep him there. Alana was, he had to admit, a good mother. She was practical and sensible, tender and solicitous. She was everything Ewan's own mother had never had the time to be, working two jobs to keep them both housed and fed without a husband in the picture, and this should have made Ewan love Alana more. Except that from the moment Rebecca was born, Alana's focus was purely on her. Mother and baby made an inviolable unit, whole and perfect in themselves. They sat on the sofa, Alana feeding their daughter with her body, the two of them gazing at each other with the purest love Ewan had ever seen. And he would watch them from the doorway.

They needed more money and Ewan's mate Joel knew a band who were seeking a session guitarist at the last minute for a tour. The money was good, Rebecca was two months old, and Alana was so competent, so confident as a parent. There seemed little reason not to go.

And go again, when he was asked. And go on the next tour, too. He sent the money home and Alana saved for a deposit, applied for a mortgage and got him to sign the forms when he was between work. Every time he came back Rebecca was bigger, could do more things that he had missed her doing for the first time. Being absent was what his own mother had done, what she'd had to do, except that Rebecca was with her mother who loved her instead of with childminders as Ewan had been. What other choice did he have, but to keep taking work?

This was what love was, love in the real world: responsibility and obligation, the money sent home, phone calls when the time zones matched, milestones missed, and the real life lived out on the road.

When Rebecca was four he came home for her birthday. He brought a giant cuddly kangaroo he'd purchased for her in a toy shop in Sydney. It had been the biggest toy in the shop, designed to be bought by fathers who needed something impressive to make up for their inadequacy. The house was full of children he'd never met, running around and screaming in their party dresses. Alana had had her hair cut; for a moment, when she'd opened the door to him, he'd not recognized his wife. He could pick out Rebecca right away in the sea of children, by her mass of red curls, the way she skipped across the room. When he handed over the kangaroo, Rebecca gave him a swift hug and was gone before he had time to register the feeling of her little arms around him.

That evening, when the other little girls had gone home and Rebecca was tucked up in bed with her kangaroo, her face still sticky with cake, Alana told him that she'd met someone else, someone who wanted to stay, who would be a good stepfather, who wanted more children. All he remembered feeling was relief.

The next morning he said goodbye. Not goodbye for good, not yet; he'd visit whenever he could, for the next few years. Until he couldn't bear to do so any more.

Rebecca was eager to get to her toys, but he held her for a moment longer than she wanted to be held. He closed his eyes and he breathed in the scent of her hair, felt its warm silk against his cheek, her little lithe body struggling to be set free and play, and he felt what he had felt in the moment when she was born. When the midwife had handed her, hot and slippery, into his arms and she had looked straight up into his eyes as if she knew him already. He had held her and she had curled her tiny hand around his finger and he knew he belonged entirely to her. This grip around his finger that made him want to laugh and cry, to find a dragon and fight it for her, to change the world so that it would keep her safe and happy.

Ginge met him in Camden for a pint. 'Glad to see you,' said the big, redheaded tour manager, as soon as Ewan walked through the pub door. 'I thought you'd disappeared off somewhere.'

Ewan had a sudden, humiliating memory of the letter he'd written, and which Felicity had posted. Thank God that Ginge had never got it. What an embarrassing suicide note. And the cheap whisky, too; that was another embarrassing thing. If he was going out, he would go out with twenty-five-year-old Laphroaig. For fuck's sake, some things you only did once, and they were worth doing right.

Possibly it was a good sign that he was thinking about his own contemplated suicide as embarrassing. He wondered what Flick would say.

'I'm back now,' he said. 'Guinness?'

At the table, Ginge raised his glass. 'To Lee.'

'To Lee.' It was easier than he'd thought it would be, to say Lee's name to Ginge. But not by much.

'We missed you at the funeral,' said Ginge.

'I couldn't do it, mate.'

'What happened wasn't your fault.'

'Maybe one day I'll believe that.' The pub was loud. It wasn't something he'd normally notice, but it had been so quiet lately, everywhere except for in his own head.

'I talked to Petra when we went up there. She'd like to speak to you.'

'I'll bet.'

'She doesn't blame you either. You were the last person to see him. I think she wants to know what happened, from your point of view.'

Felicity had said he should do that, too. Ewan gulped his pint and said, 'I'll think about it. So what's been going on with you?'

Ginge filled him in on the usual: stroppy artists, venue disasters, merch problems. On their second pint, he asked Ewan, 'So where have you been? You haven't replied to any phone calls or emails. Or is it just me you're avoiding?'

'It's not you. I've been . . . trying to get my head together.'

'Any luck?'

'I'll let you know when I find out.'

Ginge tugged at the collar of his T-shirt. 'It's a big thing. It could have been you on that Texas highway.'

'I wish it had been.'

'You should have someone to talk to. You know? You can't keep this bottled up. It'll do you in.'

'I think . . . I think I might have found someone.'

'Ah. I see. You've been out with the *women* getting your head together.' Ginge turned back to his pint, but not before Ewan saw his contempt.

'Not like that. It's someone I knew before. She turned up out of the blue, when I needed her most.'

'And she's helping you? Not distracting you – helping you? Because I know about you and distractions, remember. I've been your TM enough.'

'She's incredible. I'd forgotten how incredible. She makes me feel that I want to be a better person.'

'Good. Well, that's good.'

'Also, she made me sign up for counselling. I'm seeing someone next week.' It sounded lame, but he knew from experience that if he didn't tell anyone about the counselling, he wouldn't go. And he thought he needed to go, if only because he owed it to Felicity.

'Even better. That's a great idea. But listen, I'm always around too, yeah? Always on the end of the phone, or up for a pint. I'm off to Thailand, but not till October. And I can put the word out that you're looking for studio work, if you want. Whenever you're ready.'

'Thanks, mate. Not yet, but maybe one day.'

Ginge settled his bulk back into the leather-covered bench, making it groan. He wrapped his slab of a hand around his pint. From all appearances, he was getting ready for a session. 'So, tell me about this girl then. Fit? Funny? Mad? She's not married, is she?'

Chapter Twenty-three

The restaurant is my choice. This is not always a good idea; usually I let Quinn decide these things because he is more likely to choose a restaurant due to good reviews and an appealing menu, and I am more likely to choose a restaurant due to a quirky name or having a waterfall in the dining room. This restaurant doesn't have a waterfall, but it does have a little fountain in the centre with lotus blossoms floating in it. And it had a good review from *Time Out* Sellotaped to its front window, so I booked it when Quinn agreed to meet me for dinner, and hoped it would turn out to be the best of both worlds.

Now I wish I'd let Quinn choose, because it feels too heavy a responsibility. It seems as if too much is hinging on this dinner, the first we've had together since I left Tillingford. We arranged it the same day Suz turned up and talked about my hurting him, quickly or slowly. The same day I'd spent most of with Ewan. Quinn rang me to see how my hangover was and I asked him if he'd like to come to London for dinner with me in two nights' time.

When I opened Lauren's door to him, we both paused, uncertain of what to do. A hug, a kiss, a handshake? He smiled at me and said, 'Hello, love, I'm glad to see you,' and I could tell he was waiting for me to decide, so I kissed him on the mouth, only briefly, anxious that he might be able to taste how I'd kissed Ewan all those days ago. And then, because the kiss had been so brief, I kissed him on the cheek as well to make up for it.

His hair looked much the same and his face was still carefully stubbled, and he was wearing the blue shirt I liked best, the one that had been washed so many times it was buttersoft, and a silk tie that I had bought him because it was the purple of the foxgloves that grow outside our cottage and went so well with his hair and eyes. He'd said he would come on the train straight from work, but I could tell he'd gone home and changed first, washed his face and hands, brushed his hair and chosen his clothes, like a man nervous about a first date.

I was glad to see him and then I thought of what I had to say and my hands began to sweat, despite the air conditioning.

Time apart had made me more able to see his features. He was handsome, not the kind of handsome that made you look twice, but the kind of handsome that grew on you with time. I could see the effect of my leaving him in his face, which was thinner. I could probably see the changes better than Suz could, since she saw him nearly every day. He gave me a bouquet of white roses, their scent clean and pure, their stems wrapped in tissue and plastic film so the thorns wouldn't bite.

'I'd forgotten how nice this flat was,' he said. 'Lovely and cool, too.'

'Oh well,' I said, 'you know Lauren. I'll find a vase for these. They're beautiful.'

I'd tidied up. Even in a flat as spacious as Lauren's, even with as few belongings as I'd brought, the clutter had started to show. I'd put away all the clothes I'd put on and discarded, as if I, too, were nervous about a first date. I'd lined up Molly's cards on a side table. I left all my drawing materials out as a visible display of how much work I was doing, though I'd put the sketches of Quinn the robin and Ewan the crow into a bedroom drawer.

I'd gone through the flat's rooms again and again, making sure there were no traces of what I knew was untraceable: every time I'd lain in the bed or staggered onto the sofa, or just stood, transfixed, looking out of the window at the unremarkable street, smelling frangipani and feeling in love.

Yesterday, it happened three times. I didn't leave the flat at all, partly worried that I'd make a fool of myself in public, mostly wanting to be alone to feel it, to offer myself up to it. Drunk with bliss. At one point it occurred to me that this must be how drug addicts feel — as if the rest of the world is irrelevant next to what they're experiencing inside their own heads. The drug isn't an escape from real life; it *is* real life, so much more real than any other life could possibly be.

Suz and Ewan both asked me if I was stoned, when they saw me afterwards. Yesterday I wallowed in it. I gave myself a full day, which could be why it happened so often, if I was willing the feeling to occur. Ewan texted me once, something silly about practising the ukelele, and I responded in a dizzy haze. Fortunately I didn't send it. When I read the text over later, it didn't make much sense; autocorrect had changed nearly every word I'd misspelled into something irrelevant.

The sight of the text alarmed me. I thought that if I tried hard enough, I could control my actions when I was in the midst of this feeling, but the text is evidence that I can't. That there's another me inside, someone who wants to act on my love. I stared at the text for a long time and then I dialled Dr Johnson's office. The phone rang on the end of the line, miles away in Tillingford, and I pictured the chain of events I was setting in action: consultation with my GP, an urgent neurology appointment, explanations to Quinn about how I've been feeling about another man. Or maybe I wouldn't have to explain it to Quinn. Maybe Dr Johnson would run into Molly in Waitrose again and explain the whole thing to her in the bakery aisle.

I hung up before the receptionist could answer.

Today it's happened only once, this morning when I was doing some laundry, a good seven hours before Quinn came. I sat with my back against the washing machine and closed my eyes until it was over. I don't know what I'll do if it happens while Quinn is with me. I can't run away from him without explanation. And I can't bliss out in front of him without explanation, either.

While I filled a heavy glass vase with water, he looked around the flat in the way that he looks at everything. I saw him taking in the straightened cushions on the sofas, the lack of dirty tea mugs, the rugs geometrically positioned parallel to the walls, the stacks of sketches and pencils, the logged-off laptop. He looked at this, and he looked at me, and he frowned.

'I had a bit of a tidy,' I said.

'It looks like you've been able to do some work. That's good. Does the quiet help?'

'Yes, I think so.'

'How's my friend Igor coming along? Has he solved the puzzle yet?'

'All right. Slowly. I'm a bit stuck.'

'Can I help?'

I shook my head. 'What time is it? I made a reservation for seven.'

And now we sit, separated by a white-clothed table, listening to the burble of the restaurant's water feature. It's just as well it's here, because they aren't playing music and there aren't any other diners and it helps to fill the silences.

Though it doesn't.

'White or red?' Quinn asks me, looking at the wine list.

'I don't mind, whichever you prefer.'

'You like white better. Sauvignon or Chablis?'

'I won't be drinking much anyway.' I gesture in a way that's meant to mean I have to draw and make up stories tomorrow, but really it's because I want to keep control of what I say. Of what I feel.

Quinn orders a bottle of Sauvignon blanc and the waitress brings us prawn crackers. 'How are your mum and dad?' I ask.

'Fine, they're fine. They say hi.'

'Tell them I say hi too.'

'I hear Suz came to visit you on Thursday while she was in Town.'

I look up sharply at that, but then I go back to my menu. 'Yes, it was really nice of her to pop by.'

'She's been keeping busy.'

How much have they discussed? Has my entire conversation with Suz about inequality been relayed back to him?

No. Suz wouldn't do that.

'I'm sure she's been very busy,' I say. 'She always works so hard.'

The waitress brings the wine, asks Quinn if he'd like to

taste it. She pours us each a glass and takes our orders for food. 'Do you want a starter?' Quinn asks me, and I say, 'If you do,' so we don't order one. 'Maybe dessert,' Quinn says.

'So what have you been doing?' he asks, as he asks on the phone.

I should tell him now. If I had any guts, if I were strong enough to be fair, I would tell him, *I have met up with my former lover. I have searched him out and kissed him, I have spent the night in his flat on his sofa. He says I saved his life. I've felt that I've been in love with him for some time. Sometimes when I was with you.*

I would tell him, *I'm so sorry. So very sorry, Quinn.*

'Working,' I say, my throat dry. 'Mostly working.'

'Have you seen Lauren at all?'

'No, she's been in Brussels. She's due back in September.'

'I can't believe how warm it's been. It's more like Spain than England.'

'Yes, it's incredible.'

'It's supposed to last another week, at least. Maybe two. Right through August.'

Quinn is exactly the same as he has always been. He's the same man who made me laugh when I should have been crying, the one who asked my permission before the first time he kissed me. The one who took me on a picnic in the rain and who undressed me, back in our cottage, as if he were uncovering a treasure. Dropping each item of clothing on the floor in the puddles made by our dripping hair. The man who swore to love me for ever under a canopy of umbrellas and who slept with his phone next to his cheek so I could listen to him breathing. He names the flowers in our garden and the features of the moon. Those hands holding his chopsticks, twisting his wine glass and refilling it, have held mine and held me and performed a thousand little kindnesses for my sake.

On our wedding day I walked into the church late, my hand slippery around my bouquet of freesia and roses, and Quinn was waiting there at the altar, straight and slender. From the back he looked almost like a stranger. In the car I had been worrying, fidgeting, pleating my dress, looking at the storm clouds through the window. I'd felt my mother's absence like a blade. But here in the church, the music started and he turned around and I was happy. Purely happy, in that one moment, with no room for anything else.

Why can't that moment stretch and keep? Why don't I smell roses and freesia?

We decide against dessert. The waitress gives him back his debit card and he folds the receipt carefully into his wallet. He drinks the last bit of wine in his glass. Mine is still half full.

He spreads his hands on the white tablecloth. 'Shall I stay the night tonight?'

'I . . . I don't think it's a good idea, Quinn.'

He nods. He meets my eye, looks away, and meets it again. 'Are you feeling well?'

'I'm a little – I've been having a little bit of dizziness. It's okay. Dr Johnson said it was migraine.'

'Maybe you should see him again.'

'If it gets worse, I will. I promise.'

'When . . . when were you thinking of coming home?'

'I don't know.'

He reaches out and takes my wrist, as if we're being pulled apart, falling.

'Let's go,' I say.

He releases me. 'Yes. All right.' He holds the door of the restaurant open for me going out, as he did going in. He gives me his arm and I take it. Outside, London has shifted into darkness, or as dark as London gets. The Thames is flat and black; I can't see the moon. Either it hasn't risen yet, or it's new, or it's hiding behind a tower block. Here in London, I've lost track of its phases.

People in shirtsleeves or strappy dresses congregate outside the pubs, smoking and laughing and yelling conversation at each other. Between Quinn and me there's silence.

Ask me, I think, as hard as I can. *Ask me if there's someone else. Ask me if I've betrayed you. Don't settle for silence, please.*

If he asks me, I will give him the truth. Because he deserves to know it, even if I am too cowardly to give it to him unprompted.

But he doesn't ask.

Chapter Twenty-four

'Oh, good morning. I have an appointment with you and I'm afraid I've lost the letter with the date on it, so I'm ringing to check when it is.'

'Name?'

'Felicity Bloom. I mean, Felicity Wickham. That's my married name.'

Mouse and keys clicking. 'Your appointment was on the fourteenth.'

'Of next month?'

'Of this month. It was last Friday.'

'So . . . I've missed it?'

'Yes.'

'Oh. Bother. I've sort of moved house, you see, and I didn't have the letter to remind me. Can I reschedule it?'

'One moment.' More clicks. 'The first opening I have is for the sixth of November.'

'But that's months away.'

No reply.

'The thing is, the problem is, that my symptoms have become more . . . complicated. And frequent. And I wasn't really concerned about them before but now I'm starting to think that maybe I should be.'

'Perhaps you should go to your GP and get another referral?'

'Oh. Maybe. The thing is – I'm not really, I don't really want to – isn't there any way I can get an urgent appointment without seeing him first?'

'We only take referrals, I'm afraid.'

I frown at the sofa cushion. What am I supposed to do? Present myself at an A&E here in East London? And say what? I'm getting these weird feelings of being in love?

'So shall I book you in for the sixth of November or do you prefer to see your GP first?'

'I . . . I don't know. Maybe it can wait. I mean – do you think I need to be worried that it's happening more frequently?'

'You'd have to see the doctor, I'm afraid.'

'But you must see a lot of people—'

'I can't possibly comment, I'm afraid. I can only book you the appointment if you want it.'

'Um . . . I . . . yes. Okay. Thank you. The sixth of November. I'll write it down this time.'

It is wonderful to be in love in late summer.

In the late summer in London with the traffic like a symphony. In the late summer when you leave the broad windows open and rain soaks the wooden floors and the smell is like being in a forest. In the yelling and the screach of brakes and the brave birdsong, in the flicker of shadow cast by a plane tree, in the car radios coming closer and fading away into a series of bass heartbeats. When you're in love,

people smile at you, they walk on their way smiling and the next person catches it, and you spread a ripple of love all the way from your throbbing centre to the next street, to the next one, all the way outwards through E14, across the Thames and into other people's windows, to the places where they are having their tea, watching television, washing up. It will touch them, your love, it will make them get up from their sofas and join hands with each other, join hands and dance, fling their shoes into the street, throw the soapsuds into bubbles in the air and cry out singing with the rapture of being in love
   in love
   in love

Chapter Twenty-five

'Hello, love, you're not answering. I hope it's because you're sleeping. Anyway, give me a ring, will you? And don't forget to drink plenty of liquids. Bye.'

'Don't you *ever* answer emails? Listen, I'm in London on a flying visit next week for a meeting, back to Brussels next day. I have a feeling we have to chat. Make sure there's milk in the fridge. Okay, ciao, call me. And *answer emails*, dammit.'

'Oh hello, Felicity? It's Molly. I just saw Quinn and he says you're not feeling very well, dear. I wondered if you wanted me to give him some soup to bring to you? I'm sure it would be no trouble for him to pop up to Town this weekend. I shall send you a card in the meantime to cheer you up! Take care and get lots of rest. Maybe it would be more relaxing to be at home in your own bed, do you think?'

'Flick. I can't stop thinking about you. Call me.'

'Felicity? It's Madelyne, just ringing to see how you're getting on with the book. Please ring me back as soon as possible.'

★

'Hello, love, I'm wondering if you've lost your phone? Pointless question to ask, really. Anyway, give me a ring when you've got a moment. I hope you're feeling better. Bye.'

'Flick, I mean it. Call me. You turn up out of nowhere and then you disappear. You've got me worried now. Call me. As soon as you get this. Do you hear?'

Ewan

Surely this wasn't right. He checked the address on his phone again, and then checked the number of the building. It was the same. He punched the button for the flat number she'd given him and waited for a reply through the intercom. But all he got was the buzz of the door as it opened.

The lobby was ten degrees cooler than the outside, floored in granite, full of mirrors and plants. He'd been in shabbier five-star hotels. It didn't fit in with what he knew about Felicity at all, that she would live in a place like this. This was the sort of building that wanker City-types lived in, or that sat mostly empty as pieds-à-terre for wealthy foreign nationals.

In the lift going up, he thought again how little he knew about Felicity Bloom. He didn't know her new last name. He knew none of her friends. Nothing about her current life, really, other than that her mother had passed away a couple of years ago and that she was married to a man she didn't talk about, and that she drew children's books. He'd picked one up in a shop a couple of days ago: *Igor the Owl and the Earwig Enigma*. It was charming, and warm, and funny, and very Felicity in a way that this building wasn't.

It was probably her husband's flat. Before the lift doors opened, he fantasized that she was married to some rich arsehole who had dragged her into this sterile Canary Wharf world, and when she'd come to find him it had been a cry for help. That he was supposed to save her as much as she'd saved him. The daydream lasted for about as long as it took him to step from the lift into the corridor with its thick carpeting, its discreet numbers on the doors, and realize that if this was what Felicity was used to now, he didn't have much to offer in return. Seeing as he was unemployed and flirting with depression.

And he was only coming to check on her. For a week, since she'd met him in Greenwich, she'd been around nearly every day. Knocking on his door, turning up at odd hours, sleeping on his sofa. And then, for over a week: nothing, aside from a text or two. There was no other way to check that she was all right apart from coming to her flat.

Besides, he missed her.

He rapped on the flat door, only now suddenly realizing that the reason she hadn't been in touch might be because she was with her husband, and the odds were that the husband would answer the door right now. Typical of Ewan not to have planned for this possibility. He stuck a carefree smile on his face, ready to act airily like the old friend that he was. Only that, and nothing more.

For several minutes, nothing happened. He raised his hand to rap again, when the door opened. Her hair was down around her face, her eyes blinking. She rubbed her forehead with her hand and seemed not to recognize him at first.

'Flick,' he said. 'Are you all right?'

'Hmm. Asleep.' She peered up at him. 'How did you know where I was?'

'You texted me your address.'

'Did I?' She was barefoot, in a sleeveless top and a skirt that skimmed her knees. 'I don't remember. When did I do that?'

'The day before yesterday. Flick, are you okay? You look . . . odd.'

'I told you – I was sleeping.'

'Can I come in?'

She went into the flat and he followed her. The air conditioning wasn't working as well in here as it was in the lobby and the corridor. Or that could be because the windows were open, letting in the outside air. The living area looked as if a strong wind had blown through it. There was a half-drunk glass of water on the floor near one of the two white sofas and a crumpled knitted throw beside it. A lamp lay on its side. Papers were scattered everywhere; he glimpsed several saccharine greetings cards on the floor. A drawing of an owl with glasses, scribbled out with almost vicious strokes.

He remembered what he'd suspected earlier, from the odd way she could behave, the blissed-out expression she could get. The way she looked now, groggy and disoriented. But there was no obvious evidence of drug use – no powder on the coffee table, no smell, no roaches or gear.

'Is your husband in?' he asked.

'Quinn? You mean is he here? No, he isn't.'

'It's a nice flat.'

'Yes.'

'It's customary,' he said gently, mostly to see if it made her smile, 'to offer one's guests a cup of tea.'

'I don't think you should be here,' she said. 'I don't think it's safe.'

He looked around again. No man's jacket hanging on the back of a chair, no briefcase, nothing particularly husband-like, except for the expense of everything which lay like a gloss over the flat. 'What does he do?'

'He's the editor of a newspaper.'

Ah. He could picture Mr Felicity, editor-in-chief: good suit, excellent shoes, hair thinning, belly straining the shirt from too many business lunches. The flat made more sense, now. It didn't explain why Felicity was married to him.

'Are you expecting him back?'

'No. I'm not expecting him. Why are you here, Ewan?'

'Didn't you get my messages?'

'I'm not sure where my phone is. Maybe it's in the bed-room? I don't know. When is the last time we spoke?'

'Last Thursday.'

He saw her calculating in her head. 'That was when we had ice cream for breakfast. Not since then?'

'Not except by text. Don't you remember?'

'I'm a little . . .' She rubbed her forehead again. 'And what day is it today?'

'Friday.'

'Of the following week? Oh. Oh dear.'

She didn't seem distressed, just disappointed.

'Have you eaten today?'

'Toast. I'm fine.'

'You lie very badly.' He went into her kitchen. There were, in fact, toast crumbs everywhere. There was also quite a bit of uneaten toast, much of it burnt. All of it was cold. The only empty bottle was of Lucozade.

'I think you should leave,' Flick said, following him.

'Why?' he asked, filling the kettle and switching it on. He looked in the fridge for food: champagne and a jar of jam. The milk was on the counter beside the kettle and it had clearly gone off.

'I think I might do . . .' She shook her head. 'I'm trying to do the right thing, Ewan. I'm not sure how to do it.'

'Are you ill?'

'No. No, I'm fine.' She frowned. 'Yes, I'm sure I'm fine. Actually, I feel completely normal right now. So that's good.'

'Don't take this the wrong way, but are you doing any drugs at all?'

'No.'

'You don't have to lie to me about it. I've seen almost everything you can imagine.'

'I'm not doing drugs. Listen, Ewan, I really don't think it's a good idea for you to be here.'

'I'm just doing for you what you did for me. I'm worried about you, and I want to make sure you're all right. Where do you keep the tea? We'll have to have it black.'

'Don't bother, please.'

'Just as well – everyone tells me I make a shitty cup of tea. Let's talk.' He pointed through the kitchen door to the living room, and she sighed, went to one of the sofas and sat down. She looked small in this big flat, and as if she didn't belong. He sat beside her. Said, 'You haven't changed a bit since I knew you.'

'I've changed in some ways.'

'Do you love him?' he asked. She'd been looking down, pulling the throw over her bare feet, but at that she raised her head.

'I . . .'

'I can't believe you love him,' he said, surprised at the rush of emotion, the jealousy. 'If you loved him, you wouldn't have come to find me.'

'It's complicated, Ewan. I don't think I can really explain it to you. I can't explain it to myself. But yes, I do love him. Otherwise, I wouldn't have married him.'

But she sounded uncertain.

'You told me once that you wanted to be extraordinary. Does he help you do that?'

'That was a long time ago.'

'If you love him, why are you attracted to me?'

'I – I'm not.'

'Yes, you are. That's why you don't want me here. You're married to him, but you're attracted to me. And you don't trust yourself not to do something about it. Is that why you haven't seen me for a week?'

Her hands were clenched in her lap. 'I don't want to talk about it.'

'You can't deny it, Flick. You know it as well as I do. There's still something between us. You kissed me.'

'I didn't mean to.'

'But you did. It's still there. What we felt all those years ago.'

He touched her face, stroked her cheek. He took her chin in his fingers and made her look at him. Her eyes were as he remembered them, soft and green.

'We shouldn't have split up,' he said. 'It didn't get us anywhere. We're not happy without each other, are we? Be truthful.'

'I don't know. I'm not sure what happiness is any more.'

'I'm sure. Because the only time I've felt it lately is when I've been with you.'

She swallowed. He felt it through his fingers, all through his body. She'd always shown every emotion she felt, imprinted on her face. He could see the desire there now. The doubt.

'We hardly knew each other,' she said. 'We don't know each other at all, now. We've only spent a few hours together.'

'So why did you find me, at exactly the right time? If it wasn't for this?' He stroked her bottom lip with his thumb.

'I'm not even sure I like you very much,' she said. But she was breathless. He could hear it. He knew what it meant.

'I'm falling in love with you,' he told her. For a moment, he saw her real answer in her face. Then she shook her head.

'No. You're not. You can't be.'

'I didn't care about anything. I'd thrown away everything. But you gave me back my life. You gave it meaning again.'

'That's not true. You still have a daughter. You can still have a job if you want it. I'm not the only thing. I'm not that important to you. It's just— I just happened to be there.'

'You sound like you're trying to convince yourself.'

She pulled back from him. But she didn't get off the sofa. 'If you want meaning in your life, you should get in touch with your daughter. She's the one who needs you.'

'It's too late for me and Rebecca. It's not too late for me and you. We've been given a second chance.'

'Ewan, I can't. This wasn't meant to happen.'

'I think it is meant to happen,' he said, and he took her face in his hands again and kissed her.

Chapter Twenty-six

I'm not feeling anything but Ewan's hands on me, his lips on mine. My mind and heart aren't playing any of their tricks; I'm nowhere but here on Lauren's sofa, on a Friday afternoon when I thought it was Wednesday. I am in my right mind. I have no excuse.

I kiss him back. I feel the second chance he was talking about: the present, the past, our bodies, no thought of anything else in our lives but each other. He is entirely familiar, and yet he isn't, and is it the familiarity or the strangeness which makes me wrap my arms around his neck? Which makes me respond to the sound he makes in his throat when he shifts on the sofa so that he can cover my body with his?

I know it was always this way with Ewan, this desire that we could barely control. His hands roam over my body, as if he wants to touch all of me at once. He pulls down my top to kiss my neck, my chest. I can't breathe, or rather I'm breathing so quickly that I can't feel the oxygen. I dig my fingertips into his arms and arch up against him, wrapping one of my legs around his. I feel alive. I feel every inch of my body, aware and awakening from what seems like a long sleep.

He smells of sweat and faintly of cigarette smoke, of soap

and coffee. He does not smell of frangipani. But my body still burns, and curves up towards him, and tells me yes. And his tongue in my mouth and his breath in my ear, hot shivers as one of his hands strokes up my bare leg underneath my skirt. I want him like I did when I was twenty. And I shouldn't.

Or is this what it was all for? All the scent and the longing? Back to this, the sound of his shirt tearing as I help him push it off, my body seemingly acting of its own accord to touch his naked chest?

I close my eyes and there he is, in the darkness behind my eyelids, looking at me out of the painting my mother did. The portrait of a young man in love.

I push him away and struggle to sit up. 'Ewan,' I say, my lips and tongue clumsy. 'Ewan.'

The name feels like a kiss. I hear it as if someone else has said it, and can't work out whether it's a protest or a plea. His eyes unfocused, he reaches for me again.

'Ewan, we—' I begin, but before I can say any more I hear the door of the flat open.

Chapter Twenty-seven

I don't have time to get off the sofa, to pull away from Ewan. I do have time to think, *Please let it be Lauren*, and then I hear Quinn's voice: 'Hello, love? The door was op—'

He appears, carrying two canvas shopping bags. He drops the bags on the floor. Something breaks.

I scramble off the sofa and hold my top together with my hand. 'Quinn,' I gasp. 'I didn't—'

Quinn is staring. From me to Ewan, who is still on the sofa, his shirt off. His hair disarranged from where I have tugged at it. His mouth red with kissing me.

'Who is this?' Quinn asks.

His voice is not patient and pleasant. It is low and quiet.

Ewan stays on the sofa. 'Are *you* the husband?' He appears to be as surprised as I am.

Quinn does not look surprised at all. He is pale and very still.

'Ewan,' I say. 'You need to leave, right now.'

'The door was open,' says Quinn. Beside him, a pool of clear liquid seeps from one of the shopping bags.

'I can explain,' I say, although I can't.

'I don't think you need to,' says Quinn.

'I didn't mean for you to—'

'Then perhaps you should have closed the door.' He sounds dangerous. I never thought he could sound dangerous. Ewan is still staring, his shirt crumpled on the floor. I scoop it up and hand it to him, but he doesn't take it.

'I thought he'd be different,' Ewan says.

'Ewan, please go. You're making this worse.'

'It can't get much worse,' says Quinn. 'Unless of course you'd like to take your clothes off too, Felicity.'

I have never seen him like this.

'Is this the first time, or the dozenth?' he asks us. 'Have you been doing this the entire time you've been gone? Is this the "old friend" you told me you were seeing?'

'It's not what it looks like. We weren't going to . . .' My sentence fades away under his anger. I don't know if we were going to have sex. I was about to stop Ewan.

Or was I? I was pushing him away. I was saying his name. I was going to tell him to leave. I was going to pull him closer. I was entirely myself.

I can still feel his hands on my skin. With Quinn looking at me like this, I feel as if the places that Ewan touched me, kissed me, are glowing red.

'I love her,' Ewan says. 'She saved my life.'

'You're in love with my wife,' Quinn says, in his new quiet, dangerous anger.

'He's not,' I say. 'He might think he is, but he's not. Ewan, go away. Leave us alone, please.'

'I am,' Ewan says. 'I'm in love with her.'

It's the last straw. I kick Ewan in the shin. I'm barefoot, and the impact is enough to make me wince.

'Flick! What the—'

271

'I need you to go. *Now.*'

He looks from me to Quinn. Quinn's eyes have narrowed to dark slits.

'He isn't going to hurt you, is he?' Ewan asks me.

'Oh, for God's sake. Just *go.*'

The two men stare at each other for a long moment and my crazy mind, chasing itself, thinks that they are going to start fighting. Launch into a brawl right here in the middle of Lauren's Canary Wharf flat, knocking over furniture, sending papers flying. But these things don't happen in real life.

Quinn's fists are clenched.

'I need to speak with my wife,' he says finally, in this new voice. Ewan keeps steady for another minute, and then he shrugs. He pulls his shirt over his head.

'I'll call you,' he says to me. 'I love you.'

Under Quinn's gaze, I wince.

Ewan walks past my husband without giving him another glance. He slams the door behind him. It echoes and then it's quiet.

'Quinn,' I say. 'We didn't sleep together. We kissed, and that was it. It was a mistake, a very bad mistake. I was just about to tell him to leave.'

'I don't believe you.'

I'm still holding my blouse together with my hand. I button it, my fingers trembling.

'It's been going on since you left. Or before?'

'Nothing's been going on. It – this just happened.'

'I'm stupid, Felicity, but not that stupid. Not any more. Do you know what I thought? I actually thought you might be ill. I thought you might not be taking care of yourself properly. Now I know better, don't I?'

He is still straight, his full height, no smile, no tenderness in his eyes. He is a stranger, more of a stranger than he's ever been, even when I didn't know him. There's a button missing from my blouse.

'I trusted you,' he says.

'Nothing's happened.'

'He says he loves you.'

'He's crazy.'

'Did you leave me because of him?'

'I did have to work. And I did need to think.'

'Did you leave me because of him?'

'Partly,' I whisper.

'Who is he?'

'I knew him ten years ago.'

'You were lovers?'

'Yes.'

'And now?'

'No. We're not, Quinn.'

'You are. If you haven't actually had sex, it's just a technicality.'

'I was about to tell him to stop.'

He makes a sound of contempt. I can't argue.

'Do you love him?'

'No. I don't know.' He waits. 'Sometimes I think that I do.'

'I've loved you with everything I have in me,' Quinn says. 'I've given you everything that matters. And it was never enough for you. I don't know what would be.'

'It's not that it wasn't enough. It's that it was too much.'

'How could I love you less?' he cries. 'Was I supposed to hold something back? Was I supposed to lie to you? Cheat on

273

you? Find *an old friend*? What do you want, Felicity? Do you want me to do what you've done to me?'

'No, I—'

'Ever since I've known you I've done nothing but try to please you. I thought that if I could make you happy enough, you'd keep loving me. And this is what you wanted? Someone else?' He's shouting now, gesturing at the door that Ewan has closed behind him. I've never heard him shout before.

'I don't—'

'Everyone said it. Not to my face, but I knew they were thinking it. *She's not going to stick around for long, mate. She's too different. Doesn't fit in. She'll find someone else, someone to suit her better, someone who won't tie her down in a tiny village.*' His face twists as he says it. 'When you left, I said you were working. Everyone knew, but I thought they were wrong. I said . . .' His voice falters.

'I never meant to hurt you, Quinn. I don't want to hurt you. I'm so sorry.'

'Too fucking late.'

I hold out my hand to him, hoping he'll let me touch him.

'I know what you think about me, about my job, about my family. You thought our life was too small. You thought I was your . . . puppy.' He spits the word out. 'But you're wrong. It's more than you'll ever know. It's more than you'll ever deserve. And I . . .'

This time he raises his hand to his eyes, and I step away from the sofa towards him, every part of me wanting to comfort him, even through my shame, but when he lowers his hand, his eyes are dry.

'I deserve more than you,' he says. Coldly. So coldly. 'Goodbye, Felicity.'

I watch him walk out of the door. He doesn't slam it behind him; he closes it, and that's enough.

I could run after him, try to explain. But everything he said was the truth. I did, sometimes, think that my life with him was too small. I did want Ewan. And Quinn does deserve better.

The puddle under the shopping bag has grown and started to make a small trail of liquid across the floor, like a pointing finger. I get a tea towel from the kitchen and wipe it up. It smells like elderflower, and the broken cordial bottle in the bag confirms it. He's brought me tea and cordial, cartons of fresh soup and packets of biscuits, a ripe mango and a bunch of sunflowers. There's a Mervyn Peake paperback in the bag that had the cordial, and a little pocket sketch book of the kind I like. Both of them are wet and sticky from the spill.

I unpack each thing and put it on the floor, in a line. Then I pick the pieces of glass out of the bag and put them into the tea towel. A splinter of glass cuts my finger and I put it in my mouth, tasting blood mixed with elderflower.

I don't know if I was going to stop Ewan. I'd like to think I was, but I can't be sure. But whatever choice I was going to make in that moment, it's now been made for me. I've destroyed my marriage to Quinn.

The door buzzer goes. My finger still in my mouth, I pick up the receiver.

'Flick,' says Ewan. 'Let me in.'

'It's not a good idea.'

'I know he's gone.'

Quinn is gone. I wipe my wet cheek on my bare shoulder. I recognize the sickness in my stomach, the feeling of anticipation.

'I need some time to think,' I tell him.

'But you'll talk to me? You'll see me again? I meant what I said.'

'I'll be in touch,' I say.

'How long?'

'I don't know. I have to . . . I have to work things out. A couple of weeks? A month maybe? Please don't contact me, Ewan. Let me sort this out, and then I'll call you.'

'Is that really what you want?'

'Yes.'

'We still have a chance,' Ewan says. I put down the phone.

And then the sickness in my stomach and in my heart resolves into the scent of frangipani and I lie down on the sticky floor, tears leaking from my eyes, waiting until I feel in love again, until for these few moments at least, I no longer have a choice.

Part Three

You all, healthy people, can't imagine the happiness which we epileptics feel during the second before our fit . . . I don't know if this felicity lasts for seconds, hours or months, but believe me, *I would not exchange it for all the joys that life may bring.*

Dostoevsky

Chapter Twenty-eight

It's cooler in Tillingford than it is in London; the air hangs less heavy and a breeze rustles the leaves. The common has been baked brown and dry. It's Saturday lunchtime, and there's a cricket game going on. Derek will be watching it in his portable chair, drinking tea that Molly has made him from a flask. Maybe Quinn's with him; he joins his father sometimes. If I know Quinn, he will probably want to continue with his normal life, even after what he discovered less than twenty-four hours ago.

But I'm not certain that I do know Quinn.

I hope he's still angry, though. I'd rather he were angry than sad.

If he's told anyone about discovering me and Ewan, it will be all over Tillingford by now. *Felicity Wickham left her husband for another man after only a year of marriage.* They'll love that piece of juicy news. I spot Irene Miller, the town gossip, leaving the cricket game and approaching me over the green, and I hurry to slip through the gate to Hope Cottage.

Our garden is vibrant with splashes of orange, red and purple. Despite the heat and the dryness elsewhere, here it still feels damp. Quinn's bike rests against the side wall. I haven't rung to let him know I was coming; I wasn't sure he'd want to speak to me. Now that it's too late, I need to tell him the truth, the facts that I was too cowardly to tell him all along.

Somehow I thought that if I could work out who I was truly in love with, if I could work out what the scent of frangipani meant, that everything else would fall into place. I would decide it wasn't relevant, re-commit myself to Quinn, and everything would be fine. Or I would find bliss with Ewan. It would be cut and dried, no questions possible.

But that hasn't happened. Love isn't a single perfect moment, a whiff of scent, eyes meeting. Life goes on. People get hurt, memories are tarnished. There are connections and resentments, friends and families. Maybe every happily-ever-after is someone else's broken heart. Or maybe that's too neat, even. Maybe the hearts just get broken, and that's it.

I need to tell the truth, and say I'm sorry. I don't know what comes next. I don't hold out much hope of being forgiven. Maybe I will find Ewan and see if he was right about second chances. But I still wear Quinn's ring, and I owe him an apology before I do anything else at all.

After only a few weeks away, I feel like a stranger here, but not enough of one to use the front door. I've loved this garden. I've loved this man. I take a deep breath and walk along the side of the cottage to the back.

The kitchen table has been taken outside and it stands on the overgrown grass. The Wickhams are all sitting around it: Derek and Molly, Suz and Quinn. There's a bright cloth spread on the table and there are bowls of salad, a bottle of wine, a jug of lemonade. Someone has put tall hollyhocks in a vase. The sunshine pools on the grass, sparkles on the glassware. There's no fifth chair. Molly, passing a dish of tomatoes, catches sight of me and lets out a little cry, and I know that Quinn has told them everything.

'I'm sorry,' I say.

Quinn stands up. Beside him, so does Derek, putting his hand on his son's shoulder. 'You have some nerve coming here,' Derek says.

'Not very much,' I admit. 'I'm scared to death.'

'You should be!' screeches Molly and I turn to her, surprised. She's jumped to her feet too, though she's still holding the bowl of tomatoes. 'How could you do this to Quinn? One year – one year! And you're tired of him already?'

'It's not that. I'm not tired of him.'

'Mum,' says Suz quietly, 'sit down.'

'I didn't mean to hurt Quinn. I didn't mean to hurt any of you. I just had these feelings, and I had to follow them. I've been a coward. I should have told the truth from the start. It would have been less complicated.'

'You should have stayed away from my boy!'

Molly's face is fierce. This soft woman, the woman who chatters about nothing and sends sugar-sweet greetings cards, looks as if she wants to tear my eyes out. Any minute the bowl of tomatoes is going to come flying at my head. I had no idea that she could be so passionate in defence of her young.

Good, I think. *Good for you*. Irrationally, I want to smile at her and clap my hands.

I bow my head. 'You're right. I shouldn't have married Quinn. I thought . . . I thought I could be happy with him.'

Quinn stands there, silent.

'You need to get your things and get out,' says Molly. 'I'll pack them up myself, with my own hands, and good riddance.'

Derek takes the tomato dish from his wife's hand and puts it on the table, saying, 'Molly, please.'

'We welcomed you as part of the family,' says Molly.

'I know. You've been nothing but kind. But you know I've never fitted in.'

'I knew you were having doubts,' says Suz, 'but I didn't think you would do something like this.'

I've started shaking. I'm going to take it all, everything they can fling at me, and then I'm going to walk away and I'm never coming back. Quinn isn't even looking at me. Suz's disappointment is a heavy weight in my stomach. The scent of the wildflowers in the garden is growing stronger, suffocating with sweetness.

'I wasn't one of you,' I manage. 'It wasn't any of your faults. It wasn't Quinn's fault.'

'I thought you were going to talk it through together,' says Suz.

'You don't go running to another man!' cries Molly. 'It's not what you do! Maybe in your mother's world – that artistic world that's so much better than ours. But not here. Not in my family, not to my *son*.'

My stomach's churning, acid and fire. The ground is unsteady under my feet. The flowers are growing, whitening into frangipani with golden hearts, and I'm becoming lighter somehow, lighter even though I'm burdened with guilt and regret.

'I'll just go.'

Lighter, so light I tumble up into the air.

From above, the Wickhams look like an army, fore-shortened to dark heads and sun-kissed shoulders. Derek stands near his wife, Suz folds her arms across her chest. Quinn stands straight beside the table filled with glistening food, bright colours, summer. They're magnificent – the magnificent Wickhams – and I see myself in front of them, trembling, my hair dull in the light.

'I'm sorry,' I say, though it comes from below me, where I am standing down there. How did I get up here? My lips are numb. Every breath saturated with scent. 'That's all I came here to say.'

'Felicity?' says Suz. I see her step forward, bumping the table. Her glass of lemonade tips over. I see Quinn push aside his chair. My arms fly out, my legs collapse. I see my eyeballs roll up to where I am above everything, and for a moment I am staring myself in the face. And then I'm absorbed back down into my body and I'm on the grass. There are voices. But as soon as they speak they're being pulled away from me, drained away into nothing, into darkness, into memories that are gone, a disappearing brush of a finger.

Quinn

They'd been talking about the weather breaking, about a hosepipe ban, about what was going to happen to the post office. About everything except for Felicity and his ruined marriage, although they were all thinking about her. So much so, that when she appeared in the garden, it seemed as if their thoughts had come to life.

Her hands were shaking; she kneaded them together and he didn't want to think about how alone she looked. His mother's voice cracked and rang, full of anger. He remembered a long-ago picnic, some time when he was a child, when his mother and father had argued and he had sat on the blanket, pulling blades of grass from the earth as if it could stop the fear of it all being his fault, of everything being finished. The argument was over quickly but the fear stayed, cocooned inside him, visiting him again at night, waiting for its time in the sun.

He stood beside the table listening to his mother. He was too old to let his mother defend him, but he didn't seem to be able to speak. All night he'd been consumed with anger. He'd seen them over and over again: the man on top of his wife on the sofa, his hand up her skirt. Felicity's arms around him. The blush on her cheeks, her hands on his chest. Whenever he closed his eyes he could see them, or even worse, just afterwards, when Felicity had spotted him and had jumped up, pulling her blouse together, full of panic and guilt and yet still aroused from that man's touch. That other man. The one she had gone after. The one she wanted more than she'd ever wanted him.

The anger burned at him, gnawed at him. Almost more than what she'd done to him, he hated that she'd made him feel this way.

And here she was, trembling in their garden. He couldn't quite connect this Felicity with that one in London yesterday. He supposed it was denial. It was habit. 'I'm sorry,' she said, and he wanted to go to her, despite the anger, despite the betrayal. He wanted to forget all about it and carry on as normal. If he looked at her, he would.

So he didn't look at her.

But out of the corner of his eye, he saw her fall.

She yelled wordlessly, a hoarse sound that was her and wasn't. He ran forward. He couldn't catch her before she hit the ground but he caught her afterwards as she lay there. She jerked and twitched, a rag doll pulled by invisible strings. Her eyes blinked, over and over; her mouth worked, as if trying to say something important.

'What's happening?' his mother cried.

'It's some kind of seizure,' said Suz, who was kneeling beside him. Quinn held Felicity against him, cradling her in his arms, shielding her head from the ground.

'Call 999,' he said to his sister, and she pulled out her phone. Felicity's face contorted and her body struck out, heels drumming on the grass his father had watered. One hand, her left hand, the one with his ring, escaped and slapped the side of his arm. It wasn't puppet strings but his anger making her jerk, helpless, possessed.

No, not his anger. It was a disease. Something wrong.

'What is it?' his mother asked. 'Should we put something in her mouth? To stop her swallowing her tongue?'

He shook his head. Felicity was thinner than she had been, but her brittle strength pushed at him in pulses, in twitches, testing its escape. He steadied her head but it twisted, by itself, and her breath panted against the side of his shirt. He felt it through the cotton. He was reminded of a baby rabbit, years ago, found by the side of the road, its leg broken, frightened out of its mind by the boy who was trying to help it. It had rolled its eyes, scratched him with its needle claws, tried to run.

Time stretched, he knew it was stretching, knew it was only seconds but it felt like hours, enough time for him to know he wasn't surprised by this seizure. That he'd always sensed there was this stranger inside Felicity, this being pulling the invisible strings. Her eyes fluttered closed, open, closed again; she made choking sounds but she wasn't choking, she was breathing, he could feel each breath. A silver thread of saliva hung from her lips and he brushed it away with his hand. Her dress had rumpled up over her knees so he pulled it down again.

'They're coming,' Suz said behind them, and though he didn't think Felicity heard, her body relaxed into heaviness.

'Felicity,' he said. She stared at him without recognition. 'Felicity, can you hear me?'

She wiped her mouth, rubbed her forehead. The crease appeared between her eyes that she got when she was thinking. Her mouth moved without sound and her eyes stared at him as if he were a stranger, as if he were a tree. No panic, no fear, only nothing. Every part of her was Felicity except she was not there.

One of his colleagues, years ago, had had epilepsy and he'd told them matter-of-factly what to do if he had a fit: clear a space, keep him out of danger, don't put anything in his mouth, talk to him, roll him onto his side if you could. Wait for it to be over. Don't give him a drink until he could talk. Keep calm. Don't worry. Put aside your anger and your fear.

'Felicity,' he said gently to her, 'it's me. Can you hear me?'

She sighed and closed her eyes. Quinn held her and waited for it to be over.

Chapter Twenty-nine

I'm in hospital. I see the blue curtain around my bed and hear a conversation in another language, maybe Punjabi, happening on the other side of the curtain; it smells of disinfectant here and the sheets are stiff, and somewhere something is beeping and I have a tube coming out of my left arm, so where else could I be but in hospital?

But I don't know how I got here. I'm not wearing shoes. I'm lying on my side and Quinn is sitting beside me looking into my face. My first thought is, *That's all right.* I close my eyes and go to sleep.

The next thing I know, he's shaking me by the shoulder.

'Are you awake?' he asks. I am faintly surprised that he's speaking in English, not Punjabi. 'Do you know who I am?'

'You're Quinn Wickham. You used to want to be a spy.' My voice is hoarse.

'How are you feeling?'

'Tired and thirsty.' My muscles ache, too. I go back to sleep. There aren't any dreams.

'Mrs Wickham? Are you with us?' A nurse is standing over

me. I'd rather sleep but her voice is quite insistent so I say, 'Yes.'

'Can you smile for me, love? Good. Squeeze my hand? Now this one? How many fingers am I holding up? How about now? Can you tell me what day it is? Who's this charming young man with me? Just follow this light, will you? Now look straight ahead. Good.'

Did I pass? What was the test? I don't usually pass tests. I'm not good at concentrating and even worse at spelling.

'What happened?' I ask. 'Did I fall?'

'You had a seizure,' says Quinn. 'You're in hospital.'

'How are you feeling?' asks the nurse.

'I want to sleep.'

'You can do that in just a minute. Do you remember anything about what happened?'

'I . . . remember floating in the air looking down at us. But that probably didn't happen.'

I also remember being in the garden, with my mother-in-law flinging recriminations at me. I remember what I did to earn them. I want to bury my head under the pillow and go back to sleep, so I let my eyes close again and do that.

When I wake up again, Quinn is there, watching me. I expect him to say, 'Good morning, love,' but he doesn't. Then I hear the beep. Hospital.

I try to sit up, but everything aches. 'Did I do anything stupid?'

'You fell down and had convulsions. It was very sudden.'

'I hope I didn't freak out your mum.'

'She's not bad in a crisis.' Meaning, I freaked her out.

'Poor Molly.'

Molly, her eyes blazing, telling me to stay away from her son.

289

'Are you all here? Your mum?' I look around; we're in a ward, curtains drawn around the bed.

'Just me. They stayed at home. They're waiting for news.'

'Have I been out for long?'

'You were out for a while. You had a fit, and then you lost consciousness. Sometimes you seemed awake, but not aware. You've been sleeping since we've been at the hospital. You seem very tired.'

'Yes.' Very tired, of everything. Ready to rest and not think for a while. I close my eyes and then open them. 'How long have I been out?'

'They took you for a CAT scan and you slept through it, I think. Do you remember it?'

'No. How long ago was it? Did I just ask that?'

'It's okay. It's been several hours.'

'How did I get here?'

'Suz called for an ambulance.'

'Did I say anything?' I watch his face carefully, but I can't read anything on it but concern.

'No. It's okay. All we're worried about now is that you're well.'

'What's the tube in my arm?' Mum had tubes. She had tubes everywhere, pumping in poison that was supposed to save her. I reach for it, and he stops my hand with his.

'They're giving you anti-seizure meds. And some fluids; you're dehydrated.'

'I'm tired.'

'Go to sleep.'

'I don't like hospitals, Quinn.'

'I'll be here.'

This time, I dream. I'm in my garden at Hope Cottage,

only I've built a wall around it, a high wall of mismatched stone. Around me, the plants are growing in stop-motion quickness. Sending out tendrils to pull themselves up, twining around each other. The weeds multiply with a low wet rustle of leaves. I am surrounded by green, up to my knees, up to my waist. Flowers burst, wither, fall. I see white and yellow, frangipani without scent. They brush my face, caress my cheek, burrow through my hair. A petal, soft as flesh, cool as wax. Stems and roots, pollen and sap, all these beings competing for the sunlight. I open my mouth to breathe and a leaf slips inside. It's the walls, the walls that are keeping the plants in when they want to crawl out, stretch, seek the air, be free.

I open my eyes. The curtains are patterned. Quinn sits beside me, reading a newspaper.

He lowers the paper. 'You're awake. Are you feeling any better?'

'I'm thirsty.' There's a plastic jug of water near the bed. I reach towards it, but the tube in my arm stops me.

'Here.' He pours a glass of water and pushes a button on the bed which makes it move me slowly into a sitting position. When my mother died I did the reverse; I laid her down, as if she could have the rest she'd always wanted. I take the water and drink it.

'Are you still sleepy?'

'Not so much.' The curtains are different. There wasn't a bedside table before. 'Have I been moved?'

'You've been admitted to the neurology ward. They moved you while you were sleeping.'

'And you came. You've stayed with me. Why?' I remember now, my going to the cottage, meeting Quinn and his family.

291

I was there to apologize for what I'd done. He's come in the ambulance, or after it, and he's stayed. I don't know how long.

What does it mean that he's here? Has he forgiven me? Or is it just something he'd do for anyone who happened to have a seizure in his garden – stick around to make sure they're all right? It's more likely to be the latter. He'd probably do the same thing for Cameron Bishop if the boy were struck down in the act of stealing his bicycle. Plus, he's my next-of-kin, for the time being anyway, so he'd feel an obligation. He's my only kin.

'I'm worried about you, Felicity. I'm your husband.'

I feel sick and anxious and ashamed. 'Can I have another glass of water?' He pours it for me and watches me drink it. 'I came to Tillingford to say I was sorry. I didn't mean for it to be so dramatic.'

'Half the Tillingford cricket team turned out to watch you being loaded into the ambulance.'

'Great.' A vision of myself, shuddering and twitching, on the ground next to Molly's neat shoes. 'Did I froth at the mouth? Did I swallow my tongue?'

'That's a myth. You can't swallow your tongue. It's anatomically impossible.'

'I drooled, didn't I?'

'You—'

A big man strides up, clearly a doctor, with two smaller persons standing behind him, just as clearly students or underlings. 'Mrs Wickham. I'm Dr Chin, Neurology Consultant here. How do you feel?'

'I'm all right. I'm trying to get Quinn to tell me whether I drooled.'

'That's a good sign. Not the drooling, but that you're

concerned about it. Can you smile for me, please?' Smiling, grasping, following a light, naming myself, counting fingers. It's the same routine I went through with the nurse. 'Can you answer some questions for me? Do you feel well enough?'

'I'll try.'

'Do you remember the episode that brought you here?'

'Not really. I was . . . in the garden with my husband and my in-laws, and I started feeling sick. Unreal. I could see us from above, as if I were flying. And then I woke up in hospital.'

'Had you had a fever, or were you ill? Had you taken any drugs or alcohol? Medication?'

I shake my head.

'It was rather a high-stress situation,' says Quinn.

'Have you had seizures such as this in the past, to your knowledge?'

'No. At least, not like this.'

'What do you mean, "not like this"?'

'I've never passed out, or had convulsions. Not that I know of. But I think I've had episodes. I think that might be what they were. But I'm not sure.'

'You've been having seizures?' asks Quinn. 'Since when? Why didn't I know?'

'Sometimes seizures aren't obvious to an observer,' says the doctor. 'Sometimes they're not even obvious to the person having them. You've had focal seizures, then? Episodes?'

'I thought they were migraines. Then I thought they were memories.'

'Why didn't you tell me?' Quinn demands.

'They were . . . private.'

'*Private?*'

293

'The mind is the last area of mystery,' says the doctor.

Except for maybe the heart.

'I didn't tell anyone because I was trying to work out what they meant,' I say.

'So this is your first tonic-clonic seizure – your first fit, what we used to call a *grand mal*,' says the doctor, minions scribbling behind him, 'but you may have had focal seizures before. Epilepsy run in your family?'

'No. That is, I don't know. I've never met my father. But my mother didn't have it.'

'Extended family?'

'I don't know them.'

He emits a noise that seems calculated to make me ashamed of only knowing one of my relatives, currently deceased. 'Tell me about these experiences you've had that you think may be seizures.'

I tell him about the scent of frangipani coming out of nowhere, about how at first I thought it was aftershave or perfume, or even a ghost, until I realized no one could smell it except for me. I tell him how I learned about the jumpiness that presages it, the sinking of the stomach, the warnings that sometimes allow me to make excuses and leave so I can be alone. Then I tell him about the feeling. The bliss, the wonder of being in love. How it possesses me and transforms me into a creature of pure light. And then the euphoria after it's gone, the echo that remains long enough to leave me bereft when it's faded.

I'm aware that I'm telling Quinn all of this, too. I don't watch him but I can feel him absorbing it. His pain is raw and red.

'Is the experience always the same?' asks the doctor.

'Yes. I mean, I do different things during it, depending on

294

where I am. Who I'm with.' My cheeks heat. 'Usually I just sort of experience it. I've been told I look stoned afterwards.'

'When did it start?'

'This spring. Probably . . . May? It was when we went for dinner at Cerise,' I tell Quinn. I have to look away from him immediately.

'That was the third week in May.'

'And how often does this happen?' asks the doctor.

'At first, only rarely. Once a week, maybe twice. But it's been happening more frequently. Recently it's been happening quite a lot.'

'And by quite a lot, you mean . . . ?'

'Several times a day. More than that, sometimes. It's . . . hard to tell the difference between this and my real feelings.'

'The sinking sensation in the stomach is typical,' says Dr Chin. 'So is the dazed feeling afterwards, and the fact that they're identical. These may be good indications that you've been having seizures rather than spontaneous emotions. The tests will help us work out if that's what they are.'

In the pause, I can feel Quinn gathering himself. 'What would cause symptoms like this?' he asks at last, and his voice is the semblance of a journalist's, looking for facts. If you didn't know him, you might believe it.

The students leap to attention. 'You don't have to tell us right now,' I say quickly.

'A variety of things could cause seizures, most of them treatable to a greater or lesser extent.'

'A brain tumour?' asks Quinn. 'Cancer?'

'Quinn, I don't think I want to know.'

'We need to know, Felicity.'

'A tumour is among the things that could be indicated, yes.

295

But we mustn't jump to conclusions. The CAT scan wasn't definitive. It showed something, but I can't be quite certain what it is yet, so I want to run some more tests tomorrow morning.'

'I think I'd rather go home.' Wherever home is.

'You have to stay,' Quinn tells me. 'You didn't see what happened to you, but it was frightening. Imagine if it happened somewhere dangerous? We have to find out what's wrong, so you can get better.'

'If there's the choice between feeling as if I'm in love every now and then, and finding out about a scary diagnosis, I think on balance that I'd rather feel in love,' I say.

'Would you,' says Quinn quietly.

'You need a diagnosis,' says the consultant. 'If you're having escalating seizure activity, chances are that this is something we need to take care of now, whether with medication or surgery. All being well, we'll have some answers tomorrow.' He pats the blanket beside my leg in a way that is no doubt meant to be soothing. 'Try to rest, and not worry too much. Lie still if you can. We'll keep you on the anti-seizure meds, by mouth instead of IV since you're conscious, but tell a nurse immediately if you feel something coming on. You're in the best place to be if the seizures recur.'

He turns away, the minions following him.

Quinn remains. I can't look in his face, so I look at his shirt. It's wrinkled and he has a grass stain on the elbow. Possibly from when I fell down. Would he have picked me up, or waited for the ambulance crew?

'I'm sorry,' I say, once again.

'Why didn't you tell me that all of this was going on?' he asks.

'Because . . . because I didn't know what they were. Dr Johnson said they could be migraines. And then I thought maybe it was Mum's ghost, and then I thought maybe it was just my own mind. Dr Johnson referred me to a neurologist, but I missed the appointment.'

'Why didn't you make another one?'

'I did. For November.'

'You weren't trying very hard, then.' He's attempting to stay calm, but he's angry.

'I didn't really want to hear that something was wrong with me. And besides, every time it happened, I felt happy.'

'You felt that you were in love with him.'

'I felt . . . I didn't know what it meant. It wasn't the sort of thing I could tell you about.'

'What *is* the sort of thing you can tell me about, Felicity? Is there anything?'

I bite my lip. For a moment, we listen to the noises of the ward. It reminds me of the dinner we had together, when the fountain in the restaurant couldn't cover up the silence between us.

'Is all of this the truth?' he asks me at last. 'You really can't help these feelings?'

'Do you think I'm lying to the doctor?'

'You lied to me.'

'I'm . . . it's the truth. I was having these feelings, and I didn't know how to deal with them.'

He looks as if he's tasted something bad. 'And what about *him*? He says he's in love with you. Is he having seizures, too?'

'No. I – I went to see him. I wanted to see if what I was feeling was real. And I spent some time with him. He was – he wasn't very happy.'

'So you tried to make him happier by having an affair with him.'

I swallow. 'I'm sorry.'

'It sounds very convenient. Considering what's been going on.'

'I know you're angry with me, Quinn. I deserve it.'

'I'm very angry with you. Not least for neglecting your health to the extent that you have to have a *grand mal* seizure in front of me for me to know that something's wrong. And even if all this is caused by sickness, even if you couldn't help what you felt, you didn't have to act on it.'

I wince.

'I can't believe it,' he says. 'It doesn't make sense at all.'

He leans forward and holds his head in his hands.

'You don't have to stay,' I tell him. 'I'll be all right.'

'No,' he says to the floor. 'No, you won't. You must be – you must be very frightened.'

Tears come to my eyes because he's right. I'm terrified that I may have ruined everything because of something wrong with my brain. I'm terrified that there may be something growing inside me that could rob me of myself. Kill me, by inches, like cancer killed my mother.

I can't tell Quinn this. I can't ask for his sympathy when I've wronged him. I wipe my eyes with the back of my hand before he can see I'm crying.

'I'm just very tired,' I whisper.

He clears his throat. He raises his head, but doesn't look at me.

'The doctor says you need your rest,' he says. 'Go ahead and get some sleep.' He pulls his newspaper out of his pocket where he's stowed it. It's the *Express*, not one of his normal newspapers. He must have picked it up here at the hospital. The headlines are something about Syria, something about pensioners succumbing to the heat.

He meets my gaze and I see it all: his pain, his worry, his anger, his resignation. Every bit of it my fault.

'You should go home,' I say.

'You're my wife. You're still my wife. You shouldn't be alone.' He opens his newspaper again, and that's the end of the discussion. I close my eyes. Through the noise of the ward, I can hear the tiny movements he makes.

Chapter Thirty

The ward isn't quiet at night. Beeping, shuffling feet, talking, groaning, and someone is even singing in another room. But when I wake up the air is full of frangipani. I can almost see the flowers in the dim light.

I reach for the call button but stop before I press it. This is beautiful. This is my mother, this is my lover, this is my youth and my past.

It transforms the ward into a paradise. They think it's a sickness and they want to take it away from me.

I slip out of bed. Quinn isn't here; he must have gone home to sleep. At some point I've been put into a hospital nightgown. The floor is cold under my bare feet and I pause, trying to formulate a plan. I don't have a car. I'll need a cab. But I'll have to get dressed first. Unhook myself from this IV. I check the cabinet beside the bed and find a plastic bag with my dress, my shoes, my handbag. Do I have money enough to get back to London? Will they let me go? What will happen if I pull this IV out? Will I trip some sort of alarm? They can't keep you in hospital against your will, can they? What if your husband wants you to be here?

I look around. No one seems to have noticed, not yet. I

need help. And my heart leaps and I know just who I need to see. Who will help me.

I find my mobile in my handbag, stuff everything back in the plastic bag and back in the cabinet, then get into bed. I pull the sheet up around my head so that no one will see what I'm doing. You're not supposed to use mobile phones in hospital, are you?

Ewan's phone goes straight to voicemail. 'Ewan, how do you know if you really love me?' I ask it. 'It's madness, isn't it? It doesn't make any sense.'

His voicemail doesn't answer my questions. I should be calling the nurse. I should be telling her to adjust my medication. 'Everything has become much more complicated,' I tell Ewan, via the message. 'I can't tell you about it right now. But maybe later. Don't ring me. It's not safe.'

I hang up the phone and I realize what I've done. Is this what I've done before? Did I text Ewan my address this way, when I was temporarily out of my mind? What else have I said in this state? What else have I done? My heart is pounding so fast, I feel so happy and the happiness is all wrong.

I grope for the nurse call button and press it. A nurse appears within half a minute.

'I'm afraid,' I tell her. 'I think I need some help.'

301

Quinn

Standing on the other side of the curtain, a plastic cup of tea in his hand, on his way back to his post, he heard her on her phone, asking Ewan if he really loved her.

When he'd got up to go to the vending machine, she'd been asleep. Sleep erased the shadows under her eyes, the pale sick hue of her skin, hardly different from the shade of her pillowcase. It made her look as if she were dreaming of love. He remembered the word she had used earlier to the doctor: *bliss*.

'It's madness, isn't it?' she said on the other side of the curtain, into her phone. 'It doesn't make any sense.'

Quinn turned around. He tossed the cup of tea into the bin by the ward reception desk. He rang Suz as he was walking down the corridor towards the exit.

'Can I have a lift home?' he asked her. 'I came out without enough money for a cab.'

'Ten minutes,' said Suz, although from her voice he knew he'd woken her. Because that was what you did in his family. If someone you loved needed help, you gave it. Without thinking, without questioning, without weighing the cost to yourself.

But when your wife was ringing her lover from her hospital bed, enough was enough. For anyone.

It was warm outside but cooler than in the ward. He'd gone into A&E in full afternoon sunshine, and the hours had slipped away into darkness. Even at one o'clock in the morning, there was a patient in a hospital nightgown leaning against the railing outside the entrance smoking a cigarette. She didn't look as if she was enjoying it.

Suz pulled up about fifteen minutes after the smoking patient had ground her fag end into the pavement and gone back inside. He opened the passenger side door and got in. She didn't drive away, but regarded him instead. 'You look like shit.'

'I don't feel too bad.'

'That's a lie.' She was wearing pyjama bottoms and a T-shirt. 'How is she? Any diagnosis yet?'

'They still haven't told us what's wrong, but hopefully tomorrow, once she's had more tests, they'll know more. She's sleeping a lot. It seems to be the only thing she wants to do.' Aside from ringing her lover.

'Do they think it's a brain tumour?'

'They say it could be lots of things. She's been having seizures for a while now. Mild ones. Smells, feelings. She didn't tell anyone.' He tipped his head back against the seat. 'I should have known.'

'How could you have known if she never told you?'

'She asked me if I had any particular smells that led to memories. Ones that were so strong that it felt as if you were actually living through those memories again. She had all these things she'd collected – perfume, bottles of oil, a clove-studded orange – and she was sniffing them. I thought it was just a . . . Felicity question.'

Suz kept the motor idling. A taxi pulled up in front of her, collected a passenger, and drove off. 'You've had an awful time,' she said. 'But I think she must have been frightened. Do you think that's why she's been . . .'

'The seizures make her feel as if she's in love. With that other man.'

'Oh.' Suz let that sink in. 'That's weird.'

'Apparently that's why she went to find him. She says.'

'Do you believe that?'

'I don't know.'

Suz sighed. 'What are you going to do?'

I am going to go home, have a shower, get into bed and continue the process of learning to sleep alone.

Instead he said, 'Did Dad have an affair that time?'

Suz didn't ask what time he meant. They had never spoken of it: the time of the raised voices behind doors, the time of Dad always late coming home, the time of sandwiches for supper. He and Suz had sat in the back seat of the car and tried not to listen as their parents whispered viciously in the front. They'd each kept their eyes on their own book.

Suz turned off the ignition. 'I think so,' she said.

'I thought it was my fault.'

'I thought it was mine too. I thought it was because I was different. But it couldn't have been. That's just the way children think.'

'It got better, didn't it?'

'It's better now,' Suz said. 'I tried to ask Mum about it once a few years ago, and she changed the subject. She talked about foxes getting into the bins instead.'

'I don't think they're unhappy. But how can you tell, when they're always the same?'

'I don't think Mum would ever admit to being unhappy. Can you imagine it? But no. I don't think they're unhappy. I think they rub along fine.'

'I think it was that woman who worked with him, the one with the short hair. She wasn't anything special.'

'Maybe she didn't have to be. Is . . . he? The man that . . . is he something special?'

'I didn't really see him. I don't think I'd recognize him on the street. I was more focused on Felicity.'

'I'm so sorry, Quinn.' Suz pushed her hair behind her ears. 'Mum, yesterday. I thought she was going to rip out Felicity's throat. I haven't seen her that angry in years. Not since . . . the time you're talking about.'

'What made Mum stay, if Dad had an affair? Was it vows, or did she not want to be on her own? It would have been hard for her on her own. I thought about that when Dad had his heart attack. She wouldn't be able to cope.'

'She'd have us. I think she stayed because she loved him.'

'And why didn't he leave? He must have felt something for that woman. What made him choose us instead?'

'Maybe it was habit.'

'Is that what love is, then? Just getting used to something?'

Suz put her hand on the key, ready to turn it.

'I should have known,' said Quinn. 'I should have asked her. I should have asked Felicity what was wrong. But I was too afraid of the answer.'

His sister sighed. 'It's not your fault, Quinn. We're all like that. It's what our family is like. We talk and talk and we don't ask the questions.'

'No, it is my fault. I'm supposed to be some sort of

305

journalist, but when it matters, I don't ask. Not even you. We don't talk, not about anything that matters.'

'We're talking now,' said Suz. She touched his shoulder. 'I always knew we would, if we needed to.'

'It's habit,' he said, staring out of the window. 'It's all bloody habit. It's easier than facing the truth.'

Suz squeezed his shoulder, and put her hands back on the wheel. 'Are we going?'

A deep breath. 'No. I'll stay.'

'Are you sure? You could do with some sleep.'

'I need you to bring some things for her, please. She needs a toothbrush, and some of her own pyjamas. A hairbrush and a flannel and soap. Her dressing gown. She'd probably like a book and maybe a sketch pad. Can you bring those tomorrow morning?'

Suz nodded. He opened the door and stepped back out onto the pavement, where the smoking woman had come outside for another cigarette.

Chapter Thirty-one

The doctor has four students with him today. They all have notebooks and they are all scribbling madly even before he starts speaking to me.

'Well, Felicity, it looks like we've worked out what's causing your seizures.'

The last time he spoke to me it was 'Mrs Wickham'. I suppose once a man has seen several maps of the inside of your head, he has the right to call you by your first name. He's been inside my head in almost every way possible, I think, short of cutting it open. I've been injected with dye through my arteries and inserted into machines which riddled me with bullet-firing noises; the doctors have attached electrodes to me, told me to draw pictures, asked me questions, shone lights for me to follow. The neurologist said that the mind was the last place of mystery, but I think he was just trying to make me feel as if I had a few private thoughts that the scans couldn't detect.

Quinn has read the *Observer*, the *Independent*, the *Telegraph*, *The Times*, as well as the *Oxford Times* and the *Maidenhead Advertiser*. He's done the crosswords in all of them; he's asked for my help with some of the clues, but other than that, we've barely spoken. He went home briefly while I was having my tests, to take a shower and a nap, but from the looks of him, he didn't sleep much then or last night either.

They've changed my seizure meds, and there hasn't been the faintest whisper of frangipani. I can only vaguely remember ringing Ewan last night and leaving a message. Or rather I don't remember the message itself, but I remember the facts of it, in the way that you remember the events or symbols of a dream when waking, without being able to picture them: I asked him if he really loved me. I told him not to ring me. Whilst Quinn was gone, I turned my phone back on and checked it. Ewan had rung five times, so I turned it off again.

I'm in an enormous mess. I feel as if I am two people and I don't know which one is real.

The doctor pulls up a chair; his minions remain standing a respectful few paces behind him. 'First, let me explain how we started our investigation. As you and I discussed yesterday, you've been experiencing some seizures involving olfactory hallucinations paired with the experience of an intense, unprompted emotion. Your GP diagnosed this as migrainous aura because you have had a history of migraines. By the way, as a matter of interest, would you say this emotion was attached to any particular remembered experience in your past, or was it a dissociated feeling?'

'It's associated with a time and a person from my past,' I say. 'The smell is, too. They're both about something that happened ten years ago.'

'Interesting.' The minions scribble madly. 'Well, that's another confirmation of our initial suspicion that you were experiencing temporal lobe seizures. These seizures often have an emotional or memory aspect, though not always, of course. It's a vast oversimplification, but we think of the temporal lobe as being the place where we remember and feel. Anyway, as we were saying, these seizures were often followed by a feeling of euphoria and you were able to operate normally or almost normally before and afterwards. However, recently the frequency has increased, and yesterday you experienced a tonic-clonic seizure, leading to your admission in an unconscious state.'

I'm not sure whether he's saying all of this for my benefit, or for that of the students.

'The CT scan detected a mass in the left temporal lobe. You can see it here.' He passes me a picture of an outline of a thick bright white egg shape printed on glossy black paper. The egg is filled with variegated grey. It's my skull in cross-section, seen from the top. Everything is symmetrical except for a light spot near the centre, as if someone has left a large kidney bean inside my brain.

It is terrifying. This is me.

'You said the left temporal lobe,' I say. 'This is on the right.'

'CT scans are inverted.'

'Is it a tumour?' asks Quinn, leaning over to look at it. 'She had the scan yesterday. Why didn't you show us this then?'

'We wanted to make certain we knew what it was, before alarming you unnecessarily.'

'I'm alarmed right now,' I say.

'It's not an unusual problem,' says the doctor, 'though it is quite large, and the positioning is rare. Here's a sagittal image from the MRI you had this morning. That is, a side-on image. You can see the mass clearly.'

This print-out is more of a Hallowe'en horror than the other one. I can see my skull from the side, looking more

309

fragile here, my eyeballs as round shadows, my clenched teeth, and the soft coils of my brain. There's a glowing sphere in the centre of it, a few inches behind my eyeballs. He passes me another print-out, this one from the top. The mass glows less here, and is more of a bean than a sphere. But it is still something that definitely should not be in my head.

'I can't feel it,' I say. 'Surely I should be able to feel something that's this big?'

'You have been feeling it, as a scent and an emotion. It's been putting pressure on your temporal lobe and causing the seizures. Most likely it's grown lately, which is why the seizures have become more frequent and why you had a tonic-clonic. It's been putting pressure on all of your brain, not just this little bit.'

'But what is it?' asks Quinn. 'What can be done about it?'

'Ah, so this print-out shows us exactly what it is.' Dr Chin hands over another piece of paper with a flourish. It's as if he's enjoying the slow reveal, like a burlesque dancer. I glance at the four students, who are rapt, and pretty much prove my suspicions: this is a show for them. I hope they're enjoying it.

The last picture is not recognizably mine or anyone's head. It looks like a round sac filled with water into which someone has released a slow stream of black dye; or possibly a fluid tree in autumn drawn by a watercolour artist. One of the branches has a black lump on it, a full bladder.

'This is a cerebral angiogram. A picture of the arteries in your brain. As you can see here, one of the arteries in the left posterior has ballooned out into an aneurysm.'

Quinn's hand lands on my shoulder. As he has avoided touching me – aside possibly from the time when he scraped me up from the grass – I can tell this isn't good news.

'Is that like a blood clot?' I ask.

'It's a weakness in the walls of the artery. It bulges out and fills with blood, which is why this one is growing. It's causing pressure in your temporal lobe, which in turn is causing autonomic aura – the funny tingle in your stomach you describe, which is typical of temporal lobe seizures – along with somatosensory hallucination of smell, and the psychic aura of emotion. Love,' he adds with relish. 'It's one of the great philosophical questions of the universe: what is love? In your case, the answer is right here on this angiogram. Love is caused by this malformation of the artery in your brain.'

The students are going crazy with the writing now.

'I am guessing that love caused by aneurysm is fairly rare,' I say.

'I've never heard of it before,' says the consultant, almost gleefully. I restrain myself from slapping him. 'There's a wide literature on temporal lobe hallucinations, but I haven't yet encountered this particular hallucination, and this aetiology is also rare. Ninety per cent of cerebral aneurysms are anterior, rather than posterior, as yours is. So you not only have unusual symptoms, but an unusual disease. It was probably a good thing you were admitted for the tonic–clonic seizure rather than the hallucinations, as otherwise this might have been misdiagnosed as mental illness.'

'Love is insanity,' I say quietly.

'On the contrary – your experience proves that love is not only entirely normal, but an infinitely repeatable human condition. And that any one love affair, any single emotion, can be preserved in the brain indefinitely, waiting for the right physical conditions for it to recur.'

311

I picture this: every emotion I have ever experienced, lined up in my brain like paintings in a gallery. Bundles of neurons, each one clearly labelled with its event and consequential feeling. *First kiss, age thirteen: awkwardness. Hug from mother: security. Laughed at by whole class in primary school: humiliation. Finding best friend in a youth hostel in Mumbai: discovery. Butterfly lands on hand on summer's day: serenity.*

'You're saying that everything I felt is . . . chemical? Electrical? Just impulses in my brain?'

'You say "just" impulses in your brain, but there is no emotion that isn't caused by these impulses. So as far as that goes, your seizures do create authentic emotion.'

Quinn's hand tightens on my shoulder and I glance at him. He appears as irritated with the doctor as I am. 'Leaving aside the philosophical questions for the moment,' he says, 'isn't a brain aneurysm dangerous?'

'If it ruptures, yes, extremely. A subarachnoid brain haemorrhage can cause severe brain damage and death if not treated in time.'

'So you have to take it out.'

'Of course.'

'Do you mean brain surgery?'

'I think that Felicity is a good candidate for endovascular coiling, which is much less invasive. But she'll have to be assessed by the interventional neuroradiologist before we can make any decisions.'

'Wait,' I say. 'This is my head. I have a few more questions. If you take this thing out, are you saying that everything I felt will be gone?'

'The desired outcome is that you won't have the seizures any more, though we'd also keep you on anti-convulsive medication post-surgery for some time, to help with that. And you'll have to be monitored to make sure the aneurysm doesn't recur.'

'You don't understand. I'm asking about the feelings, not the seizures.'

'You want to *keep* the feelings?' asks Quinn.

'I just want to know.'

The doctor glances back at his students to make sure they're getting this. 'The emotional kernel that you keep revisiting will still be in your temporal lobe. You most likely won't experience it in the same way, as if you're living through it again. It will be like any other memory, though perhaps a particularly strong one.'

'I'll lose it.'

'You'll keep it as a memory. Unless the pressure from the aneurysm, or the surgical procedure, causes some damage. Which isn't impossible. Despite incredible developments in our knowledge and techniques, the brain is still unpredictable.'

'Could this aneurysm have caused other symptoms besides the seizures?' asks Quinn. 'For example, behavioural changes?'

'Have you noticed those?'

'Yes,' says Quinn, at the same time that I say, 'No.'

The consultant laughs. 'Marriage, eh? Damage to the temporal lobe can change behaviour. Loss of memory, impulsiveness or lack of inhibition.'

'But that's just the way I am,' I tell Quinn. 'I've always had a rubbish memory. And I've always been impulsive.'

'How long has she had this aneurysm?' Quinn asks the doctor.

'Difficult to say. Unless they cause symptoms such as these,

313

unruptured cerebral aneurysms can go undetected for a person's entire lifetime. Some studies estimate that ten per cent of the population have them but will never suffer any problems because of them.'

'So I don't necessarily need to be treated,' I say.

'Yes, you do,' says Quinn.

'Your husband is right, you do. You may have had this weakness in your artery for years, and it could have been growing for some time without causing any perceptible problems, but it's of a size now to cause seizures, and therefore surgery is indicated. As soon as possible.'

'And it could have ruptured at any time during the past however many years?'

'An aneurysm of this size has a greater than six per cent chance of rupturing annually. As I said, a rupture can lead to catastrophic brain damage. And yours is growing with every day it remains untreated.'

I take the print-outs again and leaf through them. A glowing kidney bean. A black bladder of blood. This is where love lies. This has been my passenger for who knows how many years, lying in the folds and shelter of my brain, filling itself with blood, stretching and growing. Possibly it was there when my mother was alive. While the cancer was eating her body, this bean was pushing outwards, testing its walls. All the time I may have been nearly as close to death as she was.

What would I have done differently if I had known?

I wouldn't have let her lie in the hospital bed. I would have carried her outside; her body was light as air. I would have sat with her on the beach and run the sand through her fingers and tucked the feather of a gull behind her ear. I would have tasted salt on my lips and held her and lived our moments together as if they were our last.

I touch the shape on the egg-like CT scan. It could have been any memory, any feeling that was triggered. It could have been my first day of school, or learning to tie my shoes. It could have been my fear of what was under my bed, a drunken afternoon in Paris, a moment on the train from Cornwall to Paddington.

But it wasn't. It was frangipani, and love for Ewan. Is that chance, or an inexplicable design? Does that mean that this swelling was inside my brain when I met Ewan in that life-drawing class, when that memory of being in love for the first time was laid down? It was a part of me even then?

How much of my happiness and sadness, my impulsiveness and my joy, my decisions and actions, my me-ness, has been caused by this curled-up kidney bean of blood, nested in my brain like the embryo in an ultrasound photograph?

Quinn

Quinn had been in love three times in his life. Not counting temporary infatuations or girls he'd dated once or twice. He couldn't even really count Andi, with whom he shared a flat and occasionally a bed soon after university; she was his best mate for a time, nearly two years, picking up an on-again-off-again relationship with him in between dating other people until she found Christianity and emigrated to Australia. He cared about Andi but he hadn't been in love with her, and she not with him, although his parents had hoped, not so subtly, that he'd get more serious with her.

The first time he fell in love was a missed opportunity. He was seventeen and everyone in the sixth-form common room knew that Kathy Lewis was head-over-heels in love with Quinn Wickham. She was a pretty girl but shy, and Quinn already knew shy. He'd been shy through most of his senior-school years, being shorter and slighter than the other boys. Though he made up for his diffidence by being friendly and courteous to everyone, as his dad advised him to, he never had the confidence that many of the other pupils had, that Suz had always had. He knew shy, so he didn't notice shy, because he was too busy noticing the people who weren't shy and wishing he were more like them. The ones who could joke loudly in the hallways and make people laugh, the performers and the athletes, the fellow students he wrote about in the school newspaper which he'd set up himself, written and laid out and printed and distributed ever since he'd been in Year Nine. The news spoke for itself; he didn't have to. He could stay shy.

Then he got his growth spurt in the middle of his first year of A-levels and he found it was easier to talk to people when you could look them in the eye, or even look down at them. He started wondering if Anastasia Jenkins would notice him now, after ignoring him for the past three years. That was why he never noticed Kathy Lewis, taking the seat next to his in geography, sneaking glances at him over lunch. And then some of the girls started to giggle about it, and some of the boys nudged him and pointed. Then of course he couldn't notice her, not beyond his normal polite friendliness, because it would embarrass both of them.

Anastasia Jenkins started going out with Damien Boynton, and that was the week that Quinn started looking at Kathy's hair and noticing how shiny it was, like strands of black silk. Then one day he noticed she'd had her ears pierced twice, her nails painted with glitter. Then her handwriting, which was much more dramatic than you'd expect from a girl so shy, all spikes and flourishes like a seventeenth-century clerk's. They exchanged glances and smiles. They worked together to research a paper on the Euro Zone. She invited him to her house to revise.

For half a term, February to April, he felt a warm happiness in sitting beside her. He thought about kissing her

317

and the thought of it made him want to skip. He knew he didn't have to say anything to her, because she was in love with him. Everyone knew it. There was a secret sub-text to every sentence that they spoke to each other. It was the first time he'd been in love, properly in love, and it was wonderful.

For the Easter hols he went to visit Suz at her flat in Leeds and when he rang Kathy, for the first time, the night before they went back to school, her younger sister answered the phone. 'She's out with Mark,' the sister told him, undisguised glee in her voice. 'She says you never rang her and she was tired of it.'

Kathy went out with Mark for the rest of their school career. Quinn went out with as many girls as would have him. He kissed Anastasia Jenkins at the sixth-form leavers' do and her lips were sticky with a lipstick that tasted of too-ripe cherries.

The second time he fell in love, it was much more substantial. He met Maya during his first year at university and the two of them clicked. She was studying journalism too, was not-technically-a-virgin too, had just missed Oxbridge too, her family was also traditional, though with different traditions. She and Quinn laughed at the same films and jokes and people. They met, and dated, and soon it was Quinn-and-Maya, a double act, a team, a partnership. They drank in the student bars together, spent afternoons exploring sex together, moved in together in their third year. His parents thought they would marry. Her parents initially put up an objection, but after meeting Quinn several times were resigned, even pleased.

And then it ended. He didn't know why, and Maya claimed

not to either. They had sex less often, though when they did, it was just as good. They spent more time with other people. Sometimes they didn't speak for a day or two, maybe even a week, other than text messages or notes left to each other on the refrigerator. There was no falling-out, no argument, no appreciable difference in how they got along. But they weren't in love any more. It had drained away, almost without their noticing it. Without either of them speaking of it, or making an effort to revive it.

When Maya accepted an internship in Hong Kong after their exams, they both agreed to stay in touch but see other people. The heartbreak was there, but it was more for what they'd lost than for the ending of what they had now. He spoke with her occasionally on Facebook these days, friendly and distant.

The third time was Felicity. He'd been dating another woman when he met Felicity on the train from Cornwall. It was nothing serious, a friend of a friend, but they were meant to go to the cinema the following Friday. He'd cancelled it, apologized over the telephone, told her he had met the woman he was going to marry. She'd thought it was a joke. He and Felicity were married three months later.

His love-life CV wasn't very different from his friends', male and female: they all had the one who had got away, the one that should have worked but didn't, the one who grabbed their heart at first sight. It was a combination of factors, of well-worn stories and clichés, that was enacted and re-enacted millions, billions of times. They could be reduced down to sketches, to facts, enumerations of sexual positions tried or arguments avoided, betrayals of feeling or fidelity, mindgames or heartbreak. *Oh yes, I had a relationship like that.*

Oh yes, my heart was broken the same way. Oh yes, I know the type of person you mean.

When he thought of Maya now, or Kathy, or Andi, or any of the women who had touched him in some way, physically or mentally – not many, but no fewer than what he supposed was typical – he sometimes felt a warmth or a smile, or a pang of regret or lust. He remembered the facts: I was in love with her once. I used to want to sing just from looking at her hair or her eyes.

But he couldn't feel those emotions again; he couldn't relive them by thinking of them. They were reduced to memory. To traces, with some power, but not much.

Not enough to take precedence over what he felt now, in the corridor outside the neurology ward, still awake on coffee and nerves, waiting for his wife to go through surgery that would probably save her life, that would possibly restore her to him, but might also kill her.

He had always loved how Felicity lived in the now. He loved her impulsiveness, her ability to see what was in front of her when other people ignored it. And yet Felicity, unlike him, unlike anyone else he knew, was caught in a loop of past feeling that her brain had convinced her was as fresh as the day when it happened.

It was so strange. Something you'd read about in a health feature, tucked in the back of the Sunday supplement.

In the corridor, near the vending machine that dispensed species of vile liquids containing caffeine, he closed his eyes and tried to recall what it felt like to be in love with Maya. How was it different, for example, for what he felt for Felicity?

If Maya walked into the hospital corridor right now, he

would be able to distinguish his present emotions about her quite easily from what he felt for his wife. There was no comparison. But what if he were presented with the experience of how he felt about Maya, for example, after the first night they'd gone to bed together? Would it be the same raw emotion that he'd felt after first making love with Felicity, the same sleepless drunkenness of flesh and joy? Was there a space in his brain that carried a specific 'night after Maya' feeling, which was quantitatively different from his 'night after Felicity' feeling? Or was it more that he had a general 'Quinn is very happy after making love with someone he cares deeply about' feeling that was applied whenever the situation arose?

'Pardon me, are you waiting?'

He came back to himself with a start. The woman standing next to him was looking enquiringly between him and the vending machine.

'After you,' he said, and when she'd collected her cups of brown liquid, he began feeding coins into slots. A coffee, white, from one machine, and a packet of Jaffa cakes for his supper from the other machine. The hospital cafés were all closed by now. He considered a second packet for Felicity before he remembered she was nil by mouth in preparation for surgery tomorrow morning.

Vascular coiling, it was called. The neuroradiologist would feed a tube up through Felicity's femoral artery at her groin, up her body to the brain. Once the tube was there, the neuroradiologist would insert a coil of thin platinum wire to choke off the aneurysm's blood supply and stop it from growing. It was much less invasive than opening up her skull and clipping the aneurysm, and required less recovery time.

Yet the risks still included stroke and brain damage and heart attack, and rupture of the aneurysm itself.

He'd watched Felicity as the neuroradiologist explained the procedure and the risks. She had been looking at the print-outs the entire time, tracing her fingers over the pictures of her brain. He wasn't certain it had all sunk in. Of course, it was terrifying enough for him to think of her brain being messed around with; it would be much more so for her. For a moment or two, though, a stubborn expression had crossed her face: lips pressed together, chin set – the kind of expression she got when he reminded her she should probably leave earlier for an appointment, or when his mother started arranging their weekend plans for them.

As soon as she set her chin, he was certain that she was going to object to the surgery; that she was going to tell the doctor to stop being ridiculous, she was absolutely fine, and that she wanted to go home now.

She didn't. And thinking like that would be madness. This aneurysm wasn't merely causing her seizures. It wasn't only a disease that had come between them, turned her into someone like a stranger. It was something that could kill her at any moment.

He had prepared his arguments for when the doctor left them, but Felicity didn't say anything. She'd hardly said anything to him at all, since their argument yesterday, since she'd made the phone call to that man. She'd sighed and gone to sleep, leaving him too much time to think.

They hadn't yet spoken of what would happen after the surgery, when it was time to go home and resume their lives. That was the first thing Suz had asked about when he'd rung her to tell her about the diagnosis and treatment.

'We haven't discussed it yet,' he'd said. Meaning, he didn't want to discuss it with his family.

He unwrapped a Jaffa cake, popped it in his mouth, and checked his watch. Time dragged and flew in the hospital; it was nearly nine o'clock. Aside from going home with Suz to pick up his car and have a shower, he'd done little today but shuffle from Felicity's bedside to the café or shop. There were visiting hours but he knew the ward sister, who lived in a farmhouse outside Tillingford, and she told him they didn't mind him staying as long as he wanted to.

The other patients in the ward were connected to machines. Some of them were in comas. Some wore helmets. The elderly lady in the bed near the entrance had had a stroke, her face drooping and dead on one side, but she waved at him with her good hand, as she did whenever he passed, and he waved back. 'Lovely evening out there, Mrs Chowdery,' he said, even though he wasn't strictly certain it was, since he hadn't looked out of a window in several hours.

When he reached Felicity's bed, the curtains had been drawn shut all around it. He slipped between them, quietly, so as not to wake her. She was gone.

The sheet was folded back almost precisely, in a very un-Felicity way. He glanced back through the curtain; both of the loos for patient use were empty, their doors open. Her bedside cabinet was ajar and her shoes were missing, as was her handbag.

Quinn set off at a rapid walk. He checked the side wards, the reception desk, the waiting room. The staff were busy at a bed in one of the other side wards, an alarm beeping out. If she'd heard it going off, she'd have known this was a good time to slip away unnoticed.

And go where? Just for a walk, or to escape? To meet the man she'd rung to rescue her?

The corridors were quiet. He met two orderlies pushing a sleeping man in a bed, railings up.

'Have you seen a woman in a hospital nightgown walking by?' he asked them. 'Thirty years old, dark hair in a fringe. My wife's left her bed and I don't know where she's gone.'

'They wander sometimes after dark,' said the orderly. 'Full moon tonight. She'll be safe. I'll get some help.' He raised his radio.

Quinn bit back a response about his wife not being a dementia patient. 'I'll keep looking.'

He was close to the stairs; he flew down them and towards the hospital exit. The reception desk was unmanned at this time of night and the lobby was empty. Outside, there were two patients smoking, strangers united in addiction.

'Have you seen a patient come out? Dark hair in a fringe, slender, wearing a hospital nightgown and carrying a hand-bag? Could have got into a car, or walked off with a man?' The smokers shook their heads, but their cigarettes were still long, they had just lit them; they might not have been there, or have been distracted by lighter and packet.

The entrance was quite well-lit by streetlights and lights from the hospital itself, but he couldn't see Felicity anywhere. A small queue of cabs lined the kerb, but a quick question to each driver elicited no information.

She couldn't have been gone for long. It had probably taken him twenty minutes max to get coffee, which would be long enough, but surely if she'd been missing from her bed for some time, some of the staff would have noticed. He wished he'd thought to touch her bedsheets to see if they were still warm. If a car had been waiting behind the taxi rank, the same place that Suz had parked the night before, she could have got into it without anyone noticing. If she'd rung the other man, and asked him to come and get her.

He ran to the end of the block anyway, looking around for her. A searching glance both ways down the street, and then up in the other direction. His footsteps echoed against the hospital building.

She could be anywhere. She could be gone.

Quinn pounded on his forehead with both fists. He'd suspected she didn't want the surgery, but he'd dismissed it as too ridiculous. Why would she refuse something that would almost certainly save her life?

She'd risk it for love.

Breathing hard, he turned back to the hospital entrance. Maybe someone inside had found her. On the way, he tried ringing her phone, but he wasn't surprised when it went straight to voicemail.

If she had gone with the other man, what message could he possibly leave that would convince her to come back?

He took the stairs up rather than the lift, and was about to push open the door to the second floor where the ward was, when something occurred to him.

Full moon tonight, the orderly had said. And the stairs continued up, towards the roof.

His phone, set to silent for the hospital, vibrated with a message as he climbed. He curled his fingers around it in his pocket, but didn't pause to check it. At the top of the flight was a glass door to a rooftop garden. *Open 10.00–18.00* NO SMOKING said the letters on the door, but when he pushed it, it opened.

It was cooler out here. The garden was surrounded by walls, with light shining from some of the windows overlooking it, but it was still dark and quiet. She sat on a bench not far from the door. Silver moonlight lit her face and the white of her nightgown. Quinn sat down beside her. She was looking up at the moon, so he did too.

'I just left a message for you,' she said. 'I thought you might worry. Your phone was busy.'

'I was worried,' he said.

'I wanted to see the sky. I might never see it again. It might be the last time.' She drew in a deep breath. So did he, to taste the same air, perfumed with honeysuckle and warm asphalt.

'You don't want to have the surgery, do you?' The dark made it easier to speak to her.

She shook her head. 'I'm frightened.'

'I thought you'd run off with him.'

She sighed, but didn't answer.

'Would he rescue you, if you asked him to? Take you away so you wouldn't have to have the surgery?'

'I'm going to have the surgery. And no, I don't think he would. I think he'd be as vehement about it as you are. Because it will probably save my life.'

'Who is he? How long have you been seeing him?'

'I knew him when I was twenty. My mother painted a picture of him – I saw it when we went to New York.' Her voice was weary and sad.

'Is that when it started? When you saw the painting?'

'A little before that. I had the first seizure thing in May.'

'Had you been thinking about him before? During our whole marriage?'

'No. I didn't think about him. It came out of the blue, with the scent. And then the feeling, and the picture.'

Quinn clenched his hands on his lap. 'How many times?'

'How many times have I had the feeling? I'm not sure. A lot.'

'No, I meant how many times have you slept with him?'

'I haven't.'

He let his silence show his doubt.

'I haven't, Quinn. Not for ten years. When you walked in, I was – I was just about to tell him to stop. That we couldn't.'

He heard the hesitation. It was a lie, to spare him. And even if it wasn't, did it even matter?

'Do you think he really loves you?' he asked instead. He knew the answer, but he wanted to know what she'd say.

'He says he does. Though . . .' She paused. 'Yes, I believe that he thinks he's in love with me.'

Careful phrasing. Hesitation. It was nearly as bad as walking in on them together.

'But your feelings about him aren't real,' he said. 'They might have been real at one point, but now they're being triggered by seizures. You say you didn't think about him at all before you started smelling the flowers?'

'Not particularly. As something that happened once, but it was over.'

'So he might love you, but the way you feel about him is a symptom. It's not real. After tomorrow, it'll be gone, or it'll just be a memory. You'll be back to normal. A few days in hospital, and right as rain.'

Even to himself, it didn't sound convincing.

She gazed at the moon. He saw the glitter of her eyes and thought there were tears in them. 'You don't understand,

327

Quinn. For me, the feeling is very real. And it comes and goes, yes. But when it's there, it's the most powerful thing I've ever felt.'

'It made you leave me.'

'And that's why it has to be real. Don't you see? If it's not real, if it's just a symptom, then I left you for no reason. Ewan fell in love with me again for no reason. I hurt you, I hurt your family, your mother hates me, Suz can't bear the sight of me, because one of my arteries wasn't working properly.'

'But that's good,' he said wildly. 'That's wonderful. It means you'll be cured, and everything will be fixed. You can come home and we can begin again.'

'You don't really believe that, do you?'

Mare Tranquillitatis, Mare Serenitatis. Moon dust never stirred, it kept imprints for ever. Some hurts were too strong to be exposed to the air.

He spoke this one anyway. It had to be spoken aloud some time.

'Even though it's a disease,' he said, 'you still feel more for him than you ever have for me.'

The words hung between them.

'I've known it,' he said. 'You've never loved me as much as I've loved you. I've known it from the start.'

'I've had some doubts. I tried to hide them from you.'

'We've tried to hide a lot of things from each other.' He swallowed. 'Why did you marry me?'

'I was very sad, and you made me feel better. I wanted to marry you. I thought we would be happy. You're a good man, Quinn. You're the best.'

He made a derisory noise, an empty gesture at the moon. *Here I am. Look where it's got me.*

'You're the last person in the world who I should hurt,' she said. 'And yet if I could feel so much for a man who wasn't you, every day I stayed I was hurting you more.'

'You've never opened up to me, Felicity. You've always been keeping part of yourself separate. We've been married for a year and I love you, but I feel as if you're a stranger. I asked, and then I stopped asking, because you never told me how you were feeling.'

'I wanted to rest. I had so many things going through my head and when I was with you, I didn't need to think about them. You made it safe for me. When I first met you, I wanted to scream all the time. I missed my mother so much. I wanted to run into the street and tear my clothes and never stop crying. You made it so that I could be quiet. You made me smile again. I don't think there was anyone else who could have done that for me. I'm so grateful to you.'

'But that's not enough.'

'I thought it could be. I wanted it to be. I wanted it so much, Quinn.'

'What can I do? What can we change so that we can be happy together?'

She shook her head. 'I don't know. I'm not sure that I can trust myself.'

'Other people rub along,' he said. 'They stay together even if it's not perfect. They can move on from their problems. Why does it work for some people and not for us?'

'Maybe because we want everything.'

I could have had everything, if you'd just love me back.

The door opened and someone poked their head out. 'Hello? All okay out there?'

It was the orderly he'd spoken to earlier. 'I've found her,'

Quinn called. 'We're having a breath of fresh air and then we're coming back in, to the ward. Can you let them know?'

'Hot night,' agreed the orderly, and closed the door.

The sound echoed. Side by side, they looked up at the sky. She'd come up here to see it because it might be the last time.

Whatever happened tomorrow morning in the surgical theatre, this could be their last time seeing it together.

'Tell me what you're afraid of,' he said. 'Are you afraid that you'll die?' The neuroradiologist had gone through the possibilities in great detail: stroke, heart attack, problems with the anaesthesia. The procedure they'd chosen was less risky than opening up Felicity's skull, but like any surgery, it wasn't safe.

'I'm afraid of waking up and not being me any more,' she said. 'What am I, except for what I feel and what I do? If all of that was caused by a blood balloon in my brain, who will I be when it's gone?'

I'll still love you no matter who you are. But was that true? Had he still loved her when he saw her in another man's arms? That fury, the jealousy, the gut-wrenching pain – was that love? He dipped his face between his knees, and then looked up at the moon again.

'Tell me something about who you are,' he said. 'Tell me anything. We might never get a chance again.'

She gazed at his face. He felt it rather than saw it: how she had turned her entire attention to him.

'In my first memory,' she began, 'I was sitting on a baby elephant.'

Chapter Thirty-two

I talk to Quinn, watching his face. I tell him about my memories as I remember them, even though they might be wrong, even though they might have been created by paintings or changed over the years from recollection or anecdotes or from things unseen happening in my brain. Because one thing, maybe the only thing, that this whole experience has taught me is that the reality you carry within you is the only one you can act upon.

I may have fallen and broken my arm, or I may have been caught by my mother before I hit the ground. My mind wants me to know that I was safe and loved, never at risk from elephants. And that's the greater truth, isn't it?

I say all of this to him and more, there in the light of the full moon. His phone vibrates, but he ignores it. He listens to me. Twice he laughs; once he makes a movement that might be to take my hand before he thinks better of it.

I tell him things that happened only between my mother and me and which I've never spoken about: the feeling of her arms around me, the eternal smell of linseed, the smile on her face when I told my first *Igor* story, the way she spoke about her one true love whom I never knew but who helped to create me.

If something happens to me tomorrow, if I forget all of this, I won't know it's gone. Quinn will be the one who remembers it. Just like he'll be the one who remembers all the secret moments between him and me. And they might not be the same way that I remember them – they may be poisoned for him with betrayal and disappointment – but Quinn's reality is as important as mine. I trust him entirely.

'Why didn't you tell me any of this before?' he says. 'When I asked you? When I took you to New York? You clammed up. But these are good memories, Felicity.'

'When I think about how she lived, I can't help but think about how she died. And it was my fault that she died the way she did.'

I hardly believe I'm saying this out loud. But we're here, outside. And I might never speak like this to Quinn again. I might never speak like this to anyone. On the night before I might be changed for ever, I want someone to know what I did.

I want Quinn to know. I want him to see me truly.

'She died of cancer, didn't she?' Quinn says. 'How could that be your fault?'

I said something similar to this to Ewan, when he was telling me about Lee's death. I pretended not to understand how guilt can come in many forms. Even if it's not your fault – even if it's fate or cancer or a mechanical failure or an aneurysm in your brain – if you had a part in it, you are responsible.

'She was living in Cornwall,' I tell him. 'And I was in London, so I didn't see her as much as I should have done. She'd been feeling poorly for ages, but she didn't tell anyone. I went to visit her, and she'd lost loads of weight, and I was

332

frightened. She hadn't gone to a doctor. She didn't want to know, she said. She'd rather just carry on as she was.'

'Sounds familiar,' says Quinn, but his voice is kind.

'I made her go to her GP, and then for tests. It was stage-four liver cancer. The doctor said it was going to kill her. He gave her a month without treatment, maybe six if she had chemo. My mother just smiled and thanked him and asked me to drive her home.'

'You didn't, though, did you?'

'She told me that she'd achieved everything she wanted to, more than most people. And that she'd experienced every-thing. And that she'd seen me grow up and I didn't need her any more. So she was ready to go. She thought she'd work right up until she couldn't any more, and then she'd have a big party, maybe, with all of her friends and lovers and colleagues, and then she'd slip away.'

'Okay,' says Quinn. 'I understand. You feel guilty because you let her have the death she wanted. But you could have told me that, Felicity. I wouldn't have judged you for it.'

'I didn't let her have the death she wanted,' I say. 'I made her have the treatment. Chemotherapy made her sick. She couldn't leave her bed or use the toilet, and even then I didn't let her die at home, I brought her to hospital so that she could have another week. Another day. All that time that she didn't even want. I couldn't let her go, and because of that she had more pain than I can imagine.'

I expect him to say something: blame me for doing this to my mother, for not telling him before. Or soothing words to tell me that he would have done the same thing, if it were Molly who was sick.

He doesn't say anything and it is so quiet on this rooftop,

despite the traffic noise, filled with the silence between us again. But this silence gives me room to speak.

'And on the day before she died I was beside her bed. I was holding her hand and she looked up at me and she could barely speak then – she was on so many drugs for the pain that she didn't recognize me some of the time. But she looked at me and I could tell she knew who I was. She whispered it. She said, *Why have you done this to me?*'

My cheeks are wet. I wipe them.

'She said, *Why have you done this to me?* And I didn't have an answer, Quinn. I had no answer to give her.'

He shifts on the bench and he puts his arm around my shoulder. He pulls me to him and I curl into his warmth. It has seemed so ordinary until now, when I might lose it.

As always at night, he feels bigger than he looks during the day. More solid, more strong. He drops his head onto mine and speaks into my hair.

'Everything you've done,' he murmurs, 'you've done out of love.'

'I don't think that makes it any better.'

He holds me, this man who, for now, is my husband. I listen to his breathing and his heartbeat. I feel his arms around me and I inhale his scent, of cotton and coffee, a faint trace of damp from the cottage. I haven't known until tonight how much I missed him. How adrift I've been without him. How much he has mattered to me all along.

I take it all and try to store it away inside me, somewhere it won't be touched tomorrow, when a platinum wire will change my brain.

I don't know what I'll lose, but I hope none of this will fade. I hope I remember the seas of the moon.

Quinn

He wasn't certain what time it was when he woke up, but Felicity had fallen asleep too. Her head rested on his shoulder. His muscles were stiff from sleeping on the bench, but not very stiff, and the moon hadn't moved much, so he didn't think he had been out for long. Carefully, trying not to disturb her, he shifted her, put his arms around her, and lifted her up.

He hadn't carried her over the doorstep of their home as a new bride. It had been raining too hard; they'd been in too much of a hurry to get inside. He carried her now into the hospital, down the flight of stairs and into the ward. A nurse approached him but he smiled at her and whispered that everything was fine. She followed him to the bed and folded the sheets back so he could tuck Felicity in.

'You should go home,' she told him. 'We'll look after her now.'

The bedside cabinet was still open. 'She left her handbag up in the garden,' he said. 'I'll be back in a tick.'

Her bag was open on the ground beside the bench. Her phone was flashing inside it. Without thinking, without considering that this was wrong even in this situation, he took

335

the phone out and read the one message on it, sent less than an hour ago from Ewan.

I do love you. Meet me 12 September, in Greenwich. Our spot, at noon. I will be there. E xxx

He sat down, feeling sick. The text had come when they'd been on this bench together. When Felicity had been telling him her memories, when he'd held her. When he'd begun to think that maybe they would get through this, after all.

She'd talked with him, at last. But nothing had changed.

The phone was slender in his hands. A few keystrokes would let him know how many times she'd spoken with Ewan. It would allow him to listen to the messages he'd left, read the texts they'd exchanged. He would see enough of their relationship to be able to imagine the rest.

How long had his mother picked up the extra phone extension upstairs as soon as his father answered it downstairs? For how many months or years, even after it was supposed to be over, had she scrutinized every piece of post that came for Derek, and worried when he was late home from the office?

He'd never be able to ask her, but he thought he knew. Any time was too much. Even once was too much.

Quinn put Felicity's phone back in her handbag and brought it back downstairs. He replaced it in her bedside cabinet. She was asleep, turned away from him, her body a question mark in the bed.

'Going home for some rest?' the nurse who'd helped him asked as he passed her. He nodded.

'Yes,' he said. 'I'm finished.'

Chapter Thirty-three

In the morning, Quinn isn't there when I wake up. It's two nurses and the anaesthetist, checking my blood pressure. 'You're in theatre a bit earlier than we'd thought,' says one of the nurses. 'Just as well since you can't have any breakfast!'

'My husband isn't here yet.'

'Well, give him a quick ring and I'm sure he'll be waiting for you when you come out of theatre. Or we can ring for you, if you like?'

I find my phone and check for messages from Quinn. It's not like him not to be here early, reading his newspaper. He hasn't rung me at all, and Ewan has stopped ringing too. Although there are no unread messages, I check the list just in case I've missed something, and I see the text from Ewan on the top. Asking me to meet him in Greenwich again, in three weeks' time. Telling me he does love me.

It's marked as read. I don't think I've read it, though I can't trust my memory. But I have a sudden certainty, which may be wrong, that Quinn has read it, and that's why he's not here.

My empty stomach feels sick. It's very much like the feeling I've had before, smelling frangipani. But now I'm on the

337

drugs that stop those memories, so I know that my anxiety and dismay are real.

'Actually,' I say to the nurse, 'it would be great if you'd ring my husband for me. Thank you.'

They give me a release form to sign, to say that I consent to this surgery. There's no point hesitating; logic wins over doubt, though as I sign it, I feel as if I'm condemning a part of myself to death.

'Has anyone ever refused to sign one of these?' I ask, imagining it: the patient, detached from the IV and an obligation to his own health, puts on his clothes and walks out, free to pursue whatever delusions he chooses to take as truth.

'Not for this surgery,' says the anaesthetist. 'This surgery saves people's lives.'

My problem is not the surgery. My problem is what I'm going to do afterwards.

If Ewan really does love me, if he's counted on my love, which everyone tells me is only a symptom, what will happen to him if I don't meet him in Greenwich in three weeks' time? The first time I met him in Greenwich it was to save his life, though I didn't know it. If I don't meet him, he'll have lost his best friend and his lover, all in the space of a summer.

Maybe I should have answered his calls, or rung him again when I wasn't having a seizure and told him what's wrong with me. But I couldn't explain to him that everything I've done has been the result of pressure in the wrong part of my brain. It seemed easier to wait and see how I felt after the surgery. Ewan, for all his strong body and his stubbornness, is incredibly fragile.

338

Quinn isn't fragile. I have hurt him, but he is whole within himself. But the read text, his absence now, tells me that the feeling I had last night, talking to him, being in his arms, wasn't real either. It was only a temporary respite from the silence. Our conversation last night under the moon was the end.

'You're very quiet,' says one of the nurses, the one who offered to call Quinn. 'Are you all right?'

'Just enjoying thinking as hard as I can before you lot start messing around with my brain.' They all laugh again.

The neuroradiologist arrives. We spoke yesterday when she explained the surgery, but this morning, she regards me with more interest. 'I wasn't up to speed on your symptoms yesterday,' she says. 'I hear your PCA makes you fall in love. A wonderful sort of seizure to have, I'd imagine.'

What's the answer to that, anyway? No? Yes? Mind your own fucking business and stop envisioning professional publications?

'Maybe that's all love is,' I say. 'An imbalance in the brain.'

Everyone laughs. What a funny girl I am today.

'Well,' says the neuroradiologist, 'not to worry. When you wake up, you'll be cured.'

This well-trained and experienced woman who's so intrigued by my symptoms will insert something into an artery at the groin and it will wend its way upwards through my body, past my heart, which does not feel emotion though we say it does, up my neck and into my brain. There will be a tiny camera to guide the operator. It will carry a load of platinum and it will deposit this precious metal inside the aneurysm, choking it off. Coiling, it's called, which I think is an unfortunate word, with connotations of deadly snakes. As platinum doesn't grow, though there are probably many people who wish it did, the aneurysm should deflate and my temporal lobe should be safe from the pressure it has been labouring under. My blood flow should go back to normal.

Unless, of course, it doesn't. The success rate of these operations is 95 per cent, but that's the technical rate of whether the equipment works or not. Clinical success rate is about 80 per cent. In the other 20 per cent, the coiling ruptures the aneurysm, or there is a stroke in another part of the brain, or the coiling doesn't work and something else has to be tried. Of course, in addition there are always the complications possible from the anaesthesia. But chances are, it will all be fine.

See? I do listen to facts, I say to Quinn, who isn't here.

The anaesthesia is like warm honey in my veins, relief from a pain I didn't know I had. I asked them if I would dream while I was out, and they said no. It's not like regular sleep. It's blankness. They said you'll wake up and not remember anything; you may feel a bit sick, but that's normal. The hours you've been unconscious will be the hours that were spent making you better.

So it's probably not a dream I have, but maybe something caused by the small instrument insinuating itself into my mind. In this not-dream I see myself holding a book with a glossy full-colour cover. It's the next *Igor the Owl* book, the one I haven't produced yet, except when I open it to the first page, it's not any story I've been working on. The drawings are mine, though. I recognize the style.

On page one, Igor is lost. He's flying through a dark forest, and he can't get high enough through the canopy to see where he's going. It's the kind of picture that I usually put three-quarters of the way through, when we don't think Igor is going to find the solution to his puzzle, but when I turn back there's only the title page. That's a new idea, to start with Igor in peril, rather than somewhere safe. Why haven't I thought to start the story this way before?

Pages two and three are a spread. Igor is only a small owl, but the trees are growing tighter and tighter together, and he can't spread his wings any more. It's getting darker, too, and there are creatures in the shadows. Owls don't need to fear predators, but small owls, small puzzle-solving owls, do.

This spread is scary, but of course these stories are read at bedtime, safe under the covers. There is an unspoken contract in these books that the problem will be cured. I mean, it will be solved.

On page four, Igor alights on a branch, and on this branch there is a mouse. You and I know that mice are the natural prey of owls, but this is another unspoken contract. Besides, this is a talking mouse, and talking mice never get eaten.

'What's wrong?' says the mouse. 'Can I help you?'

'I'm lost,' says Igor. 'I'm a famous owl detective, but I can't find my way. I'm afraid my way can't be found at all.'

'If you're in doubt,' says the mouse, 'you should follow your heart.'

On page five, Igor eats the mouse. You can see its tail disappearing into his beak.

I turn back to the title page. I've seen the title, but I haven't read it till now. *Igor the Owl Follows His Heart*, it's called.

On pages six and seven, Igor follows his heart. It looks much like Igor himself, except it's even smaller, and it's pink with white wings like a cherub. The trees thin, shrink into

341

twigs, die off. On page eight, Igor is in a desert. He lands on a rock. In all directions, there is sand. There isn't another owl in sight, but the sun beats down on the fragile skulls of creatures who have wandered here and died. In each one of them, there is a small glowing spot shaped like a kidney bean.

And there he stayed, says the text.

The next page is the blank endpaper. That's the end of the book.

You can't have a book this short; it's not worth the money to print it. People will feel cheated. Children will be afraid. I flip back to the beginning and start again, but the story is the same each time: Igor is lost, he eats the mouse, he follows his heart, he ends up in the desert, alone.

This is not a good book for children. This is not a good book for anybody.

Ewan

The house was the last in a cul-de-sac, in a neighbour-hood outside of Leicester. It was a normal house. Ewan parked his borrowed car on the street outside it and sat with his hands on the wheel for a few moments, looking at the lawn in front, the red-painted door. This was what Lee had come home to, when he had come home. It was where the bedroom ceiling fell down because he'd put too much gear up in the loft; where he'd made a mess of the kitchen trying to lay tiles himself. Lee had a story about nearly every room in this house, but Ewan had never been in it. Their friendship had been on the road.

Walking up the path to the red door was one of the hardest things he'd ever done. Every single part of him wanted to turn around and get back in the car. But he had promised himself a new start. A new life of not running away. Of being responsible. Of being polite to post-office counter assistants.

He rubbed the fingers of his right hand, where he could still feel the back of Lee's sweatshirt, as it was torn away.

Petra opened the door even before he knocked. 'Mate,' she said, and hugged him on the doorstep. Then she stepped back and looked up at him, her hands still on his arms. 'You're an hour and a half late.'

'I got lost,' he said, and then corrected himself: 'I sat in the motorway services for ages trying to get up the courage.'

'I'm glad you're here now.' She wore thick-rimmed glasses, an enormous jumper that he thought had probably belonged to Lee. Worn slippers on her feet. Her hair had grown out of her crop and looked shaggy. She was quite different from the lipsticked, laughing, sexy girl he'd met with Lee. But her smile, though sad, was warm. Behind her, the house smelled of coffee.

'Petra,' he said. 'I'm so sorry. It would never have happened if not for me. I know I can never make it up to you, but whatever you need, I'll try to do it.'

'I don't hold you responsible for Lee's death,' she told him. 'And the fact that you came to see me is enough. But now that you mention it, if you're feeling like you've got a strong back, I could use a hand.'

Three hours later, the entire contents of Lee's shed were spread out on the lawn. Petra rubbed the small of her back and said, 'I have no idea what any of this shit is.'

Ewan balanced a soldering iron on top of a gutted speaker cabinet. 'He was a bit of a pack rat. But he could fix anything – not just electrics. Anything.'

'Mostly with gaffer tape and spit, if our house is anything to go by.' Petra plopped herself down on the lawn next to the speaker cabinet. 'You don't get the face when I mention him.'

'What do you mean, the face?'

'It's something like this.' She slackened her expression into a tragic mask. 'Except with panic in their eyes. It's what

344

everyone in my family looks like when I talk about Lee. And all of my friends around here. It's like I'm not allowed to talk about him normally, as my husband. As someone I still love. They expect me to burst into tears and freak out. Don't get me wrong: sometimes I do want to burst into tears and freak out. But sometimes I just want to talk about him.'

'Yeah,' said Ewan. 'Sometimes I do, too.'

'You were his best friend. He talked about you all the time. He said you were a total fuck-up, by the way, but he said it fondly.'

'He only ever said nice things about you.'

'Oh sweetie, I don't believe you at all.' She stretched her legs out. 'So what should we do with all of this stuff? The tip?'

'Are you sure you want to get rid of it? Doesn't it have memories?'

'These memories, I don't need. This shed is a pit to hell. Did you clock those spiders?'

'We could try eBay.'

'I wouldn't even know how to list this junk.'

'I probably know what most of it is,' Ewan said. 'If you've got a camera and a laptop, I can list it for you. Some of it's worth money.'

'Yeah. Yeah, that would be great. Thank you.' She lay back on the grass, her hands laced over her belly. 'I'm stupidly tired.'

Ewan surveyed the equipment strewn over the lawn. 'What are you going to do with the shed? Paint it?'

'It's beyond a lick of paint. I'm tearing the fucker down. I'll put up a swing set or something.'

'You're—'

'Pregnant. Yes. Thirteen weeks. It happened right before he went away. Now *you've* got the face. Stop it.'

He sat down next to her, though he had to move a roll of cable to do it. He closed his eyes and, with an effort, put aside the guilt. Because she'd told him to stop it, and she was more important than anything he could feel.

'I just . . . yeah. Okay. Did Lee know?'

'Yeah. I'm surmising that he didn't tell you.'

'He said some things. Mostly about me getting my life in order.'

'That's Lee. And you have to do it now, because it was his last request.'

'Someone else said the same thing to me not long ago.'

'It's why I don't need this shed. Or any of these things. I've got someone much more important, who will always be a connection to him. I just don't want people to get the face when this kid asks about its daddy. You know?'

'Well,' said Ewan, 'I've got a lot of stories. As soon as the kid's old enough, send him to me. Or her. I'll tell the story about the time in Memphis that I broke Graceland, and Daddy fixed it.'

'With gaffer tape, I'll bet,' said Petra, and both of them laughed, the kind of laughter where after a while, you're crying.

That night in his hotel, Ewan put on some sort of zombie film and lay on the bed, looking at his phone. Flick hadn't answered his calls or returned his message. But he liked that. She'd told him not to get in touch while she sorted out her head, and she was sticking to it. He didn't want a woman who was married to someone else. He wanted, for once and for all, to be in love with a woman who was available. Someone who would see through him. It was scary, in a way, but he was ready for that. Or at least he hoped he was.

Tomorrow he'd go back to Petra's and finish listing Lee's stuff on eBay. They'd drink coffee and tell stories. Tonight he was in another hotel room, just like all the hundreds of hotel rooms he'd stayed in all over the world. And just like he'd done in every one of them, every time for the past two years, he put down his own phone and picked up the room landline. He dialled nine to get an outside line, and then, from memory, he punched in Alana's number. All except for the last digit.

It was a zero. For the past two years, that zero had seemed to sum up an awful lot. Maybe that was why he'd never punched it.

Or maybe it was because he was, plain and simple, a coward who couldn't ring his ex-wife and ask to speak to his daughter. Who couldn't send a birthday card. Who would always have the connection, but couldn't connect.

He put down the phone and watched creatures on the screen, shambling after brains.

Chapter Thirty-four

In the desert, time passes differently. I open my eyes and it is hot, so hot, and Quinn is there looking down at me. He's blurry, but it's him. He came.

So that's all right. I'm safe.

I close my eyes again. When I open them, some hot time later, Lauren is there, eating from a bag of grapes. 'Hey,' she says. 'You look like hell.'

She's not the one who's supposed to be here. My mouth is dry. There is a nurse.

'Can you tell me your name, love?' she says.

I have to say something important to Lauren. It's far back in the corner of my head, and my head hurts. Something about trees. No, something that's made out of trees.

'Can you squeeze my hand?'

'Paper,' I say.

'You're doing really well,' says the nurse. 'Can you tell me what month it is?'

'Head hurts.' I close my eyes and when I open them again, the nurse and Lauren are still there and the grapes are all gone. There is something else missing. Someone is missing. I try to see beyond Lauren and can't.

'Papernews,' I say. There's more than that, but that's the word. That's the thing. No, it's backward. 'Newspaper.'

Lauren smiles at me as if I've been gone for months. 'Hello, Fliss, it's good to see you. How are you feeling?'

'Rotten. Dry. Is my heart still here?'

'Is she supposed to be able to speak properly?' Lauren asks the nurse.

'She'll be confused until the anaesthetic wears off.'

'I'm not confused.'

'Of course not, Fliss. Not any more than Dalí.'

'Melting clocks. In a desert.'

Lauren says, 'That's it. You're going to be absolutely fine, I can tell.'

My head is stuffed with cotton and sand and platinum, little springs that pound against my skull. The newspaper is missing, not the newspaper, but, 'Quinn.'

Lauren takes my hand. 'Quinn was here to make sure the surgery went well. He rang me and asked me to be here when you woke up properly. We had no idea you were so ill, darling.'

'Where is he now?'

She exchanges a look with the nurse. 'Just rest, okay?'

'I've got some tests first,' says the nurse cheerfully.

Please tell me your friend's name, please tell me the month, please follow this light, please open your mouth so we can take your temperature. It tires me out and I need to sleep again. It is not a blank; I am in the desert. The sun bakes my feathers and penetrates my skin. Far away, across the world, Quinn rings Lauren to be here when I wake up because he will not be here. Because he is still in the forest. Because I've flown away from him for ever.

When I wake up, I'm sobbing.

There's a cool hand on my forehead, the cool hand of a stranger, a new nurse. 'You've got a little post-operative fever – it should come down soon. We're giving you antibiotics. It's nothing to worry about. You're doing fine. The neuro-radiologist says the coiling was a complete success.'

'Where . . .'

She gives me a glass of water with a straw. I drink half of it; it tastes like the tears on my lips. 'Your friend said she'd be back later. She doesn't want to tire you out.'

Outside the window, it's getting dark. 'It looks like rain,' I say, and I'm rewarded with an approving nod.

'That's good. You're talking. You're going to be fine. Yes, my garden will be glad of it.'

She gives me a tissue, smooths my sheets, checks my lines, dims my light, tells me the doctor will be coming soon to give me a full check. When she leaves me I see what I couldn't see before: there is a newspaper, carefully folded, on the chair beside the bed.

My heart leaps. The newspaper seems an impossible distance away. Slowly, I move one leg to the edge of the mattress and over. There is a pain between my legs, a stabbing. It's where the instrument went in. I remember. My head doesn't hurt so much, only an echo. My other leg follows, and I use my arms to push up my upper body. The ward swims in front of my eyes, but my mind is clear. It has one object. I focus on the newspaper.

I reach. It's not far enough. I have to stand, propping myself up against the side of the bed, the floor cold enough to make me shiver, a plastic line attaching my arm to a bag of fluid. If the newspaper is here, I have a chance. He will wait for me after all. He's been sitting here while I slept, watching over me.

My fingers brush it, grasp it, gather it to me. The headlines are about Syria and suffering pensioners. It's a two-day-old *Express*.

He hasn't come back.

Quinn

His bloody bike was missing again. The wall it was supposed to be leaning against was empty and the garden gate was ajar. Quinn ran to the road, hoping to catch a glimpse of Cameron Bishop as he rode it round the corner, but it was empty.

'Bugger,' he said. He'd have to walk round there now, and steal his own bloody bike back, and if Cameron wasn't home yet he'd have to walk all around the village looking for him. Last time, the boy had been with a group of his friends, all with their hoods up trying to look tough and failing miserably. Still, it was a pain. More than a pain, it was disrespectful and dangerous, and he'd have to speak with Lisa and she'd speak to Cameron and it wouldn't do any good, and so Cameron's mother would end up feeling inadequate, and his bike would get stolen again. And again.

Quinn kicked the wall of Hope Cottage, where his bicycle should have been. Some of the rendering fell off and he kicked it again.

She'd looked dead. Worse than he'd ever seen her, even in the middle of the seizure because at least then she'd been moving. When she'd opened her eyes she didn't recognize him. It was as if there was no one inside her. But the neuro-radiologist said she was fine, the neurologist said she was fine. They said she was going to be as good as new.

He kicked the wall again, hard. The toe of his shoe was gritty and white, covered with flakes of rendering. There was quite a hole there now. Whoever had rendered this exterior wall hadn't done it properly, like everything about this cottage. Damp and mouldering, it was going to fall down any minute. It was a wonder it had lasted five minutes, let alone three hundred years.

'Bugger!' he yelled, loud enough so that it echoed.

He'd been angry for days.

He hit the wall with his fist and nothing came off it. It was more sound at chest height than it was below, evidently. He hit it again, and again, and then with his left hand too. All the bloody hopes. Everything he had ever wanted.

'Darling?'

His mother came round the side of the cottage, holding a canvas shopping bag and a rake. She had her gardening clothes on.

'Darling, what are you doing? You'll hurt yourself.' She put down the bag and hurried over to him. 'Your poor hand, look.'

'I'm fine.'

'You mustn't hit the wall, that's just silly. Let me look at it, we can take you inside and get you bandaged up. I'll make you a nice cup of tea.'

He jerked his hand back. 'Stop fussing! I'm a grown man!'

Molly took a step back. 'I didn't—'

'You can't make it better! So just stop. Stop! Leave me alone.'

353

Quinn turned and hit the wall again, this time hard enough to split the knuckles on his right hand and leave a smear of blood on the white.

'Quinn?' said his mother behind him, in a small voice.

She would be surprised. She would be shocked and concerned. They didn't do this: swear and yell and batter at buildings.

'I'm so angry,' he said to the wall. 'And I hate being this angry, and I hate her for making me feel this way. I hate her for being ill and I hate myself for not being able to go to her when she needs someone. I hate that everything matters so much.'

She didn't say anything, and suddenly he was sick of it. All the silence, all the smoothing over, all the fear that if you said the truth, that everything would tumble. He'd been sick of it for a long time. He turned around.

'How did you do it?' he asked. 'When Dad had the affair? How did you get through it?'

The colour dropped out of Molly's face all at once. He reached for her, certain that she was going to faint, but she steadied herself on the fence. Quinn watched as she put her hand to her mouth, as if to keep the words inside.

God. What was the use of asking? In a minute she'd be talking about tea again.

'Dad didn't have an affair,' she said.

'Mum. I know about it. I know something happened, at least. I remember all the arguments. I know it was a long time ago, and that we've never spoken about it. But I know it happened.'

'It didn't.'

He clenched his fists again. 'Can't we stop this? This

pretending that everything's all right, all the time? Because
I pretended and I pretended with Felicity. I learned it from
you. And it doesn't work. It doesn't work at all.'

'I'm not pretending.'

'But you are, Mum! Every day! But you must still be angry,
like I'm angry. Otherwise why would you have screamed at
Felicity?'

'It wasn't Dad who had the affair,' she said. 'It was me.'

He saw his mother nearly every day and he very rarely saw
her. But he saw her now: the grey in her hair, the lines on her
soft face, the way her shoulders were rounding. How age had
layered over the young woman holding the babies in the
photographs, the woman who had existed before he did.

'It was a mistake,' she said. 'A horrible, foolish mistake. It
was me thinking I could— but I couldn't.'

'Thinking you could do what?'

She shook her head. 'I don't even know any more. Have
something different, I suppose. The sort of thing you read
about in books. But that sort of thing doesn't last. It doesn't,
Quinn. Not like what I have now.'

'Who—'

'It doesn't matter. What matters is that in the end, I chose
your father. I had a home and a family, and those were more
important. And we got through it because your father is such
a good man.'

'But all the arguments?'

'It was a horrible time. But he forgave me, and we don't
talk about it. It's forgotten, a long time ago.'

Except it was happening all over again, in his life. Maybe
because he'd learned as a child how to smooth everything
over, not talk about the difficult things. If he'd asked Felicity

355

and kept on asking, would she have told him long ago about how guilty she felt about her mother's death, and would they have been closer because of it? Would she have confided to him that she was having strange feelings about someone else? If he'd asked the right question, at the right time, instead of being afraid of the answer?

'I have been thinking,' his mother said, 'that I shouldn't have spoken to – she was ill, and I – only I saw how much pain she had caused you, and I remembered that I had – and it hurt me. To know I too had caused so much pain.'

She fluttered her hand over her mouth again, and then drew herself up.

'Anyway, that's in the past,' she said.

'I'm not certain that it is.'

'Yes, yes it is. It's all finished now, and it doesn't do any good to talk about it.' She lowered her chin. 'If it's helpful to you to punch the cottage and make yourself bruised and bleeding, Quinn, then go ahead. You're a grown man with your own decisions to make. I've only come because I thought your garden could do with a bit of tidying up.' She patted his shoulder, and kissed him on the cheek. And he didn't feel like a grown man. He felt like he wanted to crawl into her arms and trust her to make it all go away.

She'd done this thing. And yet she was still his mother.

'I don't know what to do, Mum.'

'You will, darling. You're so much wiser than I ever was.' She stroked his cheek where she'd kissed it. 'Wiser and braver. I'm proud of my boy.'

He gazed at her, trying to see her. When he was a child, he'd believed she'd known everything. Could do anything. Could heal all of his hurts. But this was who she'd been all along, someone flawed and hurting, someone much more like him. She cupped his chin in her hand and smiled at him.

'I'll get started on the deadheading, shall I?' She picked up her bag and went off, busily into the garden, as if nothing had changed.

Chapter Thirty-five

They say the surgery was a success. They say I'm cured and that after I've recovered I'll be as good as new. I'll need to have regular scans, and stay on anti-seizure medications for some time just in case, but otherwise I can go on with my normal life. Lauren has taken me back to Canary Wharf with her. She's cancelled her meetings in Belgium so she can stay in London, and has ignored all of my protests that I will be absolutely fine on my own. When she has to go out to work, she arranges for friends to call on me.

I feel nothing. Lauren feeds me high-protein shakes, lean meat, soups stuffed full of vegetables. She even cooks some of it herself. None of it has any flavour. 'The antibiotics,' she says. 'They mess up your system.' She gives me small plastic bottles of drinking yoghurt full of good bacteria. I drink them in front of the television, where I've made a nest for myself so I can watch *Cash in the Attic* and *Bargain Hunt*. All these programmes about selling old things so as to be able to buy new things. Clutter and baggage. It exhausts me. Drinking yoghurt exhausts me. Changing my socks exhausts me.

The doctor said I would be tired, but this is not any

normal form of being tired. Everything is grey. Naomi and Yvonne and some of my other friends bring me books and flowers, chocolates and conversation that I can't seem to engage in. Words come slowly when I speak, and my body struggles to rouse itself. The heatwave has broken and Lauren keeps on making cheerful comments about the cool weather outside, but I feel as if I haven't breathed fresh air since that night in the roof garden under the moon. Emotion has been wrung out of me, coiled and squeezed away.

'I've been pithed,' I say to Lauren one evening when she comes home from work, bringing a fresh pineapple. I hold the fruit in my hands. Once I would have smiled at its spikiness, its outrageous armour, useless against the tempt-ation of its scent. I turn it over and put it back on the coffee table. 'Like when they take the brains out of frogs.'

'It's because you're recovering,' she says, putting her hand on my arm. 'You've been through a lot. Your body needs to conserve its energy to heal. It doesn't have any extra to cope with what you're going through emotionally.'

'I'm not going through *anything* emotionally,' I say. 'Maybe if I could see Quinn . . .'

'I don't think that's a good idea. You both need some time to come to terms with what's happened.'

'Or Ewan. I should call him. I know you don't like him, Lauren, but he's been through a difficult time too. He doesn't have anyone else.'

'Again, not a good idea. Everything's too complicated right now. Let it settle for a little while.' I've told her what's happened, of course; she may have heard more about it from Quinn. Knowing how she feels about Ewan, she's being remarkably restrained about it all. 'You're healing. Take time to heal. One step at a time. This time next week, you'll feel much better.'

'I think it's gone, Lauren. What they did to me has damaged me in some way. I can remember that I used to feel, but I can't actually do it any more. Something has gone wrong in wherever my brain makes emotion.'

'Sweetheart,' she says gently, 'if your brain couldn't produce emotions any more, you wouldn't be crying every night in your sleep.'

This is true. I have been doing this. I wake up with my pillow soaked with tears. I wake up filled with an overwhelming sense of loss.

'You'll work it out,' she says to me. 'It will become clear to you what you should do. Meanwhile, I am going to make you some fruit skewers. Pineapple stimulates dopamine production. You know, the happiness hormone?'

'How do you know all of this about food, suddenly?' I ask her.

She hugs me and kisses me on the cheek. She's a good friend, but I can't work out whether I know this logically or through feeling.

In between materialistic television shows, I try examining the facts of my life: I am separated from my husband because I cheated on him with a man whom I believed I loved. At least, sometimes I believed I loved him. I have made enemies of my in-laws and roused the concerns of my friends. I have entered into a relationship with a near-stranger and made him care about me far more than I deserve, probably far more than is good for him. I've done all of this because of a malfunction of my brain. Or perhaps I haven't. Perhaps it was something I would have done anyway, given the right circumstances. Perhaps I am naturally faithless, naturally immoral. All I know is that the world before was made of colour, and now it is made out of grey.

I poke at these facts and these possibilities, as one would a rotten tooth, and try to make them ache. Even feeling pain would be better than this. I felt pain in the hospital, after the surgery, I know I did. When I reached for the newspaper and it was two days old. When I dreamed about the *Igor the Owl* book I'll never write in reality.

I poke and poke at the tangle of facts, but I can only cry in my sleep.

During the second week of September, two things gradually make their way into my attention. One is that Lauren is spending quite a bit of time sending and receiving messages on her phone that make her laugh. The second is that 12 September is rapidly approaching, the day when Ewan arranged to meet me. I understand why he asked me to meet him in Greenwich, at the same time as before. It's a message to me that if I don't turn up, he'll do what he asked me to do originally: carry on, forget about the whole thing.

But can he forget? Can I?

On the other hand, if I do meet him, will I be doing the right thing? Should I be jumping into another relationship, and such an intense one, so quickly, when I don't know what to feel? When I'm not certain that I even *can* feel any more?

On Friday night, I walk around and around the living room. Lauren is curled up on the sofa tapping into her phone. She should be out having fun, but she's brought us a film to watch later. It's dark outside; autumn is shortening the days.

'Stop prowling,' she says to me. 'You're making me dizzy.'

I perch on the other sofa, then get up again. I want something to do, something mindless like tidying or ironing, but the flat is spotless and Lauren sends all her laundry out, and I can't stop moving around and around, like the thoughts in my head. I brush against a side table and an envelope slides off the pile stacked there, of all the post I've received and haven't bothered to open yet.

That's something I can do. I bring the stack over to the sofa and begin to open envelopes. It's mostly get well cards, from my editor Madelyne (*Don't worry about work, sweetie, just get better!*) and my agent, and friends who don't live in London. A box of expensive chocolates from Andrew and Tom. I open it and offer some to Lauren.

'How do all these people even know that I've been ill? And that I'm staying here?'

'Word travels. Lots of people love you.'

'I threw away all the cards people sent me after my mother died,' I tell her. 'I didn't even read them. I sort of think that was a mistake.'

Right at the bottom of the pile is a yellow envelope. The card is of a fuzzy yellow duckling wearing a hat. It's holding on to a rope, the other end of which has been tied around a quaint wishing well. GET WELL it says. As in, the duck has got a well. I open it, expecting an ironic message from one of my friends.

Dear Felicity,

I told you once that you should consider me your mother. I would be a poor mother if I took away my love because of

*something you had done. I'm sorry for my behaviour the last
time we met. I hope you are feeling much better.*

Love, Molly and Derek

I read the card and reread it, and then look at the front again.
It's still a duck with a wishing well. I don't know how I could
have possibly thought it was from anyone but Molly
Wickham.

All at once I miss Molly: her lily-of-the-valley-scented
hugs, her flowered teacups, the proud look she gets on her
face every time all of her family are gathered together. I
remember how magnificent I'd thought her in the garden,
defending her son. How much strength there is in niceness,
in softness, in love.

'I need to go somewhere,' I say.

'Okay,' replies Lauren. 'I keep on saying you should get out
of this flat. Where do you want to go? To the pub for a swift
one?'

'No. I need to go to St Ives.' I walk into my bedroom to
look for my shoes. Lauren follows me.

'St Ives? Cornwall? Right now?'

'Yes.' I pull on my trainers, and find a cardigan.

Lauren is smiling. 'Now this is the Felicity I know. *Finally.*
How are you planning to get there?'

'I don't know. The train?'

She checks something rapidly on her phone. 'Darling, this
time of night, you wouldn't even get there until tomorrow.
It'll have to be by car. And you're not allowed to drive, so I'll
have to come with you.'

'You haven't got a car.'

Her smile gets broader. 'I've got an idea. Just a minute.'

While she disappears to have a conversation on her phone, I pack a few clothes into a rucksack: warm things, a waterproof. The bundle, wrapped in a plastic bag, has been in the drawer with my socks since I came to Lauren's flat. It fits easily into the rucksack. Although I've assumed that Lauren is ringing a car rental agency, when I join her in the living room, she's giggling. 'See you in five,' she says into her phone, and slips it into her pocket. 'Right. You pack the chocolates whilst I make a flask of coffee.'

'You own a flask?'

'Full of surprises, me,' she says, tapping her nose.

Fifteen minutes later, her phone chirps and we're running down the stairs and out of the lobby, Lauren pulling on her cashmere jacket. 'Remember getting kicked out of that hostel in Bangkok?' she asks me, but I've stopped dead at the sight of the vehicle which is idling in front of the building. It's a green van with the words TWO SLICES CATERING on the side.

'Who's this?' I ask. The driver's door opens and a man gets out.

'This is Bill,' says Lauren. She's actually blushing. Bill, tall and with curly hair in need of cutting, offers me his hand to shake.

'I've seen you before,' I tell him. 'Thanks for this.'

'Hey, thank *you*. I didn't have any plans, and I love the beach.'

Lauren gets into the passenger seat, breathless, and I curl up in the back next to several empty plastic mayonnaise containers. As Bill drives us through London, I send her a text from the back seat to the front: *Is this one independently wealthy, too?*

She turns around. 'After careful consideration, and after watching you nearly die, I've decided with all due respect that the checklist can go to hell.'

'Here's to that,' agrees Bill, turning onto the A4.

I leave my shoes at the top of Porthmeor Beach and roll up my trousers. Lauren and Bill lag behind me, maybe because they know I want to be alone, maybe because they want to be alone too. I walk down the sand to the edge of the sea, listening to its large dark sound.

My mother isn't here. I know that she doesn't live anywhere but inside my memories. Still, I breathe in deeply, trying to catch the scent of her, trying to find a sign.

There's nothing. Nothing but the hiss of water on sand, the foaming surf. No stars tonight, no moon, only the smell of seaweed and salt. And there was never any sign anyway; that was just a bubble in my brain.

I unwrap the urn from the plastic bag and I unscrew the top. 'Goodbye, Mum,' I say, and I tip the contents out into the sea. So she can join the water cycle, swim in the ocean, fall with the rain. I imagine particles of her body dancing in the surf under the shimmer of the moon.

All she wanted was for me to be ready to say goodbye to her.

I let the water roll over my feet and ankles, here at the edge of land, where the country stops, and I know, finally, what it means to walk lightly. It's not giving things away. It's not the opposite of holding on.

It means to forgive and be forgiven. It means to hold on to love, and to nothing else.

It's taken five hours to drive here, and maybe all of my life of wandering beforehand. But fifteen minutes on the beach is all it takes for me to know exactly what I need to do next. For me to know what love is.

Whether it will work out, I have no idea.

Ewan

The rain sent the tourists running for shelter, but Ewan pulled his leather jacket up over his head and kept looking. It was quarter to twelve, and he'd been here for half an hour already, standing outside the gates to the courtyard where he could see her if she came up the hill.

For the past few days, he'd been nervous as a cat. He'd taken a Gibson out of storage and started playing again, which felt good, but he couldn't settle to it. He was too aware of the days passing, the date he'd chosen pretty much at random approaching. With every day he got more restless.

He was ready for a change. Definitely ready. But it felt like ages ago since he'd sent that message, asking Felicity to meet him here again. So much had happened since: his trip to Leicester, meeting with Ginge again, the first couple of sessions with Ali, his new counsellor. It was getting to be that he didn't have the impulse to ring Flick every time he saw something he thought she'd like.

But that would change.

He rocked back and forward on his feet, looking around, seeing her everywhere. People wore anoraks and hats, huddled under umbrellas, coming out of the Royal

Observatory Museum to stand astride the Meridian Line. It was supposedly where the world ended. Or began.

He wanted to begin again, to wash himself clean with love.

A black golf umbrella approached him, only a pair of jeans and wellies visible below. The wellies had orange spots on them. 'Flick?' he said, ducking his head to look underneath.

It wasn't Flick. But she was so familiar that it took a moment before he could process who she was.

'I wasn't sure you'd be here,' said Alana.

He could only stare. 'What?'

'It's a long way to come. So I'm glad you bothered to turn up, though you could have picked a place with a roof. Where is she?'

'Who?'

'Felicity.'

Though he couldn't process this, he glanced around, trying to spot Felicity. Greenwich park was nearly empty. All he saw was a busker, under a tree down the hill. A single person hidden under a pink umbrella watched him play guitar.

'I . . . don't know where Felicity is,' he said. 'She's supposed to be here.'

Alana shrugged. 'Okay. It doesn't matter.' Her eyes slipped past him to the busker, and then back. 'I need to know that you really want to do this. It's been hard enough already, without you mucking her about.'

'Mucking who about?'

Alana glared at him. 'You need to ask?' She looked down the hill again at the busker, who was playing that Katrina and the Waves song, and the small figure watching him play, under a pink umbrella, with pink wellies, who turned so the side of her face was visible, and her red hair.

Ewan's heart beat painfully once, and then harder.

'Two years without a word, and suddenly this. It's fine, she wanted to come, but you can't leave it for so long this time, Ewan. You need to be in her life, or out of it. And we can't come traipsing down here every time you wave your hand. *You* have to make the effort. You, yourself.'

He couldn't take his eyes off his daughter as she watched the busker. She was skinny, in a raincoat that was too short for her in the arms. Her feet danced in the forming mud.

'How . . . how do you know Felicity?' he asked.

'She was the one I spoke to? The one who sent the train tickets and told us what time to meet you? What is she, your girlfriend, or your personal secretary?'

'Felicity is . . .'

A life saver. A life changer. The person who was not coming, who was never going to come, but had known how to give him his second chance. The second chance he really needed, who was nodding her head to the music right now in the rain.

'Does Rebecca want to see me?' he asked.

'I said she did, didn't I? I've left the other two with Mike. It was lucky I could get the time off work at such short notice. But she was excited, and it's important.' Alana pointed at Rebecca. 'She's the queen of lost causes, that one. She's got a heart as soft as soft. She begged to watch that man playing guitar. Because no one else would watch him in the rain, and she felt bad, she said.' Alana turned and seized his sleeve. 'Listen, Ewan, I mean it. Only if you're going to be there for her from now on. She's growing up quickly, and you can't break her heart any more. You're in, or out.'

The song finished, and his daughter clapped, holding her

umbrella under her chin. She half-turned then, and he saw how she was searching the park, looking up the hill.

'I'm in,' he said, barely able to hear himself over the drumming of the rain and his own heart. 'I am in.'

And then she spotted him, his daughter, and he was running down the hill, jacket falling from his head, forgotten, rain in his face and in hers as Rebecca ran up the hill to meet him halfway.

Chapter Thirty-six

It's noon on 12 September, and as soon as I reach Hope Cottage I can tell that it's empty. Someone has tidied the front garden; the grass has been mowed and the hedges have been pruned. I recognize the hand of my mother-in-law, though the weeds are already starting to grow back. Quinn's car is gone.

I pause at the front gate. I knew he wouldn't be here; that he'd be at work. Quinn's habits are entirely predictable. I've told myself this was the reason I didn't ring first. I was planning to let myself in to wait for him, to be here when he got home. I wanted to be early, for once, and waiting for him. But the cottage looks deserted, as if the soul has gone out of it. Maybe it's because the garden has been trimmed. Or maybe it's something more.

The real reason I didn't ring first was because I was afraid he wouldn't answer. Or that he would answer, but he would tell me not to come.

The rain that's been threatening all morning has started to fall, a few drops at a time. I follow the path round towards the back door, but stop when I reach the side of the cottage.

Quinn's bike is leaning against it. There's a large, heavy D-lock on its wheel.

I can hardly believe it until I touch it. It's new. It looks impenetrable. A raindrop hits it and beads off. Probably in the city, a bike thief could be through it in ten seconds flat but out here, it's a gleaming black deterrent to a child's joy-rides.

'Oh Quinn,' I whisper. 'What have I done to you?'

Gravel crunches and I look up to see Quinn's car pulling into the drive. He's a shadow behind the windscreen; he probably can't see me yet, as the shed obscures half the drive and I'm behind it. The motor shuts off and I hear his door opening, his footsteps on the gravel, the boot open and close. He'll come round the shed towards the house in a minute. I listen for his footsteps, distinct from the patter of the rain.

He rounds the corner. He's wearing jeans and a blue jumper. He has a backpack slung over his shoulder and he carries a suitcase. Sunglasses have been pushed up onto the top of his head. He's let his beard grow out and he's tanned, always taller than I remember, with rain in his hair.

This is the feeling. Simple joy. A drink of water after the desert.

'Hello, love,' I say.

I know what Quinn meant every time he said it. Every single time. Because I mean it too.

He's staring at me as if he can't believe that I'm here. It's not joy on his face; it's surprise, and caution – and I've done that to him too.

'I'm so sorry,' I tell him.

'I . . .' He shakes his head to clear it and the sunglasses fall off; he catches them in one hand without looking away from me. 'How are you feeling?'

'I'm feeling fine. I'm feeling exactly the way I want to feel. A little nervous about seeing you, though.' I point to his suitcase. 'Where have you been?'

'Oh – Croatia.'

'Croatia?'

'I needed to get away. It was the first package deal that came up on the first website I visited. I took two weeks off work and went.'

'Was it nice?'

'I don't know.' He hangs his sunglasses from his collar, something I've never seen him do before, and rubs his face. It's raining harder now, the drops fatter and more frequent, but neither one of us is very concerned about getting inside. 'I thought today was the day you were meant to meet him.'

'I decided to meet you instead. If that's all right.'

He hasn't moved forward since he spotted me, and I haven't moved either. My hair has flattened to my skull, and it's beginning to drip down my neck. His eyes are the shade of the cloudy sky, the shade of the rain.

'I'll go if you want me to,' I say. 'I know I've hurt you. But I miss you so much, Quinn. I love you. I came to see if you can forgive me.'

Quinn drops the backpack, leaves his suitcase on the wet ground, and steps forward at last. He reaches past me and unlocks the D-lock with a single twist of a key. Then he throws it, in two pieces, into the bushes. There's a clunk as each piece hits the ground separately.

'Horrible thing,' he says, and then he takes half a turn towards me and I'm in his arms. I hold tight to his waist and I press my face hard against his chest where I can hear his heart, his strong, tender heart.

And this is what love is. This is what we're starting again. All the things we've done together and will do, all the extraordinary ordinary things. It's the scent of a favourite jumper, wool and cedar. It's the sound of someone in the kitchen making a cup of tea at the beginning of the day, the squeak of the gate at the end. It's arguments and partings, misunderstandings on the telephone, washing the laundry wrong so that things shrink. It's the scrawled double X on the bottom of a shopping list, the moment when you both see the sun rise and your hands meet and curl around each other, the exchanged glances at Sunday dinner that promise a conversation later in bed. It's the times his mother drives you crazy and he's remembered your best friend's birthday when you've forgotten and that's more annoying than helpful. It's wet shoes lined up together in front of the fire and a sleepy hand stroking your hair when you wake up sad. It's the silences, always broken in the end with the right words or the wrong ones, or the wrong ones that are the right ones really. It's built from nothing in layers, with sloppily-patched holes, weeds untrimmed, no corner of it perfect, all of it beautiful.

He holds me and whispers into my hair.

'Hello, love,' he says.

The Story Behind the Story

In 2010, my friend Ken told us that he had to have brain surgery. He'd been having these funny turns, episodes that felt like anxiety attacks, snatches of half-heard music or dialogue from television shows. When he consulted a doctor he discovered that he had a massive cerebral aneurysm, which had been in his brain probably for many years, and which looked unnervingly like a squid. Although he joked about it, he knew, and everyone who loved him knew, that this odd-looking thing in his brain had the potential to rob him of everything that he was.

I've always been fascinated by the power of the human brain. I read Oliver Sacks books like they're candy, and one day in *The Man Who Mistook His Wife for a Hat* I came across an account of temporal lobe seizures in an elderly woman, which manifested as her hearing music – but not just any music. She heard Irish songs from her childhood, which reminded her strongly of her mother, and where she had been, what she had felt, when she had last heard the songs in real life. The songs were distracting, and at times, very loud . . . but they were comforting too. 'Such epileptic hallucinations, Sacks explained, were real memories, accompanied by the same emotions the woman had felt during the original experiences.

Novelists are magpies, and this shiny titbit fascinated me. I immediately copied it out and stuck it on my wall – this idea that your brain can, at any point, reproduce not only the sensations of something that's happened to you in your past, but all the emotions that were associated with it as well. What if, I thought, a person were to have a seizure that felt like an emotion? Something that felt real, and more intense than everyday life? What about the feeling of falling in love – celebrated in a million pop songs, poems and love stories – the feeling that we believe is more authentic and precious than anything else?

I was introduced to Dr Dirk Baumer, Research Fellow and Neurology Registrar at the John Radcliffe Hospital, Oxford, who told me that, although it's not common, it's entirely possible to have temporal lobe seizures caused by a cerebral aneurysm. He also told me that yes, those seizures could consist of evocative phantom smells, and emotions associated with a particular moment in the past. He explained the nature and symptoms of seizures to me, and he also passed me a number of case studies. One was of a man whose cerebral aneurysm was causing him to relive, in his own brain, specific scenes from his past life.

The Dostoevsky quotation that forms the epigraph to Part Three of this novel is also in Sacks's book, and that got me thinking, too. A person sick with love may not want to get better. They may prefer to stay in love, even though their love might kill them. It might work as an addiction, an artificial euphoria that nevertheless comes from the innermost part of a person's being.

I was halfway through writing the novel when I came

376

across the quotation at the beginning of Part One, from Katherine Mansfield's short story 'Bliss'. Her heroine Bertha, a married woman, has an intense attachment to a female friend, something that makes her unbelievably happy, which lends a glow to everything. And yet the story is highly ironic (and has a masterful, cruel twist), because although we might fall in love with someone, we can never truly know what their innermost emotions are. We can only understand the reality inside our own heads.

I collected all these things together and they made me excited. I wanted to write a story with an unreliable narrator, someone who can't quite work out what love is, or what is real, or what she really wants. Someone who wants to be authentic but is at the mercy of structures in her brain. From my own experience I know that scent is incredibly evocative of the past. I've had the unsettling experience of catching a whiff of aftershave on a stranger in the street, and believing that I'd just passed the boy I used to date in high school. Quinn tells Felicity a story of opening a book and being overwhelmed by a memory because of a scent trapped between the pages, and that's happened to me, too. So many of my friends and family have said the same: that scent can hijack you and transport you.

My friend Ken's surgery was successful as far as removing the aneurysm went; he no longer has a squid inside his head, and he doesn't hear snatches of *Star Trek: The Next Generation* any more. But during surgery he suffered a stroke which caused damage to another part of his brain. He's spent the last four years learning how to be himself in a new way. Ken was generous enough to talk frankly with me about his symptoms, treatment and rehabilitation, and to give me permission to lend certain parts of his wonky brain to a fictional woman. You can read his ongoing story at www.mylifeasasemicolon.com

Julie Cohen

Acknowledgements

Thank you to Ken Shapiro, Dr Dirk Baumer, Dr Natasha Onwu, Dr Matthew Cohen, Dr Joanna Cannon, Monika Mann (RN), Jennifer Cohen (RN), and my friend Ben Pearson's mum.

Thank you to Cat Cobain who teased out the story with tea. Thanks to Gemma Sims and her mother Sue Edwards. Thanks to Lee Weatherly and Ruth Ng, Brigid Coady and Anna Louise Lucia, and all of my Reading mummy chums. Thanks to Rowan Coleman, Miranda Dickinson, Kate Harrison, Tamsyn Murray and Cally Taylor for a particular weekend near the inception of this book. Thanks to Kathy Lewis, who donated to CLIC Sargent to have her name used for Quinn's first love. Thanks to my husband, Dave Smith (aka 'The Rock God'), for information about tour buses and life on the road, and for actually breaking Graceland.

An enormous grateful slobbery hug type of thank you to my agent Teresa Chris, and to Harriet Bourton, Larry Finlay, Tessa Henderson and every single one of the team at Transworld who have made me so amazingly welcome. Thank you to Alicia Clancy in the U.S. and everyone at St. Martin's Press for making me feel welcome there, too.

Finally, thank you to my family for showing me what love is.

1. Have you ever had an experience like Felicity's, where you smelled a scent that brought up strong memories? What was it? Were you ever prompted to do something because of it?

2. What scents are the most evocative for you? Why?

3. How did your feelings about Felicity and her choices change as the book went on?

4. As you read, did you suspect that something was wrong with Felicity's health? Did the revelation of her brain aneurysm and the seizures change how you felt about her behavior?

5. Felicity made her decision to leave Quinn moments after realizing she was not pregnant. What do you think would have happened if the test results had been positive? Do you think she would have stayed, despite the feelings she was having?

6. Do you think that Felicity made the right choice in the end? Do you think Quinn make the right choice in taking her back? What do you think the future holds for them? What about for Ewan?

7. What do you think creates love? Is it a result of chemicals and electrical impulses in the brain, or is it something more? Neurologists tell us that any human emotion can be prompted by a malfunction of the brain. If this is so, how do we know what emotions are real in our own lives?

8. Felicity was disappointed when she found out that she wasn't pregnant, despite initially believing that she was only trying to conceive because her husband wanted a child. Have you ever thought you wanted/didn't want something only to realize later that you were completely mistaken? And what does this say about

St. Martin's
Griffin

sacrifices and compromises in relationships? Would you be willing to make a life-changing decision simply because your partner wanted something?

9. How did you feel when you learned about Molly's affair? Were you surprised? Why do you think love isn't always enough to ensure fidelity? Do you think it's possible to truly forgive someone for having an affair?

10. *Where Love Lies* explores several different types of love: the quiet, steady love between Quinn and Felicity; the exciting, sensual love between Felicity and Ewan; the sad and guilty love Felicity feels for her mother; the interfering, protective love Molly has for her son. How do these relationships change throughout the novel?

11. The three main characters are associated with different objects throughout the book: Quinn with the moon, Felicity with birds, and Ewan with exotic flowers. What do these symbols show us about the personalities of each of these characters?